PASSIONATE PRAISE FOR BESTSELLING AUTHOR BRENDA JOYCE

THE THIRD HEIRESS

A SELECTION OF THE DOUBLEDAY BOOK CLUB

"Brenda Joyce has crafted a genealogical thriller of family secrets and obsessions that is sure to keep you up, reading into the night!"   —*Milwaukee Journal-Sentinel*

"Joyce brings her first hardcover romantic suspense novel to an exciting conclusion."   —*Booklist*

"A tense and atmospheric thriller. THE THIRD HEIRESS adds gothic and ghostly overtones to a story of one woman's obsessive quest for truth and justice."   —*Romantic Times*

"Brenda Joyce has combined modern romance with semi-time travel, historical romance and a mystery all in one intriguing story. A must read!"   —*Affaire de Coeur*

Turn the page for more acclaim . . .

P9-DMJ-537

THE RIVAL

"THE RIVAL is an exemplary example of an author doing exquisite period research . . . I was completely enamored of the characters and their intricate personalities . . . A thoroughly entertaining and bewitching read."
—*Old Book Barn Gazette*

"Engaging . . . Love scenes sizzle . . . A well-paced, entertaining read. Ms. Joyce writes in a breathless, gripping style. . . . Passions abound in THE RIVAL . . . Ms. Joyce is a talented writer. I look forward to her next book."   —*Regency World*

"Brenda Joyce will keep you turning pages. Hot and sensual! Fantastic! 5 Bells!"   —*Bell, Book, and Candle*

"Brenda Joyce gives us an instant classic . . . Powerful, sensational, and extraordinary—clearly one of the best books of the year."   —*Under the Covers*

"Right off the bat I can say buy this book. It is fabulous! Truthfully I could not put it down. I was reading it night and day once I started . . . This story is a humdinger by Ms. Joyce. It will have you tied in knots . . . I don't know how she does it, but Ms. Joyce just keeps getting better and better. This was so good I want to read it again soon . . . Filled with so much mystery and mayhem that you may want to reread it yourself. This is definitely a 'keeper.' It's got a little bit of everything that makes a super-duper book told by a master storyteller."   —*Belles & Beaux of Romance*

"Powerful storytelling with unforgettable characters."
—*Writer's Write*

The Third Heiress

BRENDA JOYCE

St. Martin's Paperbacks

THE THIRD HEIRESS

Copyright © 1999 by Brenda Joyce Dreams Unlimited, Inc.
Excerpt from *House of Dreams* copyright © 2000 by Brenda Joyce Dreams Unlimited, Inc.

Photograph of the author by Sigrid Estrada.

ISBN: 0-312-97419-1

Printed in the United States of America

St. Martin's Press hardcover edition / September 1999
St. Martin's Paperbacks edition / August 2000

St. Martin's Paperbacks are published by St. Martin's Press, 175 Fifth Avenue, New York, NY 10010.

10 9 8 7 6 5 4 3 2 1

*This novel is dedicated to my sister, Jamie,
with love, faith, and blessings*

The *Third*
Heiress

Prologue

Jill Gallagher could not remember a time when she wasn't alone. But eight months ago Harold Sheldon had entered her life, changing it forever. He had become her best friend and confidant as well as her lover. And now she was finally starting to forget and let go of the vague, shadowy fear and bewilderment that had been deeply imprinted upon an abandoned, lonely child so many years ago. A child whose parents were killed in a car accident when she was five. Her nights of insomnia, spent staring sleeplessly at dancing shadows upon the ceiling, filled with a fear she could not quite grasp, were finally a thing of the past.

As their rental car, a two-door Toyota, sped down the Northern State Parkway, Jill glanced at Hal sitting in the front passenger seat beside her. Her mood was more than light, it was exuberant, but her grip on the steering wheel tightened. Was something wrong? Hal was absorbed in studying the map he held, which was necessary—but he hadn't really said a word since they had left Manhattan, and that wasn't like him. Even though it was early April and unseasonably cool, they were headed for the North Shore. Jill was a professional dancer, and this would be their last chance to get away before the new show, where she was in the ensemble, opened. They had booked a room at a quaint bed-and-breakfast just steps away from the Peconic Bay. Jill was looking forward to a very quiet, intimate weekend before the grueling marathon of seven performances six days a week began. She was also looking forward to long conversations about the future they would share.

Of course, nothing could be wrong. Last week Hal had asked her to marry him. Jill had not hesitated in accepting his proposal. And last night he had made love to her with even more passion than usual.

Jill smiled at the mere memory of his romantic proposal in a dark, closet-sized East Village restaurant. She thought how amazing it was that a single chance encounter could change your life forever. A year ago, before meeting Hal, she had been resigned to the path of her life, to being alone.

The map rustled. The sound seemed intrusive, odd.

Jill glanced at him, her smile fading, because his expression was so set and hard to read. The Hal she knew and loved was the most amiable and carefree of people. He was always smiling. His good nature was one of the things she loved best about him—that and his passion for photography, which mirrored her passion for dance. "Hal? Is something wrong?" The tiniest inkling of dread rose up in her.

Immediately he flashed his very white smile. Although he was dark blond and British, he had a slight and perpetual tan. His family was wealthy. Upper-crust blue bloods or some such thing. His father, Jill had been told recently, was an earl. An honest-to-goodness earl. His older brother was a viscount who would one day inherit the title. Wealthy people, Jill knew, were always tanned. It was one of the facts of life.

She was going to marry an aristocrat. Her life had turned into a fairy tale. She had become Cinderella. Jill smiled to herself.

"Jill. Watch the road," Hal said tersely.

She obeyed, her smile and sense of well-being vanishing, confused because his tone was so harsh. As she concentrated on the traffic ahead, her pulse began a slow, distinct pounding. Hal said, "We need to talk."

Jill turned to stare at him in surprise. It was a moment before she could speak. "What is it?"

He looked away from her. Not meeting her eyes. "I don't want to hurt you," he said.

Jill almost swerved into the vehicle in the lane parallel to hers. It was mid-afternoon and there was heavy traffic on the highway, but it was moving at a good clip, close to sixty-five miles an hour.

Her stomach flipped. Jill glanced at him, but he was staring straight ahead, out of the front window. His expression was so serious, so grim.

No, she thought, clenching the steering wheel so tightly her fingers began to cramp. He loves me and we're getting married next fall. This is not about us.

It couldn't be. She had already paid her dues. When her parents had died, Jill had been sent to an aunt in Columbus—an elderly widowed woman whose own children had long since grown up and had children of their own. Aunt Madeline had been distant, reserved, almost uncaring, and from a small child's point of view, unkind. Jill's childhood had been lonely. She'd had no real friends; ballet had been her refuge, her life. At the age of seventeen she had gone to New York City to become a dancer and she had never looked back once.

Hal's presence in her life now made her realize how lonely she had been.

Hal suddenly cleared his throat, as if he were about to deliver a prepared speech. Jill's head whipped around again, and this time she was acutely anxious. "What is it? Is someone sick in your family?" She managed a lopsided smile. "Oh, God, don't tell me. Harrelson refused your work!" Hal had been furiously showing his portfolio in the hopes of finding a gallery to hold an exhibition of his work. This particular SoHo dealer had been very enthusiastic upon their first meeting.

"No one is sick. Harrelson hasn't gotten back to me yet. Jill, I've been thinking. About what we discussed last week." This time he glanced at her briefly. His amber eyes were anguished. And he couldn't hold her gaze.

Jill gripped the wheel, focusing on the road with an effort. She was trying to recall what they had discussed last week, but it was impossible—her chestnut bangs were in her eyes and she was sweating. Her pulse interfered with her hearing—and her own thoughts. She did not like his tone—was he uneasy? There was only one subject she could remember them having discussed, but surely he was not referring to his wedding proposal now. *He was not.* "I'm not sure what we talked about—other than your asking me to marry you and my accepting." She flashed him a smile, but could not maintain it.

He leaned back against the seat, morosely. "I've had second thoughts."

Jill tried to stay calm but her pulse was rioting. She carefully slowed the car, glancing in her rearview mirror. She quickly began to get out of the left lane, a red sedan on her rear bumper. *This was not happening.* "You've had second thoughts?" She was in shock, thinking, I am not understanding him. "You don't mean about us marrying?" Her smile felt sickly.

"It's not about you," Hal said, his tone miserable. "My feelings for you haven't changed."

Oh, God. He was referring to their marriage. Jill remained in a state of disbelief, her mind seemed to be shutting down, refusing to function, refusing to assimilate what he was saying. She was staring at him. "I don't understand. You love me. I love you. It's that simple."

He seemed uncomfortable. He avoided looking at her directly. "My feelings for you haven't changed. But I keep thinking . . ."

"What?!" Jill's tone was harsh, a whiplash. This could not be happening!

But then, hadn't she expected this—on some deep, instinctive level? Because hadn't their love been too good to be true?

He faced her. "I don't want to live in New York for the rest of my life. I miss my family, I miss London. I miss the summer house in Yorkshire."

Jill could not believe her ears. Her hands were sweating as she clutched the wheel. Her white T-shirt stuck to her skin like glue. "Have we ever said we'd live in New York forever?" she asked hoarsely, trying to focus on the traffic ahead, but not really seeing anything. Her pulse had become deafening in her own ears.

"If this show is a hit, it could run on Broadway for years.

Don't tell me you'd leave in the midst of a smashing success. You've never had this kind of opportunity before."

Jill wanted *The Mask* to be a huge success, and she believed it would be, and until recently, her career had been the mainstay of her life, but she thought, speechlessly, Yes, I would leave, if it meant losing you. She remained silent.

Hal was also silent.

"Are you telling me that you've changed your mind?" she finally managed.

"No. I'm not sure what to do. I think we need to slow down. I think I should go home for a while and think things through."

Jill inhaled, feeling as if he'd delivered a fatal blow. She was aware now of how her limbs trembled, of a terrible sickness inside her—as if she might throw up. She turned and stared at his perfect profile, aware now of an immense pain, a heavy, dread weight in her chest. And tears filled her eyes.

Good night, pumpkin. The voice was deep, a man's. Daddy. His lips touched her hair. His hand smoothed through her bangs. *Sleep tight. We'll be home soon. By the time you wake up.*

His smile was there, shadowy, loving.

Good night, darling. A woman's soft, loving voice, her mother's slender, graceful silhouette in the doorway of her pink-and-white bedroom.

The door closing.

Darkness.

Silence.

Terror. Being alone—forever.

Because they had never come back.

"Jill!" Hal shouted.

Jill jerked her gaze to the road. To her horror, a huge pine tree was looming toward them as their car hurled toward it. Jill wrenched at the steering wheel, already knowing that it was too late . . .

Nothing in her life could have prepared her for the moment of impact. Her heart stopped. Simultaneously, Jill's entire body was snapped against her seat harness and an air bag. The vehicle, a mass of steel and fiberglass, thundered and screamed and exploded in the head-on collision. Glass shattered everywhere. Pieces of it rained down on Jill's hair and bare arms, her thighs.

And then there was absolute stillness, absolute silence.

Except for the booming sound of Jill's heart.

Her mind came to, slowly, with dread. Her heart seemed to hurt her as it pulsed inside of her chest. Jill's body felt as if it had been snapped in half; it felt crushed. She could not move, she could not breathe. Her mind was blank with shock.

An accident . . .

And then she felt the trickle of liquid down the side of her face as her lungs took in air, as her lids slowly lifted. She did not have to see it or taste it to know that it was blood—that it was her blood.

She was breathing, she was alive, they had hit a tree—oh, God.

Jill opened her eyes and saw the shattered windshield. Her side of the car was quite literally wrapped around the tree; Hal's side of the car was folded in on itself like an accordion.

Hal.

Jill gasped, fumbling with her seat belt, which she could not see, the air bag in her way. She pushed at the bag, so she could see Hal. Blood and sweat and her too-long bangs interfered with her vision. "Hal?"

She shoved at the bag and her bangs again. Jill froze. He, too, was crushed by an air bag. But his head lolled to one side, his eyes closed.

"Hal!" Jill screamed.

She turned and pushed at her door, almost beating on it until she somehow managed to wrench the handle open. Her head now throbbing, unable to breathe, Jill stumbled from the car. She staggered around the back of the sedan, tripping on the rough ground, on rocks and sticks and dirt. At Hal's door, she froze again. Blood was gushing from his neck where glass from the windshield had apparently cut a jagged hole in his throat.

"No!" Jill wrenched at his door and it flew open. Frantically, she found and unbuckled his seat belt.

Jill put her arms around him and dragged him from the car. Blood continued to stream from his neck; the front of his shirt was turning crimson. When he was on the ground, she pressed both hands against the wound, desperately trying to stanch the flow of blood. It was warm and wet and sticky, seeping through her fingers. "Help!" she screamed at the top of her lungs. "Help! Help us, please!"

She sobbed, her gaze on his deathly white face. Then she saw his lashes flutter—he was alive!

"Don't die!" she cried, pushing at his wound, the blood spreading and spreading—endlessly. "Hal, help is coming, don't die—hang on!"

His eyes opened. When he spoke, his mouth filled with blood. "I love you," he said.

"No!" Jill shrieked.

And then he said, his eyes closing, "Kate."

Part One

The Lovers

One

WHO WAS KATE?

Jill inhaled. Tears slipped from beneath her closed lids. Hal was dead and she was standing by the carousel at Baggage Claim in Heathrow Airport. It was almost impossible to believe where she was and, more importantly, why she was there. Jill was numb. Exhaustion, most of it emotional, some of it due to jet lag, did not help. Hal was dead, and she was bringing his body home to his family. The emptiness inside her, the pain, the grief, was astonishing in its intensity, and it was overwhelming.

Hal was dead. Gone, forever. She would never see him again.

And she had killed him.

It was the worst she could have imagined, a nightmare come true. She did not know if she could stand the pain and the confusion—and herself—much longer.

She did not know if she could stand the darkness much longer.

I love you . . . Kate.

Hal's voice, his dying words, pierced through her thoughts, her mind. It was a haunting litany she could not shake. Who was Kate?

Jill jerked. The baggage from the British Airways flight was beginning to come down the ramp, thumping onto the carousel, going round and round, like her own spinning thoughts. Hal's image as he died under the ministrations of a team of paramedics there on the side of the highway was engraved upon her mind. As were his last, haunting words, echoing cruelly, again and again. Words she never wanted to forget—words she never wanted to remember. *I love you . . . Kate.*

Jill hugged herself, cold and shivering. The luggage circling in front of her blurred. Jill knew, she absolutely knew, that he had been telling her, Jill, that he loved her as he died. He had loved her—the way she had loved him. Jill had not a doubt. And she knew she must seize on to and cherish this belief. But dear God, his death, and her hand in it, his speaking of this other woman, Kate, it was all horrible enough without their having had that last and final, irreversible, unforgettable exchange. If only he hadn't told her he had been having second thoughts about their future. He'd been having doubts about them, about her. Jill choked on a sob. She was in the throes of guilt and pain, grief and confusion.

Jill closed her eyes. She must not think about that conversation, it was unbearable. Everything was unbearable. Hal had been taken away from her. Just like her parents. Her love, her life, had been destroyed—a second time.

Suddenly Jill's world became too painful to bear. Blackness gathered before her eyes. Jill fought the urge to pass out, to faint. She must stop thinking, she told herself desperately, aware of tears streaming down her face, aware of the crowded terminal coming into and then out of focus. She fought for equilibrium as she swayed, her knees weak and buckling. She had to get her luggage. She had to get out of there—she had to get air. She must concentrate on the details of survival—and on meeting Hal's family, dear God. Hal's sister, Lauren, was picking her up at the airport.

And in that moment, Jill's mind went suddenly, frighteningly, blank.

For one instant, she was utterly confused. She was panic-stricken. She did not know where she was, or why. She did not know who she was. The crowd moving around her, the interior of the terminal, became more than a sea of shadows and faces. She could not identify anything or anyone. Even the letters on the signs became gibberish she could not read.

But everywhere there were pairs of eyes. Turning her way, wide and accusing, myriad hostile stares.

Why was everyone looking at her as if they wished she were dead? Jill was ready to turn and run, but run where?

Dead.

In the next moment, her mind snapped to, the shadows became walls and doorways, gates and railings, the shapes became people, the eyes, faces, and she knew everything and it was so much worse. People were staring at her, but she was crying helplessly, and she was at Heathrow, bringing Hal's body home to his family—tomorrow was the funeral. Did everyone present know that she had killed the man of her dreams? Jill wished she hadn't remembered anything. There had been bliss in the memory loss.

It had been like that ever since Hal had died—not knowing what to do, moments of terrible confusion, followed by other moments of sheer memory loss and then absolute, horrific recognition. Shock, a doctor had said. She would be in shock for the next few days, maybe even the next few weeks. He had encouraged her to rest at home and continue taking the medication he had prescribed.

Jill had thrown the antidepressants down the toilet after the first night. She had loved Hal so much and she would not sell her feelings short by trying to blunt or ignore them with Xanax. She would grieve for him the way that she had loved him, completely, irrevocably.

Jill removed her sunglasses to wipe her eyes with a tissue before replacing them. Her luggage. She had to find her single duffel bag and get out of there while she remained on her feet and in one piece. The one thing she must now do, Jill decided, was try not to think.

Her thoughts were her own worst enemy.

Jill glanced down at her feet, to find her carry-on and leopard-print vinyl tote there, along with her oversized black blazer. She turned her gaze to the carousel. To her surprise, most of the bags had been claimed. It seemed like only seconds ago she had been surrounded by the hundreds of passengers from her flight—now only a dozen people or so were waiting for their bags. Jill inhaled desperately. Had she blacked out? Somehow, she seemed to have lost time as well as her memory.

She wondered how she was going to survive, not just the next few days, but the next few weeks, months, years.

Don't think! Jill told herself frantically. She must not go where her thoughts would lead. Suddenly Jill saw her black nylon duffel bag. It was already moving past her. Jill ran after it with desperation, gripping the handle and swinging it off of the carousel. The effort cost her dearly, and she stood there for a moment, panting. She had never experienced this kind of monumental exhaustion before.

When she had regained her breath, she glanced around at the milling crowd. Now where did she go? Now what did she do? How did she find Lauren, whom she had only glimpsed in a photograph?

Jill was frozen, against her own admonitions helplessly thinking of the time Hal had so fondly and proudly showed her photos of his family. Hal had spoken often, not just of his sister, but also of his older brother, Thomas, his parents, and his American cousin. His family was, by his accounts, extremely close-knit. His love for them had been so obvious. He had glowed when he had told her tales of growing up as a child, most of them describing the summers in Stainesmore at the old family estate in the north, where as children they fished and hunted and explored the nearby haunted manor. But there had been Christmas holidays at St. Moritz, Easter in St. Tropez, and those years at Eton, playing hooky and running wild in London's West End, chasing "birds" as he called the girls, and sneaking into clubs. Then there had been his football years at Cambridge. And always, since he was a small boy, there had been his first love, his true love, his photography.

Jill knew she was crying again. He had held her close on so many nights, telling her how his family would adore her— and that they would welcome her with open arms, as if she were one of them. He had been eager to bring her home, he could not wait for her to meet them. Until that unbelievable and final conversation of theirs in the car, when he had told her he wasn't sure he really wanted to get married after all, that he wanted to go home for a while, alone.

Jill knew she must not cry again, but the tears would not stop. Shaking and weak and afraid of blacking out another time, Jill picked up her bags and started walking slowly with the crowd. She must forget about their last conversation. It was the icing on the cake, incapacitating her with bewilderment and confusion. In time, they would have worked things out. Hal would not have walked out on her. Jill knew she had to believe that.

Jill followed the crowd through a barricade where Customs officials watched them go by, relieved at least that for the moment her tears had ceased. She was about to meet Lauren and the rest of Hal's family, and never in a million years would she have dreamed that it would be this way, with her bringing Hal's body home for the funeral. She wanted, desperately, to be in control of her physical functions. She did not want to black out in front of them.

She paused as she reached a circular area where a crowd was waiting for the arriving passengers, some of them drivers holding up signs with names written boldly upon them. And Jill's gaze immediately settled on a tawny-haired woman about her own age. Jill recognized the other woman instantly. Even if Jill had not seen photographs of Lauren, she would have recognized her because she looked so much like Hal. Her shoulder-length hair was the same dark blond, spiked with lighter strands of gold, and her features were also classic. Like Hal, she was tall and slim. Lauren had that very same look of casual elegance and worry-free wealth that had nothing to do with the designer pants suit she wore but everything to do with her actual heritage—it was an aura only those born to old money can have.

Jill faltered, unable to continue forward. Suddenly she was deathly afraid to meet the other woman.

Lauren had spotted her, too. She was also motionless, and she was staring. Like Jill, she wore dark glasses. But hers were tortoiseshell and oversized, matching her beige Armani suit and Hermes scarf perfectly. She did not smile at Jill. Her face was stiff and set in an expression of . . . what? Self-control? Suffering? Distaste? Jill could not tell.

But she was taken aback and dismayed. Gripping both her canvas duffel bag and her carry-on, as well as her leopard-print vinyl tote, aware now of wearing faded Levi's and a white T-shirt, Jill walked slowly toward Hal's sister. "Lauren Sheldon?" She could not meet her gaze even through the dark glasses that they both wore.

Lauren nodded, a single jerk of her head, turning her face aside.

Jill swallowed the lump that was choking her. "I'm Jill Gallagher."

Lauren had folded her arms across her chest. Her shoulder bag seemed to be dark brown alligator. A gold and diamond Piaget watch glinted from beneath the cuff of her suit jacket. "I have a driver outside. We've already picked up the coffin. Because of the Easter holiday, we couldn't find you a decent room and you'll be staying at the house." She turned and began walking rapidly out of the airport.

For one moment Jill stared after her, trembling, in disbelief. The woman had not said hello, or asked her how her flight was. Hal had said that Lauren was kind and compassionate and more than friendly. This woman was cold and aloof, and not even civil.

But what did she expect? She had been at the wheel, and now Hal was dead. Lauren must hate her—the entire Sheldon family must hate her. She hated herself.

Far more ill than before, filled now with an accompanying dread, Jill followed Lauren out of the terminal, her mind going blank again.

Jill shifted so that she could see the highway behind her. She was in the backseat of a chauffeured Rolls-Royce, as was Lauren. Both women had taken to the farthest and opposite corners of the spacious sedan. The hearse was behind them. Jill watched it make a left turn. She continued to watch the long black sedan as it disappeared from sight. It was taking Hal's body to the funeral home, while she and Lauren were going to the Sheldons' house in London.

Jill did not want to be separated from the hearse. She almost felt like banging on the door, demanding to be let out. Her heart was thundering in her chest, and her sense of loss was, amazingly, worse. It was insane. Jill continued to stare after the disappearing hearse. She bit down hard on her lip, determined not to make a sound. She was shaking uncontrollably and afraid she might once again escape her grief by blacking out.

Jill forced herself to settle back in her seat and breathe deeply, her eyes closed, continuing to shake as she fought for equilibrium. She was not even going to make it through the next twenty-four hours if she did not somehow come to grips with herself and Hal's death. When she had regained a small amount of her composure, she glanced at Lauren. In the thirty minutes since they had left the airport, Hal's sister had not said a single word. She sat with her back toward Jill, her shoulders rigid, staring out of her driver's side window. She had not removed her sunglasses, but then, neither had Jill. They were like two hostile zombies, Jill thought grimly.

So much for kindness. They could comfort one another. After all, they had both loved Hal. But Jill did not feel up to making the first overture, not yet, and she was too aware of her role in his death. Tears burned her eyes. The funeral was tomorrow. She was booked to return home the following night. She hated the thought of leaving him behind, an entire ocean between them, yet on the other hand, if the Sheldons were all as compassionate as Lauren, it was for the best.

She opened her carry-on, a huge fake Louis Vuitton bag that she had bought for fifteen dollars from a street vendor, and searched for and found a Kleenex. She dabbed at her eyes. Lauren hated her. Jill was certain of it. She could actually feel the other woman's simmering resentment.

Jill did not blame her.

When Jill tucked the tissue back in her bag she looked up and found Lauren watching her, facing her directly for the first time.

Jill did not think. Impulsively she said, low, "I'm sorry."

Lauren said, "We're all sorry."

Jill bit her lip. "It was an accident."

Lauren continued to face her. Jill could not see her eyes through the opaque sunglasses she wore. "Why did you come?"

Jill was startled. "I had to bring him home. He spoke of you—all of you—so often." She could not continue.

Lauren looked away. Another silence fell.

"I loved him, too," Jill heard herself say.

Lauren turned to her. "He should be alive. A few days ago he was alive. I can't believe he's gone." Her words were angry and had she pointed her finger at Jill, the blame she felt could not have been more obvious.

"Neither can I," Jill whispered miserably. It was true. In the middle of the night she would wake up, expecting to find the solid warmth of Hal's body beside her. The coldness of her bed was a shock—as was the sudden recollection of his death. There was nothing worse, Jill had realized, than the oblivion of sleep followed by the absolute cognition of consciousness. "If only," Jill whispered, more to herself than to Lauren, "we hadn't gone away that weekend."

But they had. And she could not change the past few days, she could only have regrets. She would have regrets for the rest of her life—regrets and guilt.

Had he really been thinking of breaking up with her?

"Hal should have come home months ago," Lauren said tersely, interrupting Jill's thoughts. "He was scheduled to come home in February—for my birthday."

"He liked New York," Jill managed, avoiding her eyes.

Lauren removed her glasses, revealing red-rimmed eyes that were the exact same amber shade as Hal's. "He was homesick. The last few times we spoke, he told me so."

Jill was motionless. What else had he told his younger sister, whom he was so close to?

Jill thought she would die if Lauren knew about Hal's sudden change of heart about their future.

Then, angrily, she reminded herself that it had not been a change of heart. Nothing had been set in stone. Everything would have worked out, sooner rather than later.

Lauren remained unmoving also. Finally she said, "He mentioned you."

Jill jerked, eyes wide, staring now at Lauren as if she were a Martian. He had *mentioned* her? "What do you mean, he mentioned me?"

"Just that," Lauren said, putting her glasses back on. She glanced out of her window as the silver-gray Rolls sped along. "He mentioned that he was dating you."

Jill stared, stunned. They had not been dating. They had been discussing marriage—they had been on the verge of becoming engaged. She was speechless.

"How long were the two of you seeing one another?" Lauren asked bluntly.

Jill looked at her, the other woman becoming hazy and blurred. "Eight months. We met eight months ago." She was gripping the sensuous leather seat with desperation.

"That isn't a very long time," Lauren said after a pause.

"It was long enough to fall head over heels in love and to be thinking about . . ." Jill stopped herself short.

Lauren removed her eyeglasses again. "To be thinking about what?" she demanded.

Jill wet her lips. She hesitated. Everything raced through her mind—his ambivalence, her guilt, a woman named Kate. "The future," she whispered.

Lauren just stared—as if she had two heads. "He should have come home a long time ago," Lauren said finally. "He did not belong in New York."

Jill did not know how to respond. Hal had not told his sister about the extent of his relationship with her. Why? It hurt. God, it hurt, the way thinking about their last conversation hurt—the way he had hurt her by even having doubts about their future as man and wife. She lay back against the seat, severely exhausted. It hurt almost as much as his death hurt.

She needed to find a sanctuary and bury her head under a pillow and sleep. But then she would wake up and remember everything and it would be so awful . . .

The Rolls-Royce stopped.

Instantly Jill's tension increased. The Sheldon family

home was now the last place she wished to be, because if
Lauren's reception was any indication of the way Hal's family would greet her, then she was not ready to meet them, not
now, not ever.

They were on a busy, two-way street in the midst of London, Jill realized. The driver was waiting to make a right-
hand turn across the lane of oncoming traffic. Tall iron gates
were open, but the road they wished to turn onto was barred
by a mechanical barricade and a uniformed security guard.
Jill wet her lips. Past the barricade, she glimpsed a shady,
tree-lined street of huge stone mansions.

The Rolls crossed the road, the barrier was lifted without
their even slowing, the officer on duty inside of a small security booth waving them on. Jill craned her neck as the Rolls
rolled up the asphalt street, viewing palatial home after palatial home. A park seemed to be behind the homes on her
right.

Jill wanted to ask where they were. She did not.

The Rolls turned into a circular driveway on one of the
street's largest mansions and halted in the graveled drive
before the house. Jill thought she could feel her blood pressure rocketing.

"We're here." Lauren stepped out of the car without waiting for the chauffeur to assist her. Jill could not move as
quickly. The gentleman opened the door for her and Jill
stumbled out. It had started to drizzle.

Jill did not move. The fine mist settling on her hair and
shoulders, she stared at the house where Hal had been raised
as Lauren hurried up the wide and imposing front steps. Two
sitting lions, carved in stone, guarded those front steps. For
one moment, Jill was completely taken aback.

Hal had talked about his family's London home with
pride. Hal had mentioned, oh-so-casually, that the house,
built around the turn of the century, had about twenty-five
rooms and one of London's most spectacular rose gardens. It
was not the family's original London home, which had been
built in Georgian times and was part of the National Trust. Jill
had vaguely gathered that Uxbridge Hall, which was some-

where just outside of central London, was open to the public, although the family kept private apartments there as well.

Jill stared up at the city dwelling. She had expected opulence, yet she was taken aback now that she was actually confronted with the reality and the extent of it. The house was built of a medium-hued sand-colored stone and was three stories high—but the first two floors clearly had double ceilings. Thick columns supported a temple pediment over the oversized front door, and the numerous arched windows also boasted smaller pediments and intricate stone engravings. There were iron balconies on the second floor and the high, sloping roofs sported a jumble of chimneys. The stonework itself was amazing. Painstaking detail had gone into every cornice and molding. The house was surrounded by manicured lawns and blooming rose gardens; a wrought-iron fence circled the perimeter of the entire property, undoubtedly to keep the public out.

"God," Jill heard herself say. In spite of all the conversations she'd had with Hal, she could hardly believe that he had been raised in this house. And this was just their city home, not even their ancestral home, which Jill suspected was even larger and grander. She was suddenly aware of how small and shabby her own studio in the Village was. She suddenly wished she were not wearing her oldest, favorite, and most faded Levi's.

If Lauren heard her, she gave no sign, for she was already pushing open the heavy front door.

"I shall bring your bags, madam," the driver said behind her.

Jill hoped she smiled at him, thought she failed, and slowly followed in Lauren's wake. She found herself in a large entry hall with high ceilings and polished beige-and-white marble floors. Works of art hung on the walls, and the bench, marble-topped table, and mirror were all exquisitely gilded. Jill was grim. She was acutely aware of not belonging there.

Jill glanced down at her worn Levi's, and the black blazer she had put on in the air-conditioned car. The jacket was actually a man's sports jacket, but she had loved it upon sight and had bought it in a thrift store for herself. She was wearing Cole-Haan loafers, but they were very old, as soft as butter, and severely scuffed. Of course, she could only wear soft, broken-in shoes when she was not dancing because of the pain and damage her profession caused her feet.

She hesitated, afraid now to follow Lauren, feeling horribly out of place, wishing she had worn a suit like Lauren's. She didn't even remember dressing for the trip abroad. She had not a clue about what was in her duffel bag. If she was lucky, KC, her best friend and neighbor, had helped her pack, but Jill didn't remember even speaking to KC in the past few days. Suddenly she was worried about her cat, Ezekial. She would have to call KC immediately and make sure she was taking care of the tom.

Jill's gaze settled on a painting that took up an entire wall. It had to be a masterpiece, and it was depicting some kind of mythological scene that she was not familiar with. She swallowed, telling herself to take deep, steady breaths. She would meet his family, be polite. Surely they would be civil in return—unlike Lauren. In a few moments she would be shown to her room. It could not be too soon.

If only she were staying in a hotel.

Her anxiety had gotten to the point where she was ready to make a mad dash back out the front door. Jill glanced over her shoulder. The front door was solidly closed.

Her panic began mounting slowly, steadily.

Jill told herself that everything would be all right. To keep breathing deeply.

Hal's image, as he lay dying in her arms, his face starkly white, his mouth spouting blood, filled her mind.

Footsteps sounded. Jill tried to still her trembling hands and smile as Lauren reappeared. She had removed her jacket, revealing a beige silk T-shirt that probably cost more than all of the clothing upon Jill's body. "Come," she said.

Jill followed, filled with trepidation. Lauren led her into a large living room, far more lavish than the foyer. But Jill hardly glimpsed the faded but stunning Oriental rugs and the antique furnishings or the Matisse hanging on one wall.

Three men were standing in the center of the room, one elderly and white-haired, the two other men younger, in their thirties, one golden and tanned, the other dark-haired and olive-skinned. Each man was holding a drink.

Lauren stopped, as did Jill. The three men turned. As one, they all stared at Jill.

Three pairs of penetrating eyes. Three pairs of accusing gazes.

This was Hal's family.

Jill knew she was facing William, Hal's elderly father, and his older brother, Thomas, and his cousin, Alex. She did not know who each of the younger men was, although she suspected Thomas was the blond. But at that moment, she could take it no more. For their stares did not relent. Their hostility was unmistakable. But then, she had been the one driving . . .

"Some time to think . . . I love you . . . Kate."

Jill tried to clear her head. She could not. Lauren was saying something, but her tone was as cold, as unfriendly, as the regards leveled at her. Those accusing, cold, hostile stares . . . Jill watched the figures before her begin to waver and blur. Hal's ghostly white face, the blood . . . She had been driving . . . The room had dimmed, and now it lightened, and then dimmed again. And then absolute darkness came.

It was a blessing.

She heard voices first. Voices she did not recognize, male voices speaking words she could not comprehend.

Jill drifted, oddly light-headed and at peace. And then, as she became more conscious, she realized she had fainted. With that realization came the piercing comprehension that something was terribly wrong. And then her peace was shattered. By the stabbing, gut-wrenching realization that she had fainted because Hal was dead.

"What was Hal thinking?" a deep, sandy voice said. It was patrician, British, and very angry.

Jill stiffened. She had been about to open her eyes, remembering where she was now, but she kept them screwed shut.

"Hal was doing what he had to do—following his own drummer—that was Hal." Another voice, this one less hostile, but curt nonetheless. The speaker had an American accent. He must be the cousin, Alex.

"He should never have started up with her in the first place," the first voice said with the same deep pitch of anger. "He was asking for trouble. Bloody, bloody hell."

Jill didn't understand. What were they talking about? Were they talking about her?

"And look at what has happened," Lauren said, very clearly anguished. "Now he's dead. Because of her!"

Jill was tense. They all blamed her for the accident. Her stomach roiled with sickening force.

"Enough of this arguing, all of you," a third, older voice said. It was weary and it obviously belonged to William, Hal's father. "We are in a difficult time and . . ." He stopped abruptly, his voice breaking, unable to continue.

Jill's heart broke again, for him and for herself.

"Uncle William, sit down. Let me refill that."

"Thank you," William whispered, choked.

Jill wished she were anywhere but there, with the Sheldons in their living room. She should not be there. This was too personal, too intimate.

"She has nerve," the first voice cut in with its gravelly tone. It was not a compliment. "I wonder just what she knows, exactly, and why she is here." It had to be Thomas speaking.

"Your father is right. Let's not make this worse, and accusations are pointless now, without hard facts." The American was speaking again. Alex.

"Accusations," Thomas repeated harshly. "Don't tell me not to accuse her, Alex, on several counts. Damn it."

"I'm not telling you what to do. But Uncle William is right. This is a tough time, not the time to be rash."

Someone was leaning over her. Jill tensed, afraid to be discovered pretending to still be passed out. "Miss Gallagher?" It was Alex speaking again.

Jill was distressed. She opened her eyes, tears burning her

lids, despising them all now, her instincts trying to scream some kind of warning at her. Her gaze instantly met his.

His eyes were surprisingly blue, his skin swarthy, his hair short, black, and curly. They stared at one another. He soon straightened to his full height—and he was tall, perhaps six feet or more. "She's conscious." Alex continued to stare down at her. His gaze was piercing, and suddenly Jill was afraid that he knew she had been conscious for some time now—and eavesdropping on them all.

Jill started to sit up, but immediately was overcome with dizziness again.

Lauren looked down at her. "You fainted. Perhaps you should lie still for another moment or two."

"This has never happened before," Jill said hoarsely, embarrassed and wanting nothing more than to recover her strength and flee the room, and all of them. She had fainted— and that was not the same as those blackouts. "I didn't eat." How inane that comment sounded. Her gaze shifted to the three men as she tried to sit up, this time successfully. They were all gazing at her. She could identify them now. William was tall but paunchy and tired-looking, with a full head of white hair, and he was, she thought, well into his seventies, but still attractive for his age. In his double-breasted, navy blue blazer, his tan slacks and signet ring, he looked exactly the way she had expected a wealthy, blue-blooded aristocrat to look.

Thomas was his heir. He was the oldest of the siblings. Hal had mentioned more than once that his brother, whom he had adored, was an incorrigible playboy with the kind of looks and charm few women seemed capable of resisting. Jill had avoided looking his way until now, but she would have to be blind not to notice that he was every bit as drop-dead good-looking as Hal had said. His dark blond hair was sun-streaked, he was tanned, and he had the kind of muscular but not bulky body that obviously worked out vigorously at the gym. His features were more than classic, they were strong and male—the high cheekbones and strong jaw giving way to a surprisingly full and sensual mouth. He was wearing a black Polo shirt and tan trousers, a gold Rolex, Gucci loafers. Jill had expected handsome and she had expected chic. He looked like a jet-setter and a full-time playboy. Jill bet he had a dissipated lifestyle. Jill also knew that Thomas was divorced, and that his two small sons lived most of the year with their mother.

Jill realized she was staring, worse, that he knew it, for his gaze had locked with hers. She flushed. The look he sent her was cold and cutting. His message could not be louder—Jill had no doubt that he found her entirely lacking, at least in appearance. Clearly he disapproved of her faded jeans and "boyfriend" jacket, if not of her. Clearly, like Lauren, he blamed her for Hal's death.

She should have realized that this would be her reception. Maybe she was a fool for having come. But how could she not attend Hal's funeral?

"Introductions are in order," Alex said, cutting into her thoughts.

Jill met his eyes again as he stepped forward. The heat remained in her cheeks. "I'm sorry," she said, more to him, but really for everyone's benefit.

His nod was curt; his gaze shifted. Clearly he was as unsympathetic as everyone else. "Stress, shock, it happens." He was matter-of-fact.

Jill found herself regarding him. Hal had said his cousin was originally from Brooklyn, but what else had he said? He'd talked less about Alex than Lauren and Thomas. Jill thought she recalled something about Alex having lived in London for a number of years and his working in the family company. Hal had said he was brilliant, she remembered that—he had gone to Princeton on an athletic scholarship if her memory now served her.

She realized she was staring. His regard had darkened—as if he knew she was studying him, and Jill averted her gaze, managing to stand up. She folded her arms tightly around herself. Was this what it felt like to be tossed into a den of hungry wolves? She intended to beg to go to her room as soon as the introductions were dispensed with.

"My uncle, the earl of Collinsworth, my cousins, Thomas

Sheldon, and Lauren Sheldon-Wellsely," he said flatly. "And I am Alex Preston."

Jill stiffened, aware of what he was doing and incredulous that he would deliberately put her in her place as an American commoner among British aristocracy. His gaze held hers. She was not mistaking his intentional put-down. Jill was thoroughly taken aback.

Hal had said his family would greet her with open arms. That they would love her as if she were another daughter. But when Hal had said that, he had been alive. Had he really believed that?

Jill looked past Lauren and nodded warily at the other two men, who continued to regard her just as Alex continued to stare.

Thomas broke the brief silence. "You're the dancer," he said flatly, his amber eyes on hers.

Jill flinched. "Yes, I am. A *professional* dancer." She felt the need to defend herself, because his tone led her to wonder if they thought her a stripper or something. "I'm in a Broadway show. We open in ten days."

"Lovely," Thomas said. "The next time I'm in New York, I'll be certain to attend."

Jill knew her cheeks flamed. "I'm sure you will enjoy the performance. I'll make sure that you have front row tickets."

"How kind of you. I imagine it will be one smashing performance."

Jill blinked. What did that mean? She knew there were layers there, but she was too exhausted and anxious to sort through them now.

"How was your flight?" Alex cut in.

Jill was not relieved, because his tone made it clear that he didn't give a damn. But she could not hand him a platitude. "It was difficult. Very difficult." And to her horror, her voice cracked and broke. Instantly Jill turned her gaze away.

Everyone seemed surprised, but whether by her display of emotion or her declaration of the truth, Jill could not tell. Everyone, that is, except for Alex. His regard was steady but incomprehensible. He watched her fumble in her tote for a moment, and then he handed her a tissue the way he might hand a homeless person a quarter, with neither a smile nor any real sympathy at all.

William stepped forward. "Miss Gallager. We appreciate your bringing my son home."

Jill tensed, instantly feeling ill and faint again, facing William, wondering if her guilt showed—and praying that she would not have a blackout now. He was beginning to waver before her very eyes. "I am so sorry," she began. "I never thought—"

"Yes, of course, we all are. Now, if you will excuse me, I wish to retire." His smile was brief and strained; clearly he did not want her to finish. "Until tomorrow then. Good evening."

Jill watched him leave the room, walking like a very old man, his shoulders hunched over, his strides slow and heavy with effort. She had done this to him, she managed to think.

"My father is seventy-nine years old," Thomas spoke suddenly. Jill was riveted by his gaze. "This has destroyed him."

Jill did not know what to say. "It was an accident," she whispered.

"An accident," Thomas repeated harshly. "An accident."

"Tom." Alex stepped between them, gripping his shoulder. "We're all shocked and exhausted." There was a warning in his tone. "Let's skip all this." He turned to Jill. "You must be tired from the flight. Lauren will show you to a room."

Jill was so eager to flee she turned and took a stumbling step toward the doorway, but Thomas's cutting voice halted her an instant later.

"What happened?"

Jill froze.

"I asked you what happened," Thomas said. "My brother's dead. I have a right to know."

Jill had no choice but to face him. "We were going away for the weekend. There was a tree." She did not continue.

Thomas stared. Everyone stared. "I don't understand," he finally said. His nose was turning red. "I spoke extensively with the Highway Patrol. You weren't drinking. You weren't on drugs. The traffic was moderate, and moving well. The roads were only slightly damp. I do not understand!" His voice rose.

"I'm sorry," Jill whispered, trembling wildly now. "I don't know what happened . . ." But she did. Hal had upset her and she hadn't been concentrating on the road. She had killed him, and Thomas had every right to blame her, to hate her—they all did.

"Tom. Not now. Not today. Not like this." Alex's voice was hard.

Thomas wheeled to face his cousin. "Then when? Tomorrow? Before or after the funeral?"

"I expected to meet all of you under far different circumstances," Jill suddenly whispered. Tears blurred her vision. They all turned to stare at her. Lauren, cold; Thomas, visibly upset; Alex, his face an unreadable mask. "Hal spoke of you so often, so glowingly . . . he loved you all and made me love you too, and he told me how he wanted us to meet . . . it should not be this way!"

Thomas made a scoffing sound.

Jill tensed.

Thomas stared. "I am going to drop all pretense, Miss Gallagher. All pretense and all attempts at civility. My brother is dead, and had he not been in New York, he would be very much alive today. I can imagine what it is that you want, and I will tell you this. You will not succeed."

Jill was dazed. "I don't know what you're talking about."

But Thomas wasn't through. His face flushed, he said, "Hal had no intention of ever bringing you home."

Jill stiffened, unable to respond, because she was recalling their very last conversation. Horror had overcome her. And she thought, What if Hal had told his entire family that he was having doubts about us?

Alex turned, clearly intent upon ending the gathering. "Lauren, why don't you have sandwiches sent up to Miss Gallagher's room? She looks exhausted. I'm sure she wants to retire for the evening. As we all do."

Lauren stared at Alex as if she did not understand a word he said. Jill, who was almost quaking, looked from the one to the other, and watched Lauren finally, reluctantly, walk away to do as Alex had asked. "Thank you," Jill said to Alex, praying for one kind face in the family.

He just looked at her, and this time she saw the loathing in his eyes, barely disguised.

"How long did you know my brother?" Thomas demanded.

Jill tensed with dread. "Eight months."

"How did you meet?" Thomas continued, his regard unwavering.

Jill found herself glancing at Alex instinctively, even while knowing that no support would be forthcoming from him. Alex looked at her and finally at his cousin. "Tom, leave it until tomorrow."

"It's a fair question," Thomas said. "They're all fair questions. She appears here with his body. He is in a coffin, God damn it. I want to know how they met."

Jill wished she had something to lean on for physical support. Before she could reply, Lauren was reentering the room and said, "I believe he first saw her in a health club."

Jill glanced at Lauren. "No. I do train at a small studio in SoHo, but we met on the subway."

"That's not what Hal told me," Lauren returned.

"It's the truth," Jill said, mildly perplexed. Lauren was mistaken.

"The underground!" Thomas was incredulous. "Just what the hell was my brother doing on the bloody damned tube?"

"It's a very good way to get around the city," Jill said defensively.

"My brother had a driver at his beck and call," Thomas returned.

"He did, but he didn't want to live that way. He rarely used the driver in the eight months I knew him."

Thomas looked at her in such a way that she knew he thought her influence was responsible for such absurdity on the part of his brother, either that, or he thought she was lying. "It's the truth," Jill cried. "Hal was down-to-earth."

"Don't tell me how my brother was," Thomas snapped.

Their gazes locked. And Jill suddenly wondered how Hal had expected her to ever fit into his family. They were from completely different worlds. His was old money, and she didn't even have a family—her aunt did not count and Jill hadn't been in touch with her in years. Financially, Jill could just make ends meet. She glanced around the huge living room. It was twice as large as her studio back home. These people were old money, upper class, and snobs. What was she even doing there?

"Look, I even use the subway when I'm in New York," Alex said calmly. "Is her room ready?" he asked Lauren, who was standing beside him.

Lauren nodded.

Surprised, Jill glanced at him, grateful for his defense, but she was not deluded, for he was hardly her champion either.

"Since when? Your fraternity days?" Thomas asked Alex with sarcasm.

Alex smiled very slightly. "When I'm in a rush, I've left my driver midtown in a traffic jam and hopped a train." He shrugged. "It is a good way to get around, if you can handle yourself."

"Hal had no business being in the tube, just like he had no business staying in New York." Thomas looked at Jill. His meaning was clear. It was all her fault. *Everything* was her fault.

She was exhausted, she was ill, and she had never felt more debilitated, but she had had enough. "Excuse me. He had every business being in New York. I loved your brother. He loved me! We were happy!" But even as she spoke, their last damned conversation was in the back of her mind, causing doubts she should not have—and how could he have done this to her? "I have never loved anyone more. I will never love anyone this way again," Jill heard herself say. She stopped. She was about to cry.

This time no one handed her a tissue. The huge salon was silent, stunningly so, and Jill found her own Kleenex. She dried her eyes, refusing to look at either Thomas, Alex, or Lauren now. But she had seen their expressions. No one believed a word she had said; they all thought her a liar.

Jill inhaled, fighting to steady her nerves, trying to control the ever-present urge to cry. "It's the truth," she said to them all.

"Well," Thomas finally spoke. "We can dispute your version of the truth all day, can we not?"

"No," Jill said. "No. You cannot."

Thomas's jaw was tight. They stared at one another. This time Jill refused to back down even though he was overpowering.

Thomas smiled grimly—it was more of a twisted curling of his lips—and he suddenly turned and strode from the room. His strides were hard and angry.

Jill realized that she was shaking—and badly. Never in her life had she had such an encounter before.

"How long will you be staying with us, Miss Gallagher?"

Jill met Alex's penetrating blue eyes. She wet her lips. "I'm scheduled to leave the day after tomorrow."

Alex nodded. "If you give me your flight information, I'll see that you have a driver to take you to Heathrow."

Jill knew he couldn't wait for her to leave, and that her departure wasn't scheduled soon enough to suit him or any of them. Yet she couldn't offer to change her flight—she could not afford to do so. As it was, the round-trip fare, booked only a day in advance, had cost her well over a thousand dollars. She did not have money like that to spare. Jill was silent, and she was angry. Why did it seem like the entire family had wanted her to send Hal home alone? She had every right to attend the funeral.

"Please come with me," Lauren said, but it was a command.

Jill glanced at her stony face. She could not wait to escape the salon. "Lead the way."

"One minute, Miss Gallagher."

Jill stiffened, facing Alex. "Yes?"

"I want to caution you," he said firmly, his stance wide, almost threatening. "This family is in shock. You're a stranger in our midst. I don't want the boat rocked, not even slightly. I'm asking you to keep a very low profile for the next two days until you leave."

Jill stared at him, her pulse pounding. "I don't think you

are asking me anything," she said through stiff lips. "You are giving me orders."

"I'm advising you," he said flatly.

Jill hugged herself. Her damn eyes were glazing over again. "I know I'm not welcome here. I guess I should have sent Hal home alone. But that was something I could not do."

Something in his blue eyes flickered. "No one said that, Miss Gallagher."

Jill shook her head. "I am sorry if my coming here has rocked your boat." She was suddenly bitter. "He died in my arms. How could I not bring him home? I have every right to be at the funeral!" She felt tears slipping down her cheeks. She glared at Lauren. "We weren't dating. We were practically engaged—a week before he died he proposed to me. *He asked me to marry him,*" she cried aggressively.

The words had erupted of their own volition, and even as they did, her confidence wavered, while her emotions got the best of her and she could not continue. There wasn't much more to say anyway.

And all she could think of was, Hal, come back, I am so alone . . . I need you!

Then she realized that Lauren and Alex were regarding her in disbelief.

"I don't believe you," Lauren said, her expression aghast. "He would never have asked you to marry him. Thomas is right about you!"

Jill started. She did not know what Lauren meant by her last remark.

"Hal and I are very close," Lauren cried. "We are—were—only two years apart in age. If he was going to affiance himself to you, he would have told me. He said you were dating. That is all. He mentioned it once or twice. I know my brother! If my brother was in love and planning on marriage, he would have told me—time and again!"

Jill's pulse was racing wildly. Her knees felt weak—she was afraid she might once again collapse. "No," she said, shaking her head. She looked from Lauren to Alex. He was regarding her with his probing blue gaze, the shock now gone from his face. He didn't believe her either, she thought.

And she was terribly, sickeningly afraid that it was pity she now saw in his eyes. "He asked me to marry him—he did," she said hoarsely.

Alex's hands were on his hips. "It doesn't matter. The point is moot. Lauren?"

A sudden determination seized Jill. She must never let this family know that she herself had doubts—that Hal had been uncertain in the end—that maybe they were all right—while she herself was wrong.

Oh, God.

Lauren stepped forward. Her eyes were red. "Come with me. I'll show you to your room." She turned and briskly left the salon, not waiting to see if Jill was following.

Jill hesitated, sending Alex one last glance. His regard was steady, and she had the uneasy feeling that he sensed her confusion and doubt—that he sensed the entire story. But that could not be the case. She was, understandably, paranoid.

"We'll talk tomorrow," he suddenly said.

There was something unyielding in his tone that made Jill hurry away from him. She had no wish to speak with him tomorrow or at any other time. She stumbled after Lauren, wishing she had never arrived at the Sheldon home, wishing she had never met any of them.

Jill followed Lauren up to the third floor. Lauren said not a word. Her shoulders seemed rigidly set. As they walked down a long corridor, carpeted in blue and gold, numerous works of art hanging on the walls, Jill suddenly wanted to find Hal's room. The room he had grown up in as a boy. The room he had used when he was in town. It would give her some comfort to go there.

They stopped at a beautifully ornate door. "Good night," Lauren said. She turned and walked away.

Jill watched her go. She knew she was not mistaking her rudeness. Then she walked into her bedroom, closing the door behind her.

Her bags had been brought up. They were neatly lined up at the foot of a huge four-poster bed with a dark green velvet bedspread, matching dust ruffles, and pillows and shams in various shades of green, blue, and gold. Jill looked around, wide-eyed.

The ceiling was pink, and intricately carved, a huge beige starburst in its center. The walls were painted a lovely, muted jade green, and numerous paintings—all of them old but small in size—hung on the walls. The room she had been given was the size of her studio in the Village—at least. There was also a working fireplace on one wall, the mantel a dark green marble, and the room's furnishings were all antique, the fabrics—brocades, silks, and damasks—rich in texture, but faded and old.

Jill wandered around, touching the beautiful porcelain lamps and a small black, green, and gold Chinese screen standing in one corner. Had Hal been insane? She would have never fit into his family in a million years.

Jill stood very still, seized with absolute understanding, with horrific comprehension.

Hal had fallen in love with her. But when their relationship had deepened, he had realized the impossibility of ever bringing her home. He had wanted to marry her—but had realized that his family would fight their marriage tooth and nail. The Sheldons would have never accepted a lowly dancer into their midst. Which was why he had suddenly had second thoughts about them.

Jill sank down onto the bed.

Hal had loved his family. From the start of their relationship he had spoken about them often, with love and pride. It had been clear to Jill that his family was the center of his existence, and because she herself had no family, it had been one of the very first reasons why she had fallen in love with him.

She closed her eyes. Hal wasn't at all like his brother, his cousin, or his sister. He had not been arrogant, and he had not flashed his money around town. Jill had not lied when she had said he had rarely used his driver in the entire time she had known him, and he had preferred jeans and T-shirts to suits and sports coats. It had never bothered Jill that he did not earn a living from his photography. He had been an artist, just as she was, and she had believed in him deeply. She had always felt certain that one day he would have had his lucky break and show his work to great critical reviews, and that would be the beginning of his career.

Suddenly the pieces of the puzzle began to fit. Hal was so different from them all. No matter that he adored them. What if he had gone to New York to escape them and the pressures of being a Sheldon—of being the different Sheldon, the near black sheep?

If so, he would have been very conflicted. But he had hidden his inner turmoil so very well—until their last and final conversation.

Jill grew frightened. She hugged her pillow, not wanting to go where her thoughts were leading her. Hal had known, at the end, that he could not bring her home without having to choose between her and his family. Jill wept.

And when her sobs finally died, she lay staring up at the ceiling, knowing she would never know how he would have solved his dilemma. Jill wished she hadn't come to London.

She wished, desperately, that Hal were alive, that they were back in New York, in the midst of their fairy tale. For now that was what it was beginning to appear to be—a foolish fairy tale.

But it was a fairy tale she would never forget, not for the rest of her life.

Jill could not sleep.

Her thoughts tormented her. And she missed Hal so badly that it hurt in every fiber of her being.

But perhaps the worst part was staring at the night-darkened ceiling, feeling so utterly alone—being so utterly alone—once again.

Jill turned on the bedside lamp. She could beg God from here to eternity, but Hal was dead, and nothing could ever change that fact. But somehow, she would survive—just as she had survived the loss of her parents twenty-three years ago. But this time the loss was different. This time she would cling to her memories. She did not want to ever forget, even if it meant living with anguish for the rest of her life. The only thing she had to do now, for her own sanity, was lay to rest her confusion and doubts. For that was a cross she just could not bear.

Abruptly Jill stood up. She could not sleep, and lying restless in bed would make her crazy, with her thoughts seesawing back and forth between her worst fears and her now unattainable hopes and dreams. She needed to do something, she needed to distract herself, for she dreaded being alone for the rest of the night.

Jill walked over to a television on a nightstand and snapped it on. She rubbed her forehead tiredly. British television with its odd humor did not interest her. What she really needed was a sleeping pill or two, which she did not have. Barring that, she could use a good stiff drink. A martini or two would do, she thought almost savagely.

Hadn't she seen a bar cart in the salon where she had fainted?

Jill glanced at the clock on her nightstand. It was a quarter to twelve. She had arrived at seven-thirty P.M. By now, the family must be well asleep. She crossed the room, pulling on a pair of jeans, for she'd been sleeping in her T-shirt and panties. She refused to consider what would happen if she were caught wandering about the house unescorted. She did not think anyone would look kindly upon the act. She knew from Hal that Lauren and Alex did not live with the family. If she stumbled across anyone, it would be that bastard Thomas. But that was too bad. She would stand up to him if he dared to confront her the way he had earlier that day. She owed the Sheldons nothing. She was alone again, and if she did not take care of herself now; no one else would.

Jill made it to the living room without seeing a soul and poured herself a scotch, which she did not usually drink and did not even like, and started back up the stairs. But on the second-floor landing she paused, sipping the neat drink. It warmed her instantly, and even better, it dulled the grief and pain and confusion immediately. Hal's bedroom, she knew, was on this floor. He had often told her how he loved the light from his bedroom facing east on the second floor.

How she wished she could go to his room and wander

among his things. On the other hand, she knew his family would be furious if she did so without permission.

But Hal wouldn't mind. Jill could almost feel him smiling at her—encouraging her.

And she didn't give a damn about the Sheldons, not after the way they had treated her that evening.

Scotch in hand, Jill started down the hall, trying to be as soundless as possible. She paused at a door, leaning her ear against it. When she heard nothing, she knocked very softly. There was still no answer.

Her heart racing wildly now, Jill turned the knob and pushed the door open. Shadows greeted her. She hit a wall switch.

A bedroom that had not been used in years greeted her, and Jill saw nothing to even remotely suggest that it belonged to a boy, much less Hal. She turned off the light, quickly backing out and closing the door. Her heart continued to thunder in her own ears.

She continued down the hall, finishing the scotch, finding three more unoccupied rooms, her pulse rampaging inside of her chest. She was beginning to question the wisdom of what she was doing, yet the scotch had given her courage. On her fifth try, she knew she had stumbled onto his room.

She inhaled, fighting to regain her equilibrium.

For facing her was a bookcase, and in it was an entire shelf of framed photographs.

The walls were also covered in photographs.

Jill began to shake. She would recognize Hal's work anywhere. She slipped into the room, shutting the door behind her, turning on the lights.

His work surrounded her, everywhere. Jill wished she had another drink.

Again, tears somehow slipped down her cheeks.

"Oh, Hal," she whispered. Her words sounded bereft to her own ears.

The royal blue draperies were partially drawn and the room was cast in dancing shadows caused by the street and house lights outside. Jill's heart was hammering wildly now as she walked over to the bookcase. She smiled, more tears coming to her eyes. Hal had mentioned to her that he had been insane as a youth, shooting everything in sight. She saw photographs of wildlife—clearly he had been on safari—of flowers, trees, landscapes, Stonehenge. And then there were photographs of his family.

Blinking to clear her eyes, Jill picked up a framed photograph of Thomas, taken perhaps ten years ago. Even then he'd had the striking looks of a model or an actor. Jill stared. Not because he had gotten better-looking with age, but because the shot was clearly a candid one, and Hal had caught Thomas leaning over an infant, with the most beautiful expression of love on his face. The child, Jill assumed, was his own.

Jill put it back. Then she froze.

On another shelf there were several photographs of Hal as a teenager and as a young man. They were not self-portraits, because Jill could recognize Hal's work. Someone else had taken them.

She started to cry, but soundlessly, the tears streaming endlessly down her cheeks.

She touched the frames. He was playing soccer in one shot, riding with the hounds in another—looking so damn blue-blooded doing so—and holding up a diploma in the last. She smiled through her tears.

She paused. There was a fourth photograph of him on a ski slope, and he was with a young woman. A terrible pang pierced through her as she studied the photo. The woman was not Lauren, she was red-haired and stunning. Of course, this photo had to be several years old and her first reaction, which was jealousy, was absurd. Staring closely at it, Jill decided that Hal looked very thin, even in his ski clothes. Had he been ill at the time this photograph was taken?

She put the frame back and glanced over at the few books filling the rest of the bookcase. Then she wandered to the bed, which was a massive four-poster in an extremely dark wood. She ran her head over the plaid quilt. He probably hadn't slept there in years.

She sat down on the bed, glancing at the photographs taped to the walls. Most were black-and-white. Many were

portraits of people she did not know, many were of his family.
Jill stared at one portrait, a head shot of a beautiful and regal
older woman who had to be his mother, the countess, whom
she had not yet met. The resemblance was unmistakable.

Jill did not move, filled up with him, and for one moment,
she almost felt him beside her, but then the moment was
gone. She lay down, more tired now than at any previous
point in the past few days. Hal's bed was more than comfort-
able—it was comforting. She could almost smell his
cologne, but that was only in her mind.

She turned her head and her gaze slammed into another
photograph—but this one was very old and in an antique silver frame on his nightstand. Jill sat up.

Jill pulled the framed picture from the bedside table where
it stood. She stared, surprised, eyes wide.

It was an old black-and-white photograph of two young
women in period dress. To Jill's untrained eye, it appeared to
be turn-of-the-century; their gowns were white and long, the
skirts slim, and both women wore boaters on their heads. The
two women were standing close to one another in front of a
wrought-iron fence. They stared at the camera, unsmiling.

Had this been Hal's?

For one moment Jill was confused, until she recalled the
several times they had visited museums in New York
together. Hal had always enjoyed pointing out the details of
late nineteenth and turn-of-the-century life—which he had
seemed quite knowledgeable about. Of course this was his.
He had undoubtedly admired the photography.

Jill looked more closely at the photo, trying to see what it
was that had drawn him to it, but for her, it was merely an old
photograph of two young women. She shrugged to herself
and laid the framed photo down on the bed. But she was
thinking now that something was odd. Hal had not collected
old photographs. He had been too intense about his own
work. Chills seemed to cover her arms.

Jill hesitated, then picked up the silver frame again.
Unsure of what compelled her, she turned it over and she
gasped. There was handwriting on the back of it.

Curious, Jill took a closer look. Her eyes widened as she read aloud, "Kate Gallagher and Anne Bensonhurst, the summer of 1906." The handwriting was Hal's.

There was no mistake about it.

Jill was frozen. She did not know what to think. But her last name was Gallagher—and Hal's last dying word to her had been "Kate."

She stared at the photo, trembling.

This was, undoubtedly, the oddest coincidence, nothing more. Jill reminded herself that Hal had loved her, had told her so before he died, and that this photograph had nothing to do with that woman named Kate, who was probably his lawyer or some such thing. Jill turned the photograph back over. Who were these women and why had Hal cared enough about their photograph to write on the back of it, to keep it?

She was grim, and in spite of her reassurances to herself, she was concerned. Oddly enough, she felt uneasy, and she was wishing that she had never come into his room.

Still, Jill continued to stare at the picture. Both women were dark-haired and fair-skinned. Of course, back in those days, women did not take sun. One of the women was neither plain nor pretty; in spite of having classic features, she somehow disappeared beside her companion, whose looks were bold and striking. It was this other young woman who suddenly commanded Jill's complete attention.

Jill could not look away. She was mesmerized. There was something compelling about her. Something so very unusual. She was beautiful, but not classically. Her nose was straight and Roman, her jaw too wide, her cheekbones very high—and there was a definite mole on her right cheek. Jill did not think it was her looks that were so commanding. Perhaps it was her eyes. They were dark and bright with intelligence, with vitality, with joy, Jill thought, and Jill received the distinct feeling that this woman had secrets she wished to teasingly share.

The woman with the mole stared back at Jill, smiling ever so slightly, Jill now saw, and her eyes were daring Jill to . . . to what?

"Just what do you think you are doing in here?" a harsh voice demanded from behind her.

Jill cried out, dropping the photograph.

"I asked you what you were doing in here," Alex Preston said from the doorway. And he flicked on the rest of the lights.

Two

Jill's palm rested on her wildly racing heart. "You frightened me," she said.

"I'm sorry. I didn't expect to find anyone in here." Alex entered the room. His expression was difficult to read now, but there had been no mistaking it a moment ago. "What are you doing in here?" His blue stare was extremely, uncomfortably direct.

Jill hesitated. "I couldn't sleep."

His gaze did not waver. "This is Hal's room. How did you find it?"

Jill flushed. "By chance. I'm sorry if my prowling around has offended you."

"You're a guest here—not a prisoner. But this is a family home." His meaning was clear—she could have disturbed the family.

"I knew Hal's room was on the second floor," Jill continued uneasily. "When I couldn't fall asleep, I went downstairs to make a drink. I sort of just wandered up here. I didn't intend to bother anyone—and I don't think I did—until now."

He was studying her very closely and he did not reply. Jill could not guess his thoughts. That increased her discomfort, as did his scrutiny. But she was given the opportunity to study him as well. He had changed into a pair of very worn, faded Levi's. They fit his slim hips snugly, like a glove. And he donned a butter-soft, yellow cashmere sweater—one that looked very expensive. Not very many men could wear canary yellow and get away with it.

Jill looked away. Hal's photography was everywhere. "I miss him," she added helplessly. "I really do. I guess that's why I came up here."

"We all miss him." Jill fidgeted as Alex glanced around the room, then at the photograph lying on the bed. "Were you looking for something?" he asked abruptly. His gaze was on the framed photograph. "What's that?"

Jill was bewildered. "No. But I couldn't help looking at his things. I almost felt him here, with me, a moment ago." Was he suspicious of her? She tried out a small smile but he did not smile in return as she picked up the old photo of the two women. Her fingers slid over the frame of their own volition. "I found this on his night table," Jill said slowly. Again, the woman with the mole caught her eye, seemingly staring at Jill. Jill stared back. One of these women was named Kate Gallagher. Something inside of her lurched unpleasantly.

She stared at the women in the photograph, having no doubt that Kate Gallagher was the one with the teasing, vivacious look in her sultry eyes. Of course her name was a coincidence. If only Hal hadn't mentioned "Kate" with his last dying breath, she thought grimly. If only her last name weren't Gallagher.

"What is it?" Alex cut into her thoughts.

She had been so absorbed that Alex's soft question startled her. She had, for one moment, forgotten where she was and who she was with. For an instant, perhaps only a second or two, she had been completely focused on Kate Gallagher. "The handwriting on the back of this is Hal's," Jill said slowly. "This is a photograph of two women, Kate Gallagher and Anne Bensonhurst, and it's dated 1906. I find this odd, because Hal was not a collector of other people's work." She finally looked up at Alex. "And isn't it strange that I have the same name as one of the women in the photo?"

"Gallagher is an extremely common name," he said without hesitation.

"But why was he keeping this? Do you have any idea?"

She would never tell Alex, or anyone, that Hal had spoken another woman's name as he died.

Alex shrugged, but he stepped closer to her and peered down at the photo she held. "Ann Bensonhurst was Hal's grandmother and my great-aunt. That is obviously why Hal kept the photo."

Briefly, Jill was relieved—that simple fact explained everything. "Anne Bensonhurst was his grandmother," she repeated. Then her relief vanished. Did it explain everything? She glanced at Alex, finding it difficult to take her gaze from the photo. "You know, don't you, that Hal was very interested in the late Victorian and early Edwardian period. In New York we used to go to museums. He was always drawn to the turn-of-the-century exhibits."

"He was a history buff," Alex said.

But Jill was suddenly remembering an afternoon spent at the Met. Afterward they'd sat outside at the Stanhope, drinking cappuccinos while people-watching, his arm around her shoulders. Suddenly it was there again, inside of her, a huge bubble of grief, the devastating sense of loss, the aloneness, the guilt. The pain was overwhelming.

"What is it?"

Jill swallowed. She must not think about Hal. She must think about Kate Gallagher. It was safer, easier. "Is Anne the one on the left with the darker hair?"

"Yes."

"She looks like you, except plainer."

"Her older sister, Juliette, was my great-grandmother."

"And how did your branch of the family wind up in America?" Jill was genuinely curious. She wiped her eyes with her fingertips.

Alex seemed to relax. "My grandmother married an American, it's as simple as that. Actually, she was very fortunate. There was nothing left for her here in Britain."

There was something in his tone that made Jill regard him closely. "What do you mean?"

"My great-grandmother died in a carriage accident as a young woman. The Bensonhurst fortune passed on to Anne. Not the title—titles can't be passed down to females, but the wealth. My grandmother, who was born a Feldston, was sent away to a girls' school when her father remarried. Most of his small fortune went to his son. My grandmother was the "poor" relation, and it was extreme good fortune that an American gentleman fell in love with her and whisked her off to a foreign land." ·

Jill wondered if he identified with his grandmother. But there was nothing penniless about this man. Even in his jeans, he had a strong aura of success, self-assurance, and power. He did not seem bitter, either, but she felt certain that he was good at hiding his emotions. "So you've returned to your roots," Jill remarked.

An extremely intense gaze pinned her down. "My roots are Luigi's, where my mother waited table her entire adult life. My roots are Coney Island, not Mayfair."

Jill didn't flinch from his stare. "How did you wind up here?"

He glanced away. "My mother passed away when I was thirteen. I was no stranger to the family—they had us out every summer. They took me in." He smiled briefly. "Hoodlum-in-training that I was." His smile faded. "It was the best thing that ever happened to me."

Jill was silent, trying to imagine this man as a young streetwise boy from Brooklyn being thrown into the midst of this family and this kind of life. "It must have been very hard."

He shrugged, clearly no longer willing to discuss the subject.

Which was fine with Jill. She glanced at Anne and Kate again. "Wouldn't it be the strangest coincidence if Kate Gallagher was a relative of mine?" The words had come forth unbidden and unpremeditated.

"The odds are a million to one."

Jill agreed with that. On the other hand, she had this inkling that there was more here than met the eye . . . "Do you know anything about her?" Jill asked curiously, studying the two women. Now it seemed to her that Kate was smiling ever so slightly at the photographer. She inspected the photograph more closely and decided that Kate was interested in the photographer, either that or she was a ham.

"No. Why would I know anything about some person in an antiquated photograph?"

"Do you know where this was taken?" Jill asked, suddenly handing it to him.

Alex studied the picture. "Frankly, I don't have a clue. It could be anywhere." Ignoring her, he put the photograph back on the nightstand, laying it down, face-up. "Hal was the historian in our family," he said. "My interests lie in the present and the future, not the past."

"Well." Jill hesitated. "I guess I'm drawn to history, too."

When he did not respond, she became aware of how late it had become, how tired she was, and the fact that she was standing barefoot in the room with him. Suddenly she noticed that he was barefoot, too. She folded her arms across her breasts. "I guess I should return to my room and try to get some sleep." She glanced back at the nightstand. For some reason, she wanted to take the photograph with her, and study it again. But it was a family heirloom and it belonged to Hal and his family. She did not think Alex would let her take it to her room.

But what if Kate Gallagher was her ancestor? Obviously she could not be her great-grandmother, because they shared the same last name. Jill was intrigued, so much so that she shivered . . . until she recalled Hal's dying words, and then she felt the weight of depression. Her life had never seemed or felt more complicated or more bereft. If only he were alive to give her the answers she desperately needed.

Alex remained silent. His lapses into silence were unsettling. Jill avoided his unwavering eyes. "Well," she said, slipping her hands into the pockets of her jeans. "If you don't mind, I'll make myself another drink before I go back to my room." She started to move toward the door.

But he did not move, and he barred her way. "What did happen, Jill?"

Jill froze. Her heart lurched.

"Or should I say, how did it happen? How did you hit the

tree?" His tone was calm, unlike his cousin's efforts to question her earlier.

Jill wanted to escape him now. "You yourself said this can wait. I don't think I can talk about it yet." She glanced at the door, wanting to flee, desperately.

"You're better off talking to me—than to them," he said, his hands on his hips. "By tomorrow, Thomas will be wanting the very same answers—again. But he is extremely upset—and very angry. Why don't you tell me instead? It will save you a helluva lot of grief."

First Thomas, now Alex, confronting her, pinning her down. Jill began to perspire. "Is this an interrogation?" Jill asked slowly, aware of the heat accumulating in her cheeks.

"No. Not unless you make it one." When Jill did not speak, he said, "Why are you so nervous? What are you hiding?"

Jill inhaled. The sound was unmistakable in the bedroom. "I'm not nervous," she shot back, a lie. "I'm exhausted, jet-lagged, and I'm sick. I've just lost someone—"

He cut her off, as if he did not believe her. "Hal was very close to the family. Although recently he wasn't calling . . . as if he were too preoccupied . . . or as if he were hiding something himself."

Jill stiffened. "I know how close he was to his family, he talked about you guys all the time. He had nothing to hide." But he had, hadn't he? He'd had their relationship to hide.

"He had you."

He was astute. Jill despised him for his candor. She hedged, buying time frantically. "What does that mean?"

"Come on," Alex said flatly. "Why beat around the bush?" His stare remained direct and intent. "You live in a cheap studio in the Village. You're a dancer. You're American. Penniless. You're not exactly the kind of girl he would bring home, much less marry."

"That was to the point," she whispered, aghast. "I take it you have never fallen in love?" She was trembling. His words hurt—maybe because they were so goddamned close to what might be the truth.

He ignored that. "Look, I'm an American, too. I grew up on the streets of Brooklyn. I know all about penniless, and I know my cousins. I know my uncle. He had plans for Hal, especially after the disappointment of Thomas's divorce and the way things are with Lauren."

Jill wondered what had happened, both with Thomas and Lauren, but did not ask.

"If you really thought Hal was going to bring you home and marry you, then I am very sorry for you," Alex said flatly.

Jill bit her lip. "He was," she said. "He was."

His look was direct and pitying. "I know what Hal was hiding," Alex said. "But I can't quite figure out what you are hiding."

She stared, becoming angry at last.

"What happened the night of the accident?"

"I don't know," she lied. "It all happened so quickly. We were talking and then I looked up and saw the tree. I've never even been in a fender bender before!"

"I know."

She stared.

"I've done my homework," he said, holding her gaze. "But not enough of it—apparently." He did not pause. "You were driving. The roads were clear. It was the middle of the afternoon. You weren't drinking and there was no sign of drugs in your blood. How does one go off the road and hit a tree, given those conditions?" He was pushing.

She found herself locking gazes with him. He made her uncomfortable and immediately she turned her head away. "Don't do this," she said, low. "Not now, not this way, not tonight. I can't handle this."

"Hal was my cousin. We grew up together. I want to know what really happened. You weren't concentrating on the road. That's my conclusion. Which means you were distracted."

Jill broke. "I am going to live with the fact that I was driving and I hit that tree and I killed Hal for the rest of my life. I don't know what happened," she cried. Jill hugged herself, finding it hard to breathe, hating Alex for pressing her this way. "I'm not hiding anything," she whispered.

"What were the two of you talking about?" he asked ruthlessly.

"I don't remember!"

"How convenient," he responded. "Were you arguing?"

Jill knew she had turned white.

"You were arguing," Alex said quietly, his gaze holding hers. "And I can guess what you were arguing about."

Tears filled her eyes. "Your family is terrible," she cried. "You are terrible. I loved Hal! Can't you see that? Can't you? You are the coldest person I have ever met! I have lost the man I love," she shouted at him. "The man I've spent my whole life dreaming of!"

"And I've lost my cousin. Thomas and Lauren lost their brother, my aunt and uncle have lost their son, God damn it," he said harshly. "Everyone is shocked, everyone is sick, we are all suffering, damn it."

Jill backed away from him.

He turned abruptly, his broad shoulders trembling. He was suddenly very angry.

Jill stared at his back. "I'm so sorry," she whispered finally. He did not turn. "I know you hate me, all of you, but I already hate myself. Please, please don't do this to me anymore."

He did not move.

Jill sank back down on the bed. Her hands were shaking—she was shaking. Briefly she covered her face with her palms, but she could not seem to stop trembling, she could not find even a hint of calm. "Tomorrow I'll find a hotel somewhere."

Alex faced her. His expression was now implacable. "Forget it. There's not a decent room available; I had my travel agent working on it all day."

It was clear that he wasn't being kind. Was anyone in Hal's family capable of compassion? she wondered. Very unsteadily, very spontaneously, Jill whispered, "Why aren't we helping one another now, sharing our anger and our grief, instead of confronting one another like this?"

"Because Hal is dead," he said simply.

Jill clapped her hands over her mouth, almost bursting into tears. How right he was. Hal was dead, and his legacy was anger and hatred and all of her lies.

"Look, let me take you back to your room," Alex said. "It's late and I'm tired."

Jill did not look up at him. She wasn't ready to look at him. She didn't answer him, either.

"You ready?" He cocked his head toward the door. "Even if you can't sleep, I suggest you get some rest. Tomorrow's going to be one helluva day."

Jill flinched. Reality crashed over her then, making her forget all about the photograph and Alex's hateful questions. *Tomorrow.* Tomorrow they were burying Hal.

"After you," he said, gesturing for her to precede him out. He touched her arm impatiently.

Jill shrugged him off. She didn't want him touching her, not even in a casual gesture. And as she moved past him, she wondered how she would get through the next day. She did not know if she had the strength to endure Hal's funeral.

Worried about whether or not she had asked her next door neighbor to look after her cat, Jill dialed New York. By her estimation, it was about eight in the evening there. But her neighbor, an unemployed actress, kept very odd hours. She went through jobs the way Madison Avenue women shopped. Jill was relieved when the phone was picked up on the second ring. "KC, this is Jill. I'm calling from London," Jill said.

"Jill! I am so worried about you. How are you?" KC cried.

Jill lay on her back in the huge four-poster bed of her room, holding the phone to her ear. She could envision KC clearly. She was tall and willowy, very attractive, with a heart of gold. Right now, Jill knew her expression was one of utter sympathy. "I'm okay," she began. Then, "God. I'm not okay. I'm not okay at all."

"I know," KC said, her tone ringing with compassion. "Jill, everything will work out—I just know it will, in time."

Jill didn't answer. The pain was stabbing through her again. But she knew KC meant what she said. As determined as KC was to become a working actress, she was even more passionate about the spiritual side of her life. She more than dabbled in everything from palmistry to Hinduism. They had met three years ago at a party in SoHo for an opening show. KC was not a guest, she was there to read people's palms and do tarot card readings. Jill had been talked into allowing KC to do a reading for her by a friend. Extremely dubious, and a little drunk, Jill had sat down opposite the blond.

To Jill's amazement, KC had taken one look at the cards laid out on the table before her and said, "You are so terribly alone."

In that excruciating instant, she'd gained Jill's complete, and suddenly sober, attention.

"You lost your family didn't you, when you were very young," she'd continued. Jill had stared, wondering who could have told her that. "And you have never quite gotten over it. But you will." KC had smiled serenely at Jill. Then her face fell. "But not soon."

Jill couldn't remember the rest of the reading, except that it had been as accurate. KC had mentioned that there was a studio available next to hers when she realized Jill was looking for a new apartment. Within a week, Jill had moved in, and they had quickly become friends.

"Why don't you try to see a doctor tomorrow in London?" KC asked now with real concern. "You know how I hate drugs, but in this case, Jill, you shouldn't have thrown that prescription out."

Jill guessed she had told KC about tossing the Xanax; she didn't remember. "I don't know. Maybe I will. I'm so tired. I can't remember if I made arrangements for Ezekial."

"Oh, you did. You asked me to look after him and I brought him to my apartment. He's underfoot all the time. He misses you."

Jill smiled slightly. "And how is he getting on with Chiron?" Chiron was KC's wiry mutt. The mixed terrier had been named after an asteroid.

"He is bullying poor Chiron," KC said with a laugh.

Jill suddenly imagined the scenario and she laughed, too. It was the very first time she had laughed in days and it felt wonderful. But then she thought about Hal and a woman named Kate Gallagher, about Alex Preston and the Sheldons, and she was grim once again.

KC said, "What's happened?"

Jill sighed. KC was also very astute—perhaps even psychic. Her intuition could be unsettling at times. Jill kept telling herself it was all coincidence, but on some deep inner level she knew that KC had some kind of extraordinary, extrasensory talent. "I don't know what I expected, but Hal's family isn't very friendly. Of course, they're all in shock." She did not tell her that they all blamed her for Hal's death, it was a topic she just could not raise. "No one believes that Hal and I were serious. I think they see me as some kind of fling. Because I'm this poor, working-class dancer."

"That sucks," KC said vehemently. "So Hal's family isn't as nice as he seemed to be?"

Jill had been thinking about her encounter with Alex. But KC's choice of words disturbed her. "Why did you say that?"

"Say what?"

"You said, as nice as Hal seemed to be."

KC was silent. "It was just a slip of the tongue, I guess. I only met him three times. I didn't really know him."

Jill was on alert. "KC, is there something you're not telling me?"

"Of course not," KC said, but she was a brutally honest person, and Jill knew she was lying. "Tell me about Hal's family," KC said quickly. "I have to go in a minute."

Jill tried to clear the confusion from her mind. She was too tired to think straight; there was no reason KC would deceive her. "They're not nice people," she finally said. "They're so rich you would not believe it. This house is a mansion, KC, and it's across the street from Kensington Palace." She stopped, about to blurt out that Hal would have been insane to try and bring her home. But she was afraid of what KC might say or, worse, see.

"Wow," KC replied. "So Hal really was loaded."

"Yeah." Jill hesitated. "KC, something odd happened." She proceeded to tell her all about the photograph of Anne and Kate.

"Oh, my God!" KC cried excitedly. "Jill, this cannot be a coincidence. Can you imagine if that woman in the photograph is your grandmother or something? Wouldn't that be cool? I mean, this family thing is so important to your life! Maybe Hal was supposed to lead you to Kate."

Jill stared at the phone. Now she was filled with unease. "I had better go," she said abruptly. "Thanks for taking care of Ezekial. I really appreciate it."

"Did I say something wrong? Jill, wait. I know you won't believe this, but the Universe has a plan for you, and it wasn't Hal." KC's tone was so earnest and fervent that Jill would have smiled under other circumstances.

But she didn't. Instead, Jill stiffened. It was a moment before she could speak, Hal's image engraved on her mind—but not as he lay dying, as he had been, handsome and happy and alive. "Not tonight. Please I've had a rough day. The Universe—God—whatever—isn't fair and this isn't just. Because Hal was good and he should be alive and we should be together and frankly, I can't figure out how God could let this happen!" Jill reached for her second scotch but she had already drunk it.

"Oh, Jill, He has His reasons," KC said earnestly. "We are all on a Path and . . ."

"I know, I know, the Universe has some magical plan for everyone," Jill said. She turned and yanked a tissue from the box that was beside her on the bed.

"There is a master plan," KC said fervently. She did not hesitate. "I tossed some cards for you, Jillian. I couldn't help myself."

Jill tensed. This was what she had wanted to avoid. "I'm really tired," she began.

"Jillian, two cards keep coming up. You must be careful."

Jill sat up straighter. Unlike her neighbor, she was not a complete romantic fool. She did not believe in fortune-telling. Not really. But KC's track record was spooky. She had to ask, "Which two cards?"

"The Fool and the Tower," she said quietly.

"Care to explain?" Jill asked tersely, not liking the sudden change in KC's tone.

"The Fool is a young man. He's skipping along quite happily with his little dog and his backpack. But he isn't watching where he's going. He is about to step off of a cliff, Jill." KC paused.

"What does this mean?"

"It's very clear. You must look before you leap."

Jill wet her lips. "I think I've already taken the free fall," she murmured, thinking about arriving at the Sheldons' home.

"The Tower is medieval; perhaps once it belonged to a castle. It's made of stone, and it's been struck by lightning. It's in flames. People are leaping off of it in terror."

The hairs prickled on Jill's nape. "I don't understand." But she did.

"The Tower stands for upheaval, for destruction. And usually the upheaval happens at the speed of light."

Jill was silent. "Maybe the Tower refers to Hal's death," she finally said.

"No. I don't think so." KC paused. Then, "I am certain this is referring to the future."

Jill disagreed, but did not say so. Her life had been destroyed by Hal's death, and it would never be the same again—if that wasn't upheaval, what was? KC was wrong. The Tower referred to the present, not the future.

KC spoke again. "Trust me, Jillian, and trust the stars, they're your allies."

"I don't think so," Jill said.

"There is a reason for everything," KC said, but gently.

"No. No, there isn't."

"Let me draw one card. To clarify things." KC sounded insistent.

"What's the point?" Jill asked, but she heard her shuffling. There was no point, because her situation was clear. Hal was dead. She was alone. And she had killed him through her neglectful driving, by God.

But then she thought about his dying words, and she thought about Kate Gallagher. And she heard the sound of the shuffling cards stop. Silence was on the other end of the line.

"What is it?" Jill whispered.

"There is a woman. It could be you, but I don't think so,

because it is the Empress. She is very powerful, surrounded by wealth, and she is very creative, perhaps in the arts."

"I'm in the arts."

"She might be pregnant," KC said slowly.

Jill stared at the phone.

"She is usually pregnant. Jill, you're not pregnant, are you?"

"No," Jill said on a deeply drawn breath. She'd had enough of fatalism for one night, and as she clenched the phone, sweating now, she thought it would be unbearable if she were pregnant. "I've got to go. I'll be home in two days. Thanks for everything."

"Jill! Be careful. And I'll see you when you get home."

Jill couldn't speak. She hung up quickly. Hal was dead. She could not possibly be pregnant.

Jill tried to recall when her last period was, but her memory was failing her now. God damn the Tower, she thought bleakly. And damn the Empress, too!

And she wasn't pregnant. She couldn't be. It would be the cruelest possible twist of fate. She had thought that life could not get worse, but if she was carrying Hal's baby, it most certainly would.

Jill cradled her head on her arms, staring up at the ceiling. She was buzzed from the scotch and exhausted and so terribly scared and finally, thankfully, numb. And as exhaustion finally got the best of her, as she suddenly, finally fell asleep, her last thought was to wonder if there was any connection at all between her and Hal and a woman named Kate.

And she dreamed about a damp, dark, crumbling tower from which there was no escape.

Jill entered the Anglican church where the funeral service was being held, trailing after the Sheldons, her shoes echoing on the centuries-old gray stone floors. Like most if not all of the churches in England, this one belonged in another place in time—it was probably five or six hundred years old. The walls were rough stone, the windows archaic stained glass, the pews scarred and well worn. Most of those pews were already filled with the family's friends and associates.

Jill felt claustrophobic.

She continued down the aisle, behind Lauren, who held a handkerchief to her face. She was crying, but silently. Her husband, a tall, thin man with beautiful dark shoulder-length hair, had his arm around her. They had met briefly at the house. Jill had gathered that he was an artist and that their marriage was fraught with tension.

Thomas walked in front of them, his arm around his mother, Margaret, whom Jill had not yet been introduced to. The few glimpses she'd had of Hal's mother outside of the church had shown her that Margaret, who was at least ten years younger than her husband, was sedated and severely stricken. She had not seemed to be aware of Jill's presence, which was probably for the best.

Jill tried not to look at Thomas's broad shoulders. It was not an easy task, because he was directly ahead of her. The nod he had given her earlier that morning had been very curt. His feelings toward her had not changed since last night.

Jill stared past him. Alex and William were walking side by side in the very front of the family, Alex gripping William's elbow quite firmly, as if afraid his uncle would collapse. The older man looked very worn and fatigued. The bags under his eyes seemed more extreme today than they had yesterday when Jill had arrived. She had not a doubt he had cried all night.

Alex and William took their seats in the first pew. Thomas was literally holding Margaret upright as he seated her beside her husband, then sat down himself. He did not look up at Jill, who slid into the second pew alone, behind the family, beside strangers who turned to glance at her.

Jill clutched her hands so hard she hurt herself. Then she caught Alex's eyes as he glanced back at her. He didn't smile; neither did she. He shifted, facing forward again.

If only the service was over. Jill closed her eyes. This was the singular most horrible moment since Hal's actual death. It felt endless. And to make matters worse, she could not forget her conversation with KC last night. And she heard someone weeping behind her, the sobs muffled but anguished.

Jill glanced around. Directly across the aisle a petite woman was sobbing into a handkerchief, her long shoulder-length auburn hair hiding her face. An elderly man had his arm around her. He was old enough to be her father.

Jill stared uneasily. The woman was young, and her fitted black jacket and skirt hugged her lush body like a glove. Jill knew her. But that made no sense, because Jill was quite certain that they had never met.

Jill suddenly realized that many people in the crowd were staring at her. She tensed, looking around, but as she did so, men and women quickly looked away from her, avoiding her eyes. There was no mistaking the fact that her presence was causing an odd and strong reaction in the crowd of mourners.

Oh, God. Too late, Jill realized that everyone must know that she had been driving, that the accident was her fault, that she had killed Hal. That was why everyone kept staring. There was no other possible reason.

Jill had never felt worse. The guilt overwhelmed her. It seemed to choke the very breath out of her.

It crossed her mind that she could get up from her seat and flee the church and all of these people with their accusing stares—flee and never come back.

But she loved Hal. She had to say good-bye.

And as the minister took the pulpit, Jill heard whispers behind her. Someone said, "Is that *her?*"

Jill froze.

Someone else replied, "Yes, that's *her*. The American girlfriend, the *dancer*."

Jill's shoulders felt like two plywood boards. She did not move. She prayed that the service would start. But the first speaker said, too loudly, "But what about Marisa?"

Marisa? Who was Marisa? Jill turned, staring at an elderly woman in a black Chanel suit, a beautiful black hat, and an extreme amount of very large, very real, diamond jewelry.

The woman smiled automatically and turned her head, gazing across the aisle. Jill did not smile back. Her stomach was curdling with dread. She followed her gaze.

And was faced with the petite redhead in the skinny black suit. The woman had stopped crying. She was staring straight

ahead. She was one of the loveliest, most feminine women
Jill had ever seen, with a perfect porcelain complexion and
dark red hair. And it was then that Jill recognized her.

From the photograph in Hal's bedroom, the one of him
and her on a ski slope.

Jill's heart fell, hard. She failed to breathe.

The priest began to speak, his somber voice cutting
through Jill's shock. "My dear, dear friends," he began, his
voice deep and resonant, "we are gathered here today under
tragic circumstances, to lay the recently departed soul of
Harold William Sheldon to rest."

Who was Marisa? What had that woman meant? Jill
fought for air. She was going to fall apart. Oh, God. This was
what she had been secretly afraid of, losing it in front of
everyone, all these strangers, Hal's family—Thomas, Alex—
everyone who despised her. She could not take any more!

Do not think about the other woman, Jill told herself. Hal
loved you. This isn't what you think it is, it is not. That
woman in the Chanel suit had meant something else—but Jill
was too distressed to comprehend what that meaning might
now be.

Jill gripped the arm of her pew. In front of her, Margaret
Sheldon was sobbing now, but softly. Thomas held her close.
Directly in front of Jill, Lauren began to weep into her hands
and then on her husband's shoulder.

The service had become a nightmare. A nightmare that
she must escape.

Jill closed her eyes, ordering herself to breathe deeply and
evenly, but she was feeling both dizzy and faint now, and
was horrified because she did not think she could cope for
very much longer. She opened her eyes, only to meet
Thomas's gaze. He was still holding his mother, and
instantly he looked away from her. The accusation in his
eyes had been unmistakable.

And Jill heard the minister saying, "One of the kindest,
most compassionate, and bravest souls I have ever known."

Brave. Had Hal been brave? He had been thinking of running out on her after his marriage proposal. Because he was
scared to bring her home to this. To these people, this

lifestyle, this arrogance and condescension. In that moment, Jill could not blame him for losing his courage. His family was cold and hostile. Oh, God. They hated her, but even if Hal were alive, they would have hated her; and Hal had known it.

Jill clenched her fists so tightly that her own short, manicured nails dug into her flesh, about to get up and run from the church. *Hal had not been brave.* She felt like the worst kind of traitor for harboring such a thought; she wished, desperately, that she had never had it. And she felt the stares again, knew she was being watched. She could not go. Everyone was already talking about her, and if she did, the gossip would become far worse. Jill stared straight ahead out of blurry eyes.

Marisa was the kind of woman Hal could have brought home. Once glance had told Jill that—she was elegant, well bred, she came from money. It was as painfully obvious as the fact that Jill was from a lower income working-class background, in her trendy rayon and lycra clothes, her thrift-store and flea-market bargains. Even her haircut was too way-out for this uptown crowd.

And most important, she was a dancer. It had been her passion since she was six years old. What had Hal been thinking?

Thomas was speaking. Jill jerked at the sound of his sandy voice, because she had not seen him rise and take the pulpit. Focusing on him now was a relief—it might even be her salvation.

He had taken the podium, which he gripped with both strong hands. A signet ring with a blood-red stone winked from his right hand. Jill couldn't help noticing that even in his pitch-black suit and with his bloodshot eyes, he had an inescapable magnetism; he still looked good.

"My brother Hal did not deserve to die," he began, and instantly he had to stop, turning his face aside, fighting for control.

Jill stared, softening a bit toward him. He might despise her, but he was also aching over the loss of his brother. Last night she had told Alex that they should be comforting one another. She still felt that way.

But with Thomas as angry as he was, he was not about to let her console or comfort him, or even share their grief and anguish.

"Hal did not deserve to die," Thomas repeated, pausing, jaw flexed. His gaze moved over the crowd, making eye contact with it. He did not glance at Jill.

"No one deserves to die," he said harshly. "But my brother was so young, he was only thirty-six, and he was also one of those rare souls that the world needs so much more of." He inhaled. "He did not deserve to die. I still can't understand why this happened." Thomas stopped. And suddenly he was looking directly at Jill.

Jill stared back at Thomas, fists clenched. Any compassion she had just felt for Thomas vanished. Had he openly condemned her for murder, he could not have made his feelings more clear. And he had openly condemned her—no one present could have mistaken his meaning, or misunderstood the accusation in his eyes. How could he be so cruel?

"Hal was one of the kindest people I have ever known," Thomas continued, still staring at Jill. "He had a heart of gold. He was a rescuer. I used to tease him about it. As kids, he was the one trying to bring home strays. We never had less than three or four cats and mutts in the house when we were growing up. Our mother used to beg him not to bring home any more strays but he would not listen."

Marisa was crying again.

In spite of his anguish, Thomas was a powerful speaker and his voice carried, but Jill no longer heard him. She stared at Marisa, who was in the throes of grief. Clearly she had been head over heels in love with Hal. Jill was sick.

"I've decided to collect all of Hal's work and hold an exhibition," Thomas was now saying. Jill's gaze swung back to the pulpit; Marisa continued to sob loudly, uncontrollably, behind and across from her. "His work is now his legacy to us, and the world," Thomas said. "I'm thinking of then exhibiting his work permanently at Uxbridge Hall. Hal loved

Uxbridge Hall. When he was alive and living in London, he practically haunted that place." Tears suddenly slid down Thomas's cheeks. And it was clear that he could not speak.

Alex suddenly was on his feet and striding onto the podium. His arm went around his cousin. Thomas shook his head. "I want to finish," he seemed to say.

Alex argued with him.

Dabbing her eyes, Jill watched the two cousins, the one lean and dark, the other so golden. Alex finally accepted his cousin's apparently stronger will, and he left the podium.

Thomas swallowed. "I'm sorry," he said harshly. "I owe my brother so much. More than I can explain here, except to say that when times became extremely difficult for me, personally, Hal never failed to call me two or three times a day. Even if it was just to say hello, to make certain I was all right, to let me know that he was there. My brother was a rare and wonderful individual."

Thomas fell silent. A long moment passed. Jill thought his eulogy was over. Her gaze remained glued to his face. Even if she had wanted to look away, she could not.

He suddenly said, smiling and crying at the same time, "When we were kids, Hal was the one playing jokes. I'll never forget the time he put a toad in our nanny's glass of water. Did she shriek, enough to wake up the dead." His smile vanished. The tears remained. "I can't believe he's gone." Thomas stopped speaking abruptly, tears sliding down his face again. "I miss him so much."

Jill was ready to get up and run away. His gaze had found hers again. She did not move.

"In Hal's name," Thomas said, "I am starting a foundation for young, struggling artists to enable them to pursue their dreams. It's what Hal would have wanted," he said.

Jill stared at him. The gesture was both noble and grand. Hal would have been pleased. She wiped her eyes. She had thought her tears finally, at long last, all used up. She was wrong.

Thomas was crying, tears sliding down his face. Jill stared even though her vision was blurry, watching as Alex went to his cousin and took him by the arm, helping him down from the pulpit.

She watched as William stood, and as Thomas fell into his father's embrace, the two men clinging tearfully. Alex hovered by them. He had one hand on Thomas, but it fell away.

The three men finally took their seats as the minister led the congregation in a final prayer. When it was over, he announced the location of the burial. Jill did not move as the guests began to rise. She was aware now of how hard her heart beat, of being absolutely exhausted, and terribly relieved that this ordeal was ended. She ducked her head, not wanting to make eye contact with anyone as they filed out, but especially not the Sheldons.

Several women cried out.

Jill leaped to her feet and turned in the direction of the cries, only to see Marisa lying on the floor of the aisle in a dead faint.

A scant second later, Alex and Thomas were there, kneeling beside her, attempting to revive her. Jill stared, watching as Thomas patted her cheeks. Alex stood, demanding smelling salts. Extending his hand over several guests, the minister, obviously well prepared, handed Alex a vial. Alex knelt beside Marisa again.

And a moment later Jill watched Thomas walking Marisa out of the church, his arm around her waist, the petite woman leaning heavily upon him. Alex followed, beside them.

Jill left the church, the last guest to do so, alone.

Jill paused on a busy London street. She wasn't sure where she was—she had been trying to find the British Library after walking about aimlessly for an hour or so, ever since the burial, not wanting to return to the Sheldon residence in Kensington Palace Gardens. It had crossed her mind that not only could she kill time in the library, she might be able to find something out about Kate Gallagher there.

Jill had bought a map from a street vendor, and now she opened it, trying to get her bearings. It was hard to concentrate. Not only had Alex and Thomas rushed to Marisa, help-

ing to revive her in the church, but Thomas had then escorted
her into the family's limousine, driving Marisa to the cemetery with all of the Sheldons. She, Jill, had arrived at the
cemetery the exact same way she had arrived at the church.
She had been chauffeured alone in a tan Mercedes sedan.

She supposed she should be grateful that the family had
not left her to her own devices. But she was not grateful, not
at all.

Clearly Marisa was a part of the family. Jill was very disturbed, and Marisa's behavior was also very distressing.
Obviously she had loved Hal. Meanwhile, the message she
had received from Thomas had been both clear and deliberate. She, Jill, was the outsider—and she always would be.
The only thing Jill was not sure of was whether Thomas
wanted to hurt her purposefully or not.

It had been one of the worst days of her life, and Jill stared
at the map, a huge headache throbbing in her forehead. As it
turned out, she was only four or five blocks away from the
British Library. She sighed and tucked the map in her tote
and started along Upper Woburn Place. She knew she was on
a wild goose chase but she did not care. She could hardly
think straight, her feelings were a jumbled, confused mess,
and she was determined not to return to the Sheldons' until
everybody was sound asleep. Thank God tomorrow she was
going home.

Jill finally saw the library, a huge modern building, on the
corner just ahead. Her steps slowed, Kate's image coming
strongly to her mind, as pedestrians hurried to and fro around
her. Jill hardly ever entered libraries. As a student, she'd
never been able to find anything inside a library; clearly she
had failed Library 101 or whatever the course had been. She
stared up at the imposing and, to her eyes, quite ugly futuris-
tic facade of the library, then decided to hell with it. She was
already there—she would give it a try. Besides, weren't
librarians there to help amateurs like herself?

She shoved a hank of too-long chestnut bangs out of her
eyes as she crossed the wide space of the forecourt and
entered the spacious, stone-floored foyer of the building. It

was astoundingly quiet. Jill approached an information booth and was told she could not use the library.

"You need a Reader's Ticket, my dear," the pleasant woman with the bluish hair said.

"A Reader's Ticket?" Jill leaned on the counter. "I only want to use the reference room—I need to look up old newspaper articles, maybe society pages, and things like that," she explained with some desperation.

"You still need a Reader's Ticket to get in," the woman explained with a friendly smile. Her name tag read Janet Broadwick and she was sixty if a day. "But we have wonderful exhibits that are open to the public," she said.

"How do I get a Reader's Ticket?" Jill asked, dismayed.

The official explained that she must submit the request in writing—and that it took four to six weeks to receive permission to use the library after that.

Jill stared almost blindly at her. "I can't believe this," she whispered. Her headache increased in its intensity, becoming almost blinding. Her knees suddenly turned Jell-O-like, becoming weak and nearly useless. Jill grew frightened. She was afraid another blackout was coming on.

"Dear?"

Jill shook her head. Tears filled her eyes. She began to shake and she knew she had better find a place to lie down before she collapsed, or worse. She had obviously pushed herself beyond her limits. Either that, or the funeral and the Sheldons had pushed her over the edge.

"Oh, dear!" the official cried in alarm, coming out from behind her desk. "Are you ill?" she asked, gripping Jill's arm.

Jill gazed at her as her face came in and out of focus. "My boyfriend died," she said unsteadily. "I just came from the funeral and I do not want to go back to his family—they blame me, you see. I was driving the car."

"Oh, you poor dear," Janet Broadwick said. "Come and do sit down."

Jill didn't protest as the woman led her into the back offices and to a chair. She closed her eyes and propped her chin in her hands, her elbows on her thighs. Her pulse finally slowed, becoming normal. "I found this photograph in his bedroom," she found herself saying. And the next thing she knew, she was looking at this kind lady with the blue-white hair and she was telling her everything.

A few minutes later, Jill was sipping a hot cup of tea and nibbling a scone. And her rescuer, Janet Broadwick, was introducing her to the head librarian, one Katherine Curtis, a young woman clad in beige trousers and a gray cardigan.

Jill realized she was starving—for the first time in days. As she devoured the scone, Katherine asked her questions about Kate and Anne. "Let me see if I can help you," she said, her expression stern but her eyes soft and blue behind the square black eyeglasses she wore.

Katherine left, her strides purposeful. Janet Broadwick patted Jill's arm. "You are looking better, dear. You were turning green, I must say, a few minutes ago."

"I'm hungry," Jill said with surprise. "I can't remember when I last ate."

"Let me bring you a sandwich. In the interim, you stay here and rest. If anyone can find what you are looking for, it is Katherine. She is quite brilliant." Janet smiled at her.

"Thank you," Jill said, overcome by their kindness. This would never happen in New York. She watched her leave, thinking that the world was filled with such surprising moments, and she glanced around at the cubicles lining the hall. She then sank back in her chair, fatigue claiming her body, wishing she had another scone and thinking that she could not get up right now if the entire library were on fire. And a moment later she was asleep.

"Miss Gallagher. Are you asleep? I do think I have found what you are looking for."

Jill jerked, realizing she had fallen asleep, and for one instant, she was terribly confused, because a young, attractive woman in oversized glasses whom she did not know was staring intently at her. She fought to focus, remembering then where she was and why, her exhausted mind so numb it wanted nothing more than to return to the welcoming embrace of sleep.

Suddenly Jill blinked, realizing what Katherine had said.

"Are you awake?" Katherine did not smile, her blue eyes behind her thick lenses very intent.

"Yes." Jill brushed her bangs away from her face. "I fell asleep."

"Yes, you did, and soundly, too. You needed it, obviously. I have been screening society pages for the year of 1906. You must see what I have found." Still she did not smile, but her eyes were eager and bright.

Jill accepted the photocopied page.

"It's from the *Herald*," Katherine explained. "Here." She pointed to a small paragraph in the middle of the page.

It was a few short lines, sandwiched between other equally terse paragraphs. "American heiress Kate Gallagher, newly arrived in London with her mother, Mrs. Peter Gallagher, from New York City, is the guest of Lord and Lady Jonathan Bensonhurst. Miss Gallagher will make her come-out at the Fairchild ball with Lady Anne Bensonhurst on Thursday, October the first."

Jill trembled, wide awake now, and reread the few lines. She glanced at the date on the top of the page. It was dated September 6, 1906. Her mind raced.

Kate was from New York City, as her own family was. A coincidence? She had just arrived in London with her mother. Jill's head felt as if it were spinning. Kate's father's name was Peter. It was the exact same name as Jill's own grandfather. How odd! That had to be another coincidence. Weren't there too many coincidences now? And how did Hal fit into all of this?

Her thoughts raced. And as Jill stared at the page, the words and letters blurred, becoming indistinct. Jill no longer comprehended the words in front of her eyes, instead, she saw the two girls, clearly, so vividly, it was as if she were there.

Their heads were close together, the one as dark as night, the other brilliantly red. Anne and Kate were two best friends, and they laughed and giggled and gossiped, choosing fabrics and accessories for the gowns they would wear to their debut, planning their lives on that single night, filled with hopes and dreams for the oh-so-bright future.

And suddenly Jill was staring at the small black-and-white paragraph again. Good God. The vision had been brief, but it had been so strong, it was almost as if Jill had traveled back in time to another magical, incandescent era.

Something strange was happening to her. She felt, with every breath she took, that this was the most important moment in her life. It was more than the desire to have a family—that feeling had always been with Jill. She felt as if her entire life had been leading to this moment: to find out who Kate Gallagher was.

One of the house's many servants let Jill in when she finally returned from the library. It was almost eight, and the house was silent. If the Sheldons had had guests join them after the funeral, they were now all gone, and Jill suspected that every member of the family was in his or her bedroom. She was relieved.

"Miss Gallagher, I was told to tell you that there will not be a supper tonight, but I can bring your meal to your room." The butler, if that was what he was, spoke matter-of-factly.

"That would be wonderful," Jill said, meaning it. She remained hungry, and she intended to eat and then dive right into bed. "What is your name?" She smiled at him.

"Jamieson. Is there anything I can get you now?" he asked dutifully.

"A bite to eat would be perfect. I'll just go upstairs, thank you." Jill watched him disappear down a corridor that undoubtedly led to the working part of the house. She was about to go upstairs, the better to avoid any member of the family, when she suddenly wished she had asked Jamieson for a glass of wine. Having helped herself to a drink last night, she did not hesitate.

The living room where she had first met the Sheldons was directly across the foyer from her, both wide doors were open, and it was lighted but empty. It was hard to believe that it had only been yesterday—a mere twenty-four hours ago—that she had met Hal's eccentric, aristocratic family.

It was even harder to believe that today he had been buried.

Swiftly, Jill crossed the foyer and entered the salon, moving directly to the bar cart. She could not think about the funeral now. It hurt too much. She quickly poured herself a scotch, this time with ice, taking a few sips. As the alcohol dimmed her grief and sorrow, she finally glanced around at her surroundings. Scotch, she decided, wasn't half bad.

She had not really paid attention to any details before. The living room had a half-dozen different seating areas, a dozen fabulous Aubusson rugs, and every item of furniture was a period antique. Some of the occasional tables had marble tops, and most of the smaller chairs had gilded arms or legs. She halted. She stared again at the Matisse on one wall, then realized there was a Chagall print not far from it.

A huge landscape was on the adjacent wall. Jill did not recognize it at a glance, but had little doubt it was by a master. She walked over to it. It was a Corot.

Jill had already accepted the magnitude of the differences between her world and Hal's. Again, grimly, she wondered, What *had* Hal been thinking? What if his family was right—and she had been a fling?

Jill refused to continue her thoughts. But, perhaps, coming to England had been a huge mistake. She was learning things, seeing things, she had no wish to be made aware of.

She thought about Marisa. Just who the hell was she to Hal?

And suddenly Jill was angry. She was angry at Hal, because he was dead and she could not get the answers that she wanted him to supply. And being angry with someone who was dead—someone whom she had loved so much at the time—was terribly wrong.

"Where have you been?"

Tensing, Jill turned. Alex had entered the room, wearing his worn jeans and another cashmere sweater, this one a red V-neck. Jill hadn't heard him approaching. She couldn't help noticing that his feet were, once again, bare. She tried to smile. It felt sickly. "This is some painting."

Alex didn't quite smile back at her. "Yes, it is. I actually convinced William to bid on it last year at Sotheby's. You didn't come back after the funeral."

Jill shrugged her shoulders, trying to relieve the tension that had been building there in the last few minutes—and the last few days. "No, I didn't. Can you blame me?"

After a moment he said, "I guess not."

Jill asked, "Is Marisa still here?" Her tone was a tad snide.

"No. She left hours ago. She's devastated." If he detected the sarcasm in her tone, he was ignoring it.

Alex walked past her to the bar cart set with crystal decanters and sterling silver utensils. As he passed her, his sleeve brushed hers. Jill watched him pour himself a vodka on the rocks. He had not used the vodka in the crystal decanter, but a bottle of Keitel One from the lower shelf of the cart.

Jill turned her back on him and continued to study the Corot. She could not even imagine what its price tag had been. Perhaps in the millions, she thought. As she stared at the shimmering landscape, she was aware of Alex behind her. She had wanted a drink, but not company—and certainly not his.

"Where did you go after the funeral?" Alex asked.

Jill faced him slowly. She did not sit down because she intended to take her drink with her and flee to her room. "The British Library." And thinking about Kate and Anne made her pulse race. Her imagination immediately took over, and once again she could see the two girls, but this time poised at the entrance to a grandiose ballroom in their evening gowns, their eyes wide and filled with both trepidation and excitement. Jill smiled slightly.

"The British Library?" His brows were high. "If you're interested in museums, why, I could have recommended far better ones than that."

"Actually I went there for a reason. Kate Gallagher."

His expression did not change. In fact, his expressions were usually flat, impassive, giving very little away. "Kate Gallagher? The girl in the photograph?"

She nodded, suddenly eager to share her afternoon with someone, even if it was him. "You won't believe what I found." She recited the short paragraph to him, having memorized it effortlessly. "Isn't that amazing?"

Alex sat down in a plush chair covered in red and gold brocade, stretching his long legs out in front of him. "What's amazing is that you went to the library in the first place. And no, I don't understand. What is so amazing about what you have found?"

"Kate was from New York. My family was from New York. The photo was important to Hal. Kate and I have the same last name. I don't know what Hal was thinking, but I can feel it in my gut that this woman is my ancestor."

He shook his head, clearly dubious. "You're overtired, and you have quite an imagination. That's what I think. Enjoy your drink." He held his glass up to hers. "Cheers."

"Do I?" Jill almost wished she could reveal to him Hal's last dying words. "You are such a skeptic," Jill said, still enthused about her discovery. "She was a guest of Anne's in September of 1906. They were to make their debut together. There are too many coincidences here, Alex."

Alex's gaze was steady. Jill realized she had never called him by his name before, and oddly, that made her cheeks heat. "I don't think there are any coincidences at all," he said finally, taking a large sip of vodka.

Jill was instantly deflated. "No, you're wrong."

"You're very romantic, Jill, that's what this is about."

Jill looked at him. "I'm not romantic. My neighbor's the romantic one, New Age, and all that. She's the one who believes life has a master plan for everyone." Jill grew silent, thinking about life's master plan. It sucked.

Alex smiled. "That's a nice thought. So what does the Universe have in store for you?" He was sprawling in his chair now.

Very surprised, she shifted to look at him. KC had said Hal was not her destiny, but she was not about to tell him that. Especially since KC was wrong.

"Well?"

"My neighbor says Hal led me to Kate."

Alex regarded her unblinkingly. "That's pushing it."

"Maybe she's right." Abruptly Jill drained her drink. "I'm really tired," she said, standing. She didn't feel like sparring anymore.

Alex stood up, but slowly. "I'll refill that for you," he said, taking her glass from her.

Jill was about to refuse, but changed her mind. Why was he being civil? Or did he wish to detain her? When Alex had filled both their glasses, she accepted hers. "Thanks," she said. "Another one of these and I'm guaranteed to pass out."

He almost smiled. They drank. For the first time since arriving in London, Jill began to ever so slightly relax as the scotch invaded her bloodstream. "Who is Marisa?"

Alex looked at her.

"Marisa is—was—Hal's childhood sweetheart—the woman we all expected him to marry," Thomas said from the threshold of the room.

At the sound of his cool, patrician voice, Jill almost dropped her scotch. She tensed even as she stepped away from Alex, turning with dread to face him. He strolled into the room. "I hope I am not intruding." His glance was directed at her, not Alex.

Jill stared at him speechlessly. They had all expected Hal to marry Marisa? She and Hal had been childhood sweethearts? Jealousy filled her. But hadn't she suspected something like this? "Were they engaged?"

Thomas was making himself a drink. He turned. "How could they have been engaged? Didn't you tell us that Hal asked *you* to marry him?"

Jill could not look away from him. She hadn't told Thomas that—she had told Alex and Lauren. Obviously there were no secrets in the family.

"Jill was at the British Library this afternoon," Alex told his cousin.

Thomas drank his scotch while regarding them both. He had removed his jacket, but still wore a custom-made shirt, a Válentino tie, and black trousers. He had very broad shoulders and slim hips. "I know. I couldn't help overhearing."

Jill did not answer, watching him. To have overheard, he must have been standing in the doorway for some time—spying upon them. Jill was angry. She felt violated. And standing there beside Alex, with Thomas staring at her, she felt cornered, she felt trapped. She did not like the look in his eyes—it was the look of a suffering animal, made mean with pain and ready to lash out.

He wanted to lash out at her—hurt her, punish her, for Hal's death. Jill was certain.

His golden gaze remained on Jill, unwavering. "So you have had an . . . interesting afternoon?" His tone was civil, nothing more.

She lifted her chin, expecting an attack. "It was very interesting."

His stare remained. "So you are a history buff—like Hal."

"No."

Both dark slashing brows lifted. "Then why the library?"

She wet her lips. "Didn't you overhear my reasons for being there while you were standing in the doorway, listening to my conversation with your cousin?"

It was hard to tell if he smiled, and if it was pleasant or not. "Actually, I do believe you said that you think this woman, Kate Gallagher, is an ancestor of yours."

"I do."

"Who is Kate Gallagher?" he asked after drinking from his scotch.

"Your grandmother was a friend and host to her in 1906," she said with some defiance and some trepidation.

"So?"

"Hal had a photo of the two women in his room. We share the same last name, and Hal asked me to marry him, and I find the whole thing too extreme to be a coincidence." She knew she was baiting him. But she could not help herself.

His expression was more than amused. "So *you* claim. Hal never told us that he was thinking of marrying you." His gaze went to her hands. "I don't see a ring on your finger."

"We didn't have time to go shopping for a ring," Jill said firmly.

"Ah, yes. Dancing must be an exacting . . . er . . . profession." His tone told her he didn't think it a profession at all.

"It is," she said flatly. "I have trained six, even seven days a week, my entire life. I started ballet when I was four—at six I was training three, four hours a day. I was seventeen when I was accepted at Juilliard, eighteen when I joined the

New York City Ballet. Being a member of the corps there is even more demanding. I can't begin to describe what it is like. A few years ago I gave up ballet for the stage."

"Are you trying to impress me?" he asked.

Jill finally flushed, with anger. "I know what you think of me. And I don't care. I also think very little impresses you," Jill said. She stopped. She had been about to descend to his level and tell him that what undoubtedly impressed him, other than his blue-ribbon pedigree and his wealth, was himself. But she was not about to become as ugly as he was.

He smiled at her. "Go ahead. Speak your mind, Miss Gallagher. Tell me what you think."

"I don't think so," Jill said. She set her half-empty glass down. "I'm going to bed."

"Hal never told you about Marisa," Thomas said too softly.

Jill faltered. Instinctively, she knew Thomas was about to deliver a brutal blow.

"I'm right." Thomas stepped closer to her. "He didn't tell you anything, did he?"

Lips pursed, she shook her head. She didn't want to hear this. But she knew she had to.

"Hal knew Marisa for most of his life. Our families are close. In essence, Hal and Marisa grew up together—they were childhood sweethearts. They started seriously dating when Hal was in his final year at Cambridge, and he only waited so long because of her age—she was only sixteen. They've done everything together—skied the Alps, safaried in Kenya, toured China, hiked India. They broke up a few times, but they always got back together. Always."

Jill didn't move. Her heart drummed heavily, loudly, in her chest. But Marisa had married someone else, she managed to think.

"Thomas." Alex stepped between them. "Leave it alone. She's splitting tomorrow."

"No," Thomas barked.

And dully, Jill thought that Alex wasn't a complete bastard after all.

Alex gripped her arm. Jill leaned into him as he propelled

her toward the door. "Come on," he said. "Enough is enough. Let's end one rotten day."

"It was Marisa who saved Hal's life," Thomas shouted from behind them. Jill faltered. And she pulled away from Alex to turn and stare across the room at Thomas.

"Yes," he gritted. "Marisa *saved* Hal's life."

Jill was trembling. "What do you mean?"

He stared. "You don't know, do you? About the drugs and alcohol?"

It was a moment before Jill could understand him. "Hal didn't drink. He didn't do drugs, either."

Thomas laughed, harshly, bitterly. "This entire family was in denial, refusing to see what was happening to Hal before our very eyes," he said. "He would come home at dawn, sleep all day, reek of alcohol, be sniffing away, but we all believed him when he said he was tired, he was working too hard, he had a cold, we believed excuse after excuse, for years and years. We all closed our eyes to what was going on. But one day Marisa found him, out cold, and it was an overdose. Cocaine, speed, and alcohol. She got the medics, she was with him in the hospital, and she held his hand for the three months he was locked up in an in-patient hospital clinic. And she continued to hold his hand the following year, when he became an outpatient—which was during the year of her own divorce. It was Hal's battle, but she was with him, in spite of her legal battles, fighting for him, every step of the way." He was still shouting. He was also close to tears.

Jill was shaking. *She hadn't known.* She was in shock.

"And you didn't know," Thomas cried.

Jill just looked at him, his anger engulfing her, and it went through her dazed mind that Hal had kept the most important fact of his life hidden from her, and that Marisa had saved Hal's life.

While she, Jill, had ended it.

Jill closed her eyes, but only for a moment. When she opened them, they were blurred. "Why didn't Hal marry her?" she managed. "When was this?"

"He cleaned up two years ago. But Marisa was in the midst of an ugly divorce. She has a child, a son, and that Italian fortune hunter she married was trying to gain custody just to have leverage against her. She and Hal were seeing each other during the divorce until it tore them apart. When Hal left for New York a year ago, it looked like Marisa's divorce might go on for years, maybe more, because of the custody battle." He smiled grimly. "But the divorce came through two months ago."

Jill reeled. Thinking, *Oh, God, he had been on the verge of leaving her to go back with Marisa* . . . "No," she cried. "He loved me. He left her. He was with me, in New York, these past eight months—"

Thomas cut her off. "Bloody right he was in New York with you. And I think the reason is obvious." His gaze slid over her body in a brutally chauvinistic way.

"I have had enough," Jill cried, turning so quickly that she slammed into Alex's chest, face first.

"You've always known how to be cruel," Alex said over her head, to his cousin, his hands closing around her shoulders.

Jill pushed away from him, rushing to the door.

"I'm not through," Thomas said, his strides sounding as he hurried across the room after her. He caught her arm from behind, whirling her around. Jill made a small sound—that of a tiny animal, caught by its much larger, dangerous predator—a sound of pure fear.

"You're here now for the same reason you went after Hal in the first place," Thomas said, his eyes filled with fury. "And don't you deny it!"

"I have no idea what you are talking about," Jill gasped.

"Don't," Alex said, hard, slamming one hand down on Thomas's wrist, forcing him to release Jill.

Jill backed up against the door.

"Why are you protecting her? Or has she gotten to you, too?" Thomas cried to Alex.

"I'll ignore that. I'm going to ignore everything that has just happened, because you are drunk on grief," Alex said harshly. "Thomas, you are not yourself!"

Thomas turned his gaze on Jill, who remained frozen against the door, ignoring his cousin—perhaps not even having heard him. He was livid. "You went after Hal because *you* are a fortune hunter. And you're here now for the very same reason."

Jill was so stunned she could not even react.

"You're here to get a piece of Hal's trust. The next thing we know, you'll be claiming you're pregnant with his child."

Jill managed to find the words she so desperately wanted. "You are wrong," she said. "You are wrong." She shoved Alex aside and fled the two men.

Three

Jill FELT LIKE A DEAD PERSON.

She slowly stepped into very skinny, gray stretch pants and a fitted black pullover, feeling as if her body had run out of fuel. Her limbs seemed to be weak and useless. She had just gotten up after a sleepless night. Terrible doubts about her own relationship with Hal had tormented her hour after hour and she had actually watched the sky lightening with the sunrise. She had been haunted by Thomas's accusations, by the fact that Hal had kept such a monumental secret from her about his battle with drugs and alcohol, and by her own very real worry that Hal had intended to marry Marisa.

Thomas had to be wrong.

But the facts were inescapable.

Jill finished dressing. She had never been more grim—or more glum. Now she understood why Hal's family hated her. It wasn't just that she had been driving the car, or that she was a dancer. They all assumed her to be a fortune hunter. It was unbelievable.

Jill had never once in her life met a fortune hunter in the flesh. How dare they think her to be such a conniving piece of trash. But even her anger failed to replace the hurt. It was the most awful of accusations.

Marisa had saved Hal's life. She, Jill, had ended it.

Had Hal loved Marisa? Or had he loved her, Jill?

Jill sank back down on the bed, her head in her hands,

exhausted. Her mind wouldn't quit, worse, she felt like crying again. KC was right. She needed drugs. Just for a few days, maybe a few weeks.

Until she adjusted to being alone again, until she adjusted to the fact that she would never have the answers she would always seek.

There was a knock on Jill's door. Jill assumed it was a housemaid and she looked at the clock beside the bed. It was almost noon. Not that she cared. Her system had taken a beating, and although she had been in London for two days now, she had yet to adjust to the time change. Nor did she want to. Jet leg meant she had already lost the morning, and that was fine with her.

Tonight she was going home. She could not wait, even though it meant leaving Hal behind—a vast ocean separating them. Even though it meant she wouldn't be able to visit his grave for years and years.

She did not know how she felt anymore. A part of her that still believed, hated leaving Hal, would hate being so far away from him. But she could not bear being among the Sheldons anymore. She could not stand up to any more brutal discoveries about Hal's life—she was afraid to learn that there were more secrets he had kept from her.

Jill grabbed her purse and leather jacket, having just applied a beige-hued lipstick, and answered the door. To her surprise, Lauren stood there, impeccable and elegant in pressed blue jeans, a navy blue Escada blazer, a white button-down shirt, and J.P. Tod's loafers.

"Good morning," Lauren said, her hands in the pockets of her blazer. She didn't quite smile, but she wasn't scowling like the day before yesterday. "When you didn't come downstairs I thought I should check on you."

Jill did not relax. "Hoping I died in my sleep?" she said, before she thought the better of it.

Lauren stared. "That's very unfair."

"You're right. But let's not pretend. You didn't come upstairs to check on my health." Jill knew she was being terribly rude, but she was also being honest. She was too tired to play games anymore.

Lauren followed her down the hall. "Jill. We spoke last night at length about you."

Jill faltered, and on the landing, she turned to face Hal's sister.

"Thomas regrets his terrible outburst. I'm here to apologize for us all."

Jill could not believe her ears. And she did not believe, not for a New York minute, that Thomas had had a change of heart. He believed she was a trashy fortune hunter. He blamed her for Hal's death. What was going on? "Okay," Jill said cautiously.

Lauren's hands remained in her pockets. "I'm sorry, too. This is very difficult. I don't mean apologizing. I mean everything. But Hal was dating you, and you did bring him home—" Suddenly tears filled Lauren's eyes, her nose turned red, and she could not continue. "Oh, God!" She turned away, her shoulders shaking.

Tears filled Jill's eyes as well. Here, at least, was common ground. Jill dug into her purse for a tissue, laid her hand tentatively on Lauren's shoulder. Lauren shook her head, continuing to cry. Jill waited, and when she finally repressed the sobs, Jill handed her the tissue. Lauren wiped her eyes carefully—avoiding mascara.

When she looked up, it was to meet Jill's own eyes, which remained moist. "Thank you."

It was a moment before Jill could speak. "Maybe he didn't love me completely, but I loved him with all of my heart and all of my soul."

Lauren stared.

Jill put her purse strap over her shoulder. "Thomas is wrong about me," she said impulsively, immediately regretting her words. Something was up, and she didn't want Lauren to know that she suspected anything.

"Thomas is in shock and in grief, we all are. He blames himself for Hal's death."

"How is that? He blames me."

Lauren shook her head. "I know you think he is a monster, but he's not. Try to understand. Please. We're a very close family. Our lineage goes back hundreds of years. Thomas is

Father's heir. But Father is seventy-nine. Thomas is the head of this family. He is almost the patriarch, he makes all the decisions, he is CEO of the company, and even the executor of Hal's and my trusts." Lauren suddenly realized what she had said and her face crumpled.

Jill understood. It was so easy to forget that Hal was dead—to think, for a moment, that he was living among them. Jill handed her another Kleenex. Lauren blew her nose. "For some reason, I thought Alex ran the company," Jill said.

Lauren gave her an odd look. "They are both very involved," she finally said. "Alex is a president, and on numerous boards, actually, but Thomas is CEO." She smiled slightly. "Thomas has the final say—in everything, and that is as it should be."

Hal had said that Thomas was a playboy. His weekend home was probably on Mykonos. She could not help being snide. Nothing Lauren said would make her change her feelings about her older brother.

Lauren continued, obviously wanting to impress Jill with her case. "Thomas is a very protective chap. He has always felt that we were his responsibility, and I do mean myself, Alex, and Hal. You know, when we were children, he was our champion. We would always go to him if we had difficulties—and he would always solve our problems. If a boy teased me at school, Thomas would appear to set things right. I remember when Alex first came to live with us—when his mother died. Mother and Father put him in the same school as Hal. Obviously he had problems. He was an American hoodlum, really, and he was miserable—all the boys ostracized him. Until Thomas dropped in on the school. To this day, I don't know what he said to a handful of the boys, but Alex was reluctantly accepted after that."

"Okay," Jill said, even though the story about Alex Preston was interesting, "I get the drift. Thomas is a knight in shining armor."

Lauren ignored that. "We all still defer to him, today. Now, though, he is also taking care of Mother and Father, too. Mother has not been well." Lauren's expression was tense. After a pause, she said, "I know Thomas is blaming himself for Hal's death. Last night he said he should have gone to New York himself to bring him home. He thinks he shouldn't have ever allowed Hal to go to New York in the first place."

Jill did not understand. "Hal was a grown man. Thomas certainly didn't run his life."

"Hal is an artist. I told you, Thomas is executor of his trust."

Jill stared. So Thomas held the purse strings. So Thomas could have manipulated Hal had he chosen to do so. It was to his credit that he had not.

"Hal and I were extremely close. He told me everything, I think." Jill's heart lurched at that. "We're only two years apart in age. But I think, perhaps, this is hitting Thomas even harder than myself." She trembled. "We're all in shock. Please forgive him his rudeness. Please forgive us. We are sorry."

Jill found herself responding to Lauren's plea. How could she not? She was not hateful by nature, and she wanted to feel compassion for Thomas—because Hal had adored him. She wanted to like Lauren for the same reason. On the other hand, this whole impassioned diatribe was contrived and strangely ill-timed. And why hadn't Thomas apologized himself? Jill had no doubt it was because he wasn't sorry for anything he had said. "I guess we can bury the hatchet." Her gaze locked briefly with Lauren's—for the merest of seconds. Jill wasn't sure who looked away first—Hal's sister or herself.

"Good," Lauren said. She smiled. Her nose and eyes were still pink.

Jill felt that her return smile was lopsided. The problem was, she did want to make peace. It was just that she knew Lauren wasn't being completely honest with her.

"Are you still leaving tonight?" Lauren asked.

Jill nodded.

"Do you want some company today? I can show you London, if that's what you want, and take you to lunch."

Jill almost gaped. She quickly rearranged her face. "I think I'll hoof it alone."

Lauren looked chagrined. "But I thought you accepted my apology for everyone?"

"I have." Jill had no choice but to smile. "I'm not feeling so great," she began.

"How about lunch and a guided tour of London?" Lauren smiled again. "We have some very nice neighborhoods here. I'd love to walk you through Mayfair, show you the Houses of Parliament, Buckingham Palace, and all that wonderfully touristy stuff."

Jill hesitated. "Actually, I have plans for the day." But she was wondering if she should accept Lauren's offer. Lauren had mentioned that the family's history went back hundreds of years. Jill was only interested in as far back as 1906.

"What kind of plans?"

"Hal mentioned to me that Uxbridge Hall is your ancestral home. He said it's open to the public. I want to go there, and I was wondering if your grandmother Anne had an ancestral home that I could visit, too."

Lauren's tawny brows lifted. "Uxbridge Hall does have a few rooms on the ground floor that are open to the public. It's not far from London—thirty minutes by car. I'd be happy to take you there."

"That would be great," Jill said slowly. Why was Lauren being so nice to her?

"But I'm afraid you won't have any luck when it comes to visiting my grandmother's home. Anne grew up at Bensonhurst Hall. She was the last Bensonhurst, and she was a great heiress when she married my grandfather, Edward, who became the ninth earl of Collinsworth. Bensonhurst, and the entire estate, came into our family at the time of the death of her parents, and I believe that was just after the First World War. But the house was demolished by order of Parliament even prior to the war—to make way for a rail station."

"You're kidding," Jill exclaimed.

"No. Those things happen. It was an old house, impossible to keep up, and it was, frankly in the way." Lauren smiled. "Let's drive out to Uxbridge. I can't remember the public hours, but we do keep an entire wing for our private use, and we can get in even if Uxbridge Hall is not open to the public today."

"That's wonderful," Jill said, feeling a rush of excitement.

"Why do you want to go there?" Lauren said curiously as they descended the stairs.

Jill hesitated before answering truthfully. "I keep thinking about Kate Gallagher. I can't get her off of my mind. There's something about her that is so compelling." Jill paused. "And I have this gut feeling that she is a relative of mine, and I just can't shake it." But she didn't tell Lauren that "Kate" was the last name Hal spoke. Jill would have no peace until she found out what that meant.

"But what does this feeling of yours have to do with Uxbridge Hall?"

"Kate was Anne's friend, after all," Jill said as they entered the spacious foyer. "She stayed with Anne at Bensonhurst in 1906. Anne married Edward. I guess Uxbridge Hall is as close as I'll ever get to Anne's family home. I really don't know why I want to go there, or what I expect to find. I just have to go." And even as Jill spoke, she felt chills creeping up her spine.

"Well, it is a lovely house," Lauren replied. "And quite a few mementos from the Bensonhurst side of our family are there. But I am quite sure you will not find anything there of value to you if you are researching Kate—unless, of course, it is Kate's ghost."

Jill glanced sharply at her. The hairs on her nape seemed to prickle again. "Whatever made you say that?"

Lauren smiled. "Don't you believe in ghosts? This is Great Britain, Jill. Our history is very rich—and actually quite bloody. We have ghosts everywhere."

Visitors were required to leave their cars in the car park and walk some distance to the house. But that was not the case for the family, Lauren had explained, as their chauffeured Rolls paused before high iron gates that were closed. On the opposite side of those gates—set in a huge brick wall—was an expanse of rolling green land, a few trees, and, in the near distance, what appeared to be a huge brick house. Jill stared as the gates were opened by an electronic device and the Rolls proceeded through. She would have never dreamed to find this pastoral enclave in the midst of London's suburbs.

"That house belongs to your family?" Jill asked rather breathlessly as the sprawling mansion came closer into view.

"Actually, it now belongs to the National Trust, but our family has the right to use it as we wish. Occasionally we even hold parties here," Lauren said.

"There's a lake," Jill said, noticing a tree-lined lake before one side of the rectangular building. Towers with spires graced the four corners of the house, and as they drove up the curving driveway, Jill was faced with an extravagant portico as tall as the house and a similarly sized temple front.

"Most of these old homes have lakes or moats—most of them man-made."

The car halted before the portico's wide, imposing front steps. As Jill slowly climbed out of the car, her pulse pounding, she was aware of the height of the six pillars holding up the pediment—they were as tall as the building itself. "Is the house three stories?" Jill asked.

"Yes. But as you can see, the ground floor has very high ceilings."

Jill remained amazed. She glanced around. To her left were another set of huge brick buildings. "Let me guess. The stables?"

Lauren nodded. "Now, of course, it's a shop and café for tourists."

"The family actually comes here—lives here—from time to time?"

"Not very often," Lauren confessed. "Hal used to come and stay here for weeks at a time when he was in town. He was the most attached to Uxbridge Hall of any of us. And when Thomas was married, he and his wife and children lived here most weekends. He used it as a kind of country home." She smiled.

"How far are we from London?"

"Not even ten miles," Lauren said cheerfully. "In the past, when this was our family's primary residence, it was very convenient."

"When was this the family's primary residence?" Jill asked as they started up the front steps. Once within the portico, they were on a slate-floored, open courtyard. The front doors of the house were at least fifty feet beyond.

"A long time ago. Before I was born, at any rate."

"Did they live here in Kate's time?"

Lauren glanced at her. "Which was?"

"About 1906."

"I believe my family still spent a good portion of their time here at the Hall. The house in Kensington Palace Gardens was also built around that time, I believe."

They crossed the courtyard. A tall, somewhat stocky woman with short, iron gray hair and oversized tortoiseshell frames, clad in a black turtleneck and trousers, had appeared to stand on the threshold of the Hall. She seemed surprised to see them. "Mrs. Sheldon-Wellsely, how are you, my dear?"

"Lucinda, I hope I should not have telephoned first."

"Of course not," the older woman said, still smiling. "This is your home, my dear." Her smile disappeared. "I am so sorry about your brother. I cannot get over what has happened. He was the nicest young man."

Jill flinched, reality washing over her. She didn't want to think about Hal now, she wanted to think about Kate. But there was no denying the stabbing ache the mere mention of him brought to her chest.

"Thank you," Lauren murmured. She quickly changed the topic, introducing them. "Lucinda Becke is the custodian, and has been so ever since I was a little girl. This is a visitor from America, Jill Gallagher."

"I almost consider myself a member of the Collinsworth family," Lucinda said pleasantly to Jill, offering her hand. If she knew anything about Jill's relationship with Hal—or about the accident—she gave no sign. "I have been the director here since '81. Actually, I was just filing some interesting papers—letters from your grandfather to his valet."

"This house is incredible," Jill said as they paused in a huge, empty room. Pillars supported the high, bluish gray and white ceiling. The center boasted a sculpted circular pattern, mirroring the mosaic on the floor, while square panels bordered it. The floors were blue and white marble, done in myriad patterns. The walls were divided into huge frieze work panels with a Roman military motif. At each end of the room were two alcoves, each with a fireplace. There were statues standing next to the room's many pilasters, and periodically there were square panels with frieze work in an arabesque motif. Gilded benches and stone pedestals with sculptures lined the far and near walls of the room.

"This is the hall," Lucinda explained. "Although in an earlier time, it was used for entertaining. Balls were held here, extremely lavish affairs." Lucinda smiled widely. "In fact, the family also had a tradition of holding the heir's wedding ceremony here. Unfortunately, that tradition did end with the eighth earl." She smiled at Lauren. "Your greatgrandfather was the last Collinsworth heir to be married in this room. What a shame."

Jill studied Lucinda's animated expression as Lauren asked, "Could you give us a brief tour? Jill is interested in the history of the house."

"I would love to." Lucinda's eyes brightened. "There is nothing I would love more."

As they walked through the hall, Lucinda pointed out the details of the various panels they passed. Jill could hardly absorb what she was saying. Excitement filled her.

Anne Bensonhurst, later the countess of Collinsworth, had certainly visited here after her debut, for she had eventually become engaged to Edward Sheldon, heir to the Collinsworth estates. She had undoubtedly been a frequent guest in this house. Had she brought along her friend, Kate Gallagher? Jill could image the two girls in this spectacular room, in their evening gowns, perhaps with raised fans—did the ladies use fans then?—surrounded by other guests. Perhaps, she thought, her mind spinning, Kate had visited Anne here after her marriage to Edward. Perhaps she had even spent the night.

As they walked into another room, which Lucinda referred to as the "eating room," she asked, "Would visitors have stayed overnight? Ninety years ago?"

"Weekend parties were quite popular, but longer visits

usually took place in country homes during the High Season," Lucinda explained.

"The High Season?"

"The summertime."

They had all paused in the eating room. It was also huge, but perhaps only a third the size of the hall. The carpet was rose-hued with a diamond pattern in gold and green, the walls were a lighter shade of rose, trimmed with pale green, and the ceiling was also pale green, with more painstaking frieze work. Paintings hung on the walls. Many were portraits.

Jill felt dazed. Her pulse was pounding too swiftly for comfort, and far too loudly, as well. Lucinda was avidly explaining that the family and its guests would take breakfast in this room. "Are those portraits of the family?" Jill asked, her lips feeling almost and oddly numb, due, she thought, to her excitement.

"Oh, no. Those two are portraits of the Duke of Northumberland from the mid-eighteenth and early nineteenth century. That portrait is of William and Mary. That one there is of George IV." Lucinda smiled eagerly. "That far portrait is of one of the early earls of Collinsworth, from the mid-seventeenth century, and the one beside it is William, the eighth earl. It is quite common in houses like this for the family to hang portraits of royalty—so one might think that the family, by association, is as majestic and as noble."

Jill was disappointed. There were some portraits of ladies among the gentlemen and she had hoped to espy Anne. She finally looked at Lucinda directly. "Oh."

"Dear, is there something you are looking for? Something you specifically wish to see?"

Jill wet her lips. "I was hoping to find a portrait of Anne, perhaps with Edward. And maybe even with her friend, the American heiress, Kate Gallagher."

Lucinda stared.

Jill realized that Lauren's regard was divided between them both.

"Come with me, into the gallery," Lucinda said, her strides brisk.

They passed through two lavish rooms and were then

faced with a vast and extremely long room. French doors opened along one of the long walls to a terrace and spectacular gardens outside. Huge crystal chandeliers hung from the ceiling, armless chairs with blue velvet seats lined the room's perimeter, and dozens of paintings were hanging on the walls. Lucinda did not pause, crossing the carpeted expanse, passing several fireplaces with white marble mantels. She finally halted in front of a large painting.

Jill gripped Lauren's sleeve. She was faced with a painting of a couple having a picnic in a meadow, near a tree. The woman was seated at the gentleman's feet, and she was dark-haired, young, and neither pretty nor plain. But her eyes were shining. "That is Anne, correct me if I'm wrong." Jill was trembling. She had also grown very warm.

"Yes." Lucinda moved closer. "She was very young, no more than eighteen. This was painted during the first year of her marriage."

Jill stared. Anne sat on a blanket in a lovely white dress sprigged with blue, beneath a large, blossoming cherry tree. On the red paisley wool blanket were the accoutrements of a picnic—a wicker basket, a bottle of wine, two goblets, and several plates. Pieces of fruit—an apple, two pears, a cluster of grapes—had spilled from the basket. A book lay open beside her skirts, and a cocker spaniel lay at her blue-slippered feet.

Standing beside Anne was a tall, dark, striking man with a very patrician, quite stern expression. He was wearing riding jodhpurs and high black boots, a white shirt and a long tweed jacket. He held a crop in one hand. A burgundy cravat was around his neck. His stare was dark, unwavering, relentless. He was handsome and charismatic. He appeared every inch the aristocrat. He looked as if he had been born to command a hundred servants—and he also looked as if he did not know how to smile. Anne seemed too young and very fragile, seated there at his feet. "So that's Edward."

"Yes."

"They make a striking couple," Jill mused. "Anne is so young."

"Many girls married at that age back then," Lucinda

explained. "This was quite the union. Edward Sheldon was *the* catch of his times. And Anne, of course, was a great heiress herself. All of London was agog over the alliance—and rightly so."

Lauren was staring at the painting as well. "I've seen this many times, but it almost feels like I'm seeing it for the first time, today." She did not smile. Jill thought her expression tense. "I never knew him. He died a long time ago. Around World War Two, I believe."

"When did she die?" Jill asked, studying Anne in the portrait.

"I was nine when she died," Lauren said.

"She lived to the ripe old age of eighty-five," Lucinda said. "She became ill quite suddenly, and passed away in her sleep, in 1975. I recall the funeral quite clearly."

Jill regarded Lauren. "You must have a lot of memories of her."

"Not really." Lauren was emphatic. "She was very brusque—and very busy. We stayed out of her way. We were all frightened of her."

Jill was surprised, and she looked at the young girl seated at Edward's feet, her eyes shining with love. "She looks fragile to me."

Lauren did not reply.

"Did she ever talk about Kate?" Jill knew it was a long shot.

"What I do remember," Lauren said, suddenly smiling but red-eyed again, "was that Hal and Thomas used to play wildly in this house when we were children." She smiled, her eyes moist. "We spent some vacations here—even a few weekends, when we were very young. Perhaps I was five or six. They excluded me." Lauren was choked up.

"There, there," Lucinda said, patting her back.

Lauren shook her head. "I'm fine. It was so long ago. I had forgotten all about it. They had their own secret language and it made me so mad, because they could spell and I could not. They used words spelled backward. Just to tease me."

There wasn't anything to say, so Jill remained silent, studying the painting, almost feeling as if Hal were standing right there beside them—or beside her, looking over her shoulder at the portrait, too. She folded her arms across her breasts. "Where do you think this portrait was painted?" Jill asked Lucinda. He was going to haunt everyone for a very long time, she realized.

"It was painted at Stainesmore," Lucinda replied. "The family's country home."

"In the north of Yorkshire," Lauren added. "It was once a huge, working estate. It's rather run-down now, actually. We still summer there sometimes."

"Hal mentioned that he summered in Yorkshire as a child," Jill said. She continued to stare at Edward. For some reason, she had gotten chills, raising the fine hairs on her arms. He looked vain, arrogant, cold, and difficult. Jill thought that it had been a poor match. Anne did not look like the kind of woman who could hold such a man's attention for very long, no matter what Lauren had said.

"I think your grandmother was in love," Jill remarked.

Lauren did not reply.

"No one married for love in those days, Miss Gallagher," Lucinda said with a smile. "Not when titles and estates were involved. But it is no secret—Anne was smitten with her bridegroom."

Jill doubted that Edward had been smitten with his bride. He did not appear to be the kind of man capable of great passion or deep feelings. "Did the Sheldons need Anne's fortune?" Jill asked.

Lauren's eyes widened. Clearly she was taken aback. "Of course not," she said quickly.

Jill hadn't meant to be impertinent. "Sorry."

Lucinda rushed into the awkward moment, for Lauren's cheeks remained flushed. "Hal was very fond of this painting in particular, you know. He used to spend hours here, right in this gallery, in fact. Not that he did not appreciate all the works of art in this house."

Suddenly Jill imagined Hal wandering around this huge house by himself—and it did not quite make sense. There was something sad and lonely about it. But there was also something else, a sense she was trying to grasp, but could not quite identify. He'd kept the photograph of Anne and Kate—and he had spent far too much time at Uxbridge Hall. She thought about all of the evenings they had shared. It suddenly seemed to Jill that not an evening had gone by that he hadn't mentioned his family, or told her some amusing tale about them, at least once. "How much time did he spend here, actually?" she asked Lucinda.

Lucinda glanced at Lauren. "He used the private apartments whenever he was in town," she finally said. "There is something I wish to show you."

A little tiny warning bell was going off in Jill's brain, but she could not quite decipher it. She followed Lucinda and Lauren down the gallery to a beautiful marble-topped table. Several framed photographs were on top of it—current photos of William and Margaret, and then several of Thomas, and one of two young boys in school uniforms who looked so much like him that they had to be his sons. "The earl, the countess, his heir, and his grandsons," Lucinda remarked.

Then Lucinda pointed at a small display case on an adjoining bureau. Inside were a variety of small objects—a painted porcelain egg, an enameled snuff box, teardrop jet earrings, an inkwell and quill, several old leather books, a locket.

"My dear, look at that locket right there," Lucinda said with a soft but triumphant tone.

Jill cried out. The locket was open. Each half contained a small, perfect portrait. One was of Anne. The other was of Kate. "Anne and Kate," Jill breathed.

"They were obviously good friends," Lucinda said. "According to the Bensonhurst house records, which we have, Kate and her mother were guests at Bensonhurst for some time."

Jill could hardly breathe. "It was in September of 1906 that they arrived," she whispered.

"Was it? You have an excellent memory, my dear. This locket was given to the museum by Anne herself, shortly before her death."

Jill did not want to leave the display case with its locket.

She was experiencing chills again, and while the sensation was disturbing, it was not entirely negative.

And then, as clear as day, she could imagine Anne and Kate seated together at a dining table in an eating room like the one she had just passed through, their heads close together, giggling and whispering, telling one another about their flirtations and successes at the Fairchild ball. Outside, the sun was high, casting the girls in a warm but ethereal glow. Both girls were too excited to eat. Both girls had never been happier. They were the best of friends.

Jill hugged herself. The hairs on her nape had just risen and her heart had lurched. The sensation was distinct. It was one of impending darkness, and it was not pleasant.

"The rumor is that she had a lover."

Jill and Lauren whirled and regarded Lucinda with equally wide eyes.

"I beg your pardon?" Lauren asked stiffly.

"Not Lady Anne." Lucinda smiled at them both. "Kate."

Jill stared. "Kate had a lover?"

"The gossip is that she used to sneak out of the window of Anne's bedroom at Bensonhurst while she stayed there, using tied-together sheets to climb down to the gardens below."

Jill's ears seemed to ring.

Lauren was cool. "Are you passing down gossip that is almost a century old, Lucinda?"

"Actually, I am passing down gossip that came from Anne herself." Lucinda smiled, unperturbed.

Jill could not believe her ears. "*She* told you that?"

"She told my predecessor. Uxbridge Hall was reopened to the public in 1968 after extensive renovation. Just before the opening, Anne came here to inspect the house and give her approval for the opening. She was the dowager countess then. Apparently the visit invoked many memories for her. Or so Janet Witcombe claims." Lucinda continued to smile.

"Is she alive?" Jill asked in a rush. "Janet Witcombe?"

"She most certainly is."

"I would love to talk to her, find out if it's true, find out what Anne actually said." But even as Jill spoke, in the throes of excitement, she realized that this might be a dead end. 1968 was thirty years ago. Who could remember a thirty-year-old conversation?

"She's a bit senile right now. But she has moments of extreme lucidity. If you are fortunate, you will catch her at a good time. I'm happy to give you her listing."

Jill turned to Lauren. "Can you believe this?"

Lauren frowned. "No. I can't. And what difference does any of this make? Even if Kate did have a lover and climbed out of the house with sheets, it's just quaint gossip, Jill. Let's go. I have had enough for one day of my dead ancestors."

Jill did not want to leave. There was an entire house to explore, and if she did not do so today, she would never be able to do so, because tonight she was going home. But Lauren was clearly finished with the outing. Very reluctantly, she followed Lucinda and Lauren out of the gallery and through a room filled with chinoiserie.

Once again in the cavernous hall, the trio paused. Jill had one last question. "Do you know if Kate came here to visit Anne after she married Edward?"

"No. She did not. That would have been impossible, I'm afraid." Lucinda stared at her. "You look like her, you know."

Jill started. "What?"

"I noticed the moment we met. Before we were even introduced."

Jill did not think there was any resemblance at all between them. Kate had been so striking—Jill was aware that she was attractive, but in a far more ordinary way. But Lucinda was being sincere. Didn't that mean that they might be related? Was Kate Gallagher a long-lost ancestor, or even her own great-grandmother? "Why are you so certain that Kate never visited Anne here?" She asked.

Lucinda was no longer smiling. She was somber. "She never visited Anne here, my dear, because she disappeared when she was eighteen, and she was never seen or heard from again."

Four

Jill walked slowly downstairs. She had put on her jeans for the flight home, and her bags had been taken out to the car by a servant. Her strides slowed. Standing in the marble-floored foyer was Alex Preston.

His back was to her. For one moment Jill faltered, debating going back upstairs in order to avoid him. On the other hand, she didn't want to miss her flight. She studied him. When Lauren had given her the long spiel that morning, she hadn't really mentioned Alex as being a part of the apology package.

Alex must have heard her or sensed her presence, because he did turn. His gaze immediately settled on her features.

Jill continued down the stairs, pausing before him. He had a way of looking right through her, or into her, that made her tense. "I'm on my way to the airport," she said, stating the obvious. She was eager to leave and didn't care if he knew it.

"I know." He smiled slightly at her. "I'm here to wish you bon voyage."

Jill assumed he was more than eager for her to depart, as was the entire family. "Are you a messenger for the family?"

"Should I be?"

She was startled. Didn't he know about Lauren's apology on behalf of the Sheldons? "I guess not. Thanks for your hospitality." She was trying to be polite so she could go. She did not know what else to say, but her words sounded slightly sarcastic to her own ears.

His slanting black brows lifted. "We've hardly been civil. And the Brits are famous for their civility."

"I'm not going to complain." She was impatient to leave. She glanced at the open front door, and the sedan idling in the driveway.

"You don't seem like the kind of woman to turn the other cheek."

"I'm very tired, Alex," Jill said tersely, in no mood to spar. "It's been a rotten couple of days." Kate Gallagher had disappeared at the age of eighteen. Nothing could have prepared Jill for such a fact.

And now she had a dozen questions on the tip of her tongue, questions she'd been too shocked to think of before, when Lucinda had dropped that bombshell upon her. In any case, Lauren had been insistent that they leave and go to lunch. They had left shortly afterward, but Lucinda had invited Jill to drop by anytime—and she had given her both Janet Witcombe's telephone number and her own.

Jill almost wished that she were not leaving London.

"Yeah, it sure has," Alex said. Then, "I heard you had a helluva day at Uxbridge Hall."

Jill started. Did he read minds? "What are there—football huddles in this family?"

"We're close-knit," he said wryly.

"It was very interesting." Jill hesitated, the urge to tell him what she had learned quite compelling. But she resisted it. "How long have you been living over here, Alex?"

He eyed her. "Why?"

"I was just wondering if you knew anything about the family's history."

"The family's history—or the alleged disappearance of Kate Gallagher?" His blue gaze held hers.

She thought she flushed. So he and Lauren had been sharing notes. She did not have to wonder if Lauren had also told Thomas all about their day. Of course she had. "Can you blame me for being curious?"

"I think you need to distract your mind, and a preoccupation with this Kate Gallagher does just that. But to answer your question, I was taken into this family when my mother died. I was fourteen. I left London a few years later only to go to Princeton, followed by grad school at Wharton. I returned exactly ten years ago. And no, I know next to nothing about her."

"You must know something about Anne," Jill persisted.

"Not really." He remained silent.

Jill found that hard to believe. On the other hand, Hal had told her once that Alex was driven by his work. Jill recalled that so clearly now. Maybe he lived in a vacuum. But she did not think so. She was a decent judge of character, and Alex seemed sharp, clever. "I know what it's like," she said slowly, "to have very little family."

He stared.

"My parents were killed when I was five and a half years old." She was grim. "It was a car accident. Can you believe it?" Suddenly she felt that damned stabbing anguish again. For a short while she had had a family—Hal had become her family—and she'd always assumed that they would eventually have children of their own. All of those dreams were now gone, forever. "The worst part of it is, I really can't remember them. I have no damn memories of my parents." But she had memories of Hal. And somehow she had to hold on to those memories, not letting anything or anyone taint them.

The task felt overwhelming.

A silence had fallen. "What's the point?" Alex asked finally.

"Your mother died, and the Sheldons became your family. I think they are extremely important to you. When Anne died, wasn't she well into her eighties?" Jill met his gaze.

"Yeah."

"And you must be, what? Thirty-three? Thirty-four? Thirty-five?"

"You're a little bulldog," Alex said, but not with rancor. "I was nine when she died. I knew her, but slightly. She was the kind of old woman a kid would avoid whenever possible."

That was interesting. Lauren had said the same thing. "Why?"

"She was strict and bossy. She was a real matriarch. We

were all afraid of her. Everyone was afraid of her. Even the servants."

Jill stared. That was not the impression she had received either from the photograph of Kate and Anne or the portrait of her and Edward. She had seemed young, soft, not quite pretty, and passive. But people changed over time. Life could do that.

Jill thought about how her life had changed—changing her—irrevocably—in one split second of a car accident. Twice.

The injustice of it all could be overwhelming. She fiercely shoved all self-pity aside.

"What is it?" Alex asked, a bit too sharply.

She shook herself free of her thoughts. "Nothing. I have a plane to catch." She glanced at her watch, a red and black Swatch affair, and shifted her vinyl tote to her shoulder. It crossed her mind that if Alex and Lauren had been comparing notes, Alex might merely be backing up Lauren. But why do that? "Well, thanks again. And you can pass that along to your aunt and uncle and cousins." She refused to think about Thomas now. Hopefully she would never see him again. It did not surprise her that no one else had come to say good-bye.

To Jill's surprise, Alex fell into stride beside her. "I'll take you to Heathrow." His gaze locked with hers. "A bit of American civility," he said.

When Jill opened the front door to her small studio, a small blur of gray fur leaped across her path. Last night she had called KC to tell her she was coming home, and KC had understood. Nothing would have been worse than to return now to an empty apartment. But her studio wasn't empty.

"Ezekial!" she cried, reaching for him.

But her gray tom was thoroughly annoyed at her—he hated being left alone—and he had already disappeared, to sulk and hopefully teach Jill a lesson.

Jill sighed. She'd needed comforting. Returning home was bittersweet. Jill set down her bags, not moving out of the doorway. She couldn't move. She was struck by how tiny her studio was. It was impossible not to have vivid contrasting images of both the Sheldon mansion in Kensington Palace Gardens and Uxbridge Hall.

Jill turned and slowly closed her door. She would probably never return to either the Sheldons' London home or their ancestral one again—and that was for the best. Wasn't it?

In a way, she felt as if she had just stepped out of a fairy tale—yet it had hardly been that. It had definitely been the worst few days of her life.

But she could not quite shake the feeling that she should not have left London just yet. But that was nonsense—there was nothing for her there.

Immediately images of Hal's family and Kate Gallagher came to mind.

Jill brushed her bangs out of her eyes, crossing the studio. According to Lucinda Becke, Hal had loved Uxbridge Hall. She thought about the portraits in the eating room—one had been of a seventeenth-century ancestor of his. It was so amazing—to be able to trace one's roots so far back—to know without a doubt who one was, where one came from. Hal, Jill thought, and people like him, undoubtedly took such knowledge for granted.

She looked around at her studio, aware of being absolutely alone in the world. Then she thought about the beautiful, compelling Kate Gallagher, who had disappeared at the tender age of eighteen. What had happened to her? Had something terrible happened? Or had she really had a lover, and had she run away with him to live happily ever after?

Was Kate her ancestor? Could she even be her great-grandmother?

If such a twist of fate was possible, then that meant Kate had never married, because they shared the same last name.

"Shit," Jill muttered, crossing the room. It was painted a pale melon color, except for the far wall, which an artist who was a friend of hers had painted as a mural. It depicted many different scenes from New York City in vibrant primary colors. Several colorful kilim rugs were underfoot, which she had collected over the years at garage sales and flea markets. Her bed was a simple queen-sized mattress and box spring, but it was covered with a royal blue quilt and a half-dozen large peach, blue, and gold pillows. A single orange couch faced the mural, a wicker chest serving as a coffee table.

The eating area was by the small open kitchen, and her tiny pine table could just seat two. Director's chairs with red canvas seats balanced that side of the room.

Jill walked into her kitchen area, shrugging off her leather jacket. She hadn't been able to sleep on the flight home. Her mind hadn't stopped, her thoughts shifting from the Sheldons and Alex Preston to Kate Gallagher and back again. And there had been the sick feeling she could not shake that had to do with her leaving Hal so far away—and with his having, perhaps, loved another woman, Marisa Sutcliffe.

She opened the refrigerator for ice water and froze. On the top shelf, which was mostly bare, was half of a leftover pizza, and in the refrigerator door was an opened bottle of white wine. She and Hal had shared that pizza just last week, Jill drinking the wine.

She slammed the door closed.

She almost expected to see him come sauntering out of the bathroom, a grin on his handsome face.

Had he loved Marisa? Had he been about to break up with Jill in order to marry the other woman? Could she have been so deceived? Could she have been so stupid?

It happened all the time, Jill thought grimly.

And why had he kept that photograph of Kate and Anne, beside his bed, of all places?

Jill gripped the counter. "This is not fair, Hal," she cried angrily. "None of this is fair!" She felt like ripping Marisa's gorgeous hair right out of her head. But that wasn't fair, either. What had Marisa done, except to love Hal over the course of her lifetime? If Hal had duped Jill—if he had been using her—then he was the bastard, not her.

But how could she be angry at, even hate, someone who had just died?

Jill realized that she could let her mind spin around and round in circles, or she could lay her confusion and anger to rest, right alongside Hal. Maybe, for the sake of her own mental and physical well-being, that was what she would have to do.

She'd done it before. When her parents had died. She'd attacked ballet with her entire being, living it and breathing it and even being it, until there was nothing else in her life.

But Jill was now exhausted, and she had no ambition to dance. She knew she'd have to force herself to go back to work—immediately. But what she really wished, desperately, was that Kate was her relative, that she was her great-grandmother, and that she knew it for a fact, that she had proof.

Jill wished she were back at Uxbridge Hall, exploring the rest of the house, looking for clues about the woman who had so tragically disappeared at such a young age.

Jill turned on the faucet, filled up a glass with tap water, and drank it thirstily, eyes closed. She did not want to be home after all. Her studio was horribly empty. She felt more alone now than ever before—even than when she had been a guest at the Sheldons, as rude and uncivil as they had all been.

Ezekial pressed against her ankles, purring.

Jill opened her eyes, which were moist, smiled, and bent to scoop up the cat. Thank God for Zeke, she thought. But temperamental beast that he was, he hissed and leaped out of her arms. He hated being held, but loved being petted—when it suited him. "Thanks, Zeke," Jill said shakily.

Jill suddenly picked up her kitchen phone. From the front pocket of her jeans, she pulled out the scrap of paper with Lucinda's telephone numbers. She glanced at her watch. It was two in the morning in New York, which meant it was seven in London. She quickly dialed Lucinda's home phone.

The phone was answered instantly.

"Jill! This is such a surprise."

"I hope I didn't wake you," Jill said swiftly.

"My dear, I'm up at six," Lucinda said cheerfully.

"I can't stop thinking about Kate Gallagher," Jill told her. "I wish Lauren hadn't rushed me out of Uxbridge Hall like that."

Lucinda was silent. Then, "Yes, that's a shame."

"What happened, Lucinda, after she disappeared?" Jill asked. "And when exactly did she disappear?"

"It was the autumn of 1908, just before the holiday season," Lucinda told her. "There was an investigation, but she was never found. I do believe there was some suspicion that she did run away with her lover. I have some old clippings filed away somewhere, Jill. I would have to look for them, though."

"That would be great," Jill said enthusiastically. "Was her lover ever identified?"

"No, I don't think so. I'm sure I would remember his name if I had read about him. It was a big to-do, Jill, dear, back in 1908. A very big to-do."

Jill was silent, thinking about what it must have been like back then. She couldn't even begin to imagine how people close to Kate would have reacted to her unsolved disappearance. "Do you think she ran away with her lover?" she finally asked.

"Dear, I have always wondered about that. But frankly, I have no idea. Even though Anne did tell my predecessor that there was a lover, what if she was wrong? Maybe there was no one."

"Then something terrible happened to Kate," Jill said. She shivered as she spoke.

"Her family was very wealthy. Perhaps she was kidnapped but the kidnapping went awry. I do believe that was one of the theories bandied about at the time."

"Thank you, Lucinda."

"Are you planning to return to London anytime soon?"

"You know, I'm thinking about it. But I guess I should forget about Kate and get back to work." Jill felt despondent at the notion.

The two women chatted for another moment, then said good-bye. Jill's mind was whirling. And she thought, how could she *not* go back to London? Something was compelling her to return, as if she would have no peace about Hal until she found out more about Kate.

She could go back to London, or she could go back to work. There was no question about what she'd rather do.

I must be crazy, she thought, to even consider returning to London to chase after a woman who might or might not be a relative, especially when that woman had disappeared ninety-one years ago.

But how could she *not* go? Kate was practically haunting her, at least in Jill's mind, and she *had* to know what had happened to her. Jill realized that she wanted nothing more than to learn that Kate's life had had a happy ending, even if she wasn't a long-lost relative.

Right now, the concept of justice was awfully appealing—but it felt as elusive as a rainbow.

"Ezekial," she called softly.

He suddenly appeared on top of the kitchen counter to stare unblinkingly at her. His eyes were a green-gold. She walked over to the cat and stroked his fur. Ezekial began to purr.

Jill smiled slightly, a few tears gathering in her eyes. But she was feeling better, because she had to go back—and the decision felt right. She'd figure out the logistics tomorrow—including the financial ones. A moment later she walked into the bathroom, thinking to shower. But Hal's razor was lying on her sink, his shampoo was in the stall. Cursing, she walked back out of the bathroom. She had to clean out her apartment, put away his stuff. It suddenly occurred to her that he had clothing in her closet, jeans in her bureau drawer. There were probably even condoms in the drawer of her night table.

Jill knew she was not up to the task of putting away his things.

She felt ill, and it was only partly from exhaustion and jet lag. They'd shared too many good times in her studio. She couldn't stay there—not now, not yet.

She walked over to the couch and sat down, the cat rubbing against her ankles, glancing automatically at her answering machine. She had two messages. Not even thinking twice about it, she pressed PLAY.

Jill waited for the tape to start playing, reaching down to caress the tom once more.

And Hal's voice came on.

"Hi, Jill. It's me. Um . . . look, we need to speak. There's

something . . . well, how about lunch before we hit the road?
Call me, I'm at home." There was a second, longer pause. "I
miss you, Jill," he said. And then the machine said, "Friday,
eleven-ten A.M."

Jill was frozen. His voice had been vital, alive. Oh, God.
She began to shake uncontrollably.

Nothing could have been crueler than to hear his voice
now.

It was like a message from the dead.

But it was not a message from the dead. Hal had called her
that fateful morning they were leaving, and she must have
been in the shower. They had never had lunch before leaving.
And he was dead at dinnertime.

Jill's brain felt fuzzy, numb. She could not breathe. She
pressed SKIP and REPEAT. In a moment his message came on
again.

Leaning forward rigidly, Jill strained to hear every nuance
in his tone. She was desperately looking for an inflection that
would tell her that he loved her with all of his heart and his
sudden reluctance to marry had only been a brief and tempo-
rary aberration, that they would have worked it out in a matter of time. And that a woman named Marisa Sutcliffe did
not exist.

Marisa's face loomed before her. Thomas's cruel words
filled her mind. *"I know he would have married her."*

Jillian pressed REPEAT again. Surely she would find the
reassurances she was looking for in his brief message. Surely
she must.

Ezekial had stopped winding himself around her ankles
and now he meowed. Jill really did not hear him.

"I miss you, Jill . . . Friday, eleven-ten A.M."

She played the tape another dozen times.

Jill woke up the following morning thinking about Hal. She
had dreamed about Kate again. She couldn't remember her
dream, but it had felt urgent and disturbing and she was
almost certain that Hal had been in it, too, as had a dark faceless stranger.

Then she recalled her decision to return to London and

she almost felt whole again. She certainly felt better than she had during the past few days. At the very least, her hunt for the truth about Kate Gallagher would keep her preoccupied in a healthy manner. It would certainly prevent her from having a complete breakdown. She would fly standby, and her only issue was finding an extremely cheap place to stay while there, and subletting her own studio in the interim.

Jill showered, called Goldman, the choreographer of *The Mask*. In what usually happens to absentee Broadway dancers, she found out she had been replaced. Jill was oddly relieved, and she made herself some coffee and a bagel. She then reached for the phone. It was early evening in London, and Jill wanted to talk to Janet Witcombe. But the woman in the nursing home who answered the phone told her that Janet was already asleep for the evening. Jill was disappointed.

She was better off waiting to interview Janet in person, Jill decided. Even if it took her a few weeks to reorganize her life and leave. She sipped her coffee, wondering what Janet Witcombe would tell her when she managed to reach her.

Jill got up to pour herself another coffee, Hal's image competing with Kate's in her mind. She shivered. There had been a question she had been avoiding asking, even herself. It was a question she had been afraid to acknowledge, much less ask. Had Hal's interest in Uxbridge Hall been solely in his ancestors? Or had he talked about Kate Gallagher, too?

Jill was afraid of the answer.

She told herself that she was being a fool. She had no reason to fear the answer to that question, none. Jill shivered again. Her studio seemed cool, as if the temperature had suddenly dropped, and she closed the windows and slipped on a huge sweatshirt. Had he, like Lucinda, noticed the similarity in their appearance?

Jill was uneasy. But if she really did look like Kate, that was some kind of proof of a genetic link between them. Wasn't it?

Abruptly Jill slid her plate and mug aside. She stood and walked into her bathroom. She flicked on the light and stared at herself in the mirror.

She had never looked worse, but that was from grief and

fatigue, and a little makeup would help. She studied her own reflection. She had hazel eyes—she was certain Kate's were a very dark brown. Her hair was chestnut, and Kate's was red. Perhaps there was a resemblance though. Jill had a straight, delicate nose—Kate's had been a bit Roman. Still, Jill had a similarly strong jaw, wide forehead, and high cheekbones. And then there was the mole.

Jill's birthmark was the color of a freckle. It wasn't dark like Kate's. Kate's mole had been near the corner of her mouth. Jill's was a bit higher, more toward her cheek. Suddenly Jill reached below her sink where she kept a basket filled with makeup. She pulled out a brown eye pencil and dotted it on the mole.

Jill regarded her reflection, almost mesmerized. Abruptly she turned, feeling almost disembodied, walking into the single room of her studio, and directly to the drawer in the bureau beside her bed. She rummaged through it. A long time ago she had bought an old pendant at a thrift shop. The pendant was an engraved garnet stone set in gold very plainly, dangling from a velvet ribbon. To this day Jill had no idea why she had bought it—it was not her type of jewelry. She preferred clean, modern pieces, usually in sterling silver.

The pendant spilled into her hand. Jill returned to the bathroom as she put the necklace on.

The wine-colored stone winked at her from the hollow of her throat. It was such a period piece, Jill thought.

It was the kind of piece a woman might wear in the nineteenth century—or even at the turn of the century and a few years later, in Edwardian times.

Jill's hands were trembling. Slowly she took her jaw-length hair and pushed it back, away from her face, and up high onto her head. Kate's hair had been long and curly and she had worn it either down or twisted on top of her head.

Jill stared, her pulse beginning to pound. For one moment, she thought Kate was staring at her in the mirror. A beautiful, vitally alive, vibrant, red-haired Edwardian woman . . . and then the moment was gone.

Jill dropped her hands as if her own hair had burned her.

Her layered chestnut hair fell wildly down around her face, her cheekbone-length bangs into her eyes.

Jill inhaled, staring into her own eyes, which were wide and filled with a wild light. She had not just seen Kate in the mirror—that had been the result of her fatigue and her very active imagination. But she did resemble Kate. There was no mistaking that. Even now.

She resembled her a lot. Enough to be her sister—or her great-granddaughter.

Jill had expected to be elated. But she was not.

For suddenly the question was glaring. How could Hal have *not* noticed the resemblance? The answer was easy. It was right there in the mirror.

And a little voice was whispering inside of her head that there were no coincidences. None. It whispered, Hal and Kate, Kate and Jill, Jill and Hal. Jill wanted to clap her hands over her ears.

And she was afraid.

Five

AUNT MADELINE WAS STILL ALIVE. JILL HAD NOT SPOKEN
with her in four or five years. She did not hold any grudges,
but there had never been any real affection between them,
and it had been natural for them to drift even farther apart
than they had already been.

Her aunt was her mother's sister. Her father, Jack Gallagher, had not had any siblings. Or that was what Jill had
believed her entire life. Jill was trembling as she picked up
the phone. If she was going to try to find out if Kate was
related to her, Aunt Madeline seemed the place to start.

Jill recognized her midwestern twang and gruff tone of
voice instantly. "Aunt Madeline? Hello. It's Jill."

There was a moment of silence on the other end of the
line. "Hello, Jill. How are you?" Her tone was polite, but
reserved.

"Fine," Jill lied. Madeline knew nothing about her life;
there was no point in telling her anything now. "I was wondering if you could help me. I'm trying to figure some stuff
out about my father and his father."

"That's odd," was all that Madeline said.

Jill could envision her on the other end of the line, seated
in an easy chair in the faded green living room, clad in a
clean but outdated housedress, her dark hair streaked with
gray, her full face dour, reading glasses hanging on her
breasts. "Did Jack have any brothers or sisters?" She wanted
to make certain that her version of the truth was accurate.

"No, he did not. If he'd had, you might have gone to live with them instead of with me."

Jill felt her mouth twisting into a grimace. "Yes." She did not add that that would have been best for everyone. "Did you ever meet Jack's family? His father, Peter, or his mother?"

"No, I did not. These are strange questions, Jill."

"I'm sorry," Jill found herself apologizing. "I'm trying to find my roots. You know, trace my ancestry."

"Why?"

Jill hesitated. "I was in London recently, and I think I discovered a woman who was an ancestor of mine."

There was no reply.

Jill sighed. "Do you know anything about Jack's life? He was born in New York City, wasn't he? And didn't he marry my mother here?"

"Yes. I believe so."

Jill felt like pulling out her hair. Her mother had been a housewife, and Jack, she knew, had been a junior lawyer in a large firm. "Aunt Madeline, was Peter, my grandfather, also born in New York?"

"I have no idea."

Jill realized this was not going to be very helpful. "Is there anything that you might remember and want to tell me about my father's family?"

"No. The plumber is here. He's at the door. Hold on."

Jill heard wood creaking and realized her aunt had been in her rocking chair. She was clenching the phone. The call had been useless.

Five endless minutes passed, in which Jill debated merely hanging up, but she did not do so. Suddenly Madeline said, "There's a box in the attic."

"What?"

"Their things. Your parents'. I got rid of most everything, but some papers and some of her jewelry I kept. Don't know why."

Jill had stiffened with surprise and excitement. "Aunt Madeline, you're wonderful!" she cried.

There was absolute silence on the other end of the line.

"Could you UPS me the box, two-day air? It's not very expensive and I'll send you a check the moment I know the amount," Jill said eagerly.

"I don't know . . ."

"Please. It's very important," Jill said.

Madeline made a sound that Jill took to be an affirmative. Jill gave her address on West Broadway and Tenth Street and managed to get Madeline to promise to send the box first thing the next day. She hung up, pleased.

If she was lucky, there would be something in that box to help her discover the truth about Kate—or about her own ancestry, if it was different. And even if there wasn't, she suddenly ached to have those few possessions that had belonged to her parents. Why hadn't Madeline told her about the box years ago?

Jill shook her head. That answer was easy. Her aunt hadn't said anything because it had never occurred to her to do so.

In any case, one thing was clear. She needed to go back to London sooner rather than later. The urge had grown in its intensity ever since Jill had made the decision to go back, and was almost irresistible now.

Jill went to her bedside bureau and took out her bank book. As she had thought, she had less than three thousand dollars in her savings account. Her checking account had a few hundred in it. "Damn."

She had to get on the phone and make a few calls. One of the soundmen on *The Mask* had a wife who was in real estate. Jill couldn't afford to pay anyone a commission, but maybe they might help anyway, given the circumstances of Hal's death and her sudden unemployment. It was worth a try.

KC also knew tons of people. She might know someone who wanted a sublet right away.

Jill ran across the studio for her tote, dug out her Filofax, and found the number she was looking for. She was about to dial when her phone rang. To her surprise, it was her aunt.

"Aunt Madeline?" Jill could barely believe it.

Without even saying hello, her aunt said, "I just remembered something. I think your grandfather was born over there. In England."

Jill froze.

Madeline was silent.

Jill recovered. Breathlessly, images of Kate Gallagher dancing in her mind, Jill asked, "Are you sure?"

"No. But I seem to remember something like that. I think he might have come to America as a young man."

It was about four P.M. in London. Quickly Jill dialed the museum.

To her relief, Lucinda was still there, and in a moment she had picked up the telephone. "Jill! I am so pleased that you have called," she said enthusiastically. "I have been thinking about you. How are you?"

"I'm okay," Jill said, dying to tell her what her aunt had said. "Lucinda, do you have a minute or two?"

"Of course, my dear," the Englishwoman said. There was a smile in her voice. "Are you still haunted by Kate?"

Jill tensed. "Yes, I am. That's an odd choice of language."

"Is it? We are very proud of our ghosts over here in England, Jill."

Lauren had practically said the same thing. "She's on my mind. I just learned that my grandfather might have been born in England, Lucinda—and I had always thought my family to be American."

"That is interesting," Lucinda said. "Why don't you try to find his birth certificate? If it's not in New York, maybe we can locate it over here."

"God. I hardly know where to start. Lucinda, I'm trying to find a sublet for my studio. I want to return to London to research Kate, but I don't have a lot of money. How much would a flat cost me? Or a room?"

"London flats are expensive—in decent neighborhoods, that is. Hmm. Let me think about this."

Jill agreed and Lucinda said, "You know, Lauren came back the other day. Apparently she is now fascinated with her family, too."

For one moment, Jill was surprised and even disturbed. Then the moment was gone. "What did you tell her?"

"Nothing. She wandered about by herself. She spent some time, though, in our archives."

"Can I get into those archives?" Jill asked.

Lucinda hesitated. "I would have to ask my employer. Being as you are not family."

"Who is your employer?"

"It is someone who works for the Collinsworth Group." There was a pause. "You know, dear, I have a neighbor who has a nice flat right next door to my own flat in Kensington. I believe Allen is going to be out of town for the next few months and is looking for someone to stay and take care of his two cats. Let me check for you and see what I can do."

Jill's heart began to pound with hope and excitement; she found herself crossing her fingers. "Lucinda, if that flat is available, and it's reasonable, I'll take it. And I love cats—I have one of my own.

"One more thing, please," Jill said, sitting down nervously. "Lucinda, did Hal ever talk about Kate Gallagher? Or express any kind of interest in her at all?"

The other woman paused.

Jill stiffened. "Lucinda?"

"He was intrigued by Anne and Kate," Lucinda said. "He said he wanted to write their story one day. He used to take that locket I showed you to his apartment and stare at it while making notes. Jill, there is something you should know."

"What?" She barely breathed. Her palms were clammy.

"About a year ago, Hal told me he had found some letters, written by Kate, to Anne."

Jill almost dropped the phone. "Oh, my God. Have you read them?"

"No. I've never even seen them. In fact, I'm not sure they actually exist." Her tone was cautious.

Jill was on her feet. "What do you mean? I don't understand."

Lucinda hesitated again. "I don't really know how to say

this. I'm not sure I should even be telling you this." She did not continue.

Jill felt dread. "Whatever is on your mind, please, Lucinda, I would appreciate your sharing it with me. I have to know what Hal was up to." It was only after she had spoken that she realized how odd her own choice of words was.

"Very well. He promised to send me copies of the letters, several times, in fact, but he never did."

"But Hal wasn't a liar," Jill said slowly, very confused. "He wouldn't make up such a story."

"Jill, the day he called me to tell me he'd found the letters, it was almost midnight. He sounded quite . . . incoherent."

Jill's grip on the phone was deathly. Her heart lurched. "Incoherent."

"I hate speaking ill of the dead. He sounded soused, my dear, three sheets to the wind . . . absolutely foxed."

It took Jill a moment to comprehend her. "You think he was drunk?" She gasped.

"He was incoherent." Lucinda was firm. "I do not know what to think."

Jill could not move. "Lucinda, if he had those letters, do you have any idea where he might have found them—or where he might have put them?"

"No, I do not. But they would be priceless—to us and to the family. He would keep them somewhere very safe. They're certainly not here at Uxbridge Hall. Maybe he kept them with him."

Jill stared blindly across her studio, an image of Hal with old letters filling her mind. "Maybe you're right. What if they're in his apartment here in New York?"

"If you find them, do let me know. They belong at Uxbridge Hall," Lucinda said. "We would want the originals."

Jill promised to do so. The two women chatted for a few more minutes, Lucinda promising to call her tomorrow after she had spoken to Allen Henry Barrows, and then they hung up. Jill remained stunned. Hal had been fascinated by Kate and Anne; Kate had written letters to Anne. And Hal had sounded drunk as a skunk when he had called Lucinda to tell her about it.

No. Very adamantly, Jill decided that Lucinda was wrong. Hal had conquered his drug problem. She had never seen him drink or do drugs during the entire eight months they had been together. Lucinda was wrong.

Jill was not relieved. First Marisa, now this. Maybe Thomas was right. Maybe she did not know Hal the way she thought she had.

Hal had a co-op on Fifth Avenue. Jill still had her keys. She hadn't been there since his death, and as she approached the building on the corner of 76th Street, her steps slowed. The doorman outside recognized her and smiled.

His apartment was on the twentieth floor. It was bright and sunny, facing Central Park. Jill paused in the living room, oblivious to the view of the park and the West Side. Being there was making her feel almost violently ill.

She had to find those letters. She felt it with every fiber of her being. But she felt paralyzed. Hal's presence seemed to be everywhere.

Jill closed her eyes. Had he loved her? Or had he loved Marisa? What if he had, in some bizarre way, loved Kate?

She was never going to forget his last words as he lay dying in her arms there on the road. "I love you . . . Kate." As he lay dying, had he confused her with another woman, a woman who, had she been alive, would have been more than a hundred years old?

No. It was impossible. But why did she have that tiny whispering voice there inside of her head, one that kept repeating a litany Jill had come to hate? Hal and Jill . . . Jill and Kate . . . Hal and Kate . . .

Suddenly Jill was angry. She was furious with Hal. He had died, and his death should have been an ending. But instead of the act being final, a door forever closed, his death raised far too many questions and issues, far too much confusion and doubt.

Shoving her turbulent thoughts aside, Jill walked briskly into the third bedroom, which Hal had used as an office. She was there for a reason, and she had to stay focused—but she was trembling, her knees felt weak, and her insides remained curdled. She was also unable to shake the ridiculous feeling that Hal would walk through the door at any moment and that she would soon wake up from the worst nightmare she had ever had.

Jill sat down at the desk, trying not to think about anything other than finding the letters. She began going through the drawers, one by one, methodically, determinedly, her jaw set. She had to find the letters. She ignored his bills and receipts. His desk was neat, because his life had been photography, which meant he had spent far more time in his dark room than in his home office. She riffled through his papers, and froze when she found an address book.

Instantly Jill opened it to G. Her name and number were printed there. She hesitated, intending to close it and put it back in the drawer. But she could not help herself. She went through it carefully, trying not to feel guilty. Lucinda's number was there, both her home number and her work number at Uxbridge Hall. So was Marisa Sutcliffe's.

Jill put the address book away. Going through it had been a mistake. It had only upset her—and of course he would have had Marisa's number and address—he had known her for years and years.

But now Jill was distressed, and Kate was no longer on her mind. A small voice inside of her head told her that if she snooped into his private life now, she would be sorry. In the next instant she found his AT&T long distance telephone bill. Her heart felt like it was working its way up into her mouth. Do not look at it, she told herself. Stay focused. Look for the letters.

But Jill's hands did not obey her mind. She quickly scanned it.

There were quite a few calls to London, and not to the same number. Jill had known that he talked to his family often, and it should not be a surprise. But he had been calling three different London numbers frequently. Shaking a bit, Jill opened his address book. He had dialed Marisa's number ten times in the last month.

Jill slammed the address book shut. Her pulse raced wildly. A telephone call was not an act of deception. It did not mean that he had still loved Marisa. It did not mean that he had been cheating on her—or that she was merely a fling. It did not mean that he had not loved her, Jill, with all of his heart.

Or did it?

Jill jumped to her feet. Coming to Hal's apartment had been a mistake. She was more upset than ever, she had not been ready for this, she would come back another time, when she was calmer—she had to leave, now.

She needed air.

Why had he called Marisa ten times in the month before he died? Why?

The answer was so obvious. Thomas was right. Hal intended to marry Marisa, and once he had known of her divorce, he had broken up with Jill so he could go home and do so.

But how did Kate fit in?

Suddenly Jill could not breathe. She ran from the office, grabbing her tote and jacket and racing across the living room to the front door. She pushed it open and stood outside in the hallway, sucking down air. She would come back to search for the letters when she wasn't sick with doubt and grief, when she was stronger.

At that moment, the elevator door opened, and Thomas Sheldon stepped into the hall. Jill could not believe her eyes.

He was the very last person she wished to see. "What are you doing here?!" she cried.

"The doorman said you were up here and I could not believe it," he responded. His eyes were wide, he appeared as disbelieving as she. "What do you mean, what am I doing here? What are *you* doing here?"

Jill fumbled for a reply. "I left some things," she began. She stopped. It was clear from his expression that he was highly skeptical of her.

"You have a key to the apartment," he stated. He did not wait for a reply. "May I have it?"

She blinked at him. "What?" If she gave him her keys, she wouldn't be able to come back and search the apartment.

Suddenly his gaze became searching. "Are you ill? Are you going to faint?"

In that instant, Jill knew she was going to black out. "I need to lie down," she whispered. She could not take the stress anymore.

Thomas walked past her, unlocked the door to the co-op, and stood aside.

Jill's intention was to go right to the couch. But the moment she entered the apartment, her insides heaved and she knew she was about to lose her breakfast. Jill ran into the bathroom, where she was violently sick.

When the retching ceased, Jill clung to the toilet bowl, unable to believe what had happened. It felt like one of the singularly worst and most embarrassing moments of her life. But she did not move, waiting for the light-headedness to ease.

She heard his footsteps. Jill did not want to turn. She knew he was standing in the open bathroom doorway. She had not had time to close the door.

He was silent. Then he said, "I'll fetch a glass of water." He walked away.

Jill wondered if he was, suddenly, being kind. She doubted he had a kind bone—or a sensitive one—in his entire being. She got to her feet, shut and locked the door, and began to rinse out her mouth and wash her face. Jill stared at her pale reflection, once again noticing that her face was too thin, the circles under her eyes far too dark, her jaw-length, layered hair a mess—noticing once again her startling resemblance to Kate.

He knocked on the door. "Are you all right?" he asked, his tone absolutely neutral.

"I'm fine," she called, trying to sound normal when she was breathless and shaking. But at least she felt stronger now. She cupped her hands and drank some water, praying for more composure.

She heard him retreat.

Jill took one final glance at herself in the mirror, wincing.

When Jill stepped out of the bathroom it was to find him standing in the center of the corridor, and their gazes briefly met. "I'm sorry," she said.

He handed her the glass of ice water. Jill sipped it, sitting down in the closest chair, a huge leather affair. She watched him pace and stare out of the huge windows at the co-op's stunning views of Central Park, so green and lush, the cherry trees in full bloom.

Thomas turned. "Do you have the flu?" His hands were on his hips. His shirt was cream-colored, his tie mostly turquoise blue with a multicolored gold-and-black print. His Rolex glinted on one wrist.

Jill shook her head. "No. I'm very run-down."

He continued to regard her. "What are you doing here?"

Jill tensed. "I could ask you the same thing."

"I own this apartment," he said evenly. "I have every right to be here."

She gaped at him. "This is Hal's apartment."

"What are you talking about? I own this co-op. I bought it five years ago because I'm in New York so often. When Hal moved to New York, I told him to go ahead and move in. It would have been absurd for him to rent another flat."

Jill was stunned. "Hal told me that this was his apartment."

"You took him too literally."

Jill knew that had not been the case, not at all. He had lied to her. Why? What had he to gain by lying? Jill could not understand. Another lie, another deception . . .

"Could you be pregnant?" Thomas cut into her thoughts.

Jill gasped. "Pregnant?"

"Yes, pregnant."

Jill stared at him, thinking about KC's reading. Thinking about that card, the Empress. "No. I am not pregnant." The odds, she had told herself, were a zillion to one against it; they had always been extremely careful. But now she knew she had to face the possibility; she would pick up a home pregnancy kit on her way downtown.

"You seem uncertain," he said, studying her. "You seem nervous."

"You're scaring me," she cried. "But you want to scare me, don't you?"

Thomas's eyes darkened. "Why would I want to scare you, Miss Gallagher?"

"I don't know," Jill said honestly. "Because you hate me. Because you blame me for Hal's death."

Thomas sat down on the couch facing her, unbuttoning his jacket as he did so. Then he ran one hand through his thick, sun-streaked hair. His signet ring glinted as he did so. "I'm not trying to scare you." He looked up at her. "I thought I'd pack up his things," he said slowly. More to himself than to Jill. "But I don't know. I think I'll have someone else do it." He grimaced.

Jill knew she could offer to do it—and have an excuse to come back—but she wasn't up to that task, either. Jill hugged herself. In spite of herself, she felt a vast understanding for what he was going through. "I need to pack up some of his things at my place, too. It's terrible."

Their eyes met for the very first time.

They both looked quickly away.

"It feels like he's still here," Jill said, glancing around the sunny apartment and once again almost expecting to see Hal standing in the doorway.

Thomas jerked, his regard piercing. "What do you mean? You think his ghost is here?" He was incredulous, yet there was something else in his voice, and Jill didn't know whether it was hope or fear.

"I don't know. His energy, maybe." She couldn't smile reassuringly. "I forgot how much you Brits believe in ghosts. It's not like that over here."

Abruptly Thomas glanced at his watch and reached into his breast pocket, but came up empty-handed. He said, "I'm late and I must change an appointment. I forgot my phone."

Jill regarded his back.

Then he said, without turning, "I can't seem to keep my head on straight these days. I'm constantly missing appointments, forgetting and misplacing things." He turned, his slight smile wry, shrugging in a self-deprecating manner.

Jill had never seen him smile before and now she could

guess the extent of his sex appeal. No wonder he was a playboy. With his looks, his blue blood, his wealth, he probably had women falling over at his feet. "At least you're functioning," Jill said, thinking of her own straits.

"Well," Thomas said after a heavy pause. "Shall we go?" Clearly he did not wish to discuss either his or her behavior since Hal's death. Jill didn't blame him. She didn't want to compare those kinds of notes either. They weren't friends; they never would be.

Outside of the door, which he locked, Thomas turned to her. "May I have your key?"

Jill froze. He waited. Their gazes connected again and this time held for a long moment.

His eyes were the exact same amber color as Hal's. He was so much like Hal. The same high cheekbones, the same patrician nose, the same sensual mouth, the same hair. But there was also a vast difference. No one would ever mistake Thomas for his brother or vice versa. For it was like comparing a rough, uncut diamond with one cut and faceted and polished to perfection. But there was even more. Thomas had an arrogance and self-assurance that Hal had never had.

Still, it hurt to look at him.

"There's no reason for you to have a key to this apartment," Thomas said.

Jill turned away from Thomas, her pulse drumming, not wanting Thomas to glimpse her expression. She had no choice now but to hand over her keys. She'd never get back into this apartment without his permission, being as they got along about as well as an inbred schnauzer and an alley cat. Yet she had to find Kate's letters.

Jill dug into the pocket of her jeans and handed them to him. "I want to apologize. I shouldn't have come here without permission, but then, I didn't know the apartment was yours. If I'd known, I wouldn't have just walked in."

"Apology accepted," Thomas said. Jill believed him now. Somehow, they'd buried the hatchet—warily. She followed him to the elevator, which opened the moment he pressed the DOWN button. "Please." He stood back so she could enter first. Hal had been the same way.

The door closed, leaving them together in the small mirrored space. His reflection was everywhere, and hard to avoid. "Did you find what you were looking for?" he asked.

Jill, about to brush her bangs out of her eyes, froze. "I wasn't looking for anything," she said.

He did not reply.

Six

THE BUZZ OF THE INTERCOM WOKE JILL FROM HER DEEP SLEEP. It was five o'clock in the afternoon—she had slept on and off for most of the day. Jill had followed KC's advice, and had gone back to her doctor for a prescription to help her get through the next few weeks. Perhaps that was why she'd finally had a decent night's sleep and then slept all that day as well.

She had also let her doctor draw blood for a pregnancy test. He had called her a few hours ago with the results. Thank God, the test was negative.

Jill stumbled to the intercom and woke up fully when the voice on the other end announced himself to be UPS. The box from her aunt had arrived.

Jill opened her front door, waiting for the delivery, more than awake now—she was filled with excitement. The UPS man emerged from the single, exceedingly slow elevator and Jill quickly signed for the medium-sized carton. Then she turned and looked at the box containing her parents' things. Excitement seized her.

Good night, pumpkin.

Jill had been about to run to get a knife, but her father's voice, so loud and clear in her mind, halted her in her tracks. It was a voice, she realized, that she would never forget.

Sweet dreams.

Jill closed her eyes, leaning on the kitchen counter, suddenly able to visualize her mother clearly for the very first time. She had been petite and slim, with wavy golden hair and Grace Kelly features. Her smile had been gentle and serene.

The memory was as wonderful as it was painful. Jill did not know why, after all of these years, it had suddenly surfaced. Clinging to the image, Jill found a knife and went to the box and slit it open. Then she began to go through their things, her eyes moist, her vision blurred.

Jill sorted through slowly, cherishing every single item she withdrew. Her aunt had saved mostly papers, which Jill set aside for last. Otherwise, there was an odd assortment of their belongings, from her father's ties and cuff links to several of her mother's scarves, all vibrant early seventies prints, a crystal beaded evening bag, and a genuine pearl necklace. Madeline had saved her father's law school textbooks, her mother's cookbooks, including an early edition of *The Joy of Cooking*. There was also a book on gardening and, oddly enough, a *TV Guide* for the week of May 1, 1976.

Jill grew very somber. That was the week of the car accident.

She put aside the *TV Guide*. Madeline had saved several of her mother's dresses. Jill smiled at the sight of a mini-dress in a Pucci kind of print and then at a blond hairpiece. Why had her mother added that hairpiece to her shoulder-length hair?

And there was a map of Great Britain and an accompanying travel guide.

Jill sat down on the floor, her mother's pearls in one hand, the yellowing map and outdated travel guide in the other. She stared at the three items.

Had her parents visited England? Or had they been planning to go? And if so, why?

Jill told herself that they had gone as tourists, nothing more. But in her heart, it felt like another coincidence connecting her to Kate Gallagher.

She would never really know the reason for their trip, or intended trip, she decided.

Jill bent to the task at hand once again. She finally turned to the large manila envelopes stuffed with papers that she had removed from the box first. She opened the bulging one first and dumped the contents out on the floor beside her.

The first thing she recognized were their passports. Jill's heart began to hammer, hard.

She opened them both, first Shirley's, then Jack's. She finally had pictures of them. Tears gathered in her eyes. "Oh, God," Jill said. She realized, with a pang, that she looked like her father. And her mother was every bit as blond and beautiful as she had just recalled her to be.

Jill suddenly reached for her father's passport. She opened it to the back pages. And sure enough, she found a stamped entry that showed he had entered the UK in 1970. Her mother's passport had the same entry. They had visited Great Britain the year before she was born.

Jill shook her head to clear it of confusion. This probably was a coincidence—but she wanted it to be so much more. She wondered if she could find out more about their trip— where they had actually gone while abroad.

The next thing she saw were several of Jack's diplomas, including his law school degree. She found his birth certificate—he had been born November 24, 1936—and then she riffled through everything and came up with Shirley's birth certificate as well. She had been ten years younger than Jack.

She saw and seized their marriage license. She was surprised to find that they had been married by a judge, not in a church. There were two witnesses whose names seemed to be Timmy O'Leary and Hannah Ames.

Jill checked to make sure the envelope was empty, and then she opened the second one, which was very thin, unlike the first. A handful of photographs fell out, followed by some papers.

Jill froze. In that instant, she realized the papers were letters, the photographs were of her parents and herself. Several were baby photos of herself. Her parents were so happy in each photo, clearly they had been in love. Tears gathered in Jill's eyes.

Jill gave up trying not to cry when she saw the next picture. She was only a toddler in a ridiculously lacy dress, but her parents were holding hands and leaning over her in her high chair, their faces glowing with parental love. Jill was beaming. This, then, was what she never had.

No, this was what she'd had but could not recall.

Shaken, Jill sorted through four or five more family photographs, realizing that although she hadn't found anything to link her to Kate, she'd finally found the missing pieces of her own past, which she would cherish forever. And then she discovered that the very last photograph was of her parents' wedding party.

There were a number of people in formal dress standing around and behind the bride and groom, who were beaming and holding hands. They all seemed to be standing on the steps of a government building. For one moment, Jill admired Shirley in her billowing white wedding gown, and her father in his white tuxedo. Immediately, she recognized the Lewises, her mother's parents, directly behind Shirley, their smiles wide and happy, but she did not recognize the young man beside Jack or the young woman beside her mother. She assumed they were the best man and maid of honor.

She stared at the single, older man with gray hair standing beside her father, also in a white tux with a red carnation in his lapel. He seemed familiar—even though she had never glimpsed him before. Her heart began to pound.

Who was he? Why did he seem so familiar to her?

Jill turned the photo over and read, "Our wedding day, October 1, 1969, Jack and myself, Timmy and Hannah, Mom and Dad and Peter."

Peter. Jill flipped the photograph, on her feet now, staring at Jack's father, Peter Gallagher, with scrutinizing intensity. She still didn't know why she had recognized him. Jack didn't look like him at all. Maybe, she decided, she had met him as a toddler and had some latent memory that she could not consciously recall.

Jill sat back down on the floor, overwhelmed now by all she had found. Her gaze moved across the photographs, the letters, which she'd read at another time, the passports and birth certificates. What a treasure trove, even if she hadn't found a clue about her Gallagher ancestry.

Suddenly Jill was disturbed. Something was off here. She pushed everything around, trying to pinpoint what was bothering her—and among all the clutter she kept espying the photos of Jack and Shirley, her own baby photographs, Shirley and the Lewises, and Jack, Shirley, and the Lewises. Jill suddenly realized that her mother had all kinds of memorabilia relating to her family, while Jack had nothing at all—except for his father's presence in the single photograph of his wedding party. It was more than odd.

It was a glaring omission.

But what did it mean?

Had Jack despised his father? Had there been a falling out between them? Or had he been avoiding something from his past, from his background? Had he even been hiding something?

Jill did not have a clue. She reached for her mother's letters—and another piece of the puzzle seemed to fall into place.

As Jill unlocked the door to her studio, having gone out for groceries, she heard the stereo playing one of her CDs from inside. She froze, not pushing the door open. Had she left the CD player on when she went out? She did not think so. In fact, she was certain she had not.

In the next instant, Jill knew that KC had let herself into her studio with her spare key—as she sometimes did. For one awful moment, she had been panicked, thinking the worst, forgetting all about her best friend's penchant for just moseying on over.

Her mind was not functioning as it usually did. She had become distracted, forgetful. Last night she had not slept at all in spite of the Xanax. She had been too revved up, thinking about one of Shirley's letters to her mother.

Jill had found out the reason that her parents had gone to England. Peter had died that year of heart failure, in 1970. His death had come as a shock. He was only sixty-two, and everyone had assumed that he was as healthy as a horse. But then again, father and son were not close, and now, according to Shirley, Jack was blaming himself for their estrangement and even his father's untimely death.

It was Jack who had insisted they go abroad—he had wanted to see the country where his father had been born. Her parents had spent three weeks in Yorkshire, trekking about the countryside as tourists, with Jack in a state of grief and guilt and confusion. Peter had been born in Yorkshire, and Jack thought, but was not sure, that he had been born in the city of York. Shirley had ended the letter by telling her mother that she was thrilled they were returning home—and that she was finally pregnant.

Jill had done some quick math when she had read and then reread that letter. Peter had been born in 1908. The year of Kate's disappearance.

It could not be a coincidence, and Jill got goose bumps every time she thought about it.

Now KC was pacing the studio. She froze in midstride when she saw Jill. "I'm so glad you're back! We *have* to talk, Jill. Do you know that you left your door unlocked?"

Jill halted, having just closed her door. "You're kidding."

"No, I'm not." KC came forward. She was wearing a tiny pink tank top and a long, flowing print skirt. Her long blond hair was pulled back into a single braid. "Jill, you look terrible!"

"Thanks," Jill said. She and KC had missed each other repeatedly since Jill's return. They'd left messages on each other's machines in lieu of having had the chance for a friendly—and long—chat. "I can't believe I left the door unlocked," Jill said.

"Maybe it's that drug the doctor put you on."

Jill was suddenly relieved. "That must be it."

"Oh, you poor dear!" KC suddenly flung her arms around Jill, hugging her hard. "Britain sounded just awful!"

Jill wasn't demonstrative by nature—and she'd never had much practice at it anyway, except, briefly, with Hal. She pulled away, feeling awkward. "It was the pits." That, Jill knew, was an understatement.

"They sound like nasty people," KC said. "Jill, that last

message. I hope I didn't get it right. You're not going back to London, are you?"

"I am. But I need your help, KC. I have to sublet this place before I go. I'm pretty broke."

KC looked aghast. But then, KC was dramatic. "You can't go back. I'm really worried about you, Jill."

Jill stared uneasily. "Why?" She could hardly get her next words out. "What have you seen, now?"

KC shook her head, but tears filled her eyes. "It was just a dream, Jillian, but it was horrible."

Jill relaxed slightly, because dreams did not interest her. And KC had never talked about dreams before. They did not seem to be a part of her repertoire. But KC said, "I dreamed about that woman, Kate Gallagher. She was locked up, Jillian." KC started to cry.

Jill stared as tears ran down her friend's cheeks. "Why are you crying?" she whispered.

"It was so dark, and she was so afraid, so terribly afraid," KC whispered back. "But then . . ." She paused.

"Then what?" Jill asked sharply.

KC shook her head again. "I don't know. It was just a dream. I know what you're thinking, but I'm not psychic and I don't predict *anything* in dreams."

The two women glanced at one another. "At least," KC whispered, "I never have before."

Chills swept Jill. She hesitated. "What did she look like? In your dream?"

KC wiped her eyes. "She was young and beautiful."

"And?"

"I don't know."

Jill almost felt relief.

Then KC said, "She had beautiful hair. Long and red, curly."

Jill's pulse went wild. "She did. How could you have known that? Did I tell you that?"

"I don't know." KC stood and walked into the kitchenette and poured herself a glass of water.

Jill went and stood facing her from across the counter. She could not recall ever describing Kate's physical appearance to KC. "Kate wrote letters to her best friend, Anne. Anne was Hal's grandmother. I want to find those letters. I'm convinced Hal put them somewhere safe in his apartment."

"You still have the key, don't you?"

"Not anymore, I don't. When I went over there the other day, I ran into Thomas." Jill frowned. "He asked me for it and·I had to give it to him." Jill stared at her countertop, which was cheerfully tiled in marigold yellow. "I wonder if I could pick the lock."

"Jillian! That's against the law, isn't it?"

Jill looked up. "I know. That's breaking and entering. But Thomas is staying at the Waldorf, not at the co-op. He won't catch me." Did she dare? Was she crazy?

"I don't know if any of this is a good idea." KC was pale. "Jill, please change your mind about going back to London."

Jill was seized with a brainstorm. "I have a great idea!" She stared at her friend. "I know the doorman. I'll tell him I forgot my key, and that I lost my wallet or something. He'll let me up." Suddenly she was excited. She knew all the doormen. They would let her in. She had no doubts.

"That is a good idea," KC agreed, but she wasn't happy. "Maybe I should come with you. I could help you search."

"Would you?" Jill knew she could use all the help she could get.

But then KC's expressive face fell and she looked at her watch. "God! I forgot! I'm supposed to be playing in an hour."

"Playing?"

KC nodded. "I got a gig at this bar. It's sort of a dive. But they let me play my guitar during happy hour. It's sort of fun. I meet cool people."

Jill grabbed her purse. "KC, I gotta go." While Thomas was still in the middle of his workday—or so she hoped. "Please ask around and see if you know anyone interested in a sublet."

"Wait!" KC caught her by the elbow. "Jillian, I haven't been completely honest with you."

Jill's eyes widened. KC wasn't capable of deception. The notion was absurd. "What do you mean?"

"I saw something terrible," KC cried, gripping her arm. *"Please don't go!"*

Jill's enthusiasm vanished. KC was so distressed that she did not move, did not speak, not for a long moment. "What? What did you see?"

KC dropped her hand. "In the dream, Jillian. Kate became you."

Jill stared.

Kate became you.

Jill was haunted by the statement as she turned the key, given to her by the doorman, in the lock of Hal's apartment. KC did not know what the dream meant. But she said the darkness and shadows in the dream were terrifying, and they still frightened her. KC was convinced that Kate's fear was real, and that it was crying out to her and Jill across the sea of time.

Jill was uneasy as she let herself into the co-op. She did not know what to think. It had only been a dream. But KC was so upset. Jill couldn't remember when she had ever seen her this upset.

It was late in the afternoon and clouds had moved in, threatening rain, so Jill flicked on a light in the living room. As she did so, a man strolled out of the master bedroom.

Jill cried out.

He actually jumped, too. "Jill?" Alex Preston said, eyes wide, brows lifted.

Jill placed a hand on her thundering heart, coming out of her shock. And then she realized that he was wearing nothing but a pair of faded jeans. His chest, which was broad and muscular, was bare. His hair was wet. In fact, his entire torso seemed damp—he'd obviously just stepped out of the shower.

"Hello, Jill," he said, coming forward now.

Jill realized she had been staring, worse, that she had walked uninvited into the Sheldon apartment—and had been caught doing so a second time. She jerked her gaze to his face. He smiled at her. "I wasn't expecting company," he said.

"I'm sorry." Alex was all lean muscle—not half as thin

without his clothes as he appeared with them on. "I didn't know you were here. I . . ."

"Obviously. I just got in. Literally," he said, pausing and leaning one shoulder very casually against the wall. "How did you get in? Oh. Let me guess. Hal gave you a key."

Jill felt distracted, and wondered what she was going to do now. "I think I'm in trouble," she finally said.

"Really?" He didn't seem angry. In fact, he appeared highly unruffled by their encounter. He hadn't been exactly friendly back in London, but now, everything about him, from his posture to his expression, seemed more relaxed.

Jill bit her lip. How much to tell him? Everything she told him would get right back to Thomas. On the other hand, she could buy herself some time in the apartment. "I saw Thomas the other day," she said slowly.

"Oh?" His smile remained in place. But his gaze was probing.

Jill winced. "I meant to ask him for permission to come here and look for a series of photos which Hal was dedicating to me. But I didn't want to bother him so I just came up. I didn't realize you were here. I'm sorry to disturb you." She hated telling the tale she had just spun.

His blue gaze was steady. Jill had the feeling he knew she was making up stories. "Where did you run into Thomas?"

"Here." Jill smiled uneasily.

Then he shrugged. "Okay. Go ahead. Look for the photos. In fact, this will be our little secret." His gaze held hers. He was no longer smiling. "I won't tell."

Jill stared, doubting that. "Why?"

"Because I'm not hung up on control the way he is." Alex stared back at her. "Because I try to be kind," he said. "I think we've all been through enough, don't you?"

Jill wondered at his about-face in personality. And oddly enough, she felt unhappy with herself for having lied to Alex. She was now perturbed, but she shoved her distress aside. She did not have all day. Where would Hal have stashed the letters? She walked over to the bookcase and took a handful of hardcovers down. She began opening them.

Alex said, from directly behind her, his breath on her neck, "Why are you looking for photographs in books, Jill?"

Jill jumped, whirling. "I . . ."

He took the book from her hands. "What are you looking for?"

She could not think of a reply.

He snapped the book closed. "Maybe I can help. Obviously it's important to you or you wouldn't be here—risking my cousin's wrath."

Jill grimaced. "I'm afraid to trust you. You're on their side." The moment the words were out she wished she'd been more discreet. She decided to throw the Xanax down the toilet when she got home. It was messing up her thought processes.

"Why are there sides?" he asked.

"Because I killed Hal. Because I'm the gold digger." She met his eyes.

He did not answer her, replacing the books onto the shelf. Then he turned. "I know you loved him. Thomas will see things more clearly when he gets over the shock of Hal's death."

Jill sank down in a chair, holding her temples with her hands. "It was an accident. A horrible one. One I'll never forget." For the briefest of moments, she felt his hand, clasping her shoulder very lightly, and then it was gone. Jill slowly looked up. What the hell did that mean?

"No one can change the past. Living in it only causes pain. We all have to move on," Alex said quietly.

"It's not so easy."

"Life isn't easy, Jill, and anyone who says it is, is either a moron or a liar."

Jill smiled a little. "You have a way with words."

He bowed. "The truth? I'm okay with words. But I'm a helluva lot better with numbers."

She smiled again, a bit more.

"How are you holding up, kiddo?" he asked matter-of-factly.

Jill was taken aback. What did he care? "I'm fine."

"You don't look fine. You look like you're out of it."

"I'm on medication. I don't think I like it."

"Maybe it's a good thing, for now. Why don't you get some rest?"

"I can't. At night I dream . . ." She shrugged helplessly, feeling very fragile now. She hadn't wanted to expose herself this way. She wished he weren't being sympathetic. "Forget it." She forced a smile.

He studied her. "Maybe you should take a trip, get away."

She inhaled. "I'm returning to London."

Surprise flickered in his eyes.

"A friend of mine has two cats which need taking care of, and now that I've lost my job, it seems like a good idea." She looked away from his piercing blue eyes. Why did she have the feeling that she should have kept her plans to herself ? "I can't stay here, not right now." She stopped before she said anything else.

"I understand."

Jill met his gaze. It was soft with sympathy. She shifted to avoid his eyes, as if that would put some distance between them, hugging herself. She was starting to unravel, seeing sympathy where there should only be hostility.

"So what are you looking for?" Alex asked.

The change of topic was welcome. Jill hesitated. She did not want to lie anymore. Besides, she had every right to try to research her ancestry. "Letters." She looked at him. Their gazes locked. "Kate wrote Anne letters. I have to find them."

Alex studied her. "So you're still after Kate Gallagher. Why?"

Jill didn't answer immediately. She wanted to tell him everything. The urge surprised her—especially because it was so strong. But he wasn't a friend or a confidant, even if he was acting like one at the moment. He was a Sheldon, no matter that his last name was Preston.

"You're hoping she's your family, aren't you?"

Jill started. "Is that so terrible?" she finally said. "Unlike you, I have no family. When your mother died, the Sheldons took you in. Wholeheartedly. My parents died, and while my aunt took me in, she hated every moment of responsibility and commitment which that entailed. What's wrong with my trying to find out if a very fascinating woman who mysteriously disappeared happens to be a relative of mine?"

"It's actually very understandable," he said, as calm as she was not. "You have your work cut out for you, Jill. You know that."

Jill met his gaze. "I know."

He smiled and shrugged. "So, let's start."

Jill got to her feet. "You're going to help me?" She was completely off-balance now.

"I've got an hour to kill until my next meeting. Why not?"

"Thank you," Jill said, uncertain of just where he was coming from. It was unsettling, first Lauren and then Thomas with their apologies, and now Alex, acting kind. Maybe it was a conspiracy.

Again, she tried to shake the cobwebs from her mind. Probably the truth of the matter was that everyone was acting oddly, because when someone beloved died, the shock remained for a very long time. Jill thought she disliked Hal's family but she wasn't sure. They were probably as ambivalent about her.

She gave up trying to figure him out because he didn't matter—Kate Gallagher mattered. She went back to the bookcase. As she began inspecting each and every book, she heard him walking into the bedroom, undoubtedly to finish getting dressed.

When he returned, he had thrown on a plain white undershirt. "Jill," he said, taking her hand and preventing her from reaching for another book. "Let's get real. If Hal had old, valuable letters, he would make copies. The originals are undoubtedly in a safe-deposit box—or a safe. The copies, well"—he smiled and pulled her with him into the office—"have to be filed away."

Jill blinked at the computer, which was already on, as Alex turned on the rest of the room's lights. "Do you work all the time?" she asked, wandering over and peering down at the screen. The file that was open was some kind of financial progress report, with gross and net estimates, overheads, etc. Had the numbers on the screen been Chinese characters, they could not have been more foreign to her.

"I like my work," he said, sitting down in front of the PC. "A slight crisis brought me here, actually." He smiled then, as if he enjoyed crises. "I've been in meetings ever since I arrived—got two more tonight. I hope to catch the first flight out tomorrow."

"That's a lot of traveling in twenty-four hours."

He laughed. "I'm used to it." Then his smile vanished. His stare was scrutinizing as he exited his file and clicked another program. The screen filled up instantly with hundreds of file names.

"Those can't all belong to Hal," Jill gasped, dismayed.

"I stay here whenever I'm in town. Which is often." Alex smiled, but at the screen, not at her, scrolling through.

Jill suddenly recalled the nights when Hal had suggested they stay at her place, not his. He'd never told her that he had company in the guise of Alex or Thomas—or anyone else. He'd said, instead, that they could dine in Tribeca or SoHo, or even have great take-out and stay in. He'd called her studio "cozy."

Alex twisted to look up at her. "What's wrong?"

He was extremely astute. Jill met his gaze, feeling sick. "All the nights he stayed at my place, he never once told me the real reason—that you or Thomas were in town."

Alex regarded her unwaveringly. "How well did you know Hal?"

Jill inhaled. She did not want to answer him. But it was obvious now that Thomas was right—she hadn't known him very well after all.

"Look, Hal meant no harm. He had a heart of gold. But sometimes he reminded me of a big puppy. He wanted to please. Hal wasn't very good at telling people things that would upset them." Alex gave her a long look and turned back to the screen. "I'm doing some searches—Gallagher, Kate, etc."

Jill nodded. She said without premeditation, to his back, "He told me that this apartment was his. He lied."

Alex's fingers stilled. He shifted to face her. "I'm sorry."

She had expected some comment, but not that. "Yeah." She forced herself to stare at the screen. "I can't figure it out."

"I told you," Alex said, his gaze still on her. "He was a pleaser. He told you what you wanted to hear."

Jill met his gaze, almost wishing she hadn't come to the co-op and run into Alex Preston. Was Alex trying to tell her that Hal had only told her that he loved her because he wanted to please her?

Suddenly she wanted to cry. Hal had told her he loved her—but he had been very involved with Marisa. So it had been another lie.

An unforgivable lie.

And then there was Kate.

"Are you okay?"

Alex was staring at her. Jill nodded, even though she wasn't, and she brushed her eyes with her fingertips. "It didn't matter to me who owned this apartment," she said.

He didn't look up at her. "Your parents died when you were very young. On some subconscious level, I bet the idea that Hal owned this apartment and had that kind of stability was very attractive to you."

Jill froze. Because she realized he was right.

She was always in debt, out of work half the time, struggling to meet her bills. And she was alone. But Hal had a family he adored and spoke often of, and had money to spend as he chose. And she'd thought he owned the co-op.

"Nothing," Alex said finally, still running a search. Jill was relieved at the timely interruption to her thoughts. Then he said, "Hold on. Maybe Hal hid some files somewhere." He began typing rapidly on the screen again.

"You're very good at this," Jill remarked, still standing behind him and peering down over his shoulder. She was relieved by the change of subject.

"Yeah, I am. Eureka. Gallagher1.doc, Gallagher2.doc, Gallagher3.doc."

"Oh, God," Jill said, seized with excitement. "Those have to be the letters."

Alex twisted around again. "Unless he was keeping a file on you."

Jill started—and realized that Alex was joking. "That wasn't funny."

"Sorry."

"Pull them up. Start with the first one," Jill said impatiently.

A moment later Alex said, "I can't."

"Why not?" she cried.

"We need a password." He continued to type. Jill watched him type Gallagher, Kate, Jill, Hal. He even tried Anne, Collinsworth, Bensonhurst. The screen did not blossom.

They spent the next half hour trying every word they could think of that had some relevance to the family or Hal. "Try photography," Jill finally said, despairing of ever coming up with the right word.

Alex typed, to no avail.

"Wait a minute," Jill cried, eyes wide. "When Lauren and I were at Uxbridge Hall, Lauren said Hal and Thomas had this secret language when they were kids. It was words spelled backward! Try Etak," Jill urged, gripping the back of Alex's chair.

"Kate spelled backward. Okay." Nothing happened. "Any more suggestions?" he asked. And just as Jill was about to suggest he try Gallagher spelled backward, his fingers flew over the keys. R-E-H-G-A-L-L-A-G.

The screen filled instantly with a document. Jill found herself gripping Alex's shoulder, leaning over him, almost paralyzed with excitement.

"It's a letter," he said tersely. "Dated January 10, 1908. I'll print it out."

But Jill did not move. "Stop," she whispered, her hand covering his. Chills swept over her as she read aloud, " 'Dear Anne.' "

The next line was "I am so afraid. I am afraid for my life."

Part Two

The Empress

Seven

Dear Anne,

I am so afraid. I am afraid for my life.

Oh, my dearest friend, I know you understand me far too well, and comprehend my penchant for melodrama. I do not want to alarm you, Anne. But in this case I do not exaggerate. I am so alone, so afraid, and I have no one to confide in. I trust you with the truth.

I did not return home. I am not in New York. I am letting a pleasant little country manor not far from Robin Hood Bay. You see, my dear friend, and I am certain you will forgive me my deception, which has caused me no undue amount of pain, I had no choice but to leave the city. I am with child, Anne.

Please, do not chastise me now! I can hear your gasp, see the horror and pity in your eyes, as well as the tears. Do not pity me. I have no regrets. Anne, I love this child's father and have no doubt that we will soon be wed. His family—and it is a very good and old family—stands in our way. But he is determined to bring his father round. I know he shall succeed. He is a master of persuasion. I suppose I know that well enough. When I return to London I shall be a bride, with a beautiful baby in my arms, his baby and, I hope, his son.

Do not ask me to tell you the identity of my love. I

cannot. It would be a terrible mistake at this tender point in time.

Do not think ill of me, Anne. There have been times where I have wished I could be more like you—so proper, a genuine lady—who would never dream of having such a liaison. But I am not like you, and it is not just because I am Irish and American. I have never understood why the blood has always run so wild in my veins. I have never understood why I have always felt that life is a huge and exciting treasure chest, put there just for me, so I might open it and explore all of its many and vast and oh-so-precious contents. But I do know that I have waited my entire life for this man. He is my knight in shining armor, Anne.

Do you remember how I described to you the excitement of riding in the hot air balloon that day in Paris one year ago? The pounding of one's pulse, the breathlessness, the absolute giddiness and delight? That is how one feels when one falls in love, Anne, with one's truest love. I know. It is how I feel now, even as I write, my only company the pounding of the rain on the windowpanes.

But, dear God, I am so alone, and I am so lonely. Of course he is not here, he is abroad; it is his father's doing. I have a staff of three—two maids so simple they can barely fill my bath, and a housekeeper so grim I would sooner talk to myself than share my fears with her. I do not, obviously, go to the village. No one has ever seen me other than my staff, and I can only speculate what the gossip must be in the surrounding countryside. We have let word out that I am a grieving widow. It was his idea and I do think it perfect. But then, he is rather perfect himself.

Yes, dear Anne, I am smiling now.

Anne, I am becoming heavy with the child. Soon, by May, the physician has said, I will give birth. He anticipates no problems—I have large hips which he says are perfect for childbearing, and my health is so good, again, due to my daily rides, my bicycling, and those long walks which you have so complained about. And, of course, I have insisted upon delivering my child in the best Infant's Hospital; I refuse to be at the mercy of some village midwife! But I remain nearly terrified, no matter what the good physician says. How many women do we know who have died trying to bring new souls into the world? Remember Lady Caswell, who died just last summer? And she was told that there would not be any problem, either! What if I die trying to give birth to our child?

What if God will punish me for my sins? Not just the sin of loving a man out of wedlock, but for my entire reckless, shameless past?

And the worst part of it is, I have no regrets! And surely He knows this!

Can you blame me, dear Anne, for being terrified? How I wish that you were here.

I am trying to be strong. Truly, I am. But I am only eighteen. There is so much I want to do, there are continents to explore, oceans to traverse, people to meet, books to read, ideas to entertain and debate, balls to attend, and, yes, more skies to fly, and having this baby and becoming this man's wife is only the beginning of the rest of my life. Or so I pray. If only I could regret my past, repent my sins, but dear God, I cannot!

Please do not reproach me when we next meet. I intend to return to town shortly after the child is born. And because I must keep my whereabouts a secret—I have sworn on the Bible that I would—I cannot even give you an address with which to write me. Pray for me, Anne. Your prayers will reach me, you know I will feel them, and I will feel better just knowing that you have read this, and that you are there, caring about me, sending me your love and affection from afar.

I miss you.

With the greatest affection, your loving and loyal, most sincere, best friend,

Kate

Jill's heart was pounding wildly as she finished reading the letter. She was so absorbed in Kate's words, so stricken by her emotions, that she completely forgot where she was. She could see Kate, her belly swollen with child, gracefully dressed in a floral-sprigged white gown, as she sat at a writing table and penned the poignant letter to her best friend, in the shadows of some poorly lit country house. The salon she was in would be well furnished. Rain streaked the windowpanes. Outside the day was dark and damp with mist and fog. A fire crackled beneath the wood mantel of the hearth. And a dour-faced housekeeper in black with a starched white apron stood in the doorway, watching Kate.

"Jill? Jill, are you okay?"

Alex's voice was a rude and shocking interruption to Jill's flight of fantasy. She blinked and realized she was leaning over him so tensely that she was pressed against his back, her hand on the desk, gripping it, beside his. Their gazes met. It took Jill a long and almost painful moment to release the past and bring herself back into the present. She straightened, inhaling loudly.

She felt disoriented.

He swiveled in the seat in order to stare very closely at her. "Are you all right?" he asked.

She was aware of trembling now, and she shook her head. "Poor Kate," she whispered.

"That was a very powerful letter. I feel sorry for her, too." He turned back to the computer and moved the mouse. The printer began to whir.

Jill remained shaken. She walked away from the desk, running a hand through her hair. Kate had gone to the countryside to have her baby. She had let a small manor near Robin Hood Bay, wherever that was. The physician had said the baby was due in May. "Kate Gallagher had a child, out of wedlock, in May of 1908," Jill said slowly. Her grandfather, Peter, had been born in Yorkshire in 1908. A coincidence?

Alex stood. "Yes, that's what the letter says. You're as white as a ghost." His scrutiny was blatant, but Jill remained overwhelmed by what she had just read and the coincidence of the birth dates, and was only vaguely aware of it. "I think you need a glass of water, better yet, a glass of wine."

Jill did not answer. Had Kate ever married? What if her child had been a boy? What if Kate was more than a mere ancestor of Jill's? What if she was her great-grandmother?

Jill knew she was leaping to conclusions. She knew the odds were a million to one. Except . . . Hal had cherished that photograph, she and Hal had been lovers, she herself looked like Kate, and Peter had been born in the same year as Kate's own child, and in the same country, too.

"Jill? Where are you?"

Jill jumped out of her skin when Alex spoke. He was standing in front of her, so closely that their knees brushed. She had not heard him get up and walk to her. His hands were cupping her shoulders, and his eyes were intent, probing hers.

She pulled away from him. She did not want physical contact. "I'm fine. I just feel so sorry for her. I wonder if he ever married her?"

Alex gave her a look of incredulous disbelief.

"What does that look mean?" Jill asked, following him from the office into the kitchen, but reluctantly. The image of Kate writing at the small desk in the dimly lit room haunted her. And of course, if her lover had married Kate, then she could not be Jill's great-grandmother.

"It means that a guy who jumps through hoops for his parents and leaves an eighteen-year-old girl in the country to have his baby alone is not about to marry her." He produced a bottle of white wine from the refrigerator. "The guy was a coward. He was also a shit."

Jill watched him uncork it. She could not shake the letter from her mind, or Kate's voice, which had been mesmerizing. "That's not fair, is it? In those days, one had a very strong duty to one's parents. I believe one needed permission to marry."

Alex poured them both glasses of pino grigio. "Honey, I'm a guy. The times may change, but the rules do not. Love, honor, honesty—those sentiments are timeless. Either a man has integrity or he doesn't. That's one of the few instances in life that is black or white."

Jill stared at Alex, really focusing on him for the first time since they had discovered Kate's letter—or maybe even since they had met. He was an unusual man—self-made, successful, keenly intelligent, yet sensitive and astute. He could obviously swim with sharks or he wouldn't have the power that he had. Yet he had ethics. Or so it seemed.

Then she thought about Hal, the ache distinct. Where had Hal's integrity been? "You're an interesting man," she heard herself say.

"One of my girlfriends told me I was boring."

Jill looked at him, actually smiling. "What was her complaint? That you work too much or you didn't want to get married?"

He smiled. "Smart cookie," he said. "Both."

Jill continued to smile, until she realized that they were sharing a light moment. She turned her back on him, shaken. She did not want to enjoy his company, not his or any other man's. She wasn't looking for anything now, other than the truth about Kate Gallagher, not even friendship from Alex—especially as friendship could lead where she did not want to go and had no intention of ever going.

"Where is that mind of yours now?" Alex asked, handing her a glass of wine.

Jill started. Fortunately he could not read her thoughts. "The letter," she lied.

He eyed her with obvious skepticism, still leaning one slim hip against the granite kitchen counter, sipping the icy cold Italian wine with obvious appreciation. He had his own kind of magnetism, too, she realized. And she was only just noticing it, probably because of the shock of Hal's death and deceptions. It was not movie-star bold, like Thomas's. When he entered a room, every head would not turn instantaneously. But after a few minutes, Jill had not a doubt that the women present would start looking in his direction, wondering who he was and what he did.

"You're staring," he said.

Jill grimaced. "I was thinking."

"About Kate?"

"Yeah." What a lie. She avoided his eyes. Whatever was happening here was wrong. Hal had just died. She did not want to find him interesting or attractive, not even for an instant.

"I know you've been through a lot, but you need to loosen up, Jill." His tone made her jerk and meet his gaze. He knew she'd been thinking about him. He probably knew she was finding him attractive, too. He was smiling at her, but not really with amusement. Jill didn't know what his smile meant. But it was a smile that reached his blue gaze. It was a good, solid, genuine smile.

"Why should I loosen up?" Jill rebutted immediately. Her thoughts were straying dangerously and she was determined to go back to where she'd been before she'd run into him in the apartment. "So you can make a pass at me?"

His eyes widened. "Is that what you want?"

"Hell, no," she said, meaning it.

He stared. His expression was inscrutable. And a silence fell between them, like a heavy black thundercloud or, better yet, like a rock.

"I apologize," Jill said abruptly, turning away. He was being kind, she was being a bitch. What was wrong with her?

"It's okay. I understand." His tone was flat. Jill looked up and thought that she had angered him.

"You need some downtime—badly," he said firmly. "Drink your wine and I'll take you home."

Jill wanted nothing more than to go. It would be a relief. "What about the files?"

"I'll print the rest of the files out for you and make a copy on a floppy, too." He glanced at his watch. He did not wear a flashy 18-karat Rolex like his cousin, but a stainless-steel Audemars Piguet with a dark blue dial. It was heavy yet sleek, at once outstanding and modest. Jill stared at his watch, then at him. It suited him perfectly, right down to the tiny diamond points that indicated the face's numbers. "I'll have to do it later, after I get back from my meetings," he said. His gaze remained steady, unwavering. Was there a question in his eyes?

Jill nodded jerkily. She had to get out of there. She decided she was exhausted, maybe overly medicated. Should she even be drinking? The answer was obvious. "Will you have time? You seem terribly busy."

"I'll make the time."

She knew he would do as he said. But she thought about the letters sitting there on file on the computer hard drive. "Alex, I could go and do that while you dress—and if it takes longer, I could stay—if you don't mind leaving me here alone?"

He smiled. "You're going home—before you fall down or pass out. I'll be dressed in two minutes flat, and after my driver drops me at the Four Seasons, he'll take you to wherever it is that you live."

In a way, Jill felt relieved. She wasn't sure why—perhaps because she had absorbed as much information as she dared that night. She had so much to think about now. On the other hand, she was also nervous about leaving the letters behind. Yet what could happen to them? They were on the C drive, and Alex had promised to copy them. "Lucinda Becke, the director of Uxbridge Hall, also wants the letters. They're very important, Alex."

"That's the second time you said that," he said, setting his wineglass down. "Trust me, Jill."

Jill watched him pad barefoot into the bedroom, then heard him whistling as he dressed. It would be a mistake to trust Alex. She had trusted Hal, and look what had happened. He had been involved with Marisa, and he'd hidden a huge chunk of his life from her. No, she should not trust any man, not in this lifetime, and certainly not Alex Preston. She turned and walked back into the office, pulling the single sheet from the printer. Jill sat down and slowly reread the letter, word by painstaking word.

Alex came into the room. "You ready?"

Jill had been so absorbed by the power of Kate's voice that once again she had forgotten where she was—and even who she was. She leaped to her feet at the sound of Alex's voice.

"You're very pale, Jill," Alex said, not moving from the doorway.

Jill shook her head to clear the cobwebs of another time, another place, from it. She met Alex's gaze. "Have you ever heard of Robin Hood Bay?" she asked.

It was a moment before he answered. "Actually, I have. It's a stone's throw from Stainesmore," he said. "Our country home in Yorkshire."

The ringing of the telephone jerked Jill out of a deep sleep.

She groaned, reaching for the clock. Outside, the sun was barely up; the sky was a mauve gray. The illuminated dial told her it was six-thirty. Suddenly she was wide awake. Who could possibly be calling her at such an hour? "Hello?" She flipped on the bedside light. Perhaps it was KC, and she was in trouble.

"Jill, I'm sorry to wake you at this hour. It's me, Alex."

Jill was surprised, and she sat up against her pillows. "Alex, is something wrong? It's the crack of dawn."

"I know. I'm on my way back to London and I wanted to reach you before my flight boards."

Suddenly Jill knew that he had called about the letters. "Did you find something in the letters Kate wrote to Anne?" She was more than fully awake. Tension stiffened her entire body.

"Jill, I don't know how to say this. They're gone."

Jill did not understand. "What?"

"When I got home last night there was no power in the entire apartment. At first I thought a fuse must have blown. I'd put the desktop in suspend mode. Half the hard drive was wiped out—there must have been a power surge. I am so sorry."

Jill stared blindly at her melon-colored wall. "The files are gone?" She was in disbelief.

"I had to call you before I left. I didn't want you to wake up and start wondering if I'd forgotten you. I didn't. I'm as upset as you are."

Suddenly Jill was angry, and she felt betrayed. She tried

to calm herself. This wasn't Alex's fault. These kinds of things happened. Didn't they? Unfortunately, computers were hardly Jill's area of expertise. "Are you certain they're gone? Maybe I should bring an expert in—"

"I am an expert, Jill. I was up all night trying to locate copies, or find the files stored mistakenly in another folder. They're gone."

Jill was so upset she could not speak.

"My flight is about to board," he said. "I'll be in the office this afternoon if you need to reach me."

Jill's eyes felt moist. Kate filled her thoughts. What if they never recovered the letters themselves? No. Jill dismissed that possibility from her mind. She would find the actual letters. Hal would not have destroyed them.

Alex was saying, "When do you think you're coming back to London?"

Jill was so upset about the lost letters that he had to repeat the question. "As soon as possible. KC thinks she might know someone who needs a sublet immediately."

"That's great," Alex said, clearly in a rush. "Buzz me when you know for sure."

She really didn't hear him. Automatically she wished him a good flight and hung up. As she leaned against the pillows, her cat jumped onto the bed. Jill stroked his silky fur.

She had believed Alex when he'd said he would make copies of the letters later that night. She'd had no reason not to believe him. He had said, "Trust me." And in spite of her own instincts, she had done just that.

Jill pulled Ezekial close. She was afraid that all of her discoveries about Hal were making her paranoid. The power had gone out; the files had been lost—it was as simple as that.

It was absurd, no, insane, for her to even question Alex's version of events. Then why was she doing so? Alex had no reason to destroy old letters whose only value was to his family—and to her. Hal's death and everything that had happened since then was interfering with her ability to think clearly. Thank God she dumped the Xanax last night or her mind would be even more of a mess.

Jill put the tom down and got up, walking toward her

kitchenette and taking coffee from the freezer. She was not soothed. What if Alex had lied?

What if he had destroyed the letters himself?

BRIGHTON, JUNE 23, 1906

"Mother, don't you think these people are boring?" Kate asked.

Mary Gallagher gasped, blanching. She and her daughter were strolling down the promenade that ran parallel to and just above the beach, their long skirts swirling, parasols and reticules in hand, their complexions shielded by elaborate hats. The crowd on the promenade was vast. There were couples, pairs of young ladies with chaperones, mothers and daughters, children and nannies. There were also jauntily clad gentlemen in fine wool jackets and trousers, many of whom glanced at Mary and her beautiful daughter. "Kate! How could you say such a thing?"

Kate was craning her neck to watch several men in bathing costumes launching a skiff from the beach. All along the beach were blue-and-white beach chairs, but many were empty now, as it was late afternoon. Quite a few parties were packing up their picnics and towels and heading up to the promenade.

"Because it's true. At least back home we are not alone. There is enough society just like us. These Brits are so . . . so . . . contained," Kate said, ignoring another gasp from her mother. She was accustomed to shocking her mother; she had been doing so ever since she could remember. "New money knows how to have fun," Kate declared.

Mary moaned, reaching into her reticule and producing a handkerchief. "Do not call the English what you just called them, they will never accept us, not if you are overheard. And never call yourself new . . . you know what!"

Kate laughed. "But that's the truth, too." Her smile faded. She saw a very handsome gentleman perhaps ten years older than herself standing by one of the telescopes that looked out to sea. He made a dashing figure in his suit and bowler as he leaned upon the iron railing of the promenade, looking not through the telescope but at her. Kate wondered if he had just arrived in Brighton, because she had not noticed him in the past few days since her own arrival in town. She realized he was staring at her.

Her heart fluttered, and she ducked her head, surprised by her own sudden shyness. But he was, beyond a doubt, the most stunning man.

Kate glanced back at him, over her shoulder.

He tipped his hat, his teeth flashing white against unusually swarthy skin.

Kate could not hide her pleasure and she smiled once at him. She knew that he continued to watch her as they strolled farther down the promenade, coming abreast of the Palace Pier. She wondered who he was.

"Are you flirting?" Mary cried, aghast, glancing back over her shoulder now.

"Of course I am. There is no harm done, Mother," Kate said with some exasperation.

Mary was distraught. She was a plump woman with extremely fair skin, blue eyes, and golden ringlets. "I wish you would behave," she said, dabbing at her cheeks again. "How can we find you a husband if you act so commonly?"

"And I wish Father were alive," Kate muttered, but Mary did not hear her. Peter Gallagher had always lauded her effrontery—but he had been an ebullient man himself, not giving a damn what the Old World snots thought of him. He had little use for knickerbockers and said so, time and again. But then, he had made his fortune in rubber and the new automobile industry, so much so that he could afford not to care what anyone thought of him. He had died last year, leaving most of his fortune to her, Kate, in the form of company shares and real estate, and an ample pension had also been left to her mother. Mary would live well for the rest of her life. Kate was an heiress.

In New York her father had turned away a dozen suitors—Kate had only been fifteen. He had claimed each and every one of them was not good enough for her—but then he had asked Kate her opinion, and Kate had agreed. Kate knew that had Peter still lived, he would never have forced her to marry against her will.

But he had wanted her to come out in Britain. "It's the Irish in me," he had told her once. "As a boy they spit on me and dropped their horse manure on my feet, watching while I cleaned their streets for them. Now my little girl will marry one o' them, just you see."

It was painful thinking about him. "Let's go down to the sea," Kate said suddenly. "We can take off our shoes and walk in the water."

"We are not in our bathing costumes, and it is too late in the day to bathe in the sea anyway," Mary replied. "Besides, the beach is all stones. Look. Everyone is leaving the beach even as we speak."

"Oh, posh," Kate said, annoyed now. "I know what you are going to tell me. That we have to go back to the Metropole and dress for supper."

"Well, we do, dear."

"Supper was horrid last night. All those fat old ladies, staring at us as if we were creatures from the very moon."

"Kate, stop."

But Kate was smiling now. "Rather, they were staring at us as if we were creatures from the days of cave dwellers. Don't you care, Mother? They hate us. We are not good enough for them—savages that we are." Kate shuddered theatrically.

"If you would be less forthright, they would not stare at us that way! Everyone saw the way you went up to that gentleman and started a conversation with him yesterday," Mary cried.

"He had lost his croquet partner. Why shouldn't I have volunteered to take the other gent's place?"

"It was far too suggestive. Ladies do not offer themselves to gentlemen."

"I hardly offered myself to him," Kate said with a laugh. "I only wanted to play the game. Mother, even if I were prim and proper, they would stare. I am not a Brit, Mother. Our money is *new*. And everyone knows it."

"Do not use that word! It is so . . . so . . . crude."

"Which word? Brit . . . or new? I am going to the beach. Come if you want," Kate called, beginning to run down a ramp, her skirts lifted well above her stocking-clad calves.

"Kate. Come back! You'll get covered with sand and supper is at eight!"

Kate dashed across the beach, laughing. She ignored her mother purposefully—otherwise she feared she would turn into an exact replica of her. There was a breeze on the beach that was brisk and salty and wonderful, and she felt it tugging at her hat. She did not stop, ignoring the stares of the last few bathers of the day as they packed up their things. Ladies and gentlemen gawked at Kate as she ran by.

Everyone was so boring.

Who could live that way? Fettered and shackled by rules? Afraid of what others might think?

Her white straw hat finally flew off of her head. Kate paused to shut her white parasol, pick up the boater, and tuck it under her arm. Her hair, which was well past her shoulders, long and red and curly, was coming out of its chignon. Kate did not care. She shook her head to encourage it to fall free, and as it did, she skipped down to the water, the tiny stones of the beach finally getting caught in her shoes. As waves rushed toward her, she waited until the very last moment before running backward, out of their way. Her white kid shoes remained miraculously dry.

Kate laughed, feeling happy and free. If she was very clever, she would manage to enjoy herself this summer, and she would also manage to avoid becoming engaged to some boring Brit. Kate pranced toward the surf again. She waited until the very last possible moment before darting out of the way of another incoming wave. As she did so, instinct made her glance back toward the promenade, but not toward her mother, who waited for her on a wooden observation deck. The dashing, dark-as-midnight gentleman stood at the edge of the promenade, a tall silhouette leaning on the fancy wrought-iron railing, staring in her direction.

For one instant, Kate's heart skipped and she faltered. Breathless, she quickly gave him her back, and too late, was covered with foaming surf as a wave crashed over her shoes and the hem of her skirt. Her cheeks felt terribly hot.

He was watching her. There was no mistake about it.

And the water was cold. As the surf rushed back to the sea, retreating swiftly, Kate smiled, kicking off her shoes. There was a relief in that, and not just because of the pebbles. She hugged herself, whirling in a timeless dance of joy. Maybe Brighton—and Great Britain—would not be so boring after all. She dared to glance toward the promenade again. The stranger hadn't moved.

She played tag with the waves for some time, until she was out of breath, her cheeks flushed, perspiration gathering beneath her stays and between her breasts—conscious of him there, watching her. Her stockings were not just soaking wet but torn and shredded. The hem of her skirt was also sodden and covered with wet sand. The sun was finally beginning to lower itself—the afternoon had grown darker. Kate finally glanced toward her mother standing on the deck at the railing. Mary waved urgently at her. Kate knew what she wanted, but did not move. The stranger was walking slowly away, down the promenade, about to cross King's Road. Had he watched her this entire time? Kate smiled to herself.

She knew her mother was probably shouting at her, and with a sigh, she picked up her things and started slowly toward the promenade. The last group of ladies and gentlemen were just departing, but one young lady in a huge white hat and a pretty white lawn gown was falling behind her friends, clutching her parasol and glancing at Kate. The rest of the promenade, as well as the beach, was now deserted, although a few couples and some young boys lurked about the pier. It was later than Kate had thought.

They would be late for supper, undoubtedly, and everyone would whisper about their tardiness behind their backs. Kate sighed.

She made her way through the coarse sand to the walkway. The other young woman had paused, left behind now by her own party, and Kate saw that she was about her own age, which was sixteen. Her hair was dark, her eyes blue, her skin as fair as Kate's. The girls' gazes met.

Kate smiled.

The other girl said, cautiously, "Don't you have a bathing costume?"

"Of course I do," Kate replied with no hesitation and a friendly tone. "But why bother to put it on at this hour?"

"Your gown is probably ruined," the other girl said.

Kate looked down at herself and smiled ruefully. "I never liked this dress anyway."

The girl laughed. "You're an American."

"And you're a Br—and you're English," Kate returned swiftly.

The dark-haired girl smiled. "That's hardly unusual. We are in Brighton." She spoke with that perfectly cultivated, upper-class British accent.

"I'm here with my mother. We're on a vacation," Kate explained.

The dark-haired girl hesitated and fell into step beside her. "How lovely. Have you been to Brighton before?"

"Never. Actually"—Kate smiled at her—"my mother wants me to find a husband and that's the real reason we're here."

The girl seemed surprised, and it was a moment before she spoke. "Well . . . we all need to wed, sooner or later."

"And why is that?" Kate laughed. "Because our parents tell us that we must?"

The girl stopped, staring at her as if she were a headless chicken. "Of course we must marry and have children."

"That's very antiquated thinking," Kate said pointedly, without rancor. "You're not one of those Br—Englishwomen with a title, are you? Then there is extreme pressure, is there not?"

"Actually, I am Lady Anne Bensonhurst, and I suppose there is some pressure." Her tone was very cautious now.

"Well, I am Miss Kate Gallagher," Kate said, extending her hand, fully aware that she did so in a bold and mannish way. "And you should read Miss Susan B. Anthony."

Anne hesitated and took her hand. She smiled a little. "It is a pleasure," she said. "Who is Miss Susan B. Anthony?"

"An extraordinary woman—a woman I hope to emulate in the course of my life."

Anne Bensonhurst blinked at her.

Kate was a very impatient girl, but her patience seemed vast now, and she added, "She was a suffragette and an enlightened thinker, my dear. She believed women to be equal to men—in all ways."

Anne's eyes widened. They walked along for a moment, and Kate asked, "How long are you here in Brighton?" They were not very far from Mary, and soon this pleasant interlude would end. Kate dreaded the rest of the evening.

"Just a few more days. I have so much to do in town. I make my debut this season, you see." Anne smiled, clearly happy with the prospect.

"How lovely," Kate said, feeling sorry for her. She would be betrothed in no time at all, having no say in the matter, Kate felt certain.

Anne faltered.

"When I marry," Kate said firmly, "it will be for true love, even if I have to wait ten years to do so."

Anne shook her head. "You must be very brave," she said. "Because no one marries for love, or at least hardly ever."

Kate laughed. "I refuse to do as others do. Don't you know that life is far too short to be fettered by stupid, useless convention? Do you have a motorcar?"

Anne blinked. "No. But my neighbor does. I don't really know him, though. I mean, I know of him—he is the Collinsworth heir and he has let the cottage next to ours. His roadster is beautiful, actually."

"You should ask him to take you for a drive. Better still, ask him to teach you to drive." Kate grinned, imagining the ruckus that would cause in this very proper Englishwoman's family.

Anne's mouth dropped. "I could never ask a gentleman—much less a premier catch—to drive me . . . Do you know how to drive?"

"I do," Kate said, and it was a proud boast. "My father taught me when I was fourteen. I'm a very good driver, and my only complaint is my mother refuses to let me drive—she says it is not fitting for women, much less one my age, and she will not budge. Soon, though, I intend to buy my own automobile. I will probably buy a Packard."

Anne was silent and wide-eyed. They had almost reached the deck. "I have never even heard of a woman driving a roadster, Miss Gallagher."

"Call me Kate. I don't mind."

Both girls paused a few steps away from Mary. "Is that your chaperone?"

Kate sighed. "That," she said flatly, "most certainly is. Actually," she amended, "that's my mother. I think she is about to have a fit."

"Well, you have sand all over your face and in your hair." Anne did smile. Then her smile faded. A woman was hurrying toward them. "That is my older sister, Lady Feldston. I do believe she has just realized that she has lost me."

Kate laughed. "I'm sure you could find your way back to your cottage with little trouble."

Anne pinkened. "Of course. Kate, would you and your mother care to join us tonight for supper? It will be quite a crowd. I believe we're having twenty for dinner. It would be so lovely."

Kate did not have to think about it. "I would love to come," she said. "For I have dreaded supper at the hotel— you would not believe how rude the other guests are."

"Rude?" Anne appeared distraught. "Why, whatever happened?"

"Ever since we arrived, they have been calling me a title-hunter behind my back—but quite loudly, I must say—I could hardly help hearing."

Anne was shocked. "That is horrid! Simply horrid—and not to be tolerated, I assure you."

Kate looked at her. "But the problem is, it is true. My mother is determined that I wed a title."

Anne was so taken aback that she could not speak. After a

long pause, she said, low, "My dearest Kate. You must never admit such a thing again. You must be discreet."

Kate laughed at her. "You sound like my mother, Anne. I will see you at supper tonight."

After Anne had left, Kate joined her mother and told her about their supper invitation. Mary's eyes were wide with excitement. "Kate! The Bensonhursts are quite an old, established family! If they should befriend us, why, you shall have your debut after all!"

Kate looked at her mother, feeling sorry for her, caught up as she was with her limited views. She patted her hand. "Why don't we dwell upon the prospect, not of my season, but of a very pleasant evening?"

But Mary was murmuring, "I wonder if she has a brother or a cousin—an eligible one, that is."

Kate ignored her—a habit she had fallen increasingly into. She decided Brighton would not be so bad after all. Maybe, just maybe, she had found a new friend to while away the summer with.

Then she recalled the handsome stranger. Kate shivered. She could not get him out of her mind. In fact, she had the oddest feeling—the deepest, most certain expectation—yet it was mingled with a fearful excitement, too. Kate hardly knew what to make of her strange emotions. She had never felt this way before.

But she did know one thing. She knew she would see him again—and she sensed it would be soon.

Eight

Jill STEPPED OUT OF THE TAXICAB AND STOOD STARING AT Lexham Villas, where Allen Henry Barrows lived. The entire block was a series of attached Victorian row houses, all of them white stucco, with wrought-iron fences curtaining off the separate properties from the street. The Barrows residence, Number 12 Lexham Villas, was on the corner. A small stone path lined with purple pansies led to the front of the whitewashed house. Two tiny patches of green lawn were in front of the house as were two old, shady trees. It was positively charming.

"Can I give you a hand with your bags, madam?" the driver asked, having hefted Jill's three bags from the trunk.

Jill started. "Oh, thank you," she said, at once delighted and breathless. This was so very British, she thought, and instead of following her cabdriver to her front door, which was painted a slate blue, she walked around the north side of the house.

To her increasing delight, she found a blooming garden there, filled with tulips and daffodils, azaleas and hydrangea, that all of the villas shared. There was even an old, whitewashed swing out back. Pink and white petunias filled the flower boxes on the windowsills on the back of Barrows's home.

Jill hurried back around to the front of the house, paid the cabbie, tipping him American style and receiving a huge thank you from him in return. She stepped inside.

The entry was dark, and directly in front of her a narrow staircase with a shiny wooden banister led upstairs. She glanced around. The walls were covered in textured, cream-colored wallpaper. The wooden floors were old and scarred from years of use but were both waxed and polished. She could see directly into the parlor from where she stood. Several faded throw rugs were scattered about, and a brick fireplace was facing her. The sofa was thick, oversized, and plush, as were both armchairs. The coffee table was clearly an antique, as was the mirror hanging on one wall. She smiled to herself.

The house belonged to another time, another place, and although Jill herself was thoroughly modern, she loved it. It was warm and cozy and so very personal. She ran into the parlor. The fireplace was real—she would make a fire tonight. She went to the windows, which were covered in heavy white muslin draperies, and pushed them aside. The sky outside was clearing. The sun was trying to shine. She then opened every window, letting in what seemed to her to be impossibly fresh, clean, very sweet air. She could smell the flowers blooming in the garden, as well as the recent rain. The grass was wet.

And a bird was singing in a tree just outside of the window. Jill craned her head to try to locate the vocal culprit, and espied a red robin. As if sensing it had an audience, it sang more loudly. Jill smiled again.

Her heart felt lighter than it had since Hal's death. It had taken Jill four weeks to arrange the sublet and back out of her life in New York. In those four weeks, Jill had gone to the public library several times, looking for information about her own grandfather or Kate. She hadn't turned up anything except an obituary about a rubber tycoon, Peter Gallagher, who had died in 1905, leaving behind a wife, Mary, and a daughter, Katherine Adeline. Jill wondered if he had been Kate's father. She had no clue. But their home had been a very fashionable address for the time—Number 12 Washington Square.

She had also wondered about the coincidence of the names—the tycoon Peter Gallagher, who died in 1905, and her own grandfather, born in 1908.

Now Jill walked into a small kitchen that was very old-fashioned, with striped wallpaper and ancient, fat appliances, also noticing a vase filled with daisies on the kitchen table. Jill saw a note beside it.

"Welcome, Miss Gallagher, and do enjoy your stay in my home." Instructions on feeding the two cats, Lady Eleanor and Sir John, followed. It was signed, "Best Wishes, Allen Henry Barrows." Jill smiled and put down the note.

She heard footsteps in the parlor, assumed it was Lucinda, her neighbor, whom she had faxed with her itinerary, and she went rushing into the other room. She skidded to a halt at the sight of Alex Preston standing there in a gray, pin-striped, double-breasted suit.

He smiled somewhat sheepishly at her. "You left the door wide open. There's no doorbell. Just a knocker. You didn't hear it."

Jill found herself folding her arms protectively across her chest. Their gazes held, her pulse thundered. "How did you know I was here?" Her heart continued to thud. He had more than surprised her—she was stunned both by his appearance at her flat and his timing. She hadn't called him to let him know that she was returning to London. In fact, they hadn't spoken since he had called her from the airport to tell her the files had been lost.

She couldn't get over what had happened. She had called Computer City. Power surges were rare.

On the other hand, she had been told that what Alex had said had happened was possible.

"Lucinda told me," he was saying, his smile fading—as if he sensed that his presence wasn't really welcome.

Jill stared. He *was* like an unwelcome apparition—except that he suddenly seemed drop-dead good-looking in his oh-so-elegant custom suit. She fought that unwelcome thought. She wanted to blame it on the new prescription she was taking. Her doctor had called her and when he had found out that she had thrown out the Xanax, he'd asked her to take half the dose, and she had been giving it a shot. In the past few weeks, she had started to feel like a human being again.

Hal had lied to her, Hal had loved Marisa, but she'd been beaten up before and she could—and would—get through this. "I didn't know you knew Lucinda," she said slowly. Why was he there?

Why did she feel so completely off-balance?

"She gave me a tour of Uxbridge Hall a few weeks ago," he replied. His smile returned, but he appeared a bit embarrassed. Jill was trying to register the fact that he had been to Uxbridge, when she realized that he was holding a gift-wrapped bottle under one arm. It was obviously wine and just as obviously, it was for her.

He saw where her gaze had settled and he held out the bottle. "Champagne. A little housewarming gift. Hope you don't mind."

She took it. "Thank you." She did not understand why he had come, or why he had brought the gift. She set the bottle down on the coffee table without opening it. Was this a peace offering? But hadn't they already made peace? Was this a pass?

Jill inhaled, her back to Alex. This was not a pass. That had been an insane thought. Alex was not just Hal's cousin, but he was a powerful, wealthy man. Men like Alex could have their share of gorgeous, twenty-year-old, would-be models, especially if they were good-looking as well as loaded. Jill knew it for a fact. She saw fat old power brokers in New York with their young, flawless girlfriends all the time. It was called life and it was spelled in capital letters.

She straightened and faced him. "I didn't know you were a history buff, too."

"I'm not. Not really."

"I don't get it," Jill said. "Why did you go to Uxbridge Hall?"

He came closer, his eyes intent on her face. "Maybe Kate has gotten her hooks into me, too."

Jill held his gaze, unable to look away.

"You still want to find her, don't you?" he said.

She hesitated. "Yes, I do." More than ever, she thought silently.

"Are you still angry with me because of those lost letters?"

Jill inhaled, taken aback and suddenly wary. "I'm not angry."

"I heard it in your voice that morning. And even now, I can see doubt—about me—in your green eyes."

Why was he pressing her? Jill's caution increased. "I don't know why you're here. It's not like we're friends, and Hal's death is between us." And, "My eyes are hazel, not green."

He stared. And said, "Today they look very green. It must be the light—or that shirt you're wearing."

She was wearing a tightly fitted button-down shirt that paid homage to the seventies. It was a collage of arresting colors—different shades of blue and green. Her pants were tight, flared, and black.

He continued, "I like the fact that you speak your mind, Jill. But I thought, maybe, we were friends."

She flushed and turned away from him. "Maybe life is too short to play games." He hadn't really answered her.

"It sure as hell is," Alex said, jamming his hands in his pockets. "I came here to welcome you back to town, being as you know no one, really, and if you want, I came to help you find Kate."

Jill nodded, remaining wary. She had promised herself, after all, that she would rely on no one now but herself. Yet there was a voice inside of her that was nagging at her, tugging at her, saying, Why not? Why not be friends? Hal's death remained between them, true, but what if he was a really decent guy? She could certainly use help in navigating her way around London. He was smart and resourceful. And he appeared to be decent—if anything, he looked smart, honest, well-to-do. What if she tested him out a bit?

The notion was unnerving. It made her shaky, it made her sweat.

"You're staring at me again. Have I grown two heads?" he said.

She had been so immersed in her speculation that she jumped. "I wish I could figure you out."

He did smile. "There's not much to figure out. I'm a hard-working Brooklyn boy—transplanted to London. Period."

Jill did smile and shake her head. "Right." They both knew he was selling himself way short.

"You look like you're feeling better," he said abruptly.

"I am." Jill pushed her bangs off of her forehead. "I'm still taking some medication, but it's a low dose." She looked him in the eye. "Hal messed up. He messed me up. But I can live with it. I try not to think about it too much."

His gaze held hers. There was warmth and understanding and even compassion in it. "You're a strong woman. I think we have a bit in common, you and I."

Jill felt herself actually flush at the compliment he had given her; then she thought about what he had said. He was right in one way. They'd both come from poor backgrounds, and they'd both lost their parents as children. But that was where all similarity ended. "You're loaded and successful and you live and associate with blue bloods. I'm flat broke, I can only wear beaten-up shoes because of my profession, and I shop at thrift shops."

He smiled. Widely.

"All right," Jill said, allowing herself another small smile. "We have something in common." Then she sobered. They had Hal in common, too.

"Don't go there," he said softly, picking up on her thoughts.

Now she recalled just how perceptive he was. "Are you telepathic?"

"Not at all. I'm just good at reading people. It comes with the territory."

Jill nodded, reminding herself to go slowly if she was going to allow him to enter even the periphery of her life, even as a mere friend and acquaintance. And that, of course, was all it would be. Assuming that he was making a discreet pass at her, which surely he was not.

"How are your aunt and uncle?" she asked, wanting to know. Guilt raised its ugly little head.

He sobered. "Okay. Considering. Margaret's on medication for her heart. I'm worried about her, actually." His concern was reflected in his blue eyes. "William's doing as well as can be expected, I guess. He's tired all the time and complaining of it, but he's thrown himself into a few of the company's outstanding projects to keep his mind occupied."

Jill felt for them both. "And Thomas and Lauren?"

"Thomas is working like a dog. I've never seen him so gung-ho. Lauren's still grieving openly." His regard was piercing.

"And you?" The words popped out before Jill could rethink them.

He stared before answering. "I wish Hal had been more honest with you and Marisa. I also wish he'd had the chance to live out his life."

Jill tucked her hands into the very small pockets of her very tight pants. Did that mean that he still blamed her for Hal's death on some subconscious level? How could he not? The ugly guilt refused to go away. It left a bitter taste in her mouth. "I guess we all wish he were still here," she finally said.

His gaze was searching.

"I would have figured it out sooner or later," Jill said grimly. "I was naive. But I'm not stupid."

"The one thing you're not," he agreed. "I have something to give you."

Jill hadn't noticed his soft black attaché case sitting on the floor beside her bags, and now he produced a manila envelope that he handed to her. "Open it."

Jill obeyed, curious. Her eyes widened when she was faced with a bold headline from the London *Times*, dated January 21, 1909. "American Heiress Missing," she read. The lead-in stated, "No Clues as to Whereabouts of Gallagher Heiress." It was a copy of the old newspaper article.

Jill began to tremble, seized with excitement. She quickly glanced at the next sheet—it was another copy of an article, this one from the London *Tribune*. "Oh, God," she whispered, reading aloud, "Foul Play Ruled Out in Disappearance of Gallagher Heiress." The third article was from the New York *World*, and dated September 28, 1909. It said, "Disappearance of Kate Gallagher Remains an Unsolved Mystery."

"The case was never officially closed," Alex said quite casually, jerking Jill out of the past. "But it was dropped in the fall of 1909 when all the leads just fizzled out. Lucinda Becke was right. Kate Gallagher did disappear—as if into thin air."

Jill gazed up at him, stunned by what she had been handed. "How did you find this? Were these articles in the archives at Uxbridge Hall?"

He grinned. It was boyish. "No. I like cruising the Net. With the right software, you can go anywhere—including into the old archives of newspapers like the *Times* and the *Trib*."

"But why? Why go to all this trouble?" Jill did not understand. And she was dying to read the three articles. She could hardly restrain herself from dashing over to the sofa to do so.

"Maybe I wanted to help out—after letting you down so badly with the letters."

He wasn't smiling. He seemed very sincere—and very intense. Jill forgot to breathe. Why was he going out of his way like this?

Alex broke the tension. "Go sit down and read. I'll heat up some water and make us some tea."

Jill nodded. She sank down on the sofa, her hands still shaking. The complaint regarding Kate's disappearance had been filed by her mother, Mary Gallagher, on January 2, 1909. Jill's excitement increased. The article described Kate as being the daughter of the deceased Peter Gallagher of New York City. Surely this was the very same Peter Gallagher who lived at Number 12 Washington Square—Jill had to assume so.

Kate had apparently been last seen at a birthday party thrown in honor of Anne Bensonhurst. That event, Jill read, had been held on Saturday, October 17, and it had been held at Bensonhurst.

Chills swept over Jill. The words in front of Jill blurred. She stared down at the copy in her hands, but instead saw Kate in a black lace ball gown, ravishingly beautiful and pale with distress. The crowd around her was a kaleidoscope of gay colors, the women bejeweled, the men in black tuxedos and starched white shirtfronts. An orchestra played. Kate stood alone watching the crowd in the huge hall.

An observer, not a participant, and an unhappy observer at that.

"Her mother was insistent that Kate would have never disappeared of her own volition," Alex said.

Jill was so startled that she almost jumped from the couch at the sound of his deep voice. He stood in the doorway of the kitchen, regarding her. "Where were you just now, Jill?"

"I could see it. Her. At Anne's birthday party. That was where a dozen witnesses claimed to have last seen her. I could see her, and the crowd, so clearly. It's almost scary how vivid it was." Jill could not smile at him.

He launched himself off of the doorjamb and sauntered forward with his long, easy stride. "Obviously she had her child—or lost her child—and returned to London—only to then disappear."

Jill hadn't thought about that. "You're right."

"If you've read all the articles, you know that quite a few of Kate's friends disagreed with her mother. Seems like your ancestor, if she was your ancestor, had a reputation for being rather reckless, impulsive, and wild."

"I believe she was my great-grandmother. I believe it more and more every day."

"Why?" He sat down next to her on the sofa, and as he did so, the kettle in the kitchen began to sing.

"It's just a feeling I have. A strong one." Jill met his gaze, expecting him to laugh at her.

He did not laugh. He said, "Sometimes the strongest feelings are correct. When my gut tells me something, I listen to it."

Jill smiled slightly at his terminology. "I've learned that my grandfather, Peter Gallagher, died in 1970 at the age of sixty-two. That means he was born in 1908, Alex, the same year Kate delivered her child."

"That's interesting," Alex said. "How'd you find that out?"

"A letter my mother wrote to her mother." Jill smiled now in her enthusiasm. "My grandfather was also born in Yorkshire, maybe in the city of York."

Alex regarded her. "There's still no proof. And we don't know that Kate had a healthy child. Jill, a lot of women died in childbirth back then although Kate did not, at least not in May of 1908, because she was alive and kicking at Anne's birthday five months later. But infants died all the time back then."

"I realize that," Jill said, refusing to be swayed to pessimism. "What do you think happened?"

"Don't have a clue." He seemed cheerful as he jumped off of the sofa and hurried into the kitchen to turn off the kettle. Jill was reading the second article when he returned with two cups of black, sweet tea. He had shed his jacket and loosened a very boldly colored red and gold tie. "Hope it's not too strong."

"I'm not a tea drinker."

"Neither am I. Guess you'll have to stock some coffee in the house."

Jill found herself staring at him, but she was seeing Kate. "I think she ran off with her lover."

His blue gaze roamed her face. "To live happily ever after?"

"Yes." Jill neither blushed nor became defensive.

"There aren't too many fairy-tale endings in real life, Jill," he said slowly.

"No." She thought about Hal—with a small pang. She wondered if she would ever be able to forgive him his treachery. She wondered if she would ever want to.

"I didn't mean to raise a tough subject."

She glanced at him and finally said, "You're very intuitive."

"Does that get me Brownie points?"

She stood up. He was too tall, he took up too much of the couch. "Why would that get you Brownie points?"

"Most women like a guy with sensitivity." He continued to regard her.

"I loved Hal," Jill said very sharply. She could not believe it. He was coming on to her!

"I know you did." Alex stared at her. He didn't say what Jill felt certain he was thinking—but you loved someone who

loved someone else and now you don't know whether to love
him or hate him. "Jill, everyone has to get on with their lives,
yourself included. If you don't mind my advice."

Jill was suddenly very angry. Furiously so. "What do you
think I'm doing? Hal is dead because of me, he lied to me
about a huge part of his life, I really didn't know him, but I'm
trying to get over it—over him—to the best of my ability.
And you know what? I think I'm doing okay—and I don't
need you coming on to me or advising me or telling me that
I'm not!"

Abruptly Jill sat down, staring at her knees. She had to
face it. Hal had known Marisa for a lifetime—he had known
Jill for only eight months. Whatever bond had been between
Hal and Marisa, it had withstood the test of time. It must
have been very special.

Jill knew she could not compete, not now, in the present,
and not then, in the past. She had been a fling. An interim
fling that had only happened because of Marisa's divorce.

She did not want to acknowledge the rest of her thoughts.
But they loomed now, loud and clear, in her mind. Maybe,
just maybe, she had also been Hal's lover because of Kate.

"Look." The one word was terse. Jill had to glance at him.
He was flushed, but in control. "I wasn't trying to criticize
you. And I wasn't coming on to you, either."

Their gazes locked. Jill didn't believe him, but she kept it
to herself.

"When I come on to you, you will know it," Alex said
flatly.

Jill stiffened. There was something in his tone that frightened her.

"I'm sorry. I didn't come here to upset you, I only came to
offer you some support." Alex flashed a brief smile at her. It
seemed strained. "Maybe we need to lay more than Hal to
rest, sooner rather than later."

Jill hesitated, daring to look him in the eye—daring to be
honest. "I want to. I'm tired of this. Of being sad, of being
angry, of being fine—only to find it's an illusion. But it's so
hard. I wake up at night and my first feeling is, I miss him.

Then I remember *everything,* and I don't miss him at all. It's horrible."

His expression softened. "I can imagine. But you have no choice, Jill. You've got to let him go. You've got to let it all go."

She stared back. He didn't know. He could only imagine what her turmoil was like. No one could know—unless they'd been lied to and duped by someone beloved who was now dead.

"What is it?" he asked sharply.

Again, he'd picked up on her thoughts. Jill was tense. "There's something I haven't told you. There's something I haven't told anyone." Warning bells exploded in her brain. Like tiny fragments of blinding light. But she could not hold her tongue.

Alex waited, patient, passive, absolutely still.

"When Hal was dying, he told me he loved me, but he called me Kate."

Alex started, eyes widening slightly. "Maybe you misheard."

"No. I didn't. He said, 'I love you, Kate.' And I know, with every fiber of my being, that he was thinking of Kate Gallagher," Jill cried.

Alex just stared.

Nine

Dear Diary,
I have met the most extraordinary woman. Her name is
Kate Gallagher. I met Kate in Brighton. She is in
Britain with her mother, hoping to catch herself a titled
husband. Indeed, she confessed as much to me within
moments of our meeting—and we were not even prop-
erly introduced. But that is Kate. She is bold and forth-
right, recklessly so. I have never before met anyone
like her, neither man nor woman.

Being with Kate is like being in the center of a
whirlwind. Of course, I have only read about such
events of nature in novels, but a whirlwind must feel
like Kate. She cannot sit still for more than a few min-
utes, and is always expounding upon her ideas, which
are, to say the least, unconventional. She expects to
marry for true love! She expects me to do the same! I
understand that she does not understand our society,
or the fact that I must marry well, and that the alliance
must suit both families. I have tried to explain it to her,
but she refuses to even try to comprehend me.

Alas, I do believe that is why I am so drawn to her.
The other day we had a picnic by a pond. Kate took off
all of her clothes and went swimming in the nude. I
must say, after my shock faded, it did look like fun. But
what if other strollers had happened upon us? I shud-

der to think of how Kate's reputation would have been torn to shreds. Truly, Kate does not think twice about anything she wishes to do, and I think that is why I am so infatuated with her. I wish, for at least a day, I could be as brave as she is.

I have thrown my first extreme fit of temper. I was determined to have Mama invite Kate and her mother to Bensonhurst for the Season. I wish for Kate to come out with me, and when I told Mama as much, she was horrified. Mama does not like Kate. It is silly, but understandable, she fears Kate's wild nature will manifest itself in me! I cried and sobbed for hours, until Papa complained, which he never does, and told Mama to give me my way. I am deliriously happy. This shall be the best Season a lady could ever have. There is not a dull moment when Kate is around.

However, I do have some anxiety. You see, dear Diary, Mama's friends dislike Kate as well. I have overheard, more than once, that they think her trash. I am also afraid that her suitors do not have the most honorable intentions toward her. Have I mentioned that the gentlemen flock to her like bees to honey? A mere smile from Kate, and an admirer comes running. Most of her current beaux have horrid reputations as rakes and scoundrels. Kate is an heiress herself, but that cannot compensate for her reckless behavior. (She was caught alone in the gardens at midnight at a soirée with a much older gentleman quite recently, in spite of my warnings not to allow him near.) I fear she will only snag the worst sort of husband, a callous fortune hunter at best. And that, I know, would break my dear Kate's heart.

I must go. Today Kate and her mother arrive at Bensonhurst for their stay with us.

Jill clutched a small bag of groceries with one hand and fumbled with her keys with the other. It wasn't even seven o'clock the following morning, but her jet lag and excitement had caused her to rise hours ago. As she pushed the door open with her hip, she heard something inside crash to the floor.

Jill stiffened, alarmed. For one instant, she was afraid of an intruder, in the next instant, she saw one of the cats flying out of the salon and upstairs—a blur of silvery brown fur. She smiled. No one had told her that Allen Barrows's cats were temperamental Siamese, and she had yet to make friends with either Lady Eleanor or Sir John.

"Jill?"

Jill turned at the sound of Lucinda's voice. "Good morning," she said as the other woman came up the stone path, dressed casually in black trousers and a black wool sweater. The day was cloudy and gray, hinting of rain. The sun was barely up.

Lucinda smiled widely, as usual, wearing her oversized tortoiseshell eyeglasses. "I got home very late last night and was afraid to call because of the time change. But I saw you go out this morning and I wanted to come over and welcome you to your flat."

"I'm glad you did. I've been up for hours. Come on in," Jill said.

Lucinda followed her into the kitchen, smiling as she glanced around the apartment. "How do you like it?"

"I love it," Jill said. "Isn't this the kind of place Kate might have stayed back in 1906?"

"Well, I think Kate would have resided in a more upscale house, certainly in a more posh neighborhood like Mayfair," Lucinda said. "Don't forget, she was a guest at Bensonhurst."

"I know. But that was before she went to the country to have her child. She came back to London afterward—she was at Anne's birthday party. I only have instant coffee. Is that okay?" Jill set a kettle to boil and went to the refrigerator for milk. As she opened the door, she was faced with the very expensive bottle of champagne that Alex had brought her last night. She had opened it after he had left, unable to resist. It was a 1986 Taittinger Blanc de Blancs. He had spent well over a hundred dollars on the single bottle, maybe as much as two. Of course, he was loaded. The gesture was probably meaningless; she doubted he had thought twice about spending so much money.

"That's fine. I was so excited when you faxed me that letter, Jill."

Jill sat down with her at the kitchen table, which was covered with a heavy linen tablecloth. The daisies left by Allen Barrows remained in the center of the table in the blue and white vase. "Are there records at Uxbridge Hall that I could look at? Wouldn't it be safe to assume that Kate stayed at Bensonhurst again when she returned to London after having her child?"

"I am intimate with those records, dear. Kate was not a guest after her first stay in 1906." Lucinda's gaze was direct. "If there was even a hint of gossip about the child, she would not have been welcome in society, Jill."

Jill absorbed that and said, "Hal would have put those letters somewhere very safe. The next time I am in New York, I will search the apartment there again. But I've really thought about it. I think they must be at the Sheldon house in Kensington Palace Gardens—because that is where they belong."

"At least we now know that the letters really exist." Lucinda's eyes sparkled.

"Alex is picking me up tonight. He's going to help me search for them at the house." Jill got up to remove the whistling kettle from the stove. Alex had not been keen on the idea. He thought it would be a wild goose chase. However, he'd explained to her that all of Hal's bank accounts had been returned to the estate. Hal did not have a safe-deposit box on record with any of the institutions where he normally banked.

Lucinda turned so she could watch her. "He seems like a very nice man. He is certainly being very helpful."

"I don't know what to make of Alex Preston." Jill hesitated. "Lucinda, do you think he might have deleted those files?"

Lucinda's eyes were wide. "Why would he ever do such a thing?"

Jill set two mugs down on the table along with a pitcher of

milk and a sugar bowl. "The more I think about it, the more doubtful I am. Kate was a guest of Anne's and she got pregnant. You just said yourself that if anyone suspected, she would have been turned into an outcast—a social pariah. Correct me if I'm wrong. A young, unwed mother in those days would have been more than a huge scandal—it would have been an unacceptable tragedy."

"Yes, it would have been a tragedy. Kate was ruined from the moment she became pregnant. I feel so sorry for her—I had no idea until I read that letter."

"Well, that is a skeleton in the Collinsworth closet, is it not? And Alex's last name might be Preston, but he is a Sheldon through and through."

Lucinda was silent. "I hope you're wrong, Jill. I really do. Besides, here in Britain every old family has more than skeletons in closets, there are ghosts lurking everywhere— and we are all used to the sordid side of our history. In fact, we are titillated by it. I can't think of why Alex would delete old letters of historic value to the family."

"Maybe you just hit the nail on the head. Alex is also an American. Maybe he is misguidedly trying to protect the only family he has."

"Oh, dear," Lucinda said.

"I hope I'm wrong, too," Jill finally said. "There's one other possibility."

"There is?"

"Yes." Jill met Lucinda's gaze. "Maybe Thomas deleted them. I'll lay odds he wouldn't want any skeletons to surface in his closet."

Jill stood by her front window, gazing outside, watching several pedestrians on the sidewalk just beyond her iron gate and the single car passing in the street. Alex had promised to pick her up at seven-thirty, claiming he could not leave the office any earlier. He was late. It was a quarter to eight and it was already growing dark out.

She heard a noise behind her and espied one of the cats sitting halfway up the stairs, staring at her out of vivid blue eyes. "Hello, sweetie. Are you Lady Eleanor or Sir John?"

The Siamese continued to stare unblinkingly. Then it began delicately licking its paw. He—or she—made Ezekial seem like a mutt. Even in the act of bathing itself, the cat appeared a snooty aristocrat.

Jill walked towards the cat, hand extended, about to pet it. It leaped up and fled up the stairs. She stared after it. "Oh, well."

Then she heard the sound of a powerful engine outside. Jill walked back to the window and parted the curtains. Her eyes widened as she watched Alex step out of a very racy, very sleek, silver sports car. He was wearing a single-breasted charcoal gray suit and a very flashy pink-and-blue tie. He saw her and smiled.

Jill flushed, stepping away from the window, dropping the curtains. She wished he hadn't caught her peeking out of the window like an excited teenager waiting for her first date. She hoped he did not get the wrong idea.

She turned and slipped on her black leather jacket, picking up her tote. She was wearing a white T-shirt and a long, straight black jersey skirt. She opened the door before he could knock, abruptly coming face-to-face with him.

"Sorry I'm late. A minor problem at the office." He smiled at her.

Jill smiled back, but briefly. "That's okay. Thanks for picking me up and chauffeuring me over to the Sheldons' in the first place." She closed the door and made sure it was locked.

"That's a helluva lock. I could pick that with my eyes closed," Alex said.

"Is that a skill of yours?"

"When I was a boy growing up, I was a bit rough around the edges."

Jill stared at his face. "What does that mean?"

"I was a street kid, sort of delinquent. I picked a few locks in my time." He grinned.

"You stole from people?"

"Just the occasional six-pack."

She knew he was not referring to soda. "How old were you?"

"Eight, nine, ten. My mother worked long hours. I was your typical wild kid." Alex touched her elbow as they walked down the stone path to his car.

Jill glanced sideways at him. He could be working in some factory now, drinking beer after work while shooting pool and living in a tenement, but instead, he was a power broker in a thousand-dollar suit, driving a car that probably cost well over six figures, part of a family of aristocrats who lived in a turn-of-the-century mansion. "It's amazing," Jill murmured, "the way a life can be altered." And before the words were out of her mouth, she thought about Hal.

"Yeah. It is. If my mom hadn't died, I might not be here." He opened the door for her. "I might be ripping off a lot more than six-packs."

Jill took a long hard look at him. He was smiling. She was trying to imagine him as a street punk into petty theft. It didn't work. "More likely you'd be one of those super cons, ripping off a few million here and there from the kinds of people you work with now."

He laughed. The sound was warm. "I take that as a compliment," he said.

She slid into the car and he closed her door. She eyed the car's white leather interior as he jumped in beside her, turning on the ignition. A CD player came on, the music classical.

He turned the volume down. "Brahms relaxes me."

"Some car," Jill returned.

"I'm not very self-indulgent, but I decided I deserved this a few years ago," he said.

Jill decided not to take issue with that comment. Before leaving New York she'd stopped in a Tourneau store and learned that the watch he wore, even though it was just stainless steel, cost fourteen thousand dollars. "What kind of car is this?"

"A Lamborghini."

"Boys and their toys," Jill couldn't help herself.

He grinned. "Yep. Life sure is fun."

Jill had to smile.

"Hold on," he said, shifting into gear.

Jill's heart stopped and she gripped the seat belt, buckling it in haste. But his comment had been in jest. He winked at her.

Quickly she turned her face away. Jill stared out of her window, aware of him in the seat beside her, an image of his strong hands on the leather-bound steering wheel imprinted on her mind. He handled the sleek monster beneath them as easily as she handled her ballet slippers. He was an interesting man. Was he charming her? And why had he agreed to help her search his aunt and uncle's house? Could she trust him?

"How was your day? All settled in?" They were on a congested two-lane street. A passing sign told Jill it was Cromwell Road.

"I spent a part of the day unpacking, did some shopping, and tried to befriend two wary if not hostile Siamese cats."

He laughed. "Got your work cut out for you, don't you?"

Jill relaxed slightly. "I think they're getting used to me." She hesitated. "How many deals did you close today?" She couldn't help being curious.

He glanced at her and their gazes locked for an instant. "One. One very important deal. Something I've been working on for about eight months." He smiled. "I got a personal piece of the action. I could keep the right woman in Taittinger champagne for the next dozen years."

Jill looked away. What did that mean?

"Is something wrong?"

"No," Jill lied.

"I think you're uptight."

She froze. Then she faced him. "Why would I be uptight?"

"For some reason, I make you nervous." He didn't smile. His eyes were on the road. His profile was one of those Pierce Brosnan types—classic and very appealing. But unlike Pierce Brosnan, who played at being a hero, he was, maybe, the real thing. Jill realized she admired him for lifting himself out of the muck by his bootstraps, even if he'd had some help from the Sheldons.

"You don't make me nervous." She was lying through her teeth. He did make her nervous, because she wasn't ready to find anyone attractive, it was too soon.

Jill stared grimly out of her window. It was going to be a long time before she slept with anyone, but suddenly she could see herself in some dark faceless stranger's arms, and it would be so comforting. She could lose herself, lose reality, feel cherished and loved—even if it was an illusion that the next morning would chase away.

Her thoughts were dangerous. She shoved them aside.

"I called on Janet Witcombe today," she said.

He did not take his eyes off of the road. "What happened?"

"She was out of it. She mistook me for one of her ten granddaughters. We had a great conversation, none of which made any sense to me, about this granddaughter's husband and kids. She gave Carol a lot of advice." Jill sighed.

"Is she always like that?" Alex asked.

"Her nurse said she has some amazingly lucid days, where she even knows the day, month, and year. I was told I can drop by anytime during visiting hours. I gave the nurse my number and asked her if she'd call me the next time Janet has a good day."

"What do you expect to find?"

"I want to know what Anne told her."

Alex glanced at her. "I hope she remembers when she's lucid," was all he said.

"So do I."

A few moments later Alex drove into the driveway in front of the Sheldons'. Jill looked toward the imposing pale stone residence and she shivered. "God. It's so big. It could take a month to cover every inch of that place."

"We have to be smart," Alex said, jumping out and coming around to her side of the car. "We have to think like Hal."

Jill was already out of the car. "Do you think anyone's home?" She prayed everyone was out.

"I doubt it," Alex said as they strode up the front steps. He turned the key in the lock and let her into the spacious foyer. "Normally William and Margaret dine out or have guests to supper. Since Hal's death, they retire to their rooms."

The guilt lifted its insidious little head again. "What about Thomas?"

"I don't know." He glanced at her.

She flushed. "I wouldn't think that he'd be home at this hour." It was half a question, half a statement.

"That would be rare. Should we start in Hal's room?"

Jill agreed and they went upstairs. In Hal's old bedroom, Alex flicked on the light. Jill glanced around. Everything seemed to have been just as she had last seen it.

"Let's start," Alex said, walking over to the bed. She watched him get down on his knees, lift the bedskirts, and peer underneath.

Jill smiled. She must have made a sound because he lifted his head abruptly, banging it against the bottom railing of the bed. "Ow," he said, backing out and rising. "What is so funny?"

"You don't seem like the type to be searching under beds for century-old letters," Jill said. It was true.

"What a man will do," he said with humor.

Jill's smile vanished. She was beginning to think that he was interested in her. There had been too many offhand passes. This was not good. "What do you expect to find under the bed? Other than dust and mothballs?"

He ignored her question. "Look, Jill. I know this is a rough time for you, but a little humor can only help."

"Okay. You're right. I'll try to lighten up."

"Good girl. And I thought he might have put the letters in a box or bag and shoved them under the bed." He sat down on the bed and began going through the desk that was beside it.

Her gaze strayed across the mattress and she froze. The photograph of Anne and Kate was not on the nightstand.

"What is it?" Alex asked as she rushed to the night table.

Jill opened the drawer. "I can't believe it." She faced Alex. "That wonderful photograph is gone."

"I doubt it's gone," Alex said, coming over and staring into the empty drawer. "Probably someone in the family just tucked it away. Eventually all of Hal's possessions will be put away."

Jill was disturbed. "No. It's gone. Someone took it."

He studied her. "I'll ask Lauren and Thomas about it," he finally said.

"Why would someone hide that photograph?" she asked.

"Your imagination is running wild." He was patient. "No one hid it."

Jill turned away, filled with skepticism. She began taking the books down from the bookshelves, one by one, trying now to ignore the photos of Hal as a boy and adolescent. It was impossible to ignore the photo of him and Marisa on the ski slopes. She paused, reached for it. As Jill stared at it, she felt the weight of sadness gathering in her heart. How had she been so mistaken?

She never heard Alex come up behind her. "Don't torture yourself. That was taken ten years ago."

"I'm not. It's over. Bingo. Like that." She'd snapped her fingers and turned abruptly, coming up against the solid wall of his chest. Jill backed up a step.

He just stared at her, his eyes searching.

Jill felt uncomfortable. "Find anything?" She tried to change the topic.

He gave her a wry look. "Is this a race against time?" he asked, going back to the desk.

Jill realized that her heart was pounding in relief. "No, of course not."

Suddenly he faced her again. "Jill. There's something I want to say."

Instantly Jill became uneasy. "Let's find the letters."

"Because I like you," Alex added.

Jill met his gaze, jerked away.

"Hal wasn't strong," Alex said, his eyes dark. "I hate speaking ill of the dead, and God knows, we were friends, and when we were young, we were partners in crime, and he had a good heart. But. And it's a big But. He was confused, immature, and prone to escapism."

Jill stared at him. Her throat was dry. But she already knew exactly what he was telling her. She just didn't want it spelled out for her. Not this way. Not by him. "Are you always so smart?"

"I'm not trying to be smarter than anyone. But you only knew him for eight months. I knew him for almost thirty-three years. There are no guarantees in life, Jill. None. And no one has a crystal ball. The future almost never unfolds the way you expect it to. They say it's a journey, and in my book, it's one helluva trip."

"As if I don't know that now," Jill said. Her smile failed. "I'm okay. I am. Really." And if she wasn't, she would be, soon. It was a promise she made to herself.

He studied her. Finally he smiled, when she knew her own face was set in stone. "You're a tough kid. Let's find those letters and see if we can't find you a family."

Jill stared at his back as he turned away. His choice of words made her feel like choking up. Was he even aware of what he'd just said?

Jill returned to the task of removing the books from the bookshelf, but blindly, focused more now on the man across the room than on the titles in front of her, unable to stop recalling his words . . . prone to escapism . . . no crystal balls . . . unable to stop recalling him.

They worked silently for the next hour, going over every inch of Hal's room. She was careful to stay at the opposite end of the bedroom as they searched through Hal's things. Jill started to wish that she hadn't asked him to help her. He was making her task more difficult, not easier. Somehow he had become a distraction.

Jill finished with the books and she began going through the cabinets beneath the bookcase. She glanced across the room. Alex was up to his elbows in Hal's clothes in his closet. But he turned his head and caught her looking at him. Neither one smiled.

Jill turned away. She felt shakier than she had earlier. Shakier—and shaken.

She sat down on the floor, running her hand over the wood inside the cabinet, making sure it was empty. What if she let him make a good pass at her? What if she let him be that faceless stranger?

Jill wanted to hate her thoughts, be appalled with herself. But it would feel so good to be held in a pair of strong arms, just for a single night. Jill smiled bitterly to herself. Who was she fooling? She'd never had a one-night stand in her life. In fact, Hal had only been the second man she'd ever been with. Her first boyfriend had been a dancer, and they'd been together for almost four years when they were just kids.

She was more than discouraged. "Alex." Jill stood as he turned, their gazes colliding. "Maybe we should call it a night."

His gaze slipped over her features, one by one. "Fine. How about a nightcap? You look like you could use one."

Jill set her jaw, hard. "I don't think so." And she was proud of herself for being rational. She promised herself that she was not going to do anything rash. Not tonight, or tomorrow, or any other time.

"What is going on in here?" A woman gasped.

Jill jerked, turning, at the sound of an English-accented voice that she did not recognize. Hal's mother, Margaret Sheldon, the countess of Collinsworth, stood on the threshold clad in a red cashmere robe, her eyes wide. Jill's heart lurched with horrendous force. The evening had just, unbelievably, taken a turn for the very worst.

Ten

J<small>ILL REMAINED MOTIONLESS.</small>

Alex walked over to his aunt. "Aunt Margaret, we didn't mean to startle you."

Margaret was obviously dressed for bed. She glanced from Alex to Jill. "I do not understand." She managed a smile. "Forgive me. I'm being terribly rude. You're Jillian Gallagher?"

Jill came forward, feeling horribly awkward, quite certain that she was the last person Margaret wished to see. "Yes. We didn't mean to intrude, Lady Sheldon. I am so sorry if we have upset you."

"Actually, you should address my aunt as Lady Collinsworth," Alex said softly. "Sheldon is the family name, but the title to the estate is Collinsworth."

Jill nodded, aware of her flush deepening.

"You are not intruding . . . I am just surprised . . . I heard noises coming from his room," Margaret trailed off, unable to continue. She glanced around Hal's room as if she expected him to appear from a corner at any moment.

Jill wanted to be anywhere but there, with Hal's mother, in Hal's bedroom. She folded her arms protectively around her body. "We were hoping to find some very important letters," Jill explained lamely. "Hal put them somewhere before he died for safekeeping. I am so sorry." She wanted to explain far more than about the letters. She wanted to explain

that she had been in love with Hal and that she had not meant
to kill him. She wanted to beg this woman for forgiveness.

"Letters?" Margaret was distressed. She was pale, her
blue eyes moistening. She turned to her nephew. "I would
appreciate an explanation another time, Alex. I am really
quite tired."

"Yes, ma'am," he said. He was deferential.

"I don't think you and Miss Gallagher should be riffling
through Hal's belongings anyway, when he is not here himself to . . ." She stopped, tears slipping down her cheeks.
"When he is not here," she whispered lamely.

Jill wanted to go to the other woman and console her. She
did not move. Moisture was gathering in her own eyes.

Alex moved. He put his arm around Margaret. "Let me
help you to your room. I'll explain everything tomorrow.
Where is Uncle William?" His tone was gentle.

"In the library. Trying to read," she returned, not protest-
ing as Alex guided her to the door.

Alex glanced over his shoulder at Jill. "I'll meet you
downstairs." Clearly their evening search was, for the
moment, over.

"I'll clean up first," Jill said, still feeling terrible for having intruded upon Margaret in her grief. "Again, I apologize,
Lady Collinsworth."

Margaret actually turned and nodded at Jill, attempting a
smile that was fragile and wan. They left. Jill quickly began
putting Hal's things away, a huge lump in her chest. She had
to find the letters, but one thing was clear. She should stay as
far away from this house—and Hal's family—as was possible. Perhaps Alex was an exception. But considering her sudden awareness of him, perhaps he was not.

A few minutes later she hurried downstairs. All she could
think of now was getting a taxi—if taxis were available in
this neighborhood or by phone—and going back to her cozy
flat. She would make herself a stiff drink and curl up with the
cats. She would try to forget about the entire evening.

She faltered in the foyer. Thomas was in the living room,
making himself a drink. His back was to her.

It was the coup de grâce. There was no one she hoped to

see less. Her first thought was to sneak out of the house before he saw her. But he must have sensed her presence, because he turned. His amber eyes widened when he saw her.

Jill wet her lips, intending to say hello very politely. But she could not seem to get the single word out.

He came forward, a scotch in hand, while Jill remained frozen by the stairs. He had obviously come straight from the office or a restaurant, because he was in a dark suit and tie. His shirt was pink. Not very many men could wear a pink button-down and appear thoroughly masculine. Thomas could. "Hello, Jill."

She swallowed, more than nervous. She had not seen him since he'd found her in Hal's apartment in New York. She wasn't sure what to expect in way of a greeting from him. "Hello, Thomas." She fumbled for polite chitchat. "How are you?"

His smile was brief, cursory. "Fine." He stared, dark brows furrowed ever so slightly. "What are you doing here?"

Jill wasn't certain that it was an accusation. Her mind raced, searching for a plausible explanation. She hadn't told him about the letters, but Alex knew—and she had let the cat out of the bag with Margaret, as well. The odds were high that he would soon learn the truth about the reason for her visit. "Alex brought me here. We were looking for letters which Kate wrote to your grandmother, Anne, before she disappeared."

A long moment ensued. "I see." He smiled faintly. Jill thought he looked worn, tired. "You are still chasing ghosts."

"Yes." Jill wasn't defensive.

"Come in." He gestured at the room. "Care for a drink while you're waiting?"

Jill was surprised, and she hesitated. He wasn't particularly warm, but he was not being hostile, either, and he had no reason to offer her a drink. "Maybe I'll just wait for Alex in the foyer," she began.

"I don't bite," he said abruptly. And he smiled slightly at her again.

Their gazes locked. "All right," Jill capitulated. The urge to imbibe—to escape, forget, relax—won.

He waved her into the salon. "What do you fancy? Scotch? Gin? Vodka?"

Jill came forward, less uneasy now. "A glass of wine?"

"Red or white?"

"Whatever you have," she replied.

"I have both."

"White."

He went to the door of an armoire and opened it, revealing a built-in refrigerator. He extracted a bottle of white wine and uncorked it, pouring her a glass. It was Pouilly-Fussé, and when Jill sipped it, it was icy cold and delicious.

"I was surprised to find you here," Thomas finally said.

"About as surprised as I was to see you," Jill returned.

"This is my home."

"But you look like the type to be at some fancy supper club with a model or two."

He laughed. "I've done that. So where is my brilliant cousin?"

"He took your mother to her rooms." Jill heard her own tone change, becoming cautious.

"Why?"

Jill avoided his eyes. "We were looking for the letters in Hal's bedroom. Your mother happened in upon us."

Thomas's expression changed. Quickly Jill said, "I apologized. I'm really sorry. The last thing I want to do is cause more distress to your family."

"Mother is not well," Thomas said flatly. He did not look at Jill. His grip on his glass was white-knuckled. "Just the other day she complained of heart palpitations again. She's on medication, and tomorrow she's scheduled for extensive tests."

"I didn't know." Jill was frozen. What if something happened to Hal's mother? First Hal, then Margaret? It would be Jill's fault.

"I'm attempting to send her off to a spa. Your spas are better than ours. Maybe the Golden Door," he said.

"That's a great idea," Jill said, guilt-ridden and in complete agreement with him. Where was Alex? She wanted to go, to hell with the drink.

He stared at her. His eyes were hard to read. "I am very protective of this family. It's my duty."

Jill sipped her wine again, looking away. She did not know what to say. "Duty is a very noble sentiment. We don't think much about duty back home."

"I'm Father's heir," he said simply, as if that explained everything. After a pause, he added, wryly, "As an American you probably think me old-fashioned. But the Collinsworth title goes back hundreds of years—five hundred and seventy-two years, to be exact. My father is the tenth earl, you see." He smiled, but it was faint. "We are old-fashioned. I believe in old-fashioned values—duty, honor, loyalty. It's my duty to make sure that this family endures through the centuries." He shrugged slightly. "Some here in Britain call us aristocrats antiquated, or worse."

Jill tossed down some wine. He was protective of his family, and that was admirable. But why the speech about values? Was there an innuendo in his words? Was he warning her that he still blamed her for Hal's death—for all that she had done to disrupt the family whose standard he held? Jill couldn't decide. But he looked depressed, she realized, and she felt even more sympathetic than she had earlier. More sympathetic, and more out of place than ever.

It wasn't just that he was rich, blue-blooded, elegant, powerful. His mindset was dynastic. The Sheldons were a dynasty. Did Alex feel the way that Thomas did?

"I really have to go," she said, setting her empty wineglass down, disturbed for reasons she could not fathom. "Can I call a taxi?"

"Have I made you uneasy?" His gaze locked with hers.

Jill started, wondering if there was a small challenge there. "Actually, you have. I admire your sentiments. But they are foreign to me." She hesitated. "You have a very big burden on your shoulders," she added quietly.

He regarded her unwaveringly. "It's not a burden. It's who and what I am."

She stared at him. It was like looking into Hal's eyes, but he wasn't in the least bit like Hal. "You can't be Superman. Only Superman would think lightly of such a task."

Thomas gave her a self-deprecating shrug.

Jill was uncomfortable. She glanced toward the doorway, and cringed inwardly at the sight of Lauren entering the foyer. This was not her lucky day.

If Lauren was surprised to see her, she gave no sign. She smiled and shook Jill's hand. "Alex mentioned you were back in town. Are you settled?"

"Almost, thank you," Jill said. She couldn't help noticing that even in a pair of jeans, Lauren looked wealthy and elegant. On the other hand, she looked much worse for wear than Thomas. There were huge circles under her eyes, and Jill could see that she'd lost a good ten pounds since they'd last seen one another.

"Where are you staying?" Lauren asked, as if they were friends.

Jill replied and they chatted for a moment about the Kensington neighborhood and Jill's good fortune in finding such a charming flat on such short notice.

Suddenly Thomas sighed. "I've become maudlin. I take it you did not find what you were looking for?" he asked Jill.

Jill started, recalling the letters. Well, their existence was no secret now. "No, we didn't." She offered no more. She didn't really want to discuss the letters with him.

"Have you met Lucinda Becke at Uxbridge Hall?" he asked. "She might be helpful. You should talk to her. She's the museum director. You know, I used to reside at the Hall when I was married, mostly on weekends and holidays. Sometimes I think Lucinda loves my family—and the Hall—more than I do."

Jill smiled with him. "I have met her, actually. When Lauren and I went over to Uxbridge together."

He nodded. "I'm sure she might help you if you really want to find those letters."

"What letters are you talking about?" Lauren asked, glancing from her brother to Jill.

Thomas answered. "Jill is still interested in that woman, Kate Gallagher. Apparently Kate wrote our grandmother some letters."

Lauren looked at Jill. "Why?"

Jill hesitated. She had been put on the spot. Thomas was looking at her, too. But not with intensity or interest. Still, Jill had the distinct feeling that the question was one they both wanted answered.

She felt her cheeks heating. Her heart racing, she said, "I think Kate might be an ancestor of mine."

Thomas sipped his scotch. "Actually, I seem to recall you saying that the last time you were here, now that I think about it. It is a long shot, Jill."

"I know." Jill smiled at him, then glanced at the doorway. Where the hell was Alex?

"More wine?" Lauren asked.

Jill shook her head. "No, thank you. As soon as Alex comes down, he's going to drive me home."

Lauren started. "You came here with Alex?" She seemed very surprised.

"Yes. What a car," Jill enthused, hoping to change the subject from Kate Gallagher.

"He has a beautiful car," Lauren agreed. "I tried to talk him out of buying it, he might as well plaster the amount of his bank accounts right on his forehead, but he would not listen to a word I said. Of course, every eligible woman in the city is after him anyway, but now, so is every ineligible one—the moment they see him in that car."

Jill could not mistake Lauren's meaning. "I am not after Alex Preston," she said flatly. "A month ago, I was nearly engaged to your brother."

Lauren did not reply.

Jill tried to tamp down her anger—and her impatience. She was getting ready to walk home, for godsakes. But Thomas patted her arm.

"My little sister is also very protective of this family." He looked at Lauren. "One day Alex will bring someone home, and I don't think any of us will have a vote, knowing Alex as I do."

"I don't expect a vote," Lauren said coolly. "But I've been with him too many times to count where women assume I'm his girlfriend and they still send him every possible signal. I mean, he's been handed phone numbers on slips of paper, Thomas, right under my very nose!"

Jill was glad she was hearing this. Hopefully it would end her incipient attraction to a man way out of her league. She wondered if he was a heartbreaker himself. Hal had said he was a type A workaholic, which meant he would have little time to play the field.

But Thomas was amused. "He's single," he said, as if that explained everything.

"My ears are burning," Alex said, striding into the room.

Jill was happy to see him. As pleasant as Lauren and Thomas were, there was stress just being with them. "Apparently you have most of the female population of London running after you," Jill said.

He actually laughed as he went to the bar cart, pouring himself a vodka. "Did either of you remove the photograph of Kate and Anne from Hal's bedside table?" he asked.

Thomas seemed to start. "What photograph?"

Alex sipped the icy vodka with obvious appreciation, leaning against the armoire, studying his cousins. He repeated the question.

Thomas regarded Alex. "Why would I take that photograph? I hate to be rude, but I have no time to chase ghosts." He smiled with some degree of apology at Jill. "My interests lie in the present and the future, not in the past."

Jill wasn't sure that she believed him. Hadn't he just spoken vehemently of the need to ensure his heritage for centuries into the future? Would not his past heritage be as important to him? She was sure of one thing, though. He would protect the Collinsworth family. It was his duty to do so. Would he also feel it his duty to protect them from resurrected ghosts with buried scandals?

"I've never even seen that photo," Lauren said. "Who cares what happened to that photograph? Mother probably tucked it away."

Jill wet her lips. "That photograph would be a family heirloom of sorts, for me."

"Only if Kate is your relative," Thomas said pointedly.

"Actually, Kate got pregnant while she was Anne's house guest," Alex said, still lounging against the armoire.

Jill almost gaped at him. What was he doing?

Thomas almost dropped his drink. "What in God's name are you talking about?"

Jill couldn't help it, she saw the two men lock gazes, and she was more than dismayed, she had a distinctly bad feeling. "Alex, it's late. Shouldn't we go?"

"Have another glass of wine, Jill," he said. "I thought you wanted some answers."

She gaped at him.

"Even if this Kate Gallagher got pregnant while she was my grandmother's guest, what does that have to do with anything?" Thomas asked. He was ruffled now.

Alex, as unruffled as Thomas was not, smiled at Jill. "Care to share your theory?" he asked.

Why was he antagonizing his own cousins? It crossed her mind that he might be sabotaging her—then she wondered if he wasn't going for the jugular, instead. Not hers, but his cousins'—or anyone who knew the truth.

Jill inhaled. "Maybe Anne was an accomplice of sorts to the affair—or a go-between. Who knows? Maybe Anne was ruined by association. For a time. Then Kate disappears. Whether she ran away or something terrible happened, Anne was involved because they were good friends. I'm surprised no one in this family knows anything about it," Jill said, looking around at the three faces turned her way. "It would have been a terrible scandal for everyone involved. It's the kind of legend that is passed down through generations."

A dumbfounded silence greeted her words. Thomas said, "I beg your pardon, and I do hate to disappoint you, but that is not the kind of legend, as you put it, which has been passed down in our family." He was angry.

"My grandmother was a noble woman, and highly esteemed by society," Lauren said firmly. "And even if she was some kind of go-between when she was a child, what difference could it make, now or then? When she married my grandfather, she became the Viscountess Braxton." Lauren looked at Alex. "Anne was your great-grandmother's sister, Alex." Disapproval filled her tone.

"I know," he said, clearly unrepentant.

Jill looked at Lauren.

"She became one of the preeminent women in this land," Alex said. "Preeminent and extremely powerful."

Jill met his gaze. She could not decode it, except that he might be enjoying himself. If Lauren or Thomas knew anything, they were great actors, she decided, worthy of the London stage.

Thomas turned to her. "Is there a reason you want to unearth a scandal about my family?" he asked very bluntly.

She shook her head. "No. I don't want to hurt your family, I've already done enough. I hope there is no scandal." Her smile felt like plaster about to crack. "I believe Kate ran off with her lover and her child to live happily ever after."

Lauren looked at her as if she had spoken Chinese. Thomas drank more scotch. Alex said, "Fairy tales." Jill caught the drift and felt like hitting him. Not hard, but hard enough.

"How is Lady Collinsworth?" Jill asked instead.

"She's gone to bed. She's okay," Alex said.

Thomas set his drink down on an end table with a white marble top. "I told this to Jill and I'll tell it to you. Mother isn't well right now and I don't want her upset."

"I don't want my aunt upset either," Alex said, as firmly.

"You never leave the office before ten," Thomas returned.

"I didn't know we kept a time clock."

Jill blinked, glancing from one cousin to the other.

"If the two of you are going to argue, I'm going to bed," Lauren said. "Unless you both want to make an awful day even worse?"

"Of course you don't have to explain yourself to me. Unless you affect the family in some way that is hurtful. How upset was my mother?" Thomas spoke as if Lauren were a fly on the wall that could not even bite.

"She's okay. I'm sorry about that. I intend to apologize fully—and explain—first thing in the morning," Alex said.

"Don't. I'll do it." Thomas responded in the kind of voice that was not to be brooked.

Jill watched them. Was there a rivalry between the two of them that she had not previously suspected to exist?

"Be my guest."

Thomas looked at his watch again. "I have some calls to make." He turned to Jill. "Drop by my office sometime. I'll take you to lunch." Suddenly he smiled. "I apologize for the family tiff."

Jill smiled slightly. "Okay." She was bewildered. Did he want something from her? Surely he was not asking for her company because he wanted to be friends? She had caused the accident that had killed his brother. Jill knew Thomas would never forget that fact, not until the day he died.

She decided she must be witnessing the civility the British were so famous for. He obviously was not earnest about the invitation.

"Thomas." Alex's tone was harsh, and it halted Thomas in his tracks.

"Yes?"

Alex walked across the room and stopped in front of him. His stance was rigid. "Did you delete those files?"

Jill almost fainted. Her eyes wide, she took in Alex's hard expression and watched Thomas's gaze become as cold as ice. "No." The one single word was harsh. "Did you?"

Alex's jaw tightened. "No."

They stared at one another and then Thomas was gone, striding from the room.

Her flat was ten minutes from the Sheldon mansion, but there was an accident on the road—a van had overturned—and they were sitting in stalled traffic. Jill was stiff with tension. Was Alex innocent? Or had he asked Thomas about the files in order to mislead her?

Someone had deleted the files, but she could not tell which of the two men had done so. It had not been a power surge. She knew that now. Because if it had been, Alex would not have attacked Thomas that way.

Jill was starting to believe that Thomas was the culprit. He had appeared not to know about the letters until she had told him of their existence that evening. In which case, he should not have understood what Alex had meant when he'd asked him if he'd deleted the files.

But he had understood.

The hairs on her nape were prickling. Jill shivered.

"Cold?"

Jill looked at Alex, seated just inches away from her, relaxed in the driver's seat of the exotic car. His question had been casual but direct. His blue gaze was as direct, but there wasn't much casual about it. It seemed brilliant.

Jill nodded. She folded her arms around herself and wished he'd let her call a cab. She'd asked again; he'd refused. At that moment his car was too small for them both.

Jill forgot about the letters. She thought about him dropping her off at her new flat. And that was what he was going to do—drop her off on the sidewalk, wave good-bye, drive away.

She reminded herself that he had hundreds of women rolling over at his feet. She reminded herself that Hal had been dead less than five weeks. She reminded herself that she was still on a low dose of antidepressant. Then she gave it up.

His arms would be strong and for a few hours, safe. God, deep inside of herself, she still hurt. Because of Hal's duplicity. Because of her own guilt. For a few hours she could touch and taste, be touched and tasted, and she might actually forget *everything*.

It was unbelievably tempting.

Jill suddenly realized that he was staring at her. "Why are you staring at me?"

"You know why," he said softly.

Something inside Jill turned over, far from unpleasantly. "I don't even want to know what you're talking about."

"You don't have to be scared," he said in that same low murmur.

She flinched, refusing to look at him. Not about to rebut. But she was fully aware of sitting like a rigid, frozen block of ice beside him, stiff with tension, afraid of herself more than she was afraid of him.

"You're more uptight now than ever. Why does being alone with me make you nervous?"

Jill felt a flaring of anger. She thought he might be more than coming on to her, and his seduction made her feel trapped, cornered, pinned down. And afraid. "Maybe it's because I hardly know you, and I cannot decide whether to trust you or not."

"But you trust Thomas?" He smiled.

Jill jerked. "Hardly."

He spoke without rancor. "There's far more to Thomas than meets the eye."

"So?"

He smiled again, faintly. The traffic was moving on the other side of the road, and the glare of oncoming headlights were reflected onto his face. "I saw the way you were looking at him. I see the way all women look at him. Most women never get past those movie-star looks. Then you add in the title. It's a flashy package, hard to resist. Most women don't have a clue who he really is. Thomas is a complicated man. With an agenda."

"Most people have agendas," Jill said. She had no intention of getting into a debate over her feelings for Thomas. Not just because it was nobody's business but her own, but because they remained highly ambivalent.

"But his is hidden," Alex said. His hands moved over the steering wheel once before gripping it. Jill didn't know if it was deliberate or not. "I think there's another reason I make you as jumpy as a cat." He twisted to face her.

She lifted both brows. If her expression was cool, it was a miracle. "What could that be?"

He smiled. "I'm a man . . . you're a woman. Yin and yang. It's pretty ancient stuff."

She inhaled. "I wouldn't give a damn if you were Paul Newman when he was forty." Did he have to be so direct? "Are you trying to say that you think there's some attraction between us?" She intended to lie until she was blue and deny it. She was not going to do anything rash. Not now—not ever.

He gave her the most disbelieving of looks. "I'd say there is. I'd say there's a helluva lot of yin and yang going down about now." He smiled again.

As if he liked her. As if he was confident of the outcome of the situation. Jill stared back at him, breathless and recognizing what that meant.

"I loved Hal," Jill said, enunciating every word very clearly, as if being succinct might make her love come back, might make him go away. This was the worst possible time for her hormones to be flowing. Worst time, worst place—worst object of affection.

"Hal is dead. Ghosts make poor lovers."

Her eyes widened. "Lovers? How did we get on the subject of lovers?"

"I don't know," he said. He was not smiling. "Maybe I do have telepathy after all."

She stared. Had she been sending signals all night long without even realizing it? "I'm going to walk," she decided, reaching for the door handle.

"As I said, as jumpy as a cat." He reached across her and prevented her from opening the door. His hand was large, firm—unyielding. "I want to give you some advice," he said very softly.

"I'm sure I don't want to hear it," Jill said, meaning it.

"I'm giving it anyway." He met her gaze. His was, as usual, far too penetrating. "Timing is a funny thing. Sometimes chances present themselves only once. The brave know when to seize the moment."

"I'm not brave."

"No?" He smiled, and it was genuine. "That's a crock, Jill."

She looked away from him. His arm remained extended across her chest, his hand remained on her door. She wasn't brave. He was wrong. She was a coward, because he was different from Hal in every way, and she was afraid, afraid of a one-night stand, afraid of more, afraid to get involved, afraid to trust and be hurt. "Damn it," she breathed, feeling close to tears. "May I please get out of the car?" she asked.

"No. I'm taking you home. And you can go to bed all by your lonesome, if that's what you want."

"That's what I want," she shot back, faster than any machine gun.

"Yeah?" Skepticism filled his tone. And his easy smile appeared again.

She pushed at his arm; he dropped it.

"Of course," he said softly and the traffic finally started to move, flagged on by two policemen, "this is one of those times in life when the opportunity is not limited. If you know what I mean."

Jill twisted to meet his eyes. "I'm not your type."

He started and laughed. "Like hell you're not."

He had turned his attention back to the road. With both dread and anticipation, Jill saw that they were not far from Lexham Villas. Oh, shit. If only he hadn't spoken with such utter conviction.

"You know," Jill said, squirming to the farthest corner of her seat, "you spoke about everyone's agenda but yours."

He steered the Lamborghini smoothly around the corner and to the sidewalk in front of her flat. The engine purred; he cut it and faced her. "Damned right I have an agenda," he said. And he was staring right into her eyes. "And mine isn't hidden, now is it?"

Jill stared back.

Neither one of them moved.

Eleven

THE NIGHT WAS BLACK AROUND THEM. JILL DIDN'T BREATHE and she didn't move. But neither did he.

Now what? Jill thought, her heart hammering against the walls of her chest. Should she . . . or shouldn't she? And why was she even having an internal debate?

"Jill."

She had to look at him. His tone had been half question, half command. Their eyes met and held. "I've gotta go," she blurted, and then, unthinkingly, she leaned across the small distance separating them and she kissed his cheek.

Not a peck. But a caress of her mouth on his beard-roughened skin.

He smelled great.

Jill pulled away, fumbled with the door, thrust it open, and leaped out of the car. She slammed it closed, waved, and dashed across the sidewalk up the path to her house, as if her clothing were on fire.

As she fumbled with her keys, shaking, she heard the Lamborghini's engine roar to life. But the sleek monster car did not pull away. Jill was aware of it idling on the street behind her.

She finally shoved open her door, stepping inside while hitting the lights, and as quickly closing it. As she locked the door, she glimpsed his night-blackened silhouette inside the sports car through the tiny window and parted curtains. Only then did she hear him drive away.

She leaned her forehead against the smooth wood. Now why in hell had she done that? Like a fool, she was sending the wrong signals, all right, she was leading him on and just asking for trouble.

Worse, her flat seemed more than empty. It felt lonely, too.

The following morning was bright and clear. As Jill made herself a huge plate of scrambled eggs, she refused to think about what had happened last night, instead trying to decide how to resume her search for Kate Gallagher. Maybe she would go back to Uxbridge Hall. Lucinda would probably have some suggestions about how she should begin.

But one question haunted her. Who had stolen the Gallagher letters? In the light of day, she thought both men had good cause for not wanting to let a skeleton out of the Collinsworth closet.

"And that is just too bad," she said to Lady Eleanor, who had appeared in the kitchen and was now waiting patiently for her food, sitting on the kitchen counter, her eyes on Jill. "Because Kate has a story to tell and I am going to tell it."

Lady E. began daintily cleaning her paws.

Jill only hoped, and fervently, that Kate's story was a happy one.

The telephone rang. Jill couldn't imagine who would be calling her, except perhaps for Lucinda. She started when she recognized William Sheldon's voice.

He was brief and to the point after a polite but restrained good morning. "I was wondering if you could come by the house, Miss Gallagher. I would like a word with you and I will be at home until noon."

Jill went on alert. She could not imagine what he wanted. "I would be more than glad to." She was afraid to ask what this was about. Had he heard about her disturbing his wife last night?

"Can you stop by this morning?" Lord Collinsworth asked. "You are in Kensington, are you not? Would eleven be convenient?"

Jill agreed. As she darted back upstairs to change, her breakfast half-eaten and forgotten, the ringing of the phone halted her in her tracks again. Alex's image came to mind as she quickly picked it up. "Hello?"

"Jillian, are you all right?" KC cried.

Jill gripped the phone. "I'm fine. Is something wrong, KC? Is Ezekial okay?" It was the middle of the night in New York, but KC was not big on sleep. Jill could hear her TV in the background.

"Ezekial is having a grand old time hissing at Chiron and then putting himself just out of poor Chiron's reach."

Jill smiled, relieved. She could imagine how Ezekial was toying with the little dog. And then, abruptly, her relief vanished. "That's not why you called."

"You need an answering machine. I tried to get through to you several times yesterday and last night." KC sounded distraught.

Jill's relief was replaced by anxiety. She reminded herself that KC knew how to make mountains out of molehills better than anyone she knew—she was a born dramatist with a touch of hysteria thrown in for good measure. "What happened?"

"Jillian, I called because someone was snooping in your apartment yesterday morning."

Jill started. "What?!"

"I had just taken Chiron out for a walk and when I returned I saw this fellow letting himself out of your studio. It wasn't your sublet, Jill. I pretended not to see, of course, and went right on into my own apartment. The moment he was gone I ran downstairs—and saw him driving away in a BMW. I got half of the license plate number, Jill. Then I went over to your place. Nothing appeared to have been touched," KC finished breathlessly.

Jill was in a state of disbelief. "KC, he's probably a friend of Joe's." Joe was the new sublet.

"Jill, I spoke with Joe. He's upset. He said no one has keys except for himself. This guy, Jill, was acting totally weird—all sneakylike."

Jill stared blindly at the parlor where she stood. "But this makes no sense," she finally said. "Someone broke into my apartment? But why? It's a crummy building. I don't have good stuff—and Joe isn't exactly loaded." Joe was an aspiring actor, i.e., he was a waiter.

"He probably picked the lock. I looked at it. He was a pro, Jill. The lock isn't even scratched." From KC's tone of voice, Jill knew she had something else she wished to say.

Then Jill stiffened. Alex had said he could pick locks. Then she felt a vast rush of relief—Alex was in London, not New York City. Wasn't he? "When was this?"

"Yesterday morning at seven-thirty."

That would have been at half past noon yesterday. Alex was not the intruder. Not unless he had taken a Concorde over first thing and then returned immediately afterward—in time to help her search the Sheldons' last night. And why was she suspicious of Alex? He had no reason to snoop in her apartment. "This must have been a mistake," she finally said. "I mean, I have nothing valuable, we live in a dump. Did the guy look like a drug head? Did you call the police?"

"I did, and they said you would have to go down to the station in person to file the complaint. I didn't get a good look at him, Jill, he kept his head low and he had a hat on. He was of medium height and build and his hair was dark brown, I think. But he was clean and sober. I'm sure."

Jill did not know what to think. "This is bizarre," she finally said.

"Jill, this man was not a burglar. This has something to do with your quest."

Jill froze. "My *quest?*"

"Your search for the truth about Kate Gallagher," KC said firmly.

Jill stood very still. "That's a strange choice of words."

"But you're searching for the truth. And that, Jillian, makes it a quest."

"I guess you're right," Jill said slowly. "How do you know this guy is a part of my quest?"

"I can feel it, Jill. It was so weird. The minute I saw him, I thought of *her*. Not you—her."

Jill was silent, her anxiety having increased, trying to tell herself to dismiss everything KC was saying as nonsense. But she couldn't. She said, "You haven't had any more dreams lately, have you?" She heard how wary her own tone was.

"No. Jill, I had to do a big spread for you."

Jill stiffened. A big spread meant that KC had done another layout with tarot cards. "You've told me, from time to time, that the cards can be wrong."

"No. The cards are never wrong. It's the reader who screws up," KC rebutted impatiently.

"What do you want to tell me?" Jill asked with dread.

"There's a man, Jill. I keep seeing him. The King of Swords reversed. And he's in your path big-time."

"Big-time," Jill repeated.

"He came up with the karma card—and with the Lovers," KC said.

"KC, I am not about to have an affair," Jill said. And of course, she was thinking of how close she had come to leaping into bed with Alex.

"The Lovers are karmic, too. It doesn't mean you'll have an affair with this guy, but you did, once, in another lifetime. Of course, you could get involved again, in this lifetime—"

"KC," Jill said sharply, wanting to cut her off. She did not want to hear any more.

But KC wasn't through. "He's brilliant, Jill. Brilliant and strong, powerful, the best at what he does. He's probably an air sign. Or he has a lot of air in his chart."

Jill glanced at her watch. If she didn't leave now, she'd be late. "KC, I have to go."

"I think you've already met him," KC said in a rush. "And if you haven't, you will. Soon. There's no avoiding this guy and I'm so worried!"

Jill was standing, but she did not hang up. "What did you see?"

"Something's wrong with him," KC said, sounding choked. "His communication. It's not okay."

Jill just stared at the phone.

"He's not being honest with you," KC said passionately. "He can't be honest with you. And you cannot trust him. *Jill, don't trust him.* If you do, something terrible will happen, I saw it in the cards, I felt it too, it's so strong—Jill, you should come home!"

Jill did not move. KC's words echoed. There was no mistaking her panic. Finally she said, "I can't go home. Not yet."

"Good morning, Miss Gallagher." William Sheldon stood up behind his massive, leather-topped desk.

Jill had been ushered into a large library with a high, domed ceiling painted pastel green. One wall was covered entirely in floor-to-ceiling books. A huge fireplace with a green marble mantel and a stunning gilded mirror above it dominated the central wall. Huge paintings, mostly eighteenth- and nineteenth-century landscapes, were hanging on the adjacent walls. There were several seating areas in the room and William's desk was at one end. Most of the furniture was covered in old and faded fabrics, gold brocades, dark green silks, darker blue velvets, and beige damask. Behind his desk the entire corner of the room was taken up by huge windows that looked out onto the rose gardens. Those gardens were carefully tended and in a rainbow riot of blooms.

"Good morning," Jill said nervously, smoothing down her knee-length black skirt. But she could hardly focus on the upcoming interview. The King of Swords reversed. A man who was powerful and brilliant, a man she could not trust. Was it Alex? Or was it Thomas?

Something terrible will happen . . .

"Miss Gallagher?"

Jill started. William was gesturing for her to sit down in one of the chairs in front of his desk. Jill hastened to obey.

His smile was cordial. Jill crossed her legs. She never wore high heels, but today she had chosen her single pair of two-and-a-half-inch pumps, which appeared spanking new from lack of use. She had wanted to convey ladylike elegance, and if she'd had her mother's pearls with her, she would have put them on, too. She was very nervous.

And to think that if she'd had all of her dreams come true, this man would have become her father-in-law. It was unbelievable.

"I understand that you were here last night, with my nephew," he said. Gold cuff links winked from the sleeves of his shirt.

Jill was already tense, now her tension increased. "We didn't think we would disturb anyone," she said. Then, "Lord Collinsworth, I apologize," she blurted out. "I apologize for everything, especially for what happened to Hal." That was not what she had intended to say. She had intended to be quiet and dignified.

He clasped his hands in front of him and looked down at them. "Yes, we are all sorry, Miss Gallagher. Thank you."

"If I could change what happened, I would," Jill continued earnestly. Jill tried to ignore the small stabbing of guilt. She wasn't sure it would ever go away.

He glanced up. "But no one can undo the past, can they? I have lived a long and fruitful life. But I also find myself filled with regrets, for choices not made, paths not taken, roads not traveled." He smiled grimly at her. "That is life, Miss Gallagher. It is never as one expects."

"Yes." Jill hesitated. "Why did you ask me here?"

He seemed to sigh. "My wife was very distraught last night."

"I know. I'm so sorry." He was going to chew her out.

"It would be better if you and she did not cross paths again. I must implore you, Miss Gallagher, to avoid my wife. She is not well, she is grief-stricken, and seeing you seems to set her back. She spent a sleepless night last night, complaining about her heart. It was her worst night since the funeral."

Of course Margaret Sheldon hated the very sight of her. Jill swallowed. "I don't want anything to happen to your wife," she whispered. Was she being banned from the premises permanently? Jill knew it was awful of her to worry about being able to finish her search for the letters, but she could not seem to help herself. "We were looking for some very valuable letters, Lord Collinsworth."

"So I understand. Valuable to whom?"

"Obviously they would be family heirlooms of a sort, for you and your family," Jill began.

"But how does that involve you?" he asked pointedly.

"Kate was my ancestor. I have some evidence to that effect." Jill knew her words were a stretch.

"Well, I suppose that is very interesting, but I must ask you to refrain from activities that distress Lady Collinsworth."

Jill wanted to ask him point-blank if she could come back when his wife was not at home in order to search for the letters. She did not. Her common sense told her that now was not the time. But it would not hurt to make a case for herself, to use in the future. Jill swallowed. "I have no family to speak of, my lord. My parents were killed in an accident when I was five years old. I was raised by an aunt who was hard of hearing and far too old to be burdened with a young child. I left home to study ballet when I was seventeen—never to return. I need to know if Kate Gallagher was my ancestor. You can trace your heritage back hundreds of years. I can't even trace mine back one generation."

"I sympathize with your plight, and if my wife were well, I would surely allow you to continue your search for your heritage, Miss Gallagher. But right now, you would only aggravate her illness and mental well-being." He glanced at his watch, which was a gold face on a black strap from Van Cleef & Arpels, as he stood up, signaling the end of their interview. "Now, I must get to the office."

Jill stood up, wetting her lips. "Kate Gallagher was a guest of your mother before she married Edward—your father. Kate had a child, possibly an illegitimate one. That same year, in 1908, Kate disappeared—and was never seen again."

He regarded her almost blankly. "I beg your pardon?"

Jill repeated what she had said, beginning to perspire.

"What is the point you are trying to make, Miss Gallagher? Why would this be of interest to myself?"

"Did your mother ever talk about Kate? Did she ever mention her? Do you know who the father of her child was? Surely you must have heard something as a child growing up here?"

"I know nothing about this Kate Gallagher, Miss Gallagher. Today is the first I have ever heard of her. My mother was a very busy woman when I was a boy. In fact, I was off at boarding school for most of the time, as was my brother. Mother was a matriarch—my father died very young, just before D-Day, in fact. Mother ran our estates, worked behind the scenes in the Lords, chairmanned every single board at the Collinsworth Group, not to mention all the charities in which she was actively involved. She was not the kind of woman to reminisce about the past. When she was alive, she lived in the present. That is what I do recollect." He did not smile as he walked out from behind his desk, extending his hand toward her.

"She sounds like a very strong and admirable woman," Jill said. She did not share the rest of her thoughts with him, that she had not appeared strong at all in either the portrait Jill had seen or the photograph.

"Yes, she was both those things. Now, if that is all?"

Jill hesitated. "Did you know that Hal had in his possession a photograph of Kate and Anne when they were girls of sixteen?"

He stared at her as if she had lost quite a few marbles. Or as if he could not quite believe that she had not shaken his hand and left, as he had prompted her to do.

"Not only did Hal have this unusual, very old photograph, he had written on the back of it, dating it—and he had it framed and standing on his bedside table. It was obviously important to him." Jill spoke swiftly.

"What does this have to do with me?"

"It was very important to him," Jill said, "and I am trying to find out why."

William shook his head. "We have all been through a terrible time," he said. "I know you were close to my son, and I know you have suffered as we all have. Perhaps this fascination you have serves a purpose, distracting you, but I would advise you to get some rest and forget about this woman. I doubt she is a relative of yours."

"What if I told you that Hal mentioned Kate as he lay dying in my arms?"

William paled.

Jill jumped to her feet. "Forgive me." She hadn't meant to

bring a graphic image to the poor bereaved man's mind. "I apologize," she said. "For imposing upon you."

Clearly shaken, William regarded her with a bewildered look. Finally he said hoarsely, "I think I must ask you to leave." He walked across the long stretch of library to the door. Jill had no choice but to follow.

But at the door, he seemed to pull himself together. Some of his ruddy coloring had returned. "Thank you for your time," he said politely. "Have a pleasant day."

Jill was startled. "Thank you."

She followed the servant from the room, thinking about their interview. William Sheldon did not know anything. If he did, she was a terrible judge of character. She wished she hadn't upset him, but she'd had to ask about Kate.

But how would she find the letters now? This house was at the top of her list of probable places in which to search. She wondered if Alex would openly defy his uncle in order to help her. Probably not.

The hall was endlessly long. As she approached the foyer, she heard female voices, one of which she recognized as belonging to Lauren. Although Hal's sister had been very civil last night, Jill tensed, shoving her worry about William and the letters from her mind.

As Jill entered the foyer, Lauren turned and saw her. Her eyes widened. And she was with Marisa Sutcliffe.

Jill could not smile. She looked first at Lauren in her charcoal designer pants suit and simple but elegant jewelry, and then at Marisa, in a short tweed skirt, a pastel green cashmere twin-set, and beige high-heeled shoes. Marisa, Jill decided, was shockingly beautiful, in spite of the fact that she looked as if she spent most of her time crying.

Both women were silent, staring at Jill, and in that split instant, Jill was fully aware of being an intruder in their midst—and a low-class one at that.

Suddenly Marisa came forward, hand extended, a smile firmly in place. "You're Jill Gallagher," she said.

Jill was taken aback. "Yes, I am."

"Marisa Sutcliffe," she said, still holding out her hand.

Jill slowly, reluctantly, took it. The handshake was brief.

Marisa had to despise her. Any other emotion would be an impossibility. So what was this? More good manners?

"This is quite the surprise," Lauren interrupted Jill's thoughts while Marisa stood mere inches from Jill, studying her the exact same way Jill supposed that she was studying Marisa. "Hello, Jill."

Jill quickly decided to tell her as little as possible and make a very hasty exit. "Good morning, Lauren. I was on my way out." She forced a smile and stepped past the two women.

"Wait."

Jill froze at the sound of Marisa's plea. And it was a plea.

"Please," Marisa said.

Jill faced her with grave apprehension.

"I don't really know what to say," Marisa said with a brief and wan smile. "This is bloody awkward. But . . . before Hal died. Did he say anything . . . anything at all?"

Jill's heart felt like a jungle drum inside of her breast. The foyer became overly warm. What was Marisa asking her? Surely she didn't know about Hal's dying words! "I'm not sure what you mean."

"Mare, don't," Lauren said, her tone soft and kind—a tone Jill had never heard her use before. "Don't do this." Lauren took her hand.

Marisa pulled it away. "Did he say anything at all— about me?" Her tone pitched upward with anxiety, with hope, with fear.

And Jill understood. How could she not? And in spite of the fact that Marisa was the other woman, in that moment she felt for her completely. Marisa wanted to know if Hal had told Jill about her, or if he had told Jill that he loved her, or wanted to marry her, or something. Then Jill thought about the fact that Marisa wasn't the other woman. She, Jill, was the other woman. "He never told me about you," she finally said, honestly.

Marisa's face fell. Lauren put her arm around her, and as Marisa dug in her alligator bag for a tissue, Lauren gave Jill a hard, angry look.

Jill froze. The look was vicious. But it was gone in the next instant.

"I had better go," Jill said, uneasy now and aware of the urge to tell Marisa the truth—that Hal had been on the brink of breaking up with her. But she hadn't expected this. She hadn't expected anything other than hatred. In fact, she had been expecting some kind of ugly confrontation from this other woman. Worse, there was something that seemed nice about Marisa. Appealing, even. How could Jill herself despise someone who was grieving like this? Her pain was horrendous. But the bottom line was that she could have behaved like a bitch. She had been more than civil.

"I miss him so," Marisa suddenly said into her tissue, her words choked. "If only he were alive!"

Lauren led Marisa to a pair of thronelike chairs on either side of a marble-topped table and she sat down in one of them. Jill watched the two women, wanting to run away now but unable to move.

Marisa looked up. "He was coming home," she cried in anguish to Jill. "He told me so. He wouldn't lie to me—we had no secrets—he even told me about you. He was my best friend in the world! How will I survive without him?!"

It did hurt. Not a lot. Just a little. Like the second day of a martini hangover, dully, listlessly. And Jill thought that if anyone knew the truth about what was in Hal's heart, it was the other woman, not Jill herself.

"How could God do this?" Marisa suddenly cried. "Hal wasn't perfect, but who is? But he was so kind! I think of so many people who don't give a damn about the poor or the ill, and they are alive! Hal cared." Marisa looked at Jill through glistening eyes. "Do you know that he never once walked past a beggar without handing him a few pounds?"

Jill knew. "Marisa."

She looked up, her nose red, her skin blotchy, her features and figure perfect.

"He was having doubts about us," Jill said with dread. "He was homesick. He told me so."

Marisa's eyes brightened.

It was the best that Jill could do.

"Thank you," Marisa said. Then she wept again.

Jill nodded grimly at Lauren and headed for the door. To her dismay, Lauren fell into step beside her. "Is Alex here?" she asked. "Did he bring you over again?"

"No." Jill paused. "Your father asked me to come."

"What matter could the two of you possibly share an interest in?" Lauren returned, obviously confused.

Jill said, "You'll have to ask him." She glanced at Marisa, who was trying to compose herself. "Tell her I'm sorry," she said.

And she walked out, leaving Lauren standing there.

Jill hurried down the drive and through the open iron gates. Once on the shady, tree-lined street, she halted, to catch her breath and compose herself. Her temples throbbed. She was beginning to understand Marisa and Hal as a couple.

And as she stood there, almost wishing that she had never encountered Marisa, her words echoed in her mind. *We had no secrets.*

Jill stared blindly across the street at a huge stone mansion and behind that, Kensington Gardens. Had Hal told Marisa *everything*?

Had he told her about Kate?

Using her hip, Jill pushed open her front door. In her hands were two shopping bags, one containing groceries, the other a brand new Sony answering machine that she'd felt she'd had to buy after her earlier conversation with KC. She smiled at Lady Eleanor, who sat up expectantly on the sofa in the parlor, regarding her unwaveringly. Another silvery brown blur disappeared into the kitchen, and presumably through the doggie door and into the gardens outside.

"Hi ya, Lady E." Jill smiled at the Siamese and carried her bags into the kitchen. As she hooked up the answering machine—reading the directions in order to do so—her mind kept skipping back to the depressing morning she'd had. After she recorded a greeting, she dialed Lucinda Becke, plopping down in one of the kitchen chairs while popping open a can of Coke.

"How are you faring, Jill?" the director of Uxbridge Hall asked.

"I feel like I'm at a dead end," Jill said. She told Lucinda how William had forbade her access to his house. "It was my best bet for finding the letters."

"I tend to agree," Lucinda commiserated. "But surely you won't give up now?"

Alex's image flashed through her mind, dismaying her. "No. I may never find those letters. Either Alex or Thomas deleted them, and I'll bet whoever did, he's got a copy himself. I'm going to Yorkshire, Lucinda. And York. My grandfather was born somewhere around there, and in any case, Kate stayed near Robin Hood Bay when she was pregnant. Which is, amazingly, just a few miles from Stainesmore. Another coincidence? How could it be one! I'm going there. I'm going to call up all of the hospitals and find out which one goes back to 1908. Maybe that's where Kate was hospitalized to give birth to her child. Maybe I can locate Peter's birth certificate while I'm at it. I'm going to find some trace of her, I swear, and I'm going to find some trace of Peter, too."

"I wish I could come with you," Lucinda said. "Perhaps you'll even find the manor where she stayed when she was enceinte. This is so exciting, Jill."

"It is exciting," Jill agreed. "And because Kate is connected to the Sheldon family through Anne, I'm going to poke around their estate, as well. God, if only I had carte blanche to search all the Collinsworth properties." Jill wondered how she could get inside Stainesmore. She'd have to come up with an awfully good story.

"I have an inkling Lord Collinsworth might not want you there, my dear. It is a private home, unlike Uxbridge Hall."

"I know," Jill said. "And that's why I'm not going to ask him for permission. I'm just going to show up." She hesitated. "Lucinda, there's something I haven't told you. In fact, I told only one person." She was half regretting telling Alex about Hal's dying words now.

"What could that be?"

Jill hesitated. "Hal mentioned Kate's name as he died. I did not mistake it. He said 'Kate' very clearly. After finding the photograph, I can only assume he was trying to tell me something about Kate Gallagher."

Lucinda was absolutely silent.

"Lucinda?"

"You gave me chills just now, Jill. I'm uncertain of what to think. You do know he spent a lot of time in Yorkshire. He was always motoring up there for days at a time."

"I thought it was strictly a summer place."

"No. That's not the impression I received. Harold took weekends there even in the winter. I remember quite clearly."

Jill absorbed that, wondering if Hal had gone alone or if he'd taken Marisa. She shoved that speculation aside, already knowing the answer. Suddenly she felt positive that the sooner she went to Yorkshire, the sooner she would have the answers she was looking for. "Lucinda, will you take care of the cats while I'm gone? I'll only be a few days."

"Of course, dear," Lucinda said.

After Jill hung up, she brooded. Even if she couldn't trust Alex yet, even if he was KC's King of Swords, he was clever and resourceful, and she almost felt like calling him and asking his advice. She wondered what he would do next if he were in her position.

"That damn King is probably Thomas," Jill muttered, eyeing the phone. She wasn't sure if she was trying to convince herself of that or if she really believed it. Besides, KC could be wrong. She was a dramatist with a capital D. Maybe she had misread her beloved cards.

But KC had upset her. Every time she thought about this man whom she should not trust, she got a sick feeling in her stomach, a feeling of unease, of dreadful expectation.

She decided to forget KC's warning for now, to put it in the back of her mind. The feeling of dread probably had more to do with how hard she kept telling herself to avoid Alex, even in her thoughts—which was just a super-indicator of the fact that her hormones were still acting up and that she feared she would cave in to her need to be held and touched sooner rather than later.

She couldn't help remembering what it had been like to

make love with Hal. It had been heaven. Of course, she had been head over heels in love with him. She wasn't in love with Alex. Not even remotely so. He was great-looking and super-smart, a total turn-on. Jill had the feeling he would be great in bed.

"Don't go there," she ordered herself firmly.

The phone rang, jerking her from her thoughts. It was Alex. Jill gripped the receiver, almost in disbelief.

"Hey, kiddo," he said. "How are the cats?"

"How are the cats?" she echoed. Maybe they shared telepathy. This was amazing.

"Lady Eleanor and Sir John."

She bit back a smile. "Lady E.'s warming up so fast she's melting. Sir John's hiding in the gardens."

She imagined him smiling on the other end of the phone. He said, "I'm sorry about last night. I came on like a Mack truck. That wasn't my intention. What can I do to make it up to you?"

Jill blinked. She became aware of her heart thundering. It was a moment before she spoke. "That was to the point."

"Life is goddamned short, Jill. I think we've both learned that recently."

Jill sobered. "Yeah." She hesitated. "You weren't really a Mack truck. More like a Humvee."

He laughed. "Thanks."

"I think you're a mind reader," she said, grinning.

He laughed again. "Not at all. Because I don't know what's on your mind now, other than your ancestor."

Jill froze. And breathed, "Is that who you're thinking about? Is Kate the reason you called?"

"I wanted to apologize, but I've been thinking about her. Something isn't right, something that I haven't figured out yet, but I have a strong feeling you are connected to her, too."

Jill felt a thrill rush over her.

"Jill?"

She was smiling at the phone. "It feels good to have someone else who is a lot more objective than myself think what I'm thinking."

"So what are you going to do?"

She hesitated again. To tell Alex her plans, or not? If she told him, she would be trusting him yet again. Jill closed her eyes. Thomas was obviously the villain here. Thomas was the one she could not trust.

She inhaled. "Your uncle called me over to the house this morning," she said quickly. Briefly she told him what had happened.

"Ouch," he said. "It's my fault. We were two bulls in the damned china shop. Look, I've thought about it. We may never find those letters. There are other ways to proceed."

He had said, "we." Jill gripped the phone, aware of how clammy her hands were. He sounded sincere. If he was lying, if he had deleted those files, he was a sociopath. Jill didn't think he was lying. He did not seem like a sociopath. He was upright, sincere. He seemed like a man with integrity. She was going to have to make a decision, and quickly, on whether to trust him or not.

Alex broke into her thoughts. "I could drive you up to Yorkshire. We know the area where Kate stayed when she was pregnant. How many suitable manors would be in close proximity to it? And locals have long memories. Every village has its ghosts and folklore. God only knows what we'll unearth."

Jill heard herself say, hoarsely, "I'm ahead of you. I've already asked Lucinda to take care of the cats."

"Great minds," he murmured, and there was something so rich and deep in his voice that Jill stopped breathing, the bed issue completely absorbing her thoughts.

Then he said, "When do you want to leave? How about Thursday at noon? It's a good six hours from here to York. Another four to Stainesmore. The only catch is that we have to head back late Sunday or at the crack of dawn on Monday."

She felt overwhelmed. "You don't have to do this. I can rent a car—"

"Another dead Yank? Forget it. I'll drive you. And that way we can stay at the estate with no problem—I'll call the housekeeper and let her know we're coming."

Jill wet her lips. "Thank you, Alex," she said.

"No problem. In fact, it's a pleasure." He paused. "Jill. A word of advice."

"What's that?"

"Don't mention to anyone else where we're going—or why."

Jill was speechless.

"See you Thursday at noon," he said.

After he had hung up, Jill stared at the phone in her hand. Why had he stressed the need for secrecy?

Why did he think there was something they should hide?

And Jill wondered if he knew something that she did not.

Twelve

JILL SPENT MOST OF THE NEXT TWO DAYS AT UXBRIDGE HALL.
Lucinda had consented to allow her free run of most of the
Georgian mansion—including the attics and the archives.
The Sheldons' private rooms were excluded. Jill didn't
expect to find the letters there, not unless they were in the
family's wing, but she was hoping to find something, anything, connected to Kate and Anne.

She started with the attics. It was the most logical place to
begin, after all, that is where everybody stored their junk
from the past. To her dismay, the attic was spotless. It had
been cleaned out a long time ago. There were no trunks lying
around, locked or otherwise, no boxes, no bundled-up
papers, nothing but dusty floors and a few mouse droppings.

Anne's bedroom also contained no clues about the past.
Every drawer had been emptied out long ago. Jill had been
hoping to find letters, notes, mementos, or even a diary. She
was very disappointed.

The rest of the public rooms were the same. Every drawer
and closet was startlingly and purposefully empty.

The archives, located in the basement, were not at all what
Jill had expected. She had hoped for an extensive treasure
chest of documents, but she was able to read through the
material in an entire afternoon. Much of it pertained to the
comings and goings, births, marriages, and deaths, of previous generations of Sheldons, which Jill skipped over.

The most interesting discovery was that Edward Sheldon,

the ninth viscount, William's father, had a penchant for sending instructions to his staff and family. There were notes to the foreman of his iron mine ordering new lights to be placed in all shafts. There were notes to the head gardener at Stainesmore. The roses were not thriving, something must be done, the viscount recommended bringing in a horticulturist. There were notes to his valet, his housekeeper, his butler, and there were notes to his sons, Harold and William, and a daughter, Sarah.

Jill hadn't realized that Edward and Anne had had another son, much less a daughter. But in 1932, Edward wrote a brief and terse note to Sarah, informing her of her engagement, and ordering her back to London in order to prepare for the wedding. He included a list of instructions—who she must call on, where she must go, what she must do and have done by the wedding.

On October 15, 1930, Edward wrote William, one of several letters sent to him over a five-year period while he was a boy at Eton.

I understand that there are times when duty must break down, when respect fails, when boys behave as mere boys. However, that is no excuse for your behavior. I have agreed with Mr. Dalton that a suspension is in order. Prepare yourself to depart for London in one week's time.

I am sure, William, that, by the time you return to Eton, you will have reflected upon your priorities, and drawn the proper conclusions.

Your father, Collinsworth

Jill blinked at the cold letter. All of his letters to William were the same—they all embodied cool reprimands. William, Jill realized, had been a little mischief-maker while a child.

There were a number of letters to Harold, during his years at both Eton and Cambridge, a series of constant reminders on how to behave and what to do when. An instant later she found herself reading a letter dated 1941. Apparently Harold had been an RAF pilot.

I am proud of you for doing your duty, for your loyalty to country and countrymen. And I know you will behave with courage and honor in the field and in the skies. Your mother and I send our blessings . . .

Jill wondered when Harold had died.

There were also brief notes sent to Anne. They were all impersonal directives. Edward requested her to oversee the new masonry at Stainesmore, the planting of new gardens in town, the arrival of a Thoroughbred stud, the dismissal of his kennel master. He asked her to meet with his banker, in lieu of himself, as he could not return to town, to discuss "the railroad matter." In fact, there were several dozen such missives, but the earliest was dated 1916. Jill could only assume that he and Anne had been married for some six or seven years by then.

The letters confounded her. There was nothing personal in any of them. Perhaps the most personal one had been that written to Harold during World War Two. But even that had a terribly cold and austere quality to it. Jill wondered if Edward had really been as cold, distant, and autocratic as he seemed.

On Thursday she was ready to be picked up by Alex, well before noon. She had made no progress in her search for the truth about Kate Gallagher, although she had learned some interesting things about the Sheldon family. Harold had died in the war, leaving William the heir to the title. Sarah, according to Lucinda, had passed away in 1985. She'd had two daughters, one of whom lived in London, both married with children.

Jill heard the roar of the Lamborghini's powerful engine just as her telephone rang. She already had her small duffel bag in hand and she decided to ignore the phone, eagerly peering out of the window. The silver monster had halted at the curb. Jill wanted to get going and she opened the front door, clad in faded Levi's, a ribbed black tank top, and her black leather jacket. Alex was striding up the walk in tan trousers and a yellow polo shirt. Clearly he had worn a sports jacket to the office that morning. He smiled at her, appearing in quite the good mood.

As Jill was about to close the door she heard, "Miss Gallagher, this is Beth Haroway from the Felding Park Nursing Home. I was hoping to catch you because—"

Jill dropped her bags and flew to the telephone, picking it up. "Beth! It's me, Jill," she cried breathlessly.

"I thought you'd like to know that Janet Witcombe is having an extremely good day, Jill. She seems entirely lucid," the young nurse said. "If I were you, I would motor out and speak with her immediately."

Jill gripped the phone, then became aware of Alex reaching for her bags in the doorway. "We'll be right there," she said. "Thank you." She hung up and hurried to Alex, who was regarding her with a lazy expression. "We have one stop to make on the way to York. Janet Witcombe is having a very good day, Alex. I have to talk to her while she is fully focused."

He was smiling; his eyes widened slightly, meeting hers. "This should be interesting." He picked up her bags and they left the house, Jill locking the door behind them. When they were settled in the silvery gray car, its engine purring, Alex said, "Try not to get your hopes up, Jill. Thirty years is a helluva long time to recall a conversation."

"I know. But I've been stuck in a rut ever since we last spoke. I've come up with nothing new. I need a lead, Alex."

He steered the car around the corner, a dimple remaining on the left side of his cheek. "What have you been doing since we last spoke?"

"I've been poking around Uxbridge Hall," she said, studying his profile. Not because he had extremely intriguing features that might be arresting, if one were at all inclined to think so, but because she wanted to gauge his reaction.

Not glancing at her, he smiled. "Sounds like fun, actually. I've been up to my neck in numbers." He sighed and shot her a glance. "Haven't got too much sleep these past few days."

Suddenly their gazes caught and held. Jill imagined him

burning the midnight oil in his office, alone in the building, and she flushed slightly and looked away. Now was not the time to think of him as an interesting man, not when they were taking off for the weekend alone together. The interruption was fortunate; Alex's cell phone went off.

He also had a car phone. The cell phone lay on the small wooden dash between his thigh and Jill. He picked it up with one hand and flipped it open, glancing at the caller ID number as he did so. "Yeah."

A moment later he said, "I decided to take some time off. I'm beat. I'll be back late Sunday or first thing Monday."

And then, "I don't know. I'm playing it by ear and heading north. The Lamb needs a good run. If there's a problem, you've got my cell and my mobile phone numbers."

Jill pretended not to listen. Who was he talking to? Suddenly she wondered if he had a girlfriend and was trying to avoid telling her where he was going. She had never asked; she would not ask now. It was not her business.

"I haven't decided where I'm staying. All right. Bye." He hung up, laying the phone back down.

In the end she could not help herself. "Who was that?"

He smiled at her, as if he guessed her suspicions. "That was Thomas. I canceled a meeting for this afternoon and he wanted to know why."

She stared. "You didn't tell him very much."

"No."

"You didn't tell him anything."

"That's right."

Jill looked back at the road. They were on Oxford Street, heading west. Why was he being so secretive? He had been secretive the other day, advising her not to tell anyone where they were off to. He wasn't even telling Thomas. Was that because he knew Thomas was guilty of deleting the files?

Was Thomas the person she shouldn't trust?

Who would want to protect the family more from the skeleton that was Kate Gallagher? Jill glanced at Alex, who was, in a way, an outsider just as she was. Except he had fought hard to earn his place inside the family. Might that not make him even more of a fervent guardian of the family's reputation?

Jill could not decide. Thomas was obvious, Alex was not. But Alex was the one who had accused Thomas of having a hidden agenda. If Alex was as up-front as he seemed, then Thomas was the offender. But what if he was not up-front at all? What if he had purposefully been misleading her? What if his agenda was the hidden one?

"Where are you, Jill?" he asked softly as they entered the A41 motorway.

She started. "Alex," she said carefully, "what do you think would happen if we discover that something terrible happened to Kate while she was at Bensonhurst? And that Anne was somehow involved?"

He did glance at her—and then in his rearview mirror. Jill studied his hands, trying to see if they gripped the leather-bound steering wheel more tightly. "You could sell the story to the tabloids for some decent dough," he said.

Jill sat up straighter. "You're kidding."

"No, I'm not. There'd be a brief sensation in the press. People would talk for a week or so at parties and in the clubs. And then it would all die down."

"An event that happened ninety-odd years ago?"

"If it was something terrible, yeah." He glanced at her. "Imagine finding out that Joe Kennedy had a mistress whom he sent away to have his illegitimate baby—and the woman and child mysteriously disappeared. Imagine he reinvented identities for them—and their descendants are uncovered and named. Wouldn't that make the tabloids at home?"

"It might make *Time* magazine," Jill said tensely, "if the story was awful enough."

"Point made," Alex said, shooting her a longer glance this time.

"Why are you helping me?" Jill asked bluntly.

He was silent. Then, eyes on the road, "Do you really need to ask?"

She hesitated. She didn't need to ask, she only had to recall the other night. Swiftly, Jill changed the subject.

"There's a hospital we should stop by in York. In 1908 it was the Yorke Infants' Hospital; women delivered their children there."

Alex looked at her and laughed. "That was a tell."

Jill didn't want to ask. "What's a tell?"

"When you're playing poker, it's something your opponent does that gives him away."

Jill settled back in her seat, folding her arms across her chest, staring out of her side window. Okay. So she'd revealed her hand. But she still had her resolve. "Let's focus on Kate."

He smiled again, to himself.

"Mrs. Witcombe, dear, you have visitors." Beth Haroway was a plump blond in her thirties, and she had just led Alex and Jill over to the little old lady sitting on a bench in the park surrounding the nursing home, a large stone building that clearly dated back a century or more. Beth Haroway was smiling and cheerful. The sky was blue, fat cumulous clouds floated by, and the sun was shining. Other nursing home patients were seated on other park benches or in their wheelchairs, others were strolling the grounds. It seemed to be a very pleasant place, but Jill only had eyes for the tiny, white-haired lady sitting on the green bench, wrapped up in a camel-colored wool shawl.

"This is Jill Gallagher from America, and her friend, Alex Preston," Beth continued cheerfully, touching Janet's shoulder. "I'm going to leave you for a moment, dear. Is there anything you need?"

Janet Witcombe shook her head, regarding Jill and Alex out of blue eyes that were far more alert than they had been the previous time Jill had met her. There was no mistaking her curiosity and interest. "Why, hullo," she said softly. "It's not often that I have visitors I do not know, much less from America." She smiled.

"I know this might seem odd," Jill said, "and I hope you do not mind. Are we intruding?" She was holding a bouquet of flowers in her hand.

"Not at all," the little old lady cried. "What a glorious day—how could anyone intrude on such a day?"

"These are for you," Jill said, handing her the bouquet of lilies.

Janet inhaled deeply. When she looked up, tears filled her eyes. "My favorite. Oh, dear. My husband used to surprise me with lilies, you know. That was years ago. He died at such a young age. He was only fifty-two."

"I'm so sorry," Jill said softly. "May I sit down?"

"Oh, please do." Janet patted the bench beside her. "Is that handsome man your boyfriend?"

Jill almost jumped out of the seat she had just taken, and she knew she flushed. "Alex is a friend," she said very firmly.

He spoke for the first time. "But only because I haven't had my say in the matter," he told Janet with a wink.

Jill ignored that.

Alex handed her a box lunch they had picked up at a neighborhood café. "I hope you are hungry, Mrs. Witcombe, because we brought you some lunch. A smoked turkey sandwich with roasted peppers, I think, with puff pastries for dessert."

"Oh, the two of you are such dears," Janet cried as Alex laid the box by her on the other side of the bench. She looked at Jill. "He is so adorable, the two of you make a beautiful couple."

Jill smiled, straightened. Tension settled on her shoulders, weighting them down like a huge dumbbell. She avoided Alex's laughing eyes. "Mrs. Witcombe, I'm actually an amateur historian and I was hoping to ask you some questions about Anne Sheldon, the late countess of Collinsworth."

Janet sat up straighter, too. "She was a great patroness," she said. "I loved working for her at Uxbridge Hall."

Jill was thrilled. "You knew her."

Janet smiled. "We met on several occasions, my dear. She was a real lady, the kind of lady one doesn't see anymore. Did you know that she never left the house without a hat and gloves?"

"No, I didn't know," Jill said with a smile. "Did she ever talk to you about the past?" she asked. "She was best friends with one of my ancestors. I mean, when they were girls of sixteen, seventeen, before she married Edward Sheldon."

Janet turned on the bench so her entire body was facing Jill. She wasn't smiling. Her eyes were direct. "Are you talking about that tragic young woman, Kate Gallagher?"

Jill inhaled, shot a look at Alex, and stared at Janet. "Yes," she said huskily. "I am." Tragic? Did Janet know what had happened to Kate? Jill began to perspire. Her fingers were tightly crossed.

Janet stared unblinkingly back at her.

"Relax," Alex said low, into her ear.

"Mrs. Witcombe, please, I am trying to find out what happened to Kate. You know that she disappeared in 1908. Without a trace. She was never seen again."

"Yes, I know, it's common knowledge," Janet said.

"It's common knowledge?" Jill raised both brows, surprised.

"It's common knowledge at the Hall. You must have seen the locket." Jill nodded. "Did you see the portrait? Of the three of them?"

"What portrait?" Jill was gripping the bench.

"At the Hall. There was a portrait of Anne and Kate and Edward. The two girls seated on the bench in front of the piano, Edward standing beside it. It was so lovely, the girls in sprigged muslin, Edward in his breeches and a hacking coat. I do think the portrait was painted in the country."

Jill glanced at Alex, who met her gaze. She turned back to Janet. "At Stainesmore?"

"Why, yes, my dear. Where else would it have been?"

"I don't recall seeing such a portrait at Uxbridge Hall," Alex said softly.

Jill wet her lips. "Janet, I have been over every inch of Uxbridge Hall. Lucinda Becke is a friend of mine. There's no such portrait there."

"Oh, my dear, there most certainly is, unless someone took it away."

"Did someone take it away?"

"Not while I was director," Janet said.

Jill nodded, making a mental note to call Lucinda immediately about the portrait. Maybe it had been sent out to be restored. "What can you tell me about Kate and Anne?"

Janet seemed to hesitate. "Very little, I'm afraid. I know what the whole world knows. The two girls were friends, and when Kate first came to London, she and her mother were Anne's guests. And Kate disappeared."

Jill found herself crossing her fingers again. "Mrs. Witcombe." She clasped the old lady's shoulder lightly. "Just before Uxbridge Hall was reopened to the public, Anne toured it to give it her stamp of approval. Do you remember?"

Janet looked her in the eye. "I could never forget." She was grim.

"What is it?" Jill cried.

"What is it that you wish for me to say?" Janet returned.

"Lucinda said Anne became very upset when she entered her old girlhood bedroom. That she wept."

"She became very distraught," Janet said, a whisper. "Not at first. At first she was so pleased with the renovations. Then, when we walked into her room, something happened to her. I saw it immediately. Her face changed. It became . . . dark . . . heavy. And she sat on the bed. I thought she was ill, but she waved me away, and she pointed to the window and told me how her friend—her best friend—Kate, climbed out of that window night after night to rendezvous with her lover."

Jill was vaguely aware of Alex having moved to stand very close beside her—as if shielding her from whatever would come next. "Did she tell you who Kate's lover was? Did she tell you what happened to Kate?"

Janet sighed heavily, and wrapped her shawl more firmly around herself. "She never talked about Kate's fate. She started to cry. Silently, without a sound. I was very frightened. I did not know what to do. She was so unhappy, my dear. So I left the room, ran downstairs, and came back with a cup of tea."

"And that is it?!" Jill cried.

Suddenly Janet's gaze was focused not on Jill, but on

some faraway horizon. Her eyes had changed, blurring, losing their brightness. Jill was afraid she had lost her lucidity. She thought the interview was over.

But Janet spoke in a soft, reminiscent, faraway tone of voice. "When I returned to the room, Anne was standing at the window. She did not hear me, even though I coughed. For one moment I was terrified, I thought she was going to jump out. For the window was wide open. She had pushed it wide open." Janet stopped.

There was a table beside the bench, and on it was a tray with a pitcher of water and several glasses. Alex handed Janet a glass of water. After she had taken a sip, she said hoarsely, "You must understand. Those windows had not been opened in years. I tried to do so once on a very hot day when I had first started my employment there. But I could not open it. And I was a middle-aged woman at the time. Anne was very old. She was close to eighty-five."

Jill didn't speak. Her gaze was glued to Janet's face. It was lined and wrinkled, and her jowls seemed to tremble. "Anne said, her voice very strange, and I will never forget her words, 'I did not know it at the time, but her lover was Edward, my Edward.' "

Jill stared at her in shock.

"Then she accepted the tea, drank it as if nothing had happened, thanked me for all the labor I had done, and she left. I saw her a few times subsequently, but the topic was never raised again. And that is all I know." Janet regarded them both. Her gaze had become bright and focused again.

Jill remained in shock.

"Well," Alex said, breaking the silence, "if Edward was Kate's lover, that certainly explains a lot."

Jill just looked at him dumbly, having no idea what he meant.

OCTOBER 1, 1906

Kate and Anne sat together in the backseat of the coach, drawn by six ebony mares, holding hands very tightly, as the vehicle rolled down the cobbled street. It was a beautiful evening, with stars winking in the blue-black sky overhead and pools of light spilling from the electric lamps lining the boulevard. Earlier that day it had rained, and thoroughly, and now the cobblestones glistened like black glass. The liveried coachman turned the team into a circular driveway in front of a vast stone mansion that was ablaze with lights. That drive was already congested with dozens of other coaches and automobiles. The coach halted, queued up now behind a line of coaches and motorcars, each vehicle awaiting its turn to pause before the front steps and let out its passengers.

Kate's and Anne's gazes met. "We are about to make our debut," Kate whispered, her fingers tightening on Anne's.

"I am so happy," Anne whispered back. "This is the beginning, dearest Kate, the beginning of the rest of our lives."

"How romantic you are," Kate whispered, smiling. "That is exactly how I, too, feel." And she turned to gaze out of the curtained window, her heart pounding, staring at the many groups of splendidly attired ladies and tuxedo-clad gentlemen ascending the front steps of the Fairchild home.

"Girls! Have you not been told, time and again, that whispering among yourselves is the rudest of behavior?" Lady Bensonhurst intoned from the facing seat. "I will not tolerate such behavior at the ball. I expect the two of you to be perfect ladies, at all times." And she glared at Kate.

Kate was wearing a silver-blue satin gown with tiny drop sleeves and a flounced hem. She raised her fan and snapped it open, using it in a simpering manner. "I beg your pardon, my lady," she said far too demurely. "We shall strive to make the most perfect effect on those present at the ball tonight."

Lady Bensonhurst's jaw ticked and abruptly she looked out of the window. Her husband, Anne's father, remained impervious to the conversation, sipping from a sterling silver pocket flask. Kate's mother, Mary, gave her a worried warning look. "Please," she mouthed silently. "Please, Kate, please."

Kate snapped her fan shut with annoyance, then realized it was their turn to disembark. Her gaze met Anne's again. All day she had been haunted by the strongest feeling that tonight

would be magical—that something very special would soon
unfold. She did not have a clue as to what might happen, but
she had been on pins and needles ever since she'd awoken,
filled with this unnerving sense of expectation.

Their group left the carriage and slowly walked up the
many steps of the house. The four ladies handed their wraps
to waiting servants, Lord Bensonhurst handed over his hat
and walking stick. They made their way to the entrance to the
ballroom, Anne moving to stand between her parents. Kate
waited with her mother just behind them, and when it was the
Bensonhursts' turn to descend to the ballroom, Anne looked
over her shoulder at Kate, her eyes at once frightened and
filled with excitement. She had never been prettier, Kate
thought, and she gave her a rough thumbs-up.

"Kate," Mary whispered, gripping her wrist. "Stop that."

The Bensonhursts were being announced. Kate looked at
her small, pallid blond mother with her continuously worried
eyes, and she wished, so very much, that her father were
there with them that night.

How proud he would be of her, Kate thought, smiling. She
had not a doubt. He would have laughed at the crude gesture.

"Mrs. Peter Gallagher from New York City, widow of the
late Peter Gallagher, and her daughter, Miss Katherine Adeline Gallagher."

Kate and her mother descended the stairs into the ballroom. Below, the vast room was filled with guests who were
clustered in large and mixed groups, sipping champagne and
conversing with friends and acquaintances. Kate held her
head high, but as she looked down at the spectacle awaiting
her, she was aware of heads turning, of ladies and gentlemen
staring up at her, of eyes widening. She felt her smile, which
was genuine. The night did feel magical, and right then, there
was nowhere she would rather be.

She and her mother were almost at the foot of the stairs.
The group behind her was already being announced. Kate's
gaze fell on a tall, dark gentleman and her smile vanished,
her eyes went wide. He was staring at her so intensely that
his eyes seemed silver.

Kate recognized him immediately. He was the gentleman

from Brighton, the one who had watched her from the observation deck while she played tag with the waves. Her pulse was thundering now so swiftly and so loudly she thought her mother had to hear it. Kate could not tear her gaze away from the gentleman, not even to see if her mother had noticed her reaction to a stranger.

Who was he?

Kate could hardly breathe. Her ears were ringing. Her heart was pounding. Was this love at first sight?

He smiled then, slightly, and bowed to her, not slightly at all.

Kate inhaled, managing a smile in return, then wanting to kick herself, certain he could see how flustered she was—as if she were some schoolgirl unused to male attention. That was hardly the case!

They rejoined the Bensonhurst group, several couples Kate had already met at other gatherings. Kate was aware of Lady Bensonhurst placing her ample back toward her, but that did not bother her. She knew Anne's mother despised her and thought her to be little more than trash. She despised Anne's mother, who was far worse than a witch. She was an absolute bitch.

She peeked over her shoulder. His gaze was on her, as intent as before. Kate sent him a quick smile. Damn it! She was flirting, but without the finesse she usually had. She must recover her composure before he judged her to be a dimwit.

Kate faced Anne. "Darling, I am going to the cloak room."

"Now? But we have just arrived." Anne became anxious. "You are not ill, Kate?"

"Hardly," Kate said. It was on the tip of her tongue to tell Anne about the gentleman, but something held her back. "I will return in a moment." She squeezed her hand and raced away, far too swiftly to be genteel or ladylike. But she had no intention of obeying Lady Bensonhurst, not about anything.

In the corridor outside of the ballroom she paused, taking a few deep breaths, struggling for composure. She *had* to learn the identity of that man.

"May I be of assistance?"

At the sound of the deep, cultivated voice directly behind her, Kate froze. She knew who it was even though they had never before spoken. Slowly, she turned.

And looked into the most amazing pair of amber eyes she had ever seen. Long lashes fringed them. He did not smile, but neither did she.

A long, silent, breathless moment passed.

He came to life. "I beg your pardon." His smile flashed, but it was brief. He bowed. "We have not been introduced, and I find myself behaving like the proverbial ass."

Kate smiled and laughed. "That is hardly possible, sir."

"No?" He was smiling now, too, but his brilliant amber eyes were unwavering on her face. "I assure you, it is. I am not usually so lacking in either words or wit. But your beauty has rather robbed me of the ability to speak."

"That is too kind," Kate began, realizing she was speaking like an ass herself.

He bowed again. "I am Lord Braxton," he said.

Kate extended her hand. "Kate Gallagher, my lord."

"Kate." His gaze took in her upswept red hair as he took her hand and kissed it. There was no mistaking the pressure of his mouth, even through the delicate silk of her white glove. "How the name suits you."

Kate smiled. "It is a very common name."

"But there is nothing common about its current owner." He smiled.

She was about to tell him, again, that he was too kind. What was wrong with her? "Thank you," she said. "I take that as high praise, coming from the source that it does."

His smile vanished. "So this source seems rather uncommon to you, as well?"

She could hardly believe her ears. "Yes," she said, quite huskily. "Very uncommon."

"I am exceedingly flattered. I do believe, Miss Gallagher, that we have laid eyes upon one another a previous time."

"Yes," Kate said, not about to play games. "In Brighton."

He stared. After a moment he said, "Do you know how many ladies would deny recollection of that day?"

"But I am not like other ladies—as you have so recently pointed out."

"No, you are nothing like the other ladies, that was evident the moment I first laid eyes upon you, when you raced the waves as would a Grecian goddess."

Kate felt herself blushing. She was at a loss for words—when she, Kate, always had a flip reply at hand. "Do you now compare me to immortals, my lord?"

"Indeed, I do, and with no apology," he said.

Kate stopped smiling. If anyone was to be compared with a mythical deity, it was him, not herself.

"You are beautiful when you blush," he said, low. Suddenly he took her gloved hand and pressed his mouth to it again. Kate's heart turned over again and again. Her knees became stupendously weak. When he met her gaze again, his eyes were brilliant. "I am being very bold, and well I know it. When may I take you driving in the park?"

"Tomorrow?" Kate said, her heart turning over yet another time.

"Tomorrow would be perfect," he said. "And tonight? Will you dance with me?"

"Yes," Kate said. Her gaze was direct. "There is nothing I wish to do more."

They were both smiling now, like besotted fools. Kate did not know how long they stood there like that, with him clasping her hand in both of his, grinning at one another. Suddenly she realized that they were not alone. Ladies and gentlemen were passing by them in the hall, and numerous necks were being craned in order to get a good look at them. She had been so immersed in his presence that she had not even noticed the other guests trafficking about them. He seemed to break free of the spell, too, glancing around. "We have been remarked," he said rather wryly.

"I am always being remarked," Kate murmured as wryly.

"Of course. No one could fail to notice you, my dearest lady."

His endearment made her heart jump wildly, and then it fell, a long, endless free fall, at a breathtaking speed, the impact at once frightening and exhilarating. Kate looked at his stunning face, at his brilliant eyes, and thought, amazed, Oh, God, I have just fallen in love!

"Are you well?" he asked sharply.

She had just fallen in love. She stared at him, for one moment, incapable of speech. "Yes," she whispered. "I am fine." But she wasn't fine. She was stunned, dazed, exhilarated. She felt as if they were cloaked in a magical mist.

He smiled, took her hand in both of his, clasping it tightly. "We should return to the ballroom, before we are excessively gossiped about."

"Yes," Kate said, wanting to stand there in the corridor with him all night. His touch on her elbow was slight but Kate also thought it was proprietary as he walked her back into the crowded ballroom. "Until the dance, then," he said.

"Until the dance," Kate replied, knowing the wait would be endless. She watched him bow a final time and stride away, pausing to enter a group of dashing gentlemen all of whom were about his own age. Kate had seen Anne standing with a group of young ladies, but she made no move to go to her, she could only stare after Lord Braxton. Oh, God. She had never thought love would feel this way. She felt as if she were floating in the clouds. She was so happy and so excited she could hardly stand it. *Oh, dear, dear God.*

"Well, we can see where she's set her red cap."

Kate was used to people talking about her behind her back, loudly enough so she could hear. She stiffened, about to walk away.

"She doesn't have a chance of snagging the Collinsworth heir. Edward Sheldon would never marry so far beneath him, and even if he would, his father would never, ever allow it."

Kate turned and was confronted by two plump matrons in tiers of diamonds. "Who is Collinsworth?" she demanded, seized with sudden panic.

"Collinsworth?" The white-haired lady smiled at her. "Why, he is one of the wealthiest earls in this land, my dear. And his son, Edward Sheldon, the Viscount Braxton, is his heir. Were the two of you not introduced?"

Kate stared blindly at her. Her pulse was deafening. Viscount Braxton . . . Collinsworth's heir . . . the wealthiest earl in the land. No. Everything would turn out right, it would, because she believed in true love, and she had just found what she had been waiting a lifetime for.

Kate turned.

Edward was watching her, clearly aware that something was wrong. His gaze was concerned, questioning.

For the life of her, Kate could not summon a smile. Nor could she go back from the precipice she now stood upon. Her heart told her that.

Thirteen

THEY REACHED YORK AT TEATIME. ALEX PARKED THE LAMborghini in front of the Ole Whistler Pub, a stone structure with wood beams that seemed out of place amid the taller brick buildings surrounding it.

Pedestrians on the sidewalk were gawking at the silver monster as they got out. A group of dirty-looking teenagers in jeans and leather had turned to stare, cigarettes hanging from their lips. Jill couldn't stop thinking about Janet Witcombe's shocking allegation that Edward had been Kate's lover.

They sat down at a scarred wooden table, across from one another. The dining room was half-full, and there was a bar in the back where several customers, male and female, were sipping pints. Jill's mind continued to race.

"Is it too late to stop at the hospital?" Jill asked. She believed the old lady's every word. Her heart lurched each time she thought about the lovers. *How had it happened? How?*

And she had to wonder, had Edward been involved in Kate's disappearance?

"Nope. Okay, Jill. Spit it out. What's on your mind?" His gaze locked with hers.

"Your mood is very good. It seems to be getting better with every passing minute," Jill remarked somewhat sourly.

"It's the air." Then he checked himself. "Maybe it's also the company."

She had been slumping, now she sat up straight as a board. Their gazes met. Alex did not look away.

Okay, Jill thought, aware of her racing heartbeat and his too-intent blue eyes. This is it. The test. Tonight they would be alone together in the same house. Would she go to JAIL, or would she pass GO? Her mind leaped ahead. To an image of herself in Alex's strong arms. And to another image, of them entwined in bed, with Alex over her, all lean hard wet muscle . . . Jill shut off her thoughts, agitated now.

He was going to make another pass at her. Jill had not a doubt. Because Alex was one hundred percent male, and he had made himself very clear.

Pass GO, she thought, realizing she was gripping the edge of the table. Stay focused on her search for the truth about Kate. Don't think about him or his body or what one wild night would be like.

"What did you mean by that comment at the nursing home? That if Edward were Kate's lover, it explains a lot?" she asked very grimly.

Alex stared. "Have you thought this through, Jill?"

"What do you mean?"

"If Kate had a child—which survived—and that child was your grandfather, fathered by Edward—then you are Edward Sheldon's great-granddaughter."

Jill stared at him, speechless.

"Of course, we don't know that Kate's child was fathered by Edward, and we don't know that that child was your grandfather." He stared at her. "I think we have to take what she said with a heavy dose of salt."

Jill remained stunned.

At that moment, their waitress appeared, setting down their teacups, saucers, and plates, smiling at Alex. Alex and Jill fell silent while she placed a platter of scones and a basket of jams in front of them, that followed by another platter of tea sandwiches. The white porcelain pot of tea was last to arrive.

While Alex poured the tea, his gaze on her, Jill picked up a cucumber sandwich and ate it, not really hungry, avoiding his eyes. Was Edward her great-grandfather? She could not digest the thought. Maybe Janet was wrong. Maybe she hadn't remembered accurately. Maybe it was better if she let this entire matter drop.

Jill was suddenly scared.

Worse, she couldn't put her finger on why—but she knew she could not let her search for Kate Gallagher go. Not yet, anyway. *Because something terrible had happened to her.*

Jill recalled KC's dream about Kate's fear. She wished KC hadn't had it. And now she was wishing that Edward hadn't been Kate's lover. How could he *not* have been involved with her disappearance?

Alex was sipping his tea.

"Would that make us cousins?" Jill asked abruptly.

"No." His vivid blue gaze locked with hers. "I'm not related to Edward at all. Anne was my great-aunt. But that would make you a distant cousin, many times removed, of Thomas and Lauren." He looked away, reaching for a scone. "Of Hal, too."

Jill froze. Her gut reaction was to be appalled, until she thought of how distant a cousin Hal might have been. "I don't know what to think."

Alex gripped her hand, hard. "Jill. We have no proof that Edward fathered your grandfather. If Kate was wild, Edward might have been one of several men—or maybe there weren't even any men at all. This is all wild hearsay and speculation."

"But she did disappear." Jill pulled her hand away.

"Yes, she did," Alex agreed somewhat gravely.

Jill stared at the plate of small tea sandwiches. Her brain felt like it was ringing—as if some heavyweight boxer had punched her one time too many. She had to face it. She already felt the truth. She had felt for some time now that Kate was her great-grandmother. She didn't just feel it, she somehow knew it, and even now, thinking about it, the hairs on her nape stood up. Oh, God. There had not been a lot of time between Kate's arrival in England and her disappearance. If Edward had been her lover, then he was the father of her child. What had happened to mother and child, dear God?

She didn't want to jump to conclusions, but if Edward was

about to marry Anne—Kate's best friend—she could only assume that he had engaged in a massive cover-up of his affair. Maybe Kate had run away out of hurt and anger, Jill thought.

Jill suddenly realized that Alex was watching her closely, a strange expression on his face. She couldn't read it, and the moment he met her gaze, it changed, becoming benign. What had she just seen in his eyes? Jill stared, pricked with unease. It had been very different from the look on his face earlier.

"Are you okay?"

"Not really." She didn't lie. Shivers swept her. Maybe she was so upset she was being paranoid. That notion was comforting. But in that moment, she thought about the split second when she had seen a vicious look in Lauren's eyes—directed at her. "Alex, I want to find out when Anne and Edward became engaged."

He absorbed that. "Well, we do know that they were not engaged in October of 1908, because that clip about Anne's birthday party would have mentioned it."

"And that was the last time Kate was seen," Jill said, at once sad and glum and confused. "I guess that means that Kate and Edward were carrying on before he was engaged, which is good news by my book." She saw his expression and added hastily, "If they were carrying on."

"I brought my Libretto. I'm happy to show you how to get on the Net and get into those archives. You might wind up searching through old files all night, Jill."

"That's okay," Jill said, pushing her plate away. "Edward didn't love her. He was using her. Otherwise he would have married Kate, not Anne."

He reached for her hand again. Jill tensed and became motionless. His hand was warm and strong. The contact didn't just feel good. There was something electric when he touched her, it made her heart flutter and lurch at the very same time. And when was the last time she had been held? Even this way?

There had been no one to hold her when Hal died. No one except KC, and Jill hadn't let her friend comfort her that way.

"You're getting too involved. Try to stay objective. Even

if she turns out to be the ancestor you are looking for, she
lived and loved a very long time ago."

Lived and loved. Jill looked up into his penetrating eyes.
Alex's choice of words often provoked her in ways she could
not identify. "I feel like I know her," she finally said. "I can't
help being involved."

"My gut tells me loud and clear that could be a big mistake. And my gut is usually right." His glance was a warning
one, but it was also brief. His tone lightened. "You done
already?"

"Yeah. I guess I wasn't as hungry as I thought."

He signaled for their check. "We might as well go on to
the hospital, because the roads get narrow between here and
the coast. Driving in the dark will slow us down even more."

Jill nodded, watching him finish his scone. Her temples
throbbed. She felt overwhelmed. But she had come to Yorkshire for a new lead, for clues, for information—and leads
certainly seemed to be popping out of the woodwork. The
problem was, the leads she now had weren't the kind of
information she had ever expected to find.

She continued to watch Alex. In the end it was fortunate
that she had let him come with her, because he had the laptop
and she would be able to stay up all night, if need be, to find
what she was looking for.

Jill froze. *The laptop.*

"What is it?" Alex asked sharply.

She stared at his handsome face without seeing him. Whoever had deleted the Gallagher files would have been a
moron not to copy them first. And neither Alex nor Thomas
fell into that category, not by a long shot.

Jill wondered if copies of those letters were filed away in
one of the folders in his Libretto.

She intended to find out.

Apparently the name Preston was hardly unknown. Although
it took twenty-five minutes to get from the hospital's front
doors into one of the hospital administrators' offices, the
moment they stepped inside, a gentleman in a suit came forward, hand extended, greeting Alex warmly.

"Mr. Preston, this is a pleasure. I do believe we met once briefly before, at a fund-raiser your uncle held in London for the hospital's research program." The administrator's name was George Wharton. The name plaque outside of his office said so.

Alex shook hands and introduced Jill. "Fortunately, I have a good memory," he said. "I attend quite a few charity events, but I do recall this one, a black tie at the Connaught."

"Your family has always been a huge supporter of this hospital. Anything I can do for you, shall be a pleasure," Wharton said, smiling.

Jill thought it was mildly interesting that the only hospital in York that had existed a century ago was supported by the Collinsworth family. On the other hand, it was the city's largest hospital, so she wasn't about to make too much of it.

Alex explained their predicament—that they were hoping to locate records from 1908.

"You are fortunate once again. We have extensive files, downstairs in the basement. I'll have someone show you down, and you can browse as you wish." Wharton did laugh nervously. "Being as the patient whose records you are looking for is long since dead, I don't have to worry about violating anyone's rights. In fact, I'll show you down myself."

They left the office, taking the elevator to the basement, Wharton and Alex chatting about the hospital's research into children's leukemia. As they stepped out into a spotless corridor, Jill said, "Dr. Wharton, has the Sheldon family always supported this hospital so extensively?"

"It's a family tradition and the earl would be the first to tell you so," Wharton said, leading them to a stainless-steel door that was not locked. He pushed it open, revealing a cavernous basement that was filled with row upon row of wall-sized file cabinets. "His father was the one who first took a serious interest in us, contributing generously to our cause and actually lifting the hospital out of near bankruptcy. Back then, it was strictly an oversized maternity ward." He smiled at Jill.

Jill managed a smile back, Alex thanked him again, and Wharton left.

"This is odd," Jill blurted. "Edward was the one who started the family tradition of supporting this hospital? Edward?"

"Jill, my family is involved in dozens of philanthropic projects. Our work is cut out for us. Let's get started."

Jill quickly walked over to the first row of cabinets. "These are alphabetized—but there are years listed on here, too," she said, staring at files labeled Williams–Woolverton, 1980–1995.

An hour later they found something. Alex had extracted a very old folder from a file cabinet and he said, "Bull's-eye. Here is a patient named Katherine Gallagher, Jill. She was admitted May 9, 1908." He paged through the contents and extended a birth certificate toward her. "Peter Gallagher, born May 10, father unknown, mother Katherine Adeline Gallagher."

Jill seized it, shaking. "But we don't know for sure that this is our Kate Gallagher—but if it is, she had a son named Peter!" Her mind was spinning. "This could be my grandfather's birth certificate. Oh, God—if only I knew for certain that he was born in York!"

"Hold your horses," he said, as calm as she was not. "She was here for three days. Attending physician, date of admission, departure, it's all here," Alex said, studying the file's contents.

"This really doesn't tell us anything," Jill almost wailed. Then she stiffened. "Alex, this is our Kate! She named her son after her deceased father!" Jill cried.

"Relax. Maybe. Here's the bill. There's got to be a copy of the receipt."

Jill tensed. "Who paid her bill?" she cried, gripping his strong, muscular arm.

He smiled at her. "That's what I like about you—you're a bright cookie." His gaze returned to the file. "Well. Here it is. Can you read that scrawl?"

Jill took the very frail, yellowed sheet of paper that listed the cost of Kate's stay as being fifty-five pounds and change. The bill was stamped Paid, and it had been signed for in the bottom right-hand corner. But the signature was not just scrawled, it was faint with age and almost illegible. She could barely make out the words. "This doesn't say Edward Sheldon, or even Viscount Braxton," she said, at once disappointed and relieved.

He peered over her shoulder, standing so closely behind her that she felt the front of his shoulder and chest against her back. "I believe the first name is Jonathan. Maybe we need a magnifying glass."

"You're right, it is Jonathan. I think the last name is Barclay," Jill said, deflating like a hot-air balloon ripped with a knife. "Damn it."

"Relax. Do you really think Edward would waltz in here and pay for the bill, then sign the receipt using his real name?"

Jill blinked at him, staring into his bottomless blue eyes. "Handwriting experts?" she breathed.

"My thinking exactly. In any case, we certainly found *something*. If this handwriting is Edward's, if he signed the receipt using the name Jonathan Barclay, we can safely assume this is our Kate."

Jill nodded, her spirits instantly lifting. "Thank you, Alex," she said. But something was nagging at her, and she couldn't quite figure out what it was. Had she heard the name Jonathan Barclay before? It seemed familiar.

"No problem." He slid his arm around her and guided her to the door. "Let's make copies and get to the house."

Jill nodded, easing away from him. Like his hand, his body was strong and warm. All lean, hard muscle. And this was not the time to be thinking about that.

But his gaze was on her, steady and searching. Jill realized there was a question in his eyes. And she damn well knew what that question was.

She knew she should look away, put up a wall, and quickly. But she didn't. For that moment, she couldn't.

The bath was steaming hot, and Jill never wanted to get out of it.

They had arrived at Stainesmore an hour ago, driving up twisting roads that were so narrow Jill knew they would have a head-on collision should another car be coming their way. The roads were enclosed by high stone walls creeping with vines and, infrequently, wildflowers, and beyond those ancient, crumbling walls, stark, barren moors seemed to stretch on endlessly to some distant point where they finally met the sky and the sea. The occasional flock of sheep could be seen grazing from time to time. Once, Jill saw a rider galloping along a distant ridge. Their ascent became steeper and steeper still. Alex had mentioned that the town of Robin Hood Bay was "that way," and he had pointed toward the coast, in a southerly direction, as his silver monster continued to climb, its engine now sounding as if it were making a vociferous protest, as if it could not withstand the rigors of the slow pace and the extreme climb.

Stainesmore belonged in a gothic novel. It certainly did not belong in the twentieth century as the millennium approached. It sat on a prominent slope of treeless land, its back to the cliffs and the sea, a towering castlelike structure of red-brown stone with an arched entryway that led into a grassy courtyard. The central roof was crenellated, and two round towers flanked the long, rectangular central portion of the building. Jill had imagined something more along the lines of a summery, whitewashed villa, and she had been slack-jawed as they had made their way to the front door, where a housekeeper and a dozen servants had appeared to greet them with curtsies, bows, and "Good day, sir. Good day, madam."

Jill sighed. The claw-footed bathtub was an antique, right down to its brass faucets. The bathroom was huge and spacious but very sparsely done, boasting little more than the ancient toilet with its rope handle, the small pedestal sink, a towel rack, and an electric heater. The floors were beige marble, though, and huge windows looked out upon the short stretch of land behind the house, containing a swimming pool and the rose gardens Edward had written his gardener about. Even while she reclined in the bath, Jill enjoyed an expansive view of the darkening gray sea and the twilight-hued sky. Jill only regretted that she did not have a glass of wine in her hand.

It occurred to her now that maybe if Hal had lived, even without the lies, she might have eventually ended the relationship first, because of the vast class and cultural differences between them.

Jill finally stood and stepped from the tub, instantly shivering, because the air was cool and she had not thought to turn on the small heater. Wrapping herself in a huge white terry-cloth robe, she imagined Alex as a boy, summering here with his cousins. Hadn't he felt very much like an outsider, as she did? She wanted to ask him what it must have been like.

A knock sounded on her bedroom door, jerking her out of her reverie.

Barefoot, still in the robe, Jill hesitated. She was certain that it was Alex, and she was immediately aware of being hot and damp from the shower, as well as being bare beneath the fluffy white robe. With some trepidation, she opened it and saw that Alex had donned his faded Levi's and the clinging yellow cashmere sweater as well as soft, scuffed loafers. His hair was damp. Obviously he'd just bathed, too.

The jeans gloved his long legs and hips, and the sweater fit his broad shoulders and muscular arms like a second skin. Jill looked away, but not before she saw his gaze slide over the fat robe she was wearing. "I'm sorry. I thought you'd be ready by now."

Jill stepped back, aware of being very alone with him on the threshold of her room in the nearly empty house. "That's okay."

"I'll be downstairs in the library. It's cozier than the living room. How does a glass of red wine sound? We keep a wine cellar and it's really well stocked."

"That sounds good," she said with a quick smile, meaning it even though she questioned her judgment in accepting such an invitation. She would focus on Kate. She would limit herself to one glass of wine, too. "Alex? Bring your laptop."

"It's a mini-notebook." He looked at her with some dismay. "You want to go on-line tonight?"

"Why not?"

His gaze veered to her mouth.

Jill was no longer smiling.

"I'll see you downstairs," he said, turning on his heel and striding down the long, bare hall.

Jill watched him go, still holding on to the door. Something was happening here, and she didn't like it. Because if she was brutally honest with herself, she would admit that she was disappointed that he hadn't tried to kiss her, touch her, and with the night falling, she was having trouble keeping her thoughts from straying to a place she was very afraid to go. She tried to tell herself that she was merely overwrought, and that it was the mystery surrounding Kate that was disturbing her, confusing her, but she'd have to be an idiot to believe her own lies.

Alex dismissed the staff and carried a tray with two glasses of a superb vintage port, two decaffeinated coffees, and two pieces of shamelessly heavy apple pie himself. Jill followed him back into the library. The room was hardly "cozy," it had high ceilings and it was at least twice the size of Jill's studio. But it was smaller than the "grand" salon with its five hundred seating areas—well, okay, there had probably been fifteen—and the dozens of faded but exquisite rugs covering the floors. Along with the fact that it was lined from floor to ceiling on three walls with books, it was rather intimate.

The fourth wall boasted a huge hearth with an outstanding and somewhat impressionistic painting hanging above that. Jill had already studied the stormy harbor scene and realized it was a Vlaminck. The furniture was old and exquisitely wrought, the fabrics elegantly, chicly faded. Jill sat down, not on the smaller of the three sofas in the room, but on the floor, her back against the worn gold damask fabric. She slipped off her Cole-Haan's and wiggled her bare toes, sighing because a half a bottle of superior wine and a few sips of port had done the trick.

"What a meal. I'm stuffed. How crass do you think it is for me to take that pie up to my room for an in-the-middle-of-the-night, I-can't-sleep snack?" she asked.

"I think that sounds like a great idea," Alex said, placing the tray carefully on the delicately carved coffee table in

front of Jill. He brought over his mini-notebook, which was
no larger than Jill's Filofax, setting it on the coffee table. Jill
stiffened. Her sense of well-being vanished.

He fooled with the modem, replacing the short cord with a
long one, which he installed in a jack. Jill watched him, saying nothing. She still wanted to find out when Anne had gotten engaged, but did she really want to snoop through Alex's
files? Did she really want to behave so shamelessly? And
what if she found the Gallagher letters there?

He booted her up. "Still game?" He smiled.

Jill met his eyes. She couldn't smile.

"Did I just ruin the evening?" he asked quietly.

He could not be a traitor to her cause. Maybe it would be
better if she did not look for the Gallagher files after all.
Then, of course she had to look. "No. Of course not. I love it
here, Alex."

He seemed surprised by her sudden change of topic. "I
guess I do too," he said after a pause. He settled down beside
her, his hands flying over the keys. "It'll take a sec or two to
get where we want to go."

He was always saying "we." Jill reached for the coffee.
She should not drink any more tonight. She was buzzed, and
they were alone. The house was huge—but his room was
right across from hers.

*There is a man . . . you must not trust him . . . if you do,
something terrible will happen . . .*

Jill could hear KC's voice as clearly as if she were speaking to her now. But KC could be wrong. She had admitted on
many occasions that while the cards did not lie, the reader
could err.

"You're into the *Trib*," he said, interrupting her thoughts.
"You can scroll each page of each issue this way," he said,
showing her which keys to use.

Jill set her coffee down and he moved aside so she could
sit in front of the Libretto. She squinted. Headlines from the
month of October 1908, jumped out at her. The month Kate
had last been seen—the month Kate must have disappeared.
"I wonder when Anne and Edward were married," she said,
and because she was so fascinated by Kate's life, it was easy

to shove her dilemma about Alex aside. For now. Besides, she could hardly search through his files with him sitting beside her.

Impulsively, she scrolled rapidly ahead, scanning pages quickly. She was aware of Alex sipping his port and watching her, even though she did not look at him. She found what she was looking for. "Alex, listen to this," she said excitedly. " 'The marriage of Anne Bensonhurst, the only surviving child of Lord Randolph Bensonhurst, and Edward Sheldon, Viscount Braxton, is to be held on Saturday, August eighteenth, 1909.' "

Jill met Alex's eyes. Her pulse raced. "I wonder if they postponed it, once Kate disappeared."

"What's the date on that?" Alex asked, digging into his slice of warm pie.

"February seventh—four months after Anne's birthday party—and Kate's disappearance," Jill said. Her gaze was already back on the small screen in front of her. "God, how do you work on this thing? It's so tiny," she muttered, scrolling as rapidly as she could through pages and pages of articles.

"With the utmost concentration," Alex said dryly.

She knew he continued to watch her, but she didn't look up, too intent on what she was doing. Jill wasn't sure how many minutes passed before she stumbled onto the wedding announcement. "They were married on August eighteenth," she said breathlessly. The article was brief and Jill read it aloud.

" 'Lady Anne Bensonhurst, the daughter of Lord Randolph Bensonhurst, was wed to Edward Sheldon, the Viscount Braxton, eldest son to the earl of Collinsworth, at St. Paul's Cathedral, yesterday at 1:00 P.M. Three hundred and fifty guests attended both the ceremony and the reception, held at the Ritz Hotel. Lord and Lady Braxton have sojourned to Marseilles for their honeymoon.' " Jill froze, her heart speeding. "Oh, God. Listen to this.

" 'Perhaps the only blight upon this lavish affair, which reputedly cost his lordship two hundred thousand pounds, is the fact that the bride's close friend, the American heiress

Katherine Gallagher, remains missing. Her disappearance was reported earlier in the year in the month of January by her mother, Mrs. Peter Gallagher of New York City.' "

Jill was silent. Then Alex touched her, lightly. "Well, they didn't postpone the wedding."

She turned to look at him. "No, they didn't." She was wide awake now. She no longer felt the effects of the wine. "I feel sick."

"You're taking this too personally," Alex said. Then, "Maybe she was pregnant, too."

Jill stared at him, and said, "Is that a joke? A bad one?"

"Not really."

"Do you think he was toying with them both?"

"He wasn't toying with Anne, Jill. She came from a premier family. She was an heiress. She was the perfect choice for a wife."

Jill stared at him, flushing with anger. "But Kate was low class, even though she was wealthy—is that your point?"

"I'm not trying to argue with you. I've lived here most of my life. Class lines still exist, and anyone who tells you otherwise is full of it."

She moved away from him and the laptop. "Kate was to Edward what I was to Hal." Then she added, "Except I don't have money, and she did."

"This is a very old, entrenched family," Alex said softly.

"Why don't you just spit it out?" Jill heard how bitter she sounded. "Hal would never have married me. Even if he had wanted to, Thomas and William would not have allowed it."

"He would have had a world war on his hands."

Jill stood. "Why do you have to always call a spade a spade?"

Alex rose slowly to his feet. He had also kicked off his shoes, Jill saw inanely. "Do you want me to lie to you? What good will that do? Isn't it better knowing the truth—so you don't make the same mistake twice?"

Jill shook her head. "Don't worry. I'm never making the same mistake again." She meant it. It was a vow that she had made to herself, one she intended to keep.

"Jill." The one word was laden with sympathy.

"I'm fine," she said. "But I think I'm going to call it a night."

"I agree." He squatted and downloaded the file. "I'll see you tomorrow, Jill."

She watched his hands flying over the keys. "What are you doing?"

"I'm filing the article for us. I've created a Gallagher folder. This file is named Anne's Wedding. Okay?" He powered off, closed the lid, and rose to his full height.

She thought about the folder; she thought about the missing letters. There would never be a better opportunity to look through his files. She started to reach for the tray.

"One of the maids will clean up in the morning, just leave it," he said. "But don't forget your pie." He smiled.

Jill took the single plate without smiling and they walked upstairs in silence. She would wait an hour, she decided, for him to fall asleep, and then she would go downstairs and see what she could find in his mini-notebook. She felt terrible, as if she were contemplating the most heinous of crimes.

They paused in front of her door; his was across the hall. Jill's shoulders had become impossibly stiff. She felt as if she were about to betray him, which was ridiculous.

He stared at her, his gaze intent, probing. Jill looked away, murmuring, "Good night."

He didn't move.

Jill's heart rate increased. Dramatically. "Oh, no," she thought, and realized her words were a whisper.

Because he was staring at her, and somehow, the angle between their bodies had lessened, becoming very acute. "Jill."

She wanted him. She was afraid.

Alex suddenly tilted up her chin and touched his mouth to hers. Their lips brushed, once, twice, three times. And Jill felt his fingers tighten, she felt his lips firm, she felt his sudden, live-wire tension.

Alex stepped back, away from her, unsmiling. "Yeah. Sleep tight," he said. And he turned. An instant later, he was inside his room, the door solidly closed.

Jill stared at the highly polished wood. She remembered to breathe. She was shaking.

Grimly—with disappointment?—she slipped into her bedroom, closing the door and leaning against it.

Her mind refused to form coherent thoughts, and Jill did not know how long she stood there, holding the plate of pie, listening to the silence of the house and the night.

She came to. He wasn't coming back, which was for the best. She set the plate down on the bureau, thinking now about her plan to break into his Libretto, feeling awful. He had just kissed her. Sweetly. If he were a liar, he would have pressed the issue, taken her to bed, there was no doubt about that.

Jill paced, glancing at the clock every few seconds, torn.

Finally her nerves snapped and she sat down. If she did not check his Libretto tonight, she might not have this opportunity again. She could not abort this damnable mission. Kate was counting on her.

Jill realized the train of her thoughts and she stiffened. Kate was dead. No one was counting on her except for herself.

She glanced at her bedside clock. It was a quarter to twelve. How long had it been since he had kissed her in the hallway? She thought maybe fifteen minutes or more had passed.

Jill kicked off her loafers and approached her door, laying her ear against it. She did not hear a thing.

She cracked it, straining to discern a sound. Again, the hall, his bedroom, the house, was absolutely silent.

Jill stole from her room and down the hall. The hall lights had been left on, and it was brightly lit. Every time a floorboard creaked her heart went wild. She kept glancing over her shoulder, but Alex did not appear.

Downstairs, she hurried through the dark house, breathless and suddenly aware of how huge it was and how empty it seemed to be. A handful of staff lived on the premises, she knew; the rest came to work daily, commuting from the town or a nearby village.

Jill started to feel as if she were being watched.

As she let herself into the library, her pulse elevated with anxiety, she told herself that was absurd. Unless, of course, ghosts were haunting the place.

She shivered, turning on one small lamp beside the sofa where she and Alex had sat on the floor. Ghosts probably did exist, but only one ghost interested her. And even so, Jill suspected she would jump out of her skin if she ever glimpsed Kate Gallagher drifting through these halls.

She settled down in front of the laptop, opening it and booting up. When the screen whirred to life, she was rewarded with a DOS prompt. That was the last thing she expected. She had assumed Windows would come on, or some kind of program with icons.

Jill stared at the blinking prompt. Then she typed in "windows," quite certain that was not going to be helpful.

The screen immediately spit back a message at her. It said, "Access denied."

Access denied?

Just what the hell did that mean? Jill stared at the message on the screen and the new prompt. She knew a few computer basics from her high school days. She typed in "Run."

"Access denied." The same message appeared.

"You need the password," Alex said from behind her.

Jill gasped, her heart dropping like a boulder, leaping to her feet. She stared at him as if he were the ghost she had just wondered about. He was standing by the library door in nothing but his jeans.

"I couldn't sleep," Jill said in a rush.

"That's pretty obvious." He slowly launched himself off of the door and came forward. He did not look at the Libretto, but at her. Only at her. "What are you doing, Jill?"

His tone wasn't friendly, and Jill froze. "What am I doing?" she echoed.

He came around the sofa. "Are you hunting Kate, or me?" he asked coldly.

Fourteen

I HAVE NO IDEA WHAT YOU'RE TALKING ABOUT," JILL SAID
tersely. She had not a doubt that her guilt was written all over
her face. Her heart continued to slam inside of her chest. "I
couldn't sleep. I thought I'd get on the Net and find the
Trib—"

"I doubt you could get on the Net, much less find the
Trib—or anything else, for that matter." His jaw was flexed.
His temples were ticking. Jill stared at him, realizing that he
was really angry.

"This isn't what you're thinking," she began nervously.

"No?" He was cold, grim. She was seeing a side of Alex
she had only witnessed once before—when they had first
met, the day she arrived in London with Hal's body. He
strode past her. The muscles in his thighs seemed to strain his
denim jeans. He shut down the laptop, closed the lid. Then he
faced her. "You know what? I don't think we should continue this discussion tonight." His eyes remained heated.

Jill could not agree more. She heard herself say, "I'm
sorry."

He detached the modem from the jack and the Libretto,
winding it up into a ball, his fingers far too efficient. He
shoved it in his front pocket, picked up the small Toshiba
machine. "Good night," he said as grimly as before.

She watched him as he crossed the library with hard
strides and left it, not bothering to close the door behind him.

Jill was shaking. She realized, too late, that Alex was not someone she wished to alienate.

She sank down on the faded gold damask sofa, her head in her hands, her heart finally slowing, a heavy weight of despondency settling over her like a grim, dark cloud. Now she would never sleep.

Not only that, she was a fool.

And then she wondered if Alex had left his laptop downstairs in order to test her.

Jill was frozen. Her mind spun. Suddenly KC's warnings were there, loud and clear. There was a man, in her path, whom she could not avoid—whom she could not trust.

The realization was searing. Alex had been unavoidable until now. Not Thomas. It was Alex who had welcomed her back to London, Alex who had helped her begin her search for the letters, Alex who was with her at Stainesmore now.

"No," Jill said aloud, trembling. The tray remained on the coffee table with Alex's piece of pie, the two port glasses, one empty, one mostly full, and two decaffeinated coffees, both ice cold by now. Jill took the port and drank it all. The burn as it settled in her stomach was welcome. Tears suddenly threatened to fill her eyes.

She lay down on the couch, flinging one hand over her shoulder. She had very few friends. And in London, her only friend was Lucinda, except that now she realized that Alex had become a friend, too, in spite of her doubts and suspicions, in spite of KC's warnings. She did not want to lose his friendship. But maybe it was better if she did.

Tomorrow. Tomorrow she would be able to think more clearly, she promised herself. Tomorrow she would figure out what to do.

And as sleep instantly overcame her, it was Alex's image that haunted her mind, not Kate's.

But not for very long.

Kate's face was vividly, achingly clear.

Her dark eyes were wide, her beautiful face so pale that her mole appeared black. Her hair cascaded freely around her shoulders but the curls were tangled, untidy. Kate stared at her with her huge eyes, unblinkingly.

Jill tossed, caught up in the dream, on some level of her subconscious knowing it was only a dream. But Kate was distressed. Her unrelenting stare was filled with . . . what? Anxiety? A plea? Fear?

Jill moaned.

Kate looked at her and began to speak.

Jill tensed. Kate was speaking urgently, her mouth moving rapidly, forming words Jill did not hear. Clearly she was more than distressed, she was frightened, pleading for something, with someone. But Jill could not hear a single word, she did not hear a single sound. Jill wanted to wake up. Something was wrong, terribly so, and she did not want to dream about it, she did not want to know.

And then Kate's face was gone. Jill was confronted with stone walls, huge blocks of gray-black stone, soaring in front of her, so close that if she reached out she could touch the slabs and feel their coarse, unhewn surface . . .

Jill touched wet, grainy dirt.

Her fingertips sank into rough earth, not stone, and she recoiled, bile filling her, wanting to step away, wanting to drop her hands, but instead, the dirt filled her palms, coarse clumps caught between her fingers, wedged between her fingernails. No, Jill thought frantically, but instead of moving away, she dug into the dirt, deeper and deeper still, the panic, the frantic urge, increasing.

No, Jill thought desperately again, I do not want to do this!

There was so much dirt! She looked down at her hands, covered with the dark brown earth, and then she saw the blood—blood everywhere . . .

Jill saw the tower then. It was a square stone structure, dilapidated and ruined, jutting out from above clusters of bent, misshapen trees, framed by a dull gray sky and a frothing sea.

I have to get out of here, Jill thought wildly. But when she tried to get up off of the bed, her fingers dug into the earth, and when she looked down, she saw the blood, and when she looked up, she saw the impenetrable stone walls . . .

The scream filled the stone chamber. Sharp, piercing, inhuman.

A death throe?

Jill jerked upright.

For one instant, as her dazed mind left the surreal dream for the actual reality of Stainesmore's library, she continued to hear the unearthly scream, echoing, resounding, around her.

It was a scream of terror and despair.

It was also filled with fury.

Jill realized her fingertips no longer dug into earth, but the fabric of the couch. Her gaze swung around swiftly, from the couch to the coffee table to the small light glowing on the side table. She was in the library, at Stainesmore. Jill realized she was trembling like a leaf.

She gulped in air. It was the worst dream she had ever had, it had been so terribly real, but it had only been that, a dream.

It had not been anything more.

But now she could see Kate's face so clearly, filled with distress, with fear. It was an expression that she was never going to forget.

"Only a dream," Jill muttered, hugging herself. Shakily she got to her feet, glancing warily around at the dark shadows of the library, but Kate Gallagher was not standing there, or at least her ghost was not, thank God. Jill glanced at her watch, realizing she was wet with sweat, and that tears streaked her face. Then she recalled KC's dream.

You became Kate.

Jill was motionless, her heart galloping again. And she was cold, chilled from the sweat that covered her body. It was only a dream. There was no point in even trying to comprehend it.

But what had KC meant?

Jill glanced at her watch. It was five in the morning. Jill knew she would never be able to go back to sleep. She would find the kitchen and make herself a cup of coffee—after a shower and a change of clothes. She was afraid to sleep—afraid of what she might dream.

Jill was reading the morning papers and sipping coffee when Alex appeared. She stiffened as he strolled into the library where she had planted herself earlier. It was only half past eight.

"Good morning," he said, clad in his Levi's and a black cableknit wool sweater. His gaze was cautious.

Jill set the newspaper down and stood. "I owe you a tremendous apology," she said nervously.

"Yeah. You do." His gaze met hers.

She scrutinized his face, staring into his eyes, trying to decide if he was trustworthy or not. His stare seemed hooded, blank. "I realize I've come to count on you. . . I don't have many friends." She stopped. She wanted to add, *But I'm afraid to trust you. Can you blame me?* She did not dare reveal exactly what she was thinking, feeling.

He was waiting for her to finish. Jill forced a smile, gave it up. "I should have asked permission to go through your files—"

He cut her off. "You don't trust me. You think I deleted those files containing Kate's letters. Don't you?"

Jill could not look away. His gaze was accusing. "I don't know what to think," she finally whispered. "I was hoping we were friends. But can you blame me for covering all bases?" She hesitated. "I didn't really expect to find those files on your laptop."

He ran a hand through his thick, short hair, appearing grim, but also rueful. "I guess I can see how, given the entire situation, it would be tough for you to trust any man."

"Thank you," Jill whispered. "I won't snoop again." And there was something there inside of her, a small place, maybe in her heart, that was relieved and stupidly pleased that they had somehow gotten past this impasse.

He regarded her. "You're a very tenacious woman," he finally said, "and it's one of the things I like about you. I don't expect you to change." He finally smiled.

It lit up his handsome face, his extraordinary blue eyes. Jill's pulse raced. He didn't quite believe her—she wasn't sure she believed her own assurances, either.

"Jill."

She met his gaze, her thoughts interrupted by the firm, commanding tone of his voice.

"You can trust me," he said. "I want to help you. We *are* friends."

Jill nodded. She wanted to believe him. But last night, his controlled anger had been far more frightening than Thomas's open displays of rage. It occurred to Jill that Thomas really was the open one; that Alex was a master at controlling—and hiding—his emotions. If he was innocent, would he have become so angry with her?

It was a horrible thought.

"Coffee warm in there?" Alex asked pleasantly, as if all were forgiven and forgotten. He was referring to the big silver pot on the coffee table in front of Jill, filled with steaming hot coffee, courtesy of the friendly kitchen staff. It was set on a silver tray with icy cold milk, a bowl of sugar, and a pitcher of fresh squeezed orange juice.

Jill wet her lips as he took her silence as a yes, pouring himself a cup of the fresh brew. His fingers were long and strong on the silver pot. And then she wondered, If he was innocent, why hadn't he offered her free run of his files? Ending her suspicions once and for all?

Jill wished she'd never had either thought. She wanted to dismiss her doubts. She could not. "Alex? May I ask you something?"

He was sipping the coffee, staring at her with his vividly blue eyes. "Shoot."

"Do you think Thomas deleted the Gallagher files?"

He lowered the cup, his gaze unwavering, but it was an instant before he spoke. "No. I do not." His voice was firm. "I think there was a power surge—a very unfortunate incident. The power was out in the apartment when I walked in, Jill. I didn't make that up."

Jill's heart beat harder than before. Had he hesitated? Had she seen a flicker in his eyes? Oh, God! The problem was, she had come to like him as a person, and she was attracted to him as a man. If only she could be objective. Why couldn't she just, blindly, trust him?

Because too much was at stake.

Jill stiffened in shock, because the voice inside of her had sounded exactly like Kate's.

"What is it, Jill? What's wrong?"

She stared at him but did not see him. What was she thinking?! She had never heard Kate speak, and she never would. There was no way she could know how the woman's voice had sounded. "I'm very tired," Jill said on a ragged breath. She pushed at her bangs again. "I fell asleep here last night and woke up at five." She decided not to tell him about the dream. It had been too disturbing, worse, it still haunted her, in a very frightening way.

"You look tired. Maybe today's a good day for a nap." He smiled, with a glance outside at the heavy, gray skies. "We're in for a lot of rain."

"Actually, I was hoping for a tour of the house and maybe the property, if it doesn't start to rain. I wouldn't mind seeing the town, too."

Now he really smiled, and it was the old Alex whom she had somehow become attached to. "I was thinking the same thing," he said. "The house tour we can do in the rain. Why don't we dress warmly and I'll take you around the property for an hour or two, and then we can grab lunch in the village," His smile flashed again. "Unless it pours. It's too steep to drive down to Robin Hood Bay and we have to leave the car and walk."

"That's fine, it sounds like fun." Jill was enthusiastic. Anything to put last night and the resulting tension behind them.

Alex had suggested they drive, being as a fine mist had begun to whisper upon the countryside. Jill had agreed, and he had forsaken his silver monster in order for them to use the house's dark green Land Rover. Rocky, barren moors stretched endlessly to the north and west of the house, as they headed south, driving parallel to the coast.

The narrow road twisted and turned as they left Stainesmore, high stone walls and hedgerows enclosing the road, making it almost impossible to see what was beyond. They were driving inland, and Jill thought it amazing how quickly the landscape changed, becoming green and verdant and dense with thick trees, grass and weeds, and wild blooms again. It was raining now, thickly.

Alex pointed out several cottages and farms, which were not visible from the road, but which small, whitewashed wooden signs with black lettering indicated. They belonged to tenants who had, for the most part, been on the estate for generations.

"How big is the estate?" Jill asked as the Land Rover dipped precariously on the rutted and, at times, unpaved road.

"About one thousand acres. It used to be larger, but a good two-thirds of it was sold off years ago," Alex said cheerfully.

Jill smiled at him, then saw, through his window, a sight that made her heart slam to a stop. "Oh, God!" she cried, seizing his arm so abruptly that the Land Rover briefly swerved to her side of the road.

"Jill!"

But Jill was staring at what she could see of a tower, a monument of black-gray stone, piercing the rain-filled sky. She began to tremble. "Stop the car. We have to get out." *This could not be happening.*

"What the hell is wrong? You look as if you have just seen a ghost," Alex said, pulling over as far to the left as he could on the narrow road. There was hardly space to do so, but the road was deserted anyway. They had not seen another vehicle in at least twenty minutes.

"Maybe I have seen a ghost," Jill said, shuddering and filled with unease. "That tower." She could not tear her gaze away. "I want to get closer. I want to go see it."

He stared at her, and Jill finally returned his gaze. "I dreamed about that tower last night," she said hoarsely. Instantly her eyes veered back to the tower. *It was exactly the same as the tower of her dreams.*

He continued to stare. "Okay. Care to elaborate?" He

flicked on the highest speed of his wipers as it had now begun to pour.

Jill folded her arms protectively around herself, aware of the alarming pace at which her heart raced. "I had this terrible dream," she said, low. "About Kate. And I saw this tower in my dream."

"I'm happy to take you there, Jill," Alex said after a pause. "But need I remind you just how many towers there are in Britain?"

She blinked at him.

"There must be hundreds, maybe thousands—just like this one."

Was he right? "Let's get out," Jill said, reaching for the door.

"Honey, I can't leave the Rover here on the road—like a sitting duck." He shifted into gear and eased forward. Jill was aware of continuing to hug herself. She craned her neck to stare over her shoulder at the tower . . . it seemed exactly the same as the one in her dream. There was no mistake about it.

A small sign on their left indicated "Coke's Way." Alex turned onto the narrow path, leaving the road behind. As they bumped over the rutted path, beneath a canopy of leafy trees, a small stone cottage came into view. It was two stories high, with a tall pitched roof and two stone chimneys. All the windows that Jill could see were boarded up.

The tower was less than a hundred yards behind it, looming up abruptly against a backdrop of wiry, twisted trees, through which glimpses of a steel gray, frothing sea could be seen. It was a ruin, but it was exactly what Jill had seen in her dream. Jill had not a doubt.

"I thought we'd gone inland," she managed through teeth that chattered. She was feeling odd, almost ill. Her emotions were so jumbled and ragged, even raw, that it was hard to pinpoint what she was feeling. She did know that she was upset, uneasy, dismayed.

"We did, but there's a small bay here. Are you cold?" Alex asked with evident concern as he halted the Land Rover in front of the cottage.

"It's no big deal," Jill murmured, already pushing open her door. Behind her, as she started forward, not toward the cottage but toward the tower, she heard the engine die. She was wearing an anorak and a baseball cap, and she did not pull up her hood. The rain continued to fall. The going was rough underfoot. Stones cropped up through the wild overgrown grass everywhere. Bushes also appeared haphazardly, which she had to slap at or detour around. Alex fell into step beside her.

"Jill," he said as they trudged toward the stone ruin, "undoubtedly you've seen towers like this before. What you are suggesting is almost impossible."

Jill didn't bother to argue with him. She was positive that she had dreamed of this tower before she had ever seen it. She had to call KC the moment she got back to the house.

Jill's trembling increased when they finally paused in front of the structure, which was four or five stories high. The tower had no roof, she realized, and from the very low stone formations around it, she realized it had once been part of a larger building.

"There was a keep here, one I believe dating back to Norman times," Alex said. "I'd like to glamorize the situation and tell you it got bombed during World War Two, but it just fell apart over the years. As a kid, I played here with my cousins. Nothing's changed."

Jill was aware that he kept glancing at her the entire time they crossed the field behind the cottage. Now she looked at him. "Are we still on Collinsworth property?"

"Yeah. This manor belongs to the estate."

Jill nodded, swallowing, her mouth dry. She did not feel surprised by that bit of information. She walked over a pile of stones and around the side of the tower. All four walls were intact. The windows were arrow slits. But the space where there had once been a door was a gaping hole.

Jill walked inside. Instantly the too-sweet smell of the earthen floor assailed her. The air changed. It was oddly airless inside, and it was also very damp and very cold. Breathless, her pulse pounding uncomfortably, Jill touched a hard slab of stone. It was rough and unhewn beneath her palm.

She stared at it. The feeling of déjà vu was acute. She had dreamed of this moment last night, but in her dream, there had been terror and desperation. . . and there had been Kate.

"What are you doing?"

Alex's voice sounded far away. Jill could see Kate again, her face strained and white, her dark eyes black and huge, and then she could hear her . . . *So much at stake* . . .

Jill inhaled, closing her eyes, feeling dizzy. She wanted to throw up.

Instantly Alex gripped her arm from behind, supporting her. She leaned gratefully against him. "Are you sick?"

She could not answer. When the dizziness had passed, Kate's face remained vividly etched on her mind, and now it was apparent that her eyes were begging Jill for help. She could almost hear her again, Help me, Help me, please . . . But Jill thought she was now imagining her voice—and maybe she was imagining everything.

The stone walls of the keep suddenly seemed to move. They leaned inward, looming over her, as if closing in upon her.

Jill shook her head to clear her vision. She was hallucinating because the dream had upset her so terribly and she was severely exhausted.

Jill pulled free of Alex's grasp, not even aware of his presence, and she squatted, touching the wet earthen floor. The earth was coarse and grainy and it filled her palms. She had felt this same wet, pebbly earth before—last night. Abruptly Jill stood. She was afraid to look down and open her hands, terribly afraid, but she did.

There was no blood.

She stared at her dirty hands, waiting for blood to cover them.

Instead, she saw Kate, panting, panic-stricken, covered with dirt and blood, her long hair wild and snarled, falling around her shoulders and down her back. And then she had screamed . . .

"I can't breathe," Jill suddenly cried, and before Alex could react, she had rushed past him, out into the clean air and the pounding rain.

She stood outside, her face uplifted to the rain, holding her hands out, letting the rain wash them clean, shivering uncontrollably.

What was happening? It had only been a wacky dream!

But her heart was telling her otherwise. Something terrible had happened to Kate. And maybe it had happened right here.

Jill realized that tears had fallen down her cheeks, mingling with the rain.

And suddenly KC's haunting words came to mind. *And Kate became you . . .*

It was a flash of insight, like a premonition. Kate hadn't just disappeared, a terrible tragedy had befallen her—and the same terrible tragedy was waiting to happen to Jill.

"Jill?" His hand closed firmly on her upper arm.

Jill flinched at his touch. She faced him without seeing him. In front of her was Kate, dirty, bloody, haggard, desperate. It was Kate gripping her arm. It was Kate who was so afraid, Kate who was in jeopardy . . .

"Jill." His tone was like the lash of a whip.

Only a dream, Jill chanted silently, but she was still sick to her stomach. She became aware of Alex shaking her. She inhaled deeply. Thànk God he could not see that she had started to cry. She finally looked at him and recoiled, because he was staring at her with such purposeful scrutiny. She did not want to share this with him, not yet, and maybe not ever.

She pulled free of his grip, still breathing deeply. Her trembling had finally lessened, she could breathe again, and looking at the walls of the tower, they appeared rock solid and absolutely motionless.

"Hey. What happened in there?"

She hadn't heard him come up behind her, and his voice was incredibly gentle and kind. Jill's heart turned over with a deep, deep need, and she realized she was exhausted and very, very vulnerable right now. She faced him slowly. What would he do, she wondered, if she walked up to him and leaned against him, laying her head on his shoulder? "I can't talk about it just yet."

"Okay." He hesitated, his penetrating gaze on hers. "Let's get out of the rain."

Jill nodded and followed him back toward the car.

"You know, I've read about people having bizarre and very strong reactions to places they've never been to before—like you've just had."

Jill stumbled. "What?" Her unease grew.

"You turned so white in there I thought you were going to faint." He was regarding her closely as they came abreast of the side of the cottage. "You seemed to be in a trance. Where were you, Jill?"

She shook her head. But she had been in a trance—or some kind of altered state.

"I was talking to you. You didn't even hear me." He stared. "You were far away. God only knows where."

Jill thought about her answer. "The tower made me feel ill," she confessed. "And it also frightened me. I told you, I dreamed about it last night." She hesitated. "I did hear you." She slowly lifted her gaze to his. Their gazes locked. "But your voice sounded far away."

A long moment seemed to pass. "Maybe we should let our hunt for Kate go for a bit. You've been through a lot recently. You'll make yourself sick—"

"No!" Her cry was sharp and loud. Even though she was afraid now, of what might happen next, of what she might find, she could not abandon her search for the truth now. Something terrible had happened to Kate. Jill felt honor-bound to expose what that something was. She realized, with a start, that she wanted justice. Kate deserved no less.

"All right. If you won't quit, you've still got my support. Want to go? It's a bit early for lunch, but we can drive around some more."

Jill didn't move. They were out of the rain now, standing on the porch behind the cottage. She looked around, at the house. He had called Coke's Way a manor. "Who used to live here, Alex?" she asked slowly.

"No one's lived here since I first came to Yorkshire when I was seven or eight. I don't know if anyone's been here since the last war."

"Didn't you call this a manor a few minutes ago?"

"It was a manor house, but you'd have to ask Thomas or

Lauren the details. Or maybe they'd know more in the village." He studied her. "What are you getting at?"

Jill was staring at the boarded-up windows on the back side of the house where they stood. Her gaze drifted upward. The windows were not all boarded up on the second floor.

"Now what's going on in that creative mind of yours?" he pressed.

She turned and realized he was smiling. "Kate stayed in a manor not far from Robin Hood Bay. Didn't we just pass a sign for Robin Hood Bay a few minutes ago?"

He was silent. "We did. It's less than three miles from here, directly to the east. There are two other old manors around here," he added. Then he sighed. "You want to go inside." It was not a question.

Jill nodded but she did not smile. Kate and Edward had been lovers. She did not have proof, only an old lady's faint recollections based on hearsay, but she believed it with all of her heart. Where better for Edward to stash his pregnant mistress than in some secluded cottage on his own property?

They walked around to the front of the cottage. While Alex went to the Land Rover to get tools to pry off the two boards nailed in an X across the door, Jill tried to peer into a window. She could make out nothing but furniture covered in cloths and shadows. She walked around the side of the house.

She discovered a door, undoubtedly leading to the kitchen, and it wasn't boarded up. But a padlock was on the door, hanging there with a thick, rusty chain. Jill grabbed the chain and tugged. It was not going to break apart in her hands.

Jill suddenly stopped what she was doing, chills sweeping over her. She could hear Alex in front of the house, prying the plywood off of the front door. The hairs on her nape felt as if they were prickling. She almost felt as if she were being watched.

Jill dropped the padlock, stepping away from the side door. She glanced around, at the overgrown lawn, the few trees in the yard, the stone wall that abutted the road. She did not see anyone, but the odd feeling remained.

If anything, it grew stronger.

As if someone were spying upon them—upon her.

Jill decided to return to the front of the house, where Alex was. She began to move away, hurrying now, glancing over her shoulder, when she tripped.

She looked down. It was only the trapdoor of a root cellar, so overgrown with grass and weeds that it was hardly visible.

Almost running, she rushed around the house as Alex pulled the last piece of plywood from the front door. "Just in time," he said merrily. Then he stared. "What's wrong now?"

"Nothing." She forced a smile, breathless, her pulse pounding. She was not going to tell Alex she had felt a presence lurking about, in the yard, perhaps, or the woods. He already questioned her judgment, he would think her a certifiable nut.

Jill told herself that if she had not been imagining things, it had probably just been a village teenager with nothing better to do than loiter and eavesdrop.

Alex twisted the heavy brass knob. It turned readily and the door swung open. Jill hurried over, peering past him.

A small parlor greeted her view, the furnishings covered in faded sheets, as she had seen before from the window. There was a stone hearth in the parlor as well. They entered, almost cautiously. The floors were dark oak. A stairwell led to the upstairs directly in front of them.

Alex sniffed the air. "Odd," he said.

Jill did not relax. She was far more tense now than before. Maybe coming to Coke's Way, maybe exploring the tower, had been a mistake. "What's odd?" she asked. She did not smell anything unusual.

"Nothing," he said with a shake of his head.

Jill walked cautiously past him, into the parlor. Only the couch and chairs had been covered. A long, not particularly exciting side table was against one wall. It was empty except for a very outdated lamp that might have been gas-lit and some old, faded hardcover books. No letters were even visible on their fabric bindings.

Alex walked past her, to the table. He picked up a book,

turning it over, opening it. "A Henry James novel," he mused. "*Washington Square.*" He flipped to a front page. "It's a first edition."

Jill was seized with excitement. She hurried to him. "I wonder if Kate read that book? Is there an inscription? Anything?"

"No." He handed it to her. His gaze was piercing. "Don't jump ahead of the game."

She decided not to offer a rebuttal. Kate had stayed here. Either that, or she had stayed in the tower.

Jill had never been more certain of anything.

Alex walked past her into a small kitchen. Jill was now inspecting the other book, which was by Thomas Melville. Then she heard Alex exclaim from the kitchen. "Christ!"

She rushed to the doorway and found him standing in the center of the poorly illuminated room, with stone floors, wooden rafters, and a large brick fireplace at one end. Then she realized why he had cried out.

There was a box of Kellogg's Corn Flakes on the wooden counter. Beside it was a container of instant coffee. Some plates and silverware were in a rubber drying rack beside the sink.

Alex faced her. "This place didn't smell as if it had been closed up for years and years. Look at this! Someone was here—recently." He picked up the cereal box and dumped some cereal into his hand. "But not that recently. This cereal's past its prime."

"Maybe it was a homeless person," Jill suggested, quite certain it was not.

"How did he get in?" Alex returned, looking under the sink. Jill realized he was inspecting the garbage—but it had been emptied.

"There's a side door, but it's padlocked," Jill told him. "Maybe someone has the key."

"Or a homeless person could have used one of the windows. We'll check when we leave."

Jill thought about the upstairs windows on the second floor of the left side of the house—which were not boarded up. "Let's go upstairs."

They left the kitchen, traversed the parlor, Alex pausing to glance at the hearth. "Charred kindling," he announced. "And ashes." He rose to his full height. "Someone made themselves right at home. I'll check to see if we leased this place out to some oddball recently."

They walked upstairs in silence, Jill preceding Alex now. She did not pause, going to the end of the corridor. "Do you know something that I don't know?" Alex asked from behind her.

"Didn't you notice the windows on this side of the house?" Jill returned. The last door was open. The other two doors they had just passed had been closed.

Uncertain of what to expect, Jill paused on the bedroom's threshold. A single bed with four low posters was in the center of the room. A blue quilt had been pulled up over white cotton sheets. An electric lamp was on the bedside table. A glass ashtray was beside the lamp and there was an electric heater on the floor.

Jill's glance swung around. There was a bureau on the facing wall with a mirror on top of it. While the bureau and mirror, like the bed, dated back perhaps a century, if not more, the items on top of the bureau, like the sheets and quilt and heater, did not.

Jill saw a pile of magazines. Her heart stopped. The top one was *Photography Today* and she recognized it immediately.

"Hal stayed here," Alex said from behind her. He, too, had seen the magazines. "I just peeked in the bathroom. There're towels, soap, shaving cream, a razor."

Jill could not move. Hal had stayed here, perhaps just before she, Jill, had met him. And this place was connected to Kate. Why had Hal stayed here? Or was the question now absurd?

He had stayed here because of Kate. Jill felt it.

She sat down on the bed, nauseous and shaken. Could she handle the truth? Could she handle more discoveries about the man she had once, completely, loved?

What if Hal had been with her because she was Kate's great-granddaughter?

Alex had moved past her and opened up the bureau drawers. They were empty. He then sorted through the magazines, his hands stilling. And Jill saw that a manila envelope lay beneath the stack.

A feeling of overwhelming dread settled over her and she stiffened, hands clasped tightly in her lap, waiting for the next blow.

As Alex opened the envelope, he pulled out a series of eight-by-ten glossies. Even from a distance, Jill could tell they were black-and-white. She did not have to see them to know that they were Hal's.

He stared at the top one, not saying a word. Jill grew concerned. His hands seemed to tremble, and a slight pink color had crept along his high cheekbones.

He slipped it beneath the others, stared at the second one, then quickly went through the dozen or so photographs.

"What is it?" Jill was standing. She hadn't been aware of rising to her feet. Her voice had sounded like a croak.

He faced her. "Here." He shoved the stack at her.

Jill took one look at the photo, instantly recognizing Hal's work, and in the next instant, she almost fainted, because she was staring at Kate, naked and so very beautiful, curled up in a plush upholstered chair. The pose was so tasteful that the photograph could have been in *Vogue* magazine. Neither her nipples nor her pubis was visible, but she was rampant femininity and sensuality rolled into one, her breasts spilling over her folded arms, her narrow waist giving way to a lush hip and curved thighs. Her head was lolling back, and there was such a suggestive and dreamy look in her eyes that it was clear that she was in love with the photographer.

But Hal could not have photographed Kate.

Instantly Jill realized she was looking at *herself*, not at Kate.

She recalled the shoot immediately, her hands shaking, and it felt as though her cheeks had erupted into fire.

She stared at herself. She did not really look this way— Hal had softened the angles of her body and her face with his skillful manipulation of light and shadow. God, for one instant, one terrifying instant, she had thought she was looking at Kate.

Her hands shaking more than before, she flipped through. The other shots were more revealing—in one she was standing, facing the camera almost but not quite directly, pushing back her hair with one hand, sunlight streaming onto one side of her body from an open window. In this shot she did not look like Kate at all—she was all lean, toned muscle, a dancer with a dancer's body. Jill grimaced and held the stack of glossies to her chest.

Her heart was pounding. She managed to meet Alex's gaze.

He did not smile. "Well, Hal was very talented—but we already knew that."

What could she say? "Yes." Then, "You're blushing." She tried to keep her tone casual. She knew she failed. "You've seen naked women before."

"Not you." Their gazes locked.

Jill stood, retrieved the envelope, shoved the photos inside, and laid it back on the bureau.

"Did you model for him often?"

Jill met his eyes again. He had tried to sound casual and he had also failed. Somehow the air had thickened in the room. "Sometimes. Actually, yes. But not always nude."

"You look great, actually," Alex said, his gaze unwavering.

Jill couldn't look away. It was a stupidly male comment, but she could not chastise him. She could not even respond. Her mind had gone blank, her feelings numb.

"Well," Alex said, "I guess you'd better keep these." He picked up the manila envelope and handed it to her. "How about lunch? I don't really know what we were looking for, but we certainly found out something." Without waiting for her, he strode to the door and through it.

Jill stared after him. It was a long moment before she could move; she could only think. *Hal had been in love with Kate.* She was certain of it.

Jill sloshed through shallow puddles in the park behind Stainesmore. Her mind refused to quit. She almost did not know what to do with herself.

Hal had photographed her in such a way that she had looked exactly like Kate—her face appearing rounder, her body more lush, and her hair, pushed untidily up, had given the illusion that it was long and curly. Oh, God.

The pieces of the puzzle were falling together—and Jill did not like it one bit.

Hal, Kate, herself. Clearly, amazingly, the three of them formed some kind of time-crossed lover's triangle. Maybe Hal had even tracked her down because of Kate. It was a horrid notion.

And Jill couldn't even begin to speculate on how Marisa fit in. But she felt sorrier for her now than she had before. Loving Hal had not been easy for either of them, apparently.

There was a small stabbing pain below her left breast. At least Alex had not noticed the similarity. She didn't know why this small fact relieved her, but it did.

She had been walking for a long time, taking small bites out of a granola bar that she had found in her pocket. The rain had finally ceased, but a thick mist hung over the grounds, making it hard to see. Jill paused, looking back over her shoulder the way she had come. She was stunned to find that she could not even see a turret or chimney of the house.

She was about to go back, but something made her glance around. The mist swirled. It lifted slightly. Jill made out the faint outlines of a chapel perhaps a hundred yards to her right.

She squinted. It must be the very same chapel she had noticed when Alex had driven her back from Coke's Way a few hours ago. She was disoriented—she had no sense of direction—but the small chapel had to be on the other side of the road, which Jill could not see.

Not that it mattered. She should go back before she got lost.

The mist continued to swirl, and before Jill could turn, she saw several headstones shimmering in the wet fog directly ahead of her. She had somehow stumbled across a cemetery.

The cemetery did not interest her, especially as it was getting darker out. But she wondered if it belonged to the family, or to the surrounding villages. Jill walked over to the closest granite stone and read the name Martha Watts Benson upon it. The dates for this particular soul were given as February 11, 1901–May 1, 1954. Well, that answered that question, she thought.

Jill turned to go, intending to head back to Stainesmore, hoping that she would not get lost. That possibility seemed distinct now, because Jill had no markers to orient herself with. Damn it, she thought.

She glanced at the old stone chapel, which she could barely make out, and tried to remember just where it had been in comparison to the house. She hoped it had been directly south of the family's summer home.

Jill started decisively forward. A moment later her foot connected with something solid and she went down with a thud.

"Ow!" Something hard—a stone—dug into her hip. She rolled away from the object, sitting in the soaking wet grass, beginning to feel the cold, thinking about the black and blue mark she would undoubtedly have. Then she looked at the stone she had tripped on.

It was overgrown with weeds, but if she did not mistake her guess, it was a small and unobtrusive headstone.

God. She'd fallen over a grave! Wasn't that bad luck or something?

Jill was about to get up. Her teeth were chattering now. Instead—and later she would have no explanation for her behavior—she crawled forward, pulling the weeds off of the small marker, which was no more than a foot and a half high.

The stone was gray-black. Like the slabs of stone from the tower.

Chills swept Jill, but then, she was wet and freezing, and it had started to drizzle again.

As she pulled the weeds off, her fingers brushed indentations in the slab—the stone was engraved. Jill crept closer. Her breath got stuck somewhere in her chest.

On all fours, she froze. Jill stared at the words swimming before her eyes, her heart careening with sickening force.

"Katherine Adeline Gallagher," it said. "June 10, 1890–January 12, 1909."

Part Three

The Tower

Fifteen

JILL STARED AT THE HEADSTONE IN SHOCK. THEN SHE GRIPPED it, the stone feeling as if it were ripping apart the flesh on her fingertips, unable to tear her gaze away from the engraved date of death—January 12, 1909. She could barely breathe; she was panting, unable to consume enough air into her severely constricted lungs.

Kate had not merely disappeared in 1908, she had died shortly after, for here was the glaring proof.

Jill suddenly sat back on her knees, in front of the headstone, closing her eyes, squeezing back hot tears. Kate, so young, so beautiful, so vibrantly alive, had died at the age of eighteen. Jill should not be surprised. She'd had an awful, dreadful feeling for some time now, especially since last night, that something terrible had happened to her. And she had been right.

What had happened? And why?

Jill choked on a sob, shaking uncontrollably. And her own image was there in her mind—but as Hal had photographed her, not as she actually was. Lush, voluptuous, like Kate.

And Kate became you . . .

Jill refused to dwell on KC's strange words. But damn it, she and Kate looked alike, and Jill was never going to forget her overwhelming and bizarre reaction to the tower. Jill was afraid.

She wiped her eyes. Hal hadn't died telling her that he loved her, he had died telling Jill that he loved Kate. It was even more difficult to breathe now. The truth was glaring, and it was unavoidable.

They had met on the subway. Or so Jill had once thought. But Lauren had insisted that Hal had met her at her club. Had he watched her there, singling her out because she looked like Kate? Had he singled her out because he knew that she was Kate's great-granddaughter?

Of course he had.

Jill did not want to cry. She had thought the tearful outbursts long since finished, her tears all used up. But they flowed freely now. She cried in silence for her other self, the Jill who no longer existed, the young woman who had naively, completely loved and trusted a very confused and troubled man.

"Jill? What is it?"

Jill recognized Alex's voice instantly as he hurried to her, his boots making a loud squishy sound in the soaking grass. She did not want him to see her like this. He would not understand; he'd think she was crying over Hal. She quickly rubbed her eyes.

He lifted her to her feet and turned her around and pulled her into his arms.

Jill did not move. She could not move. Not just because she was stunned, but because he felt very safe, very right.

She did not know how long she remained there in his embrace, but she forgot about the headstone and Kate. He was cupping the back of her head, over her baseball cap, with one large hand. It was extremely comforting, the way a mother might cup the soft, warm head of her infant.

But they both knew she was no child. His hand slid slowly down, to the bare nape of her neck. The contact was electric. And in that moment, she became aware of standing head to toe with him, of being pressed up against the length of his lean, muscular body. For another heartbeat, she remained motionless, while her mind came to life. I want this, she thought. I want him.

Reluctantly, she stepped back, away.

His gaze swept her eyes and her face, searchingly.

For one moment, she did not look away; she could not.

Then she turned and pointed, her hand trembling slightly. "Look."

He followed her gaze. He was holding a penlight in his hand, and he moved past her, squatted and shone the light on the grave. He was silent.

Twilight was falling. The drizzle had again stopped, leaving nothing but thick fog and the darkening mauve-blackened night in its place. Jill realized she was soaked to the bone. Her teeth began to chatter. Alex rose to his full height. "Holy Toledo," he said very quietly.

Jill couldn't help it, the statement was so absurd that she burst into what sounded distinctly like hysterical laughter.

He didn't smile, his gaze roaming her features, one by one. "Well, there goes your theory that Kate Gallagher ran off with someone to live happily ever after."

Jill nodded, shivering.

Suddenly Alex pulled off his own car coat, a heavy, wool-lined distressed leather affair, and he slipped it over her soaking anorak. "You'll catch pneumonia," he said. He slid his arm around her, as if he did not think her capable of making it back to the house without his support. They started across the field.

"She died," Jill chattered, their hips brushing and bumping. "And someone knew the exact date. Someone knew it and buried her, Alex. He buried her here, near Stainesmore. We have to find out what happened, and who did it!"

He did not answer. But he pulled her closer against his body as Jill began to shake uncontrollably. Kate, Hal, Marisa, Alex . . . the dynamics, the turbulence around her, was overwhelming.

"I didn't tell you about the dream," Jill said hoarsely, glancing up at his perfect profile. "Kate was in terror, imprisoned somewhere, maybe in that tower, and there was dirt all over her, under her fingernails, and there was so much blood. I *saw* her, Alex."

He started; Jill felt it. "It was just a dream." His tone was sharp. "I'm worried about you. We need to cease this quest for a few days. You must rest, Jill, before you come down with the bloody plague."

Jill's temples suddenly throbbed as she looked at him, startled by his use of such English language—and dated English language at that. "Tomorrow night we're going back to London. We can't let this go, not yet. We need to search Stainesmore for more evidence, more clues, and maybe go back to the manor and search there, too. Do you think there might be some records at the chapel? Surely they would keep records about who is buried in their cemetery?"

He regarded her as they stumbled across the soggy parkland. "What do you hope to gain?" he finally asked softly.

Jill suddenly pulled away from him, staring at him, incredulous. "What kind of question is that! She was my great-grandmother and someone murdered her!"

"We don't know that she was your great-grandmother and we don't know that she was murdered." His eyes flashed.

"Are you turning against me, now?" Jill began to tremble again, with renewed vigor. She did not want to contemplate her suspicions about Alex now. It was more than she could handle.

He stared. "I would never turn against you," he finally said. He cursed, running a hand through his hair. "What do you want, Jill? How do you want this to end up?"

"I want to know the truth. I want to know what happened to Kate, and why it happened. And what about her child, Peter—who might be my own grandfather? He didn't die. What happened to him?" Jill paused. "If your family is involved, so be it. Then there will be lots of juicy gossip in the tabloids for a week or so. They can handle it." She was bitter.

"My aunt and uncle have just lost their son," Alex said harshly. "They don't need any more unpleasantness in their lives. Not now."

She stared at him. "So you are worried that it will be something affecting the family—that it will be unpleasant?" Jill finally pressed.

He hesitated. "How could I not be worried? They're very old, they've just lost Hal. Aunt Margaret's heart is bothering her. My uncle has aged twenty years in four weeks." His tone had risen. "*I don't want them hurt.*"

Jill stared. She had never seen Alex this emotional before. Or this firm, this unyielding. It hit her hard, then, that he would never yield on this point; that his loyalty to the Sheldons was undying—that it was written in stone.

"Jill," he said, more softly, with renewed composure, "no matter what happened to Kate, she died a long time ago, and no one is going to pay for the crime—if there was a crime. I don't want to see my aunt and uncle hurt. They've suffered enough—and I know you agree with me at least on that. Let's drop this for a week or two. Especially before you become so obsessed there's no reasoning with you at all."

"I'm not obsessed," Jill said, perturbed. How far would Alex go in order to protect the Collinsworth family? He was the outsider who had always wanted in. He was "in" now. Didn't he have a lot more motivation than Thomas ever would?

"I think you're obsessed and it's damned convenient, too. Instead of crying into your pillow every night over Hal and all that he did to you, you've got this bone to chew on," Alex said, not quite calmly.

Jill couldn't respond at first. Of course Alex would feel the need to champion and defend his family's honor. Wouldn't she be as stubbornly, as fiercely loyal to her own family, if she suddenly discovered that she had one?

But she did have a family. Kate Gallagher was her family—and Kate needed her now.

Jill stumbled, bumping into Alex, trying to remind herself that Kate was dead and in spite of her gut feelings, there was no substantial proof that Kate was her great-grandmother. That it wasn't the same, not at all.

"I'm not letting this go, Alex," Jill finally said. "I can't. And it's unfair for you to want me to, especially now, when I'm making such headway—when there's so much at stake." She turned her back on him and marched in the direction they had been going. It was dark out, but the many yellow lights of the house now winked and danced through the swirling fog, beckoning her, an eerie beacon light guiding her back to Hal's home.

"Just what is at stake, Jill?" Alex called after her.

"The truth," she flung over her shoulder. She did not stop, and he made no effort to catch up to her.

A few hours later, Jill sat on the side of her bed, staring at the electric heater someone had turned on for her, having put on gray sweats and a white T-shirt, her standard wear for sleeping in cool weather. She did not want to go to sleep, even though she was exhausted. She did not think she had ever been more tired, in fact. But she was afraid to dream about Kate.

She and Alex had had a quiet dinner, each of them absorbed in their own thoughts. They'd drained a bottle of fabulous red wine—a 1982 Château Margaux—before their first course had even arrived. The tension that had arisen between them earlier that day—or perhaps even days ago—had not been dissipated by the effects of the alcohol. If anything, it had increased. The silence had become heavy, awkward. Alex had then opened a 1961 Lafite. Jill had never in her life tasted such an intense yet velvety smooth wine. They had finished that bottle, too, again hardly exchanging more than a word or two.

Jill had found herself wondering about Alex's private life—something she should have no interest in. They had both refused dessert, and had sipped decaffeinated espresso in more silence before saying good night and going their separate ways.

She had expected him to make a pass at her; to kiss her at her door. He hadn't. Jill had only been partly relieved. She found his behavior more than odd, it was highly inconsistent. She could not figure him out. Worse, there was no mistaking her own disappointment.

Jill gave it up. Instead, she concentrated on the fact that somehow Hal had led her here to this place in time—his family home in northern Yorkshire, with Alex, in the spring of 1999, searching for the truth about Kate. She had died shortly after her disappearance in October of 1908. Poor, poor Kate. The questions had haunted her since she'd found Kate's grave—what had happened? Why had it happened? And who was responsible for Kate's death?

She had only been eighteen, so it was logical to assume that she had been murdered. Recalling her terror and the way she had been pleading with someone in her dream, Jill felt sick and shaken. Had she been begging for her life?

Had Edward killed her?

It was the most horrible of thoughts, and Jill knew she should not speculate, not yet, it was too soon and it was hardly fair, in fact, it was monstrous.

Jill could not imagine Kate demurely accepting the position of mistress. Jill felt that she knew Kate. She had been a woman of passion and courage. She would have fought for her love. She would never have accepted Edward turning to another woman.

And that woman had been her dearest friend.

Jill was sick. The betrayal of Edward and Anne must have been monumental—if Kate had ever learned of it. Jill hoped she'd remained oblivious.

And Jill could not help identifying with Kate. She had been an outsider, no matter that she was an heiress, while Anne had been the perfect, suitable choice for a bride. Jill was furious at the thought.

Her determination had never been stronger. Jill reminded herself that she needed proof that Edward had been her lover, no matter that she was certain that he had been just that. She needed more than the mere recollections of Janet Witcombe—as told to her by Anne. She needed hard evidence. As soon as she returned to London, she would get a copy of Edward Collinsworth's handwriting, and have it compared to Jonathan Barclay's signature. It would be a coup if their handwriting matched.

Barclay. The name bothered her again. Hadn't she heard it, or come across it, somewhere, recently?

Jill wished she had a sleeping pill. Or another drink. Even though she'd kept up with Alex glass for glass, which meant she'd consumed an entire bottle of red wine herself, her mind continued to race, and she was still afraid of another nightmare.

She stood, paced to her door, cracked it. Alex's closed door faced her. Was he asleep?

She did not move, remembering the way he had pulled her into his arms and held her at Kate's grave. She wanted that recollection as much as she had wanted her recent, earlier speculations about his personal life.

She thought about the expression on his face when he'd looked at the nude photographs Hal had taken of her. What had that intense gaze, that blush, meant?

Jill slipped into the hall. She couldn't help glancing at Alex's closed door as she passed it. She heard no sounds coming from the other side, for he was probably asleep by now. But then, he was not trying to unearth the truth about one of his ancestors who had mysteriously disappeared and died at the age of eighteen.

Jill went downstairs. The hall was lit, as were the stairs, but the ground floor was mostly dark and filled with flickering shadows. She asssumed that everyone in the house was asleep.

Jill approached the library. Her strides faltered. The door was open, lights were on.

She saw Alex sitting on one of the sofas, sprawled out, a glass of brandy in his hand. He was staring at the fireplace, his back to her. He had not made a fire.

His head turned. "You, too?" He was wry. His mouth quirked very slightly. But his blue eyes were questioning.

Jill wet her lips. Her pulse seemed to have increased. She had already folded her arms beneath her breasts. "I'm afraid to sleep."

He accepted that, she saw it in his eyes. He stood, went to the sideboard that served as a bar, and poured her a brandy. Jill accepted it.

"Why are you afraid?" he asked after she had taken a long, heated sip.

"I don't want to dream about Kate in terror and begging for her life to be spared."

His jaw flexed. "Is that what you think you dreamed last night?"

She nodded.

"That would make you psychic, wouldn't it?"

"Yes," Jill whispered. "I have to call KC and ask her what this means. God, I'm exhausted. But my mind won't stop."

"You're overtired—and overwhelmed," Alex said flatly. He was holding his own brandy glass, and Jill noticed his knuckles whitening.

Jill thought about how easy it would be to step forward and lay her head in the crook where his neck met his shoulder. It would be so nice to be held by him again.

Then she realized she was only lying to herself. And not very convincingly at that. She wanted more than an embrace, even if she could not trust him entirely.

Jill met his gaze. Something darkened in his eyes. He turned away, moving himself back to the couch, where he sat down, his back to her.

He knows, Jill thought, trembling. He knows, but now he's the one distancing himself from me. Jill couldn't understand why.

Forcing herself to take a few deep, even breaths, she walked around the side of the sofa and sat down. He did not speak. She sipped and finally said, "Do you want to be alone?"

"No. That's okay." His smile was forced and it failed.

Jill studied her glass.

"Are you okay?"

She met his gaze, and saw that his blue eyes were trained upon her. "Not really."

"It's been a tough day."

"Yes." Jill stared at her brandy. That was an understatement. "The photographs," she said on a breath.

He was staring at his drink, perhaps avoiding her eyes. "What about them?"

She regarded him. "In that first one, I looked just like Kate."

"I saw that."

She started, her drink sloshing over the rim. "You did? You didn't say anything."

"I hadn't realized you'd noticed." His gaze slipped from her face to her bare arms, to her hands; then it slid away.

Jill did not know what such a glance meant. Her T-shirt was sleeveless; it was hardly a big deal.

Alex shifted in his seat. "What does that mean to you?" he finally said, his tone filled with caution.

She set her glass down. "Isn't it obvious?"

"No. It's not obvious," he returned very slowly.

"Don't you remember that his last dying words to me were . . ." She stopped. Their gazes locked. "I love you . . . Kate."

"You misheard." There was no hesitation. His tone was flat.

"I didn't mishear," Jill whispered, still holding his regard.

His hand gripped her shoulder. His eyes blazed. "What are you saying? That Hal mistook you for a woman who died in 1909?"

Suddenly the space between them had narrowed to mere inches. She did not know who had moved closer, her or him. And he was angry. Why? And was he angry with her or with Hal? Jill didn't dare ask.

He dropped his hand. Suddenly he looked away, cursing. "I told you once before, Hal was an escapist," he said roughly. "He knew who you were."

Jill was frozen. Desire warred with a vast trepidation and the need to know. With a very real fear. "Did he know that I am Kate Gallagher's great-granddaughter?"

He stood, his gaze shifting. "I don't know. How would I know? We don't even know that you are Kate's great-granddaughter." His gaze locked with hers. And abruptly he said, "One of us should leave, go back to bed."

She also stood. "Not too long ago, you came on to me like a Mack truck."

He stared at her. "Like a Humvee," he finally returned.

Jill smiled. "I stand corrected." And then her amusement vanished. "Alex," Jill said slowly. Ignoring the small warning voice in her head.

He continued to stare. His jaw flexed.

Why didn't he make a move? They were both drunk, or at least she was, and it was very late, the night outside was black and starless and heavy with fog, and no one would ever know. It had been so long. She needed this, him. Alex in his faded tight jeans and soft, fitted sweaters. But he did not make a move. He did not even speak.

Jill turned, drank a third of her brandy. And she faced him again. "You're making this very difficult." She cleared her throat. "Do you want to go upstairs?"

"Upstairs."

Jill could not believe what was happening. He was very clever, and very astute. He knew what she meant. He was no idiot—even if he was acting like one.

"Are you going to reject me?" she asked, trying to smile, trying to be nonchalant—and failing on both counts.

Alex gazed at her—and shoved his hands into the pockets of his jeans. "Do you even know what you're doing?" he asked harshly.

She took a step back. "Of course I do. I'm a big girl—"

He cut her off. "You're a live wire, a bundle of nerves, and unless I miss my guess, you are very, very vulnerable right now." He stared.

Jill realized he was rejecting her, and she backed away, shocked, hurt, confused, stunned. "You don't want me?"

"I want you. A lot more than a few days ago. But you don't want me."

Jill could not even think of a reply. "No," she whispered, afraid he was right. "You're wrong."

"I like you, Jill," he said grimly. "I'm also a damn good judge of character. You're not fast. You don't want a one-night stand. You're a romantic, and don't try to bluster and tell me otherwise. Tomorrow—God only knows what you'd be like. You're not ready for this. You're not ready for me."

On some level, which she did not want to face, she knew he was right. She didn't want a one-night stand, dear God, but there was no alternative. Any alternative was impossible.

"Jill," he said, his tone softening. "I'm not trying to hurt you. But I can't take advantage of you."

"Oh, God," Jill said, feeling sick. "I have just made a

complete fool of myself!" She managed a sickly smile.
"Good night."

   "No, Jill, wait. You haven't—"

   But Jill didn't stop and she didn't listen. She dashed out of
the room.

Sixteen

JILL TRIPPED AS SHE FLED UP THE STAIRS. SHE WAS ON THE landing when she realized he was behind her—his hand caught hers, halting her in her tracks.

"Jill," he said, "stop."

Jill froze, her back to him, afraid to face him and more upset than she had any right to be—except that her life had somehow spiraled seriously out of control. She was chasing a dead woman and she was chasing a guy who was way out of her league. What was wrong with her? What was happening to her?

He turned her around. "Let's not end the evening like this," he said roughly.

"I owe you a big fat apology." She managed a smile, knew it was ghastly. "I am so tired, so confused, and I'll admit I'm a wreck. I've never come on to a guy before."

"You are a wreck," he said, as softly as his hands continued to cup her shoulders. Jill became aware of his grip and renewed tension filled her. Their eyes held.

He didn't smile. "I don't want an apology. We're adults. We're attracted to one another. That's life. It's just more complicated than it should be."

Complicated, Jill thought, aware now of the one or two inches separating them, of his hands, and even aware of the heat emanating from his lean body. She knew why it was complicated for her, but why was it complicated for him?

Neither one of them spoke, and neither one of them

moved. Then he grimaced and dropped his hands from her shoulders. "I'm not really good at this," he said.

Jill met his gaze. Her heart was thudding inside her breast, slow and heavy. She wet her lips. "What does that mean?"

"It means that when I'm alone like this with a woman I like, I let nature take its course. But I don't like what's happening here. You've been through hell, and now you're obsessed with Kate. It's like you have a sickness. I'm worried."

And the worry was there in his blue eyes. Jill's heart turned over while it melted and the tension inside of her increased. "I'm not obsessed," she whispered. "I can't explain my gut feelings, or what happened in the tower, or why Hal has led me here, with you, but I just want to belong somewhere, Alex. I know if anyone can understand that, you can."

He stared.

Jill sensed he was torn—and an instant from either moving away, putting a safer distance between them, or moving closer. Hardly thinking about it, she leaned forward, eyes closing, laying her cheek against his chest.

The cashmere felt so soft. But the body beneath it was strong and hard and potently male. Even his heart was strong. She listened to its steady rhythm, eyes closed, aware of him beginning to tremble, aware of something crazy and wild and dangerous forming inside of her, overcoming her. She was breathless. And an insistence was there, building inside of her, and it was hot and sexual.

It only took him a split second to react. His arms went around her, hard. He buried his face in her hair. "You smell so good," he whispered, "like the rain. Damn it, Jill, you feel so good."

Jill had barely assimilated his words when he wrapped one arm around her, tilting her face upward with his other hand—his mouth coming down on hers.

Their lips brushed, once, twice, while Jill's heart tried to burst right through the walls of her chest.

He ended the kiss. Their gazes collided. He said, "Tomorrow, there are going to be a helluva lot of regrets."

Before Jill could agree, he kissed her openmouthed and

wet and suddenly she was off of her feet, suspended in his
arms, and he was shoving open her bedroom door with his
shoulder. An instant later she was on her back in the bed, and
he was there, on top of her, his hard groin pressed against
hers, moving against her with real insistence and urgency.
Their mouths locked.

The kiss was out of control. No one had ever kissed Jill
this way before, and it crossed her dazed mind that he really
wanted her—that no one had ever wanted her so much, so
badly, before. Not even Hal.

Their tongues met and sparred. One of his hands slid over
the fleece covering her crotch, an instant later his fingers
were inside her sweats, beneath her bikini underpants.

Jill gasped in shock and pleasure as he touched her repeatedly, finally cupping her, hard and possessive, fingers
splayed.

Jill caught his head in her hands, ending the wet, rough
kiss, shaking, dazed. Thinking, I can't wait.

"Yes, you can," he said roughly.

Jill realized she'd spoken her thoughts aloud and their
gazes locked, his blue eyes pale and starkly wild. His forefin-
ger brushed her clitoris. Jill could not move. She could only
pant—a slave to her own labored breathing and her body's
fierce exultation. Alex smiled at her, his gaze on her face,
watching her every response.

"Oh, God," Jill whispered as he manipulated her again
and again, so expertly.

Suddenly he withdrew his hand; an instant later Jill felt
him pressing her palm against the erection straining his fly.
Jill felt the huge head bulging beneath the denim and she
fumbled frantically with his zipper. "No, now," she heard
herself cry.

Alex tore the soft sweats from her body along with her
underwear. Jill wrenched open his jeans and shoved them
down his hips. She reared upward, touching her tongue to the
cotton fabric of his briefs where they covered his distended
penis, wanting to touch her tongue to him.

He ripped off the briefs and moved over her face giving
her what she wanted—Jill tasted him, all of him, sucking him

deep. She tasted salt and sweat and semen. Something inside of her burst and she felt herself begin to cry, but the sobs were not from pain, they were from need.

Jill came.

"Christ!" Alex spread her thighs and thrust into her. Instantly, Jill's contractions spiraled, heightening.

She'd never climaxed so quickly, so shamelessly, before. She was still convulsing when she felt him pull out, lift her hips, and bury his face there. His tongue flicked over her and another shattering orgasm formed in the wake of the last one.

She couldn't move, and not because his grip on her thighs was viselike. "Oh," Jill whispered as Alex moved over her again with the intention of penetrating her.

He sliced deep. "I'm the one who can't wait," he said thickly, pausing to watch her.

But she only glimpsed his strained face and eyes vaguely. She was still throbbing from her second climax, and he was hard, slick, powerful, inside of her. Shocked, Jill realized the urgency that had never quite died was building again. He moved.

Jill gripped his shoulders as if holding on for her very life—and maybe she was. He was still wearing the sweater and the cashmere was soaked through. Every muscle and tendon was clearly outlined by the wet wool. Suddenly he pulled her close, going deep and deeper still, holding her close, throbbing within her, and Jill felt the cliff coming, began to plunge and fall recklessly again.

"Turn over," he demanded, pulling out and flipping her onto her knees.

She wanted to kill him for leaving her but then he was back inside, his hands covering her crotch, opening her lips wide, and he was pumping and Jill fell, endlessly, hard, hearing her own cries with the back of her mind as he labored behind her, again and again, finally pushing her down and collapsing on top of her.

He became very still. Jill listened to her thundering heartbeat, incapable of movement. Her mind came to life and her first thought was that his body was so warm covering hers, and he was holding her in an embrace with his hands on her breasts. She smiled as he rolled off of her.

"Did I hurt you?" he whispered.

"No," Jill whispered back.

He glanced at her and she saw him smile, the smile of a sexually sated man. Then he flung out his arm and pulled her close. It was Jill who fell asleep first.

Jill paused on the threshold of the breakfast room. She saw Alex before he saw her—he was immersed in the Sunday newspaper. She could not speak. She could only stare at him. Her heart was racing like the souped-up engine of a Ferrari, and she was a bundle of short-circuiting nerves.

How could she have slept with him? She wasn't ready for any involvement, but by God, she was now involved. In fact, she was certain that she would never forget the night they had just spent together—and she still didn't understand it. He didn't love her and she didn't love him. How could two people have found such uninhibited and raw passion when they were practically strangers?

Last night had been a huge mistake. Because it had been better than she could have imagined—and already a part of her was thinking about another night in Alex's arms. She should have realized that she couldn't jump into bed with him without becoming involved, on some level, and she was involved, against her will and better judgment. And now what was she going to do?

Because making love with him didn't change anything at all. He was still a Sheldon, the truth about Kate was still out there, and eventually she was going to go home and pick up the pieces of her life.

He suddenly realized she was standing in the doorway, because his head popped up and he met her gaze, his eyes wide—and then he jumped to his feet, his chair scraping back loudly and almost turning over. His cup of coffee spilled all over the pristine white tablecloth.

Jill hoped he was as nervous as she was. Did he also have regrets? And did he care about her, just a little?

"Hi," she said nervously. She still couldn't smile as she entered the room. Matters were even worse. In the light of day, Jill kept thinking about KC's warnings and the stolen letters. If Alex was that god-awful King of Swords, then she had just made a catastrophic mistake. "Good morning."

"Good morning," he said, continuing to stand as she came forward. He was staring at her with such an intense scrutiny that Jill felt herself begin to blush.

Jill watched him pour her a cup of coffee. The gesture suddenly took on a vast significance. How many men, in this day and age, actually did such a thing? His hands were lightly tanned and steady. Oh, God. If only last night hadn't happened. If only they were just friends. Alex had been right when he'd said an affair between them was too complicated.

"Thank you," she said. Everything about last night now seemed wrong, except for the sex. He was a Sheldon, she was a nobody. Even if there were no other barriers between them, that single one would be enough.

"Can you believe it? The sun is shining," Jill said far too brightly. Her cheeks felt like twin fireballs.

He regarded her, his face a mask she could not read. It was as if she had spoken in Chinese. Finally he said, "Yeah."

Jill drank her coffee, eyes downcast. She wondered if they should discuss what had happened last night, or if they should pretend nothing had happened at all. He made the decision for her, saying, "What's the agenda for today?" Digging into a plateful of fluffy scrambled eggs.

Jill reached for a raisin muffin, less relieved than she was disappointed. He was going to pretend that last night hadn't happened. That was fine with her. She was not going to allow herself to feel hurt. "The chapel."

"I thought so." He leaned back in his chair. An expression she could not read crossed his face. "Okay, I'll drive you over after we eat."

"Thank you," Jill said slowly. She wished she had an inkling about how he was feeling. But she didn't. There was only this incredible tension between them. "I can drive myself, if you'd prefer." She told herself she would not be stricken if he told her to go her own way.

"I'll drive you." He was firm.

"Why?" Jill knew her smile was sickly. "This is my quest. You're not very enthusiastic today. I don't mind if you stay behind."

He stood. "I'm not unenthusiastic. I'm tired." The look he gave her was pointed.

Jill flushed. But at least he was referring to last night.

"I'd still like you to hold off on this, Jill. For a while." He paused. "I don't like what happened to you in the tower."

Jill hoped that he was trying to tell her that he cared. "I can't. I mean, at least not now. We're here, in Yorkshire . . . who knows when I'll have a chance to come back?"

He sighed and shrugged. He was so serious. "I have a ton of work to do this week, so I can't help you when we get back to town." He hesitated.

"What?"

"I'll admit it. I am curious, too, Jill, about what happened to your great-grandmother." Their gazes met. Alex was the first to look away. She could not understand why. He was not the kind of guy to be embarrassed by the kind of sexual encounter they had shared.

And out of the blue, a thought she did not want struck her. He wasn't being honest with her. Something was wrong. *He was lying to her.* Jill could feel it.

Alex and Jill stepped down from the Land Rover, approaching the small, old stone church. It was set just off of the road, behind a stone wall, surrounded by a pretty and lush green lawn, rose hedges, and old thick oak trees. A few steps farther away was the vicar's stone cottage, separated from the church by a stone path and more thick hedges. The church resembled thousands of other centuries-old chapels that Jill had seen both in tour guides and in movies. It was not much bigger than her studio back home.

Stepping inside was like stepping through the window of time. The chapel was empty now and achingly silent, with that powerfully peaceful feeling Jill had encountered in churches before. They stood in the aisle, blinking, blinding sunlight pouring through the windows behind the knave. The pews lining up on either side of them were worn smooth from usage and the passage of so much time. The wood smelled sweet and well oiled.

Incense also sweetened the air, Jill thought, either that or the wisteria blooming outside was extremely fragrant. As she stood there with Alex, their hips not quite touching, Jill glanced around and suddenly imagined what the church must have been like when Kate was alive. The pews would have been filled with the local villagers, the men clad in somber ill-fitting suits with high-collared shirts and fedoras, the women in long dark dresses and heavy black shoes, the boys in suspenders and knickers, the girls with their lacy drawers showing beneath wide knee-length dresses. She could almost hear horses wickering outside, and the occasional stomping of a hoof. Then she saw Kate, standing in the doorway, her face shockingly pale behind an opaque black veil, holding a swaddled infant to her bosom.

Of course Kate would have come there to pray and to hope.

Jill shivered, glancing cautiously around. The chapel was empty, but for one moment, she had glimpsed another place in time. It had almost felt as if she had been there.

"May I help you?" The vicar was approaching them, clad in a dark suit and a white clerical collar.

"Vicar Hewitt?" Alex asked, coming forward, his hand extended. "I'm Alex Preston, Lord Collinsworth's nephew. I called a few minutes ago."

The two men shook hands and Jill was introduced. Jill was surprised, for the vicar was very young—not much older than she was. Alex explained their business and Hewitt led them into a small, book-lined room behind the chapel where the church records were kept. He found the ledger they were looking for and laid it out on the old, scarred table in the center of the room. It was the size of an atlas, its dark maroon cover worn and faded with age, its pages yellowing and torn. "Anyone who died in 1909 and was buried here in our cemetery would be listed in this volume," he told them. "The listings are in chronological order, of course."

Alex thanked him and as he and Jill bent over the volume, the vicar left the room. The two windows were open and birdsong filled the silence. Alex turned the pages, running his finger down date after date, finally pausing as May 17, 1908, appeared before their eyes.

"One week after my grandfather was born," Jill murmured. A man named George Thompson had died that day and been buried in the chapel cemetery.

The ensuing date was for September 30, 1908. The next date was for December 3 of the same year. After that, the dates were for 1909.

Jill's heart raced. She ran her finger down to May 21, the next entry for that year. And as abruptly, her heart dropped. January 12, 1909, was not listed. Katherine Adeline Gallagher was not listed.

"There must be a mistake," Jill said, scanning the names of those who were buried and then dismissing them all, as Katherine Adeline Gallagher was not one of them. "Go back, Alex," she urged.

He shot her a wry glance, turned back a page, but they were already in 1907. Then they went forward, flipping to the summer of 1909. Katherine Adeline Gallagher was not listed; clearly she had not had either a service or a formal burial at the Hinton Vale Chapel Cemetery.

Jill stared at Alex as he shut the volume, the sound echoing in the stone room. "This is odd."

He did not reply.

"Someone buried her, Alex, but did so in great secrecy."

"That would seem to be the case," he said.

"What did they do, come here in the middle of the night with shovels and spades?"

"I doubt she was buried in broad daylight. I didn't expect to find anything, Jill. The police never solved the case. Of course she was buried in secrecy. The question is, why? Someone took a great risk to bury her here."

"Yes," Jill returned, clenching her fists. "Undoubtedly it was her killer who buried her—which would indicate some lingering fondness for her on his part."

Alex looked at her. "So who are you accusing?"

Jill bit her lip. "Look, Edward was fooling around with Kate, but he married Anne. I imagine Kate caused him quite a bit of grief. I mean, I don't think she wished him well and politely walked away so he could marry her best friend."

"Jill, hold your horses. What if she died in childbirth? Maybe she got pregnant again. That kind of scandal would also be covered up. You're going off the deep end."

Jill looked at him, then looked out into the chapel and toward the doorway. "She came here to pray. To pray, and to hope for the solution to her dilemma."

He studied her. "And how do you know that?"

"Don't you think she stayed at Coke's Way? It's across the road, for godsakes! Why wouldn't she come here?"

"Why are you shouting?"

"I'm not." She took a breath. "I'm just upset." That was the truth. She was distressed, and not merely about Kate.

He spoke very quietly. "If you're going to continue this quest of yours, so be it. But to make yourself sick is insane. She died ninety years ago, Jill. Nothing you find out will change what happened to her."

He was right. Why was she so emotional? Jill pulled away. "I don't know why this whole thing is getting to me this way. I almost feel as if Kate is watching me, expecting me to solve this." She looked at him, but he did not respond. "I think your family knows a lot more than they've let on."

His eyes widened. Then he resumed absolute control of his expression, and it became as flat as an overbeaten pancake. "Really."

"Yes. Most families have all kinds of folklore that's passed down through the generations. Everyone seems totally ignorant of even the existence of Kate. I don't buy it, not for a New York minute," Jill said. "You know, if Edward was the father of Kate's son, Peter, he was only twelve years older than William."

He just looked at her. "Are you trying to make a point?"

"How could William not have known about an older bastard brother?"

Alex was silent. "Maybe there was no older bastard brother."

"Maybe," Jill said, not believing it for an instant.

"Do you intend to confront him?"

Jill stared back at him. Suddenly he did not seem to be the man whose arms she had lain in last night. Suddenly it felt as if they were warily eyeing one another from opposite sides of the fence. And she could pretend all she wanted to, but that did hurt. "I did confront him—but mildly, when I first returned to London." Alex's expression did not change. "He said he knew nothing. At the time, I believed him."

"But now you do not."

"No. Now I do not."

"My uncle is an honest man. He's not a liar."

"But I'm an outsider, and responsible for Hal's death. I'm sure he wouldn't want me to know the family dirt." Jill's mind was racing, and suddenly an idea occurred to her that she should have had before—could not believe she hadn't had before. "Let's go back to the house. Don't these old estates have ledgers that go back hundreds of years? Let's get Edward's signature. First thing Monday I'm going to have it compared to Barclay's. If they come up the same, Alex, then that is proof that Edward was Kate's lover and that he had her bastard."

"All right," Alex finally said.

Jill shrugged. "You are a spoilsport."

He smiled then. "Someone has to keep a tight rein on you, kid, or God only knows where you'd be rocketing off to. Did anyone ever tell you that you could be termed a loose cannon?"

She stopped smiling. There was affection in his tone. It was also teasing. But she did not like being called "kid" after last night. "Should I be flattered?"

"Only if you like having someone looking out for you," he said, his own smile fading. "Let's go back to the house and find those ledgers you're talking about."

Jill nodded. Excitement swept over her again. But with it came trepidation. She felt as if she was on the verge of finding the answers she was looking for, but she also felt as if she were on the edge of a cliff, and that one misstep would send her plunging into an abyss.

Alex carefully tore a page out of a huge ledger, a volume far bigger than the chapel's tome. He folded it and handed it to her.

"I hope nobody notices that you did that," Jill said, glancing over her shoulder at the open doorway. They were in what Alex referred to as the study. It was not the same room as the library. This room was much smaller, it was dark and somber with wood paneling, and had only one window, which looked out on the rocky cliffs and the sea. It had clearly once been used as a home office. Jill did not think it had been used in twenty or thirty years, if not more. It was too dark, too airless, and it smelled old and musty.

"I doubt anyone comes in here, except for the odd maid to clean," Alex said, replacing the ledger onto a bookshelf filled with a dozen other ledgers. The estate records went back to 1495. Jill found that amazing.

She was cheerful. "Ready for a tour of the attics?"

He started. "You want to go up to the attics? Today?" The sun continued to shine so brightly that one might mistake their location for Florida. "You haven't been to Robin Hood Bay yet. We can have lunch at the pub."

"How about a late lunch?" Jill smiled. "Alex, everyone shoves their old stuff in their attics. I can't even begin to imagine what's up there in your attic. We can't possibly leave tomorrow without checking it out."

Alex sighed. "Follow me." As he led her through the house and upstairs, he told her that, as children, they had explored the attics at Stainesmore too many times to count. "When we were caught, we were always scolded," he said with a smile.

They were on the uppermost floor where a few of the staff slept. At the end of the hallway was a narrow door, which Alex pushed open. Jill peered past his shoulder and saw very narrow stairs ascending into darkness. "Any lights?" she asked hopefully.

"You've got to be kidding," he said. He pulled his penlight out of his pocket. "But there are three windows, if I recall correctly, and the sun is bright today." He gave her a look that indicated he'd rather be out in the sun than inside, with her, going through a musty attic searching for clues about the fate of her supposed ancestor.

Jill shoved past him, walking cautiously up the narrow stairs, hoping there were no mice scurrying about. She paused on the landing, glancing around at a long space with slanting, low ceilings. It was filled with boxes and trunks, varying in size from the kind of cartons one would pack books in, to crates that could hold clothing or even linens. She sighed. "It would take a month to go through everything up here."

"Robin Hood Bay?" Alex asked hopefully.

Jill ignored him and stepped forward. He was right, they didn't need an interior light at this time of day, in spite of the clutter. She went to a stack of old leather traveling trunks, trimmed in brass, and began pulling the top one down.

Alex immediately came forward. "Hold on before you break something—like your foot."

She watched the muscles popping out of his arms as he hefted the trunk, grunting, and moved it to the floor. Jill saw that it had a small padlock on it. She knelt and jiggled it. "Do you think we can break this lock?" she asked.

He knelt beside her. "It's been a while, but I'll try."

Jill watched him extract a Swiss Army knife from his pocket, flip open a file, and fool with the padlock. Suddenly she found herself thinking about the intruder KC claimed to have seen leaving her studio in New York. Her sense of levity vanished. When he did not have success, she was oddly relieved. "I guess you're out of practice."

He looked at her as the lock snapped open. "Voilà."

"I guess not," Jill said, unsmiling. She told herself to forget about that earlier incident—KC had probably imagined it—and Alex had been in London anyway. She needed to focus on the task at hand, and she watched Alex open the lid of the trunk, revealing carefully packed women's clothing. Then she thought about the fact that these were not her belongings. They belonged to William and Margaret. "Will you tell on me?" Her gaze met his.

"No. We're in this together."

Jill dug into the trunk. She had been hoping that the items were old—dating back to Edwardian times, but they were not. The suits were designer, and mid-calf length. She held one up. "This must be from the fifties," she said. "God, look at the fabric—at how this is made."

"Might even be from the forties," Alex returned. "Look at those shoulders."

She smiled. "So you know fashion?"

"I'm an insomniac. I like watching the classics in the wee hours." He smiled back.

Their eyes locked. Jill looked away. "Let's get to work," she said, refusing to think about their relationship now.

"I can see there's no deterring you," Alex remarked, hauling another trunk down to the floor.

"No, I am a woman with a mission." She stood. "You open up the trunks. I'm going to go through the smaller boxes. I'm a chauvinist," she added.

"Obviously." He was wry.

As Jill started toward a pile of boxes she noticed a huge object covered with a white canvas cloth, lying behind the stacked boxes, propped against the wall. "What's that?" She spoke aloud, but more to herself than to Alex. She shimmied herself in between the stacked boxes and lifted a section of the tarp. It was a painting.

A chill swept her as she dragged the entire cloth off.

The life-sized oil painting had been laid on its side. But there was no mistaking who the subject of the portrait was. Kate was sitting in the grass in a garden that was overflowing with tulips on a very sunny day. She was breathtakingly beautiful. "Alex!"

"I see," he said, coming up behind her.

"Help me get this out," Jill cried excitedly, turning to move the boxes. A moment later they had cleared a space in the attic and set the painting right side up against the boxes. "This is stunning," Jill said, her heart thundering wildly. "Oh, my God. Look at what we've found!"

Alex was silent.

Jill stared at Kate, and suddenly realized just how sensual the expression on her face was. She became motionless. Her dark eyes were almost black, sultry and beckoning. Her full mouth was parted, as if she had just drawn in her breath, or was about to speak. Kate was fully clothed, but her expression made the painting far from innocent. There was no question about what was on her mind.

And suddenly Jill recalled the photographs Hal had taken of her. She stepped away from the painting, shaken. Her expression had been identical to Kate's.

"What is it?"

The cheer of the day was gone. Jill's stomach had curdled and she could not move or even answer Alex. She was so much like her great-grandmother, she thought, staring fixedly at the painting.

Staring fixedly at Kate.

"Jill? Where are you?"

His voice sounded distant. Jill ignored it. Kate stared out from the garden, but not at her, Jill. She was staring, Jill knew, at Edward, who was beside the portraitist, watching the work of his mistress in progress. Jill could see them so clearly. Edward in a pale waistcoat and his shirtsleeves, his head bare, his eyes going back and forth from Kate to the canvas, repeatedly. He was smiling, satisfied and pleased. The artist, a younger man, working feverishly, having eyes only for Kate. And Kate, that half smile, that dreamy, sultry look, having eyes only for her lover.

The chemistry between them was electric.

"Jill."

Jill started. Alex was beside her, and she had not been aware of his presence until just then. She faced him. "What a work of art."

"Yes."

"She's so beautiful. Of course Edward—any man—would fall madly in love with her."

"Is beauty only skin deep?"

She finally looked at Alex, really looked at him, into his eyes. "Of course it's not. But we already know that she was brave and reckless, and that she defied convention—she was very admirable. In a society ruled by strict moral codes, she must have been a breath of fresh air. Men probably flocked to her like bees to honey."

"I agree."

There was something in his tone that made her stare at him. "Would you have fallen in love with her?" Jill asked impulsively. "If you had lived back then?" She hoped—desperately—that his answer was a negative one.

"I don't know. I can't say. Maybe. If she were really all of those things."

"She was all of those things." Jill was certain.

"You're a romantic, Jill, with a capital R. Has anyone ever told you that?" His gaze was riveted on her face.

"I'm hardly romantic!" Jill wasn't amused.

"You've romanticized Kate. Glorified her. Maybe she was just a wild, rebellious eighteen-year-old, as immature as most girls her age are." His brows lifted. "Maybe she made a stupid, childish decision, not thinking anything through, getting involved with her lover in a day and age when that kind of affair could only bring heartache and self-destruction."

"Don't," Jill said quietly. She faced the painting again. Alex's words echoed in her mind—heartache and self-destruction. Jill had no doubt that it was her love affair that had destroyed Kate. "Is there any harm in my romanticizing her?" she finally asked.

For a moment, he was quiet. Then he said, "I'm beginning to think so."

She did not want to know what that meant. She studied the painting, now noticing the details, the care given to every fold in Kate's satin dress, the elegance of her hands, the locket around her throat. "I can't believe that no one knew this was up here."

Alex, behind her, did not speak. Suddenly a notion seized her. "Or someone did know this was up here—and it's hidden up here for a reason!" Jill faced Alex, eyes wide. Her accusation seemed to linger, echoing, in the long, low space of the attic.

"I've seen this before," he said quietly.

She blinked. "What?"

"When we were kids, we came up here from time to time—I told you that." His hands were in his pockets. His gaze was sober. "The day we found this, we were all together, the four of us, me, Thomas, Lauren, and Hal."

Jill's heart picked up its beat. "The four of you found this," Jill repeated slowly.

He nodded.

"Hal saw this," she said.

He nodded again.

"And?" Why was she not surprised? She felt ill. Hal had seen this portrait as a child, and so had Alex. But he'd never said a word.

Alex shrugged. "That's it. The end of the story. The housekeeper yelled at us for going into the attic in the first place."

Jill stared at him, the sick feeling in her stomach heavier now, wondering at the flicker in his eyes. He wasn't telling her something, but what? "Was that the first time Hal saw Kate?"

He hesitated. "I don't know."

He was lying. Jill wet her lips. "Do you remember his reaction to this painting?"

"Not really," Alex said. "I'm starving. You ready yet?"

He had changed the subject. Jill stared at him, uneasy. He knew something he wasn't telling her, and she was so damn sure of it. "Did Hal's obsession start the day you found this portrait?" she heard herself ask.

"I have no idea," he said. "Are you finished with the interrogation?"

Jill smiled hastily. "I'm not interrogating you. I'm just surprised that you never mentioned the existence of this portrait before."

"I forgot about it," he said flatly.

Jill nodded. But maybe she was wrong. Maybe he was telling the truth and KC's nonsensical tarot card reading, her warnings, had subconsciously influenced Jill's perceptions. "Let me go through a few boxes before we quit up here," she finally said.

"You haven't had enough?"

"No." Abruptly Jill went to a stack of cartons and pulled the top one down. As she went through an assortment of odd knickknacks, Jill wondered who had hidden the painting. It should be at Uxbridge Hall, hanging there in one of the public rooms. She couldn't wait to tell Lucinda about it.

Then she realized why the painting had been hidden. Kate had died—and there had been a cover-up. Of course someone in the family would hide her painting, otherwise every time a tour went through the hall, tourists would ask about Kate, keeping the mystery alive.

Jill wondered if she was getting in over her head.

Her stomach growled. Jill ignored it, opening the sixth box, grim now. She realized it contained glassware. She was about to move on, tell Alex she was ready to go, when she looked down at the goblets, each one separated from the other by cardboard. There was no reason for her to do so, but she couldn't shake from her mind that someone had hidden the painting away in the attic, that someone did not want the truth about Kate to ever be known, and she pulled out four of the goblets, followed by another four. A set of eight snifters was below. She also removed those. The bottom of the box was lined with scraps of newspaper.

"What are you doing?" Alex asked curiously, coming over. "The trunks contain clothing—children's clothing."

"I don't know," Jill said, about to replace the glasses. "I'm ready for lunch, too." But she stared into the box, which was now empty except for the shreds of paper at the bottom. Without thinking, Jill reached down and dug through the scraps of paper, but nothing was hidden there. She was being foolish, she decided, a handful of newspaper in her hand. Then she went still. Realizing that the paper wasn't shredded at all, even though the pieces were hardly uniform in size. She appeared to be looking at differently sized articles, each one carefully and completely cut out of different newspapers. Then she noticed the date on top of one piece of a page—and it was 1909.

Jill no longer believed in coincidence.

Her pulse racing, she smoothed out a piece of paper and

saw that it had been cut out of the page with scissors, so that it formed a perfect square, and it was a clipping of an entire article, four paragraphs long. The small but boldface headline read: "HUNT FOR GALLAGHER HEIRESS WINDS DOWN." It was dated September 15, 1909.

Breathless, Jill reached for another segment of newspaper. Again, it was a clipping, this one rectangular in shape and a mere two paragraphs. The smaller yet boldface headline read, "MOTHER OF MISSING HEIRESS SWEARS FOUL PLAY."

"Alex! The bottom of this box is filled with newspaper clippings—and they're all about Kate's disappearance!" Jill cried hoarsely, smoothing several pieces out at once. And as she did so, it clicked in her brain that these clippings had been hidden, too.

There were more headlines, and another one had a date— January 15, 1909. "SECRET TESTIMONY OF BEST FRIEND REVEALS NO CLUES ABOUT KATE GALLAGHER."

Alex squatted beside her. "Well, well," he said. "Somebody was collecting souvenirs."

Jill flinched, meeting his eyes. "The question is, who?"

JUNE 1, 1907

Laughter trickled across the meadow, interspersed with the playful shouts of children and the yappings of dogs.

"This is so idyllic," Kate sighed, speaking to Anne. The two girls were standing not far from a dark, gleaming pond as a bevy of ducks drifted by, followed by two gorgeous white swans. On the other side of the pond was Swinton Hall, Lord Willow's hunting box. The hall was actually an old Scottish castle, square and bulky with ancient parapets boasting flags with Willow's blue and gold coats of arms, the flags rippling in an exceedingly blue sky. About a dozen ladies, gentlemen, and a few children were scattered about the two friends, partaking of an afternoon picnic.

The ladies sat upon plaid blankets, two and three to each tartan, nibbling cold chickens and shepherd's pies, fresh, crusty bread, and fruit tarts. Gentlemen strolled with one another or a lady friend, except for a group of four who were playing badminton in their waistcoats and shirtsleeves. Several children raced about, the boys in their knickers chasing the girls in their straw hats. Two small dachshunds had joined in the game of tag, and were barking frantically on the heels of the children.

"I have always had a particular fondness for Scotland," Anne said with a smile. She and Kate both wore long, cool white silk dresses, Kate's sprigged in yellow, Anne's in green, the hems flounced and detailed in French lace. They were holding hands as they strolled along the perimeter of the pond. Neither girl had bothered to open her parasol. "I have always wished that Father would let us a place somewhere in the north country, but he refuses. He is, I think, the only Englishman in this world to despise hunting."

"And that is so very odd," Kate said with a laugh.

"Anne!"

Kate stifled a sigh at the sound of Lady Bensonhurst's strident voice. The two girls turned around, Anne as reluctant as Kate.

Lady Bensonhurst approached them, her strides rather martial. Another lady was in tow, a beautiful woman of forty or so whom Kate disliked as much as she did Anne's mother. Lady Cecilia Wyndham smiled at Anne, but looked through Kate as if she did not exist. Kate arranged her mouth into a cold smile in return. Kate knew that the striking baroness did not like Kate because she diluted the male attention Cecilia was so accustomed to enjoying.

"Anne, Cecilia and I are off to the village to buy some of those marvelous little wind chimes we saw the other day. Do you wish to accompany us? Won't it be quaint to hang them at home in the gardens?" Lady Bensonhurst smiled at her daughter, practically ignoring Kate.

Anne glanced at Kate.

Kate gave her a look.

"Oh, I beg your pardon, you may join us, too, Kate," Lady Bensonhurst said. "I would so dislike leaving you by yourself, especially as Mary was too ill to join us for the weekend."

"I think I shall pass," Kate said, well aware she was using a phrase that the gentlemen used in their poker games.

Lady Bensonhurst recognized the slang, and she scowled. "Do speak proper English, dear Kate."

"But I am not a proper Englishwoman," Kate said with wide, innocent eyes, knowing she should have resisted temptation to indulge herself in a bit of scathing wit. After all, Lady Bensonhurst might be her patroness, but she was also, behind Kate's back, her biggest detractor, and Kate was not fooled for a moment. Just the other day she had overheard Lady Bensonhurst exclaiming about Kate having had the audacity to stroll the East End waterfront and sketch sailors without their shirts.

Actually, those sketches were some of the finest Kate had ever done.

"A tart like that will soon fall, don't you think so?" she had intoned. "If only Anne were not so fond of her and if only Lord Bensonhurst were not blinded by that red hair and those black eyes!"

"Dear, I do not think we could forget your Irish-American antecedents," Cecilia was saying now, smiling the smile of an ice queen.

"And how is Lord Howard?" Kate smiled back slyly.

Cecilia's smile vanished. "I beg your pardon?"

Kate knew that Lord Howard Dunross had crept into Lady Cecilia's bed last night—and the night before that, as well. Of course, Lord Wyndham had been in Lady Georgina Cottle's bed, so everyone must have had quite the jolly time.

"Lord Howard asked me to stroll with him after tea," Kate lied. She smiled. "I thought, out of respect for you, I should decline."

Cecilia stared at Kate, her winged black brows raised. Abruptly she turned her back on her and marched away with a loud huffing sound.

Kate managed not to laugh.

Lady Bensonhurst stared coldly. "That was extraordinarily rude."

"I fail to see why," Kate said, thinking that it was even

ruder to make love so loudly that one kept the occupants of
the adjacent chamber awake.

Anne's mother turned to Anne. "You shall join us. Kate
may do as she pleases." Lady Bensonhurst followed in her
friend's wake. Her ample hips swayed from side to side, giving one the impression that she waddled like the ducks just
now strutting upon the pond's muddy shore.

"I do not want to go to town," Anne moaned.

But Kate was frozen, her heart suddenly slamming in her
chest, not hearing her best friend. Lord Braxton had just rid-
den a beautiful bay hunter into the group, clearly having just
arrived from London. Kate placed her hand, which was shaking, on her breast. She had not known he was coming for the
ten-day sojourn in the country. Oh, God. She could hardly
breathe; she was ecstatic, she must not show her feelings, she
did not know what to do!

She had not laid eyes upon him in months. His father had
sent him to Charleston just after the Christmas holidays,
where his family apparently had several properties.

"Kate? Are you unwell? Is something amiss?"

Edward had not dismounted. He was smiling, speaking
with a group of young bachelors, some of whom, Kate knew,
had horrid reputations as rogues about town. She could not
look away from him. And then he looked up and saw her.
Their gazes locked.

For a long moment, they stared at one another. Kate did not
know who smiled first. But she was smiling, and so was he.

Then she looked away.

Edward had called on her twice in London since they had
met at the Fairchild ball, but that had been ages ago—before
his journey to America. He had taken her for a drive in the
park, and to a country fair just outside of London, in a small
village called Hampstead. Both afternoons had been glorious, and had passed far too swiftly. Unlike the past several
months, during which he had been away. Never had time
passed more slowly.

And at every fête and soirée that Kate went to in the
interim since he had been abroad, she had her ears pricked
wide, and she had learned that he was the premier catch in

the land, and that just about every girl making her come-out last season had been hoping to snare him as a husband. He was twenty-six. He seemed in no rush to marry. He had never, since he had reached his majority, courted anyone seriously. And he had called upon no one else since he had called upon her before leaving the country.

"Kate! Is that Lord Braxton?" Anne asked, low but wide-eyed.

Kate followed her gaze and saw Edward, who had dismounted, approaching them. "Indeed it is," Kate said, smiling as if she were serene, calm, and unmoved by his appearance at Swinton Hall. Kate hardly knew what to do. She twisted her gloved hands nervously.

He paused before the two girls and bowed. "Ladies." His gaze was on Anne. "Lady Bensonhurst, I believe?"

Anne had not been home on either of the occasions when he had called on Kate. Now she lowered her eyes while extending her hand. "We have not been properly introduced," she murmured demurely.

"I am happy to make the introductions," Kate said, sharing a glance with Edward while Anne's gaze was lowered. "Viscount Braxton, my dear friend, Lady Anne."

He bowed over her hand, then took Kate's, bowing over that. His clasp on her fingers was a warm squeeze, and it seemed overly long. "How lovely the two of you are," he said, smiling into Kate's eyes, not even looking at Anne. "When did you arrive at Lord Willow's box?"

"We only arrived the day before yesterday," Kate replied, trying to keep her tone even. How very hard it was. "And we shall be staying another week."

"How fortunate for me," he said, teeth flashing white against his swarthy skin. "As I, too, stay an entire week."

Kate's heart did a series of rapid somersaults. "How wonderful," she whispered. "I had not heard that you were back, my lord."

"I returned home but a few days ago," he said, his tone as low, his gaze unwavering.

Their gazes held. Kate could not look away. She forgot about Anne, standing beside them. When would he kiss her?

she wondered. He had almost kissed her that day he had driven her to the fair in his motor car. He would be in Swinton for a week. She would be there for a week. This then must be heaven. Surely at some time this week he would hold her passionately, the way she had been dreaming of being held and touched by him.

Surely this time, it would be their beginning, the beginning of something vast and magnificent, of something soul-shattering and eternal.

"Anne! We are to depart!"

"I am afraid I must go," Anne said. She smiled at Edward and curtsied. "It has been a pleasure to meet you, Lord Braxton."

"The pleasure has been mine," he said with a bow.

They both watched Anne hurry away, climbing into a carriage with her mother and Cecilia. As the carriage drove past them, Kate was aware of both ladies staring directly at her and Edward. Then they put their heads together, and Kate knew they were speaking about her, discussing her prospects of catching England's most sought-after bachelor, and dismissing the possibility as ludicrous.

"They are such witches," she said.

"I beg your pardon?"

She was briefly horrified by the slip of her too-bold tongue, but then she saw the laughter in Edward's eyes, and she laughed, too. "They talk about me behind my back. I'm Irish, I'm American, and I am not fit to be in the present company," Kate said without bitterness. She was smiling. "I would respect them more if they would speak openly. How narrow-minded they are."

"Hypocrisy is an ugly thing," Edward agreed, "as is such condescension. Unfortunately, I have found out that the wealthiest people tend to be the most judgmental. It is a shame, is it not?"

"Yes, indeed," Kate said happily. "But I do try to feel sorry for Lady Bensonhurst. Clearly, in spite of her wealth and her position, she is very unhappy with her lot in life."

"How astute you are. You do know that Lord Bensonhurst is quite the man about town?"

"I had guessed." Kate smiled archly. "Does he really keep a French actress as a mistress?"

"I shall never tell," Edward vowed with a grin.

"Ah, I can see the truth in your eyes. Well, then, we must feel sorry for Lady B. Not only must we feel sorry for her, we must hope that she continues to shop her life away. After all, that is the only satisfaction she seems to receive in life, is it not?"

"It is," he said. "Many women would be happy with such an arrangement, a titled husband who goes his own way, not bothering them with his more pressing needs, but leaving them with a carte blanche for the shops and stores." His gaze was searching.

"Not I! I care not one whit for shopping, and one day, I expect my husband to be as smitten with me as I am with him." Kate smiled boldly.

Edward stared. "One day, beauteous Kate, you will undoubtedly have your wish."

Kate felt herself blushing. "I do, perhaps, have odd expectations for a marriage. I fail to understand why more men do not take their wives seriously. Why bother to shackle oneself to a mate if one intends to go about life as if one were not so coupled?"

"Ah, well, we all have our duty to perform," Edward said, holding out his hand. "We have titles to pass down—heirs to conceive—alliances to mold. Walk with me, Kate. Being with you again is like being let out of an old, musty closet and finding oneself on the seashore."

"You are a poet, sir." Kate laughed as they strolled through the picnic.

"Hardly." Edward laughed as they left the meadow behind. A small trail led them through a cluster of birch trees and into another field. "But let me say again, dear Kate, that you are a sight for sore eyes. Your beauty ties my tongue in veritable knots."

Kate knew she blushed. "You overpraise me, my lord. Do not forget, my tongue is too sharp, my freckles too dark, my nose far too Roman—I am hardly en vogue."

Edward roared with laughter. He halted, as did Kate. The

picnic party was no longer in sight. Ahead of them was a shimmering green valley, crisscrossed with stone walls. Beyond that, a series of stark hills faced them, covered in purple gorse. The sky overhead was perfectly blue, and the sun was shining, warm and bright, down upon them. "I like the fact that you are woman enough to know yourself, that you accept yourself with true grace."

"Ah"—Kate smiled—"so you admit I am flawed."

"I admit no such thing! I think your freckles endearing, your nose striking, and should you mince words, you would bore me as most of those debutantes have done before."

Kate's smile faded. As did his. A long moment passed. Kate said, "Has there been no one, then, in all these years, who has caught your eye and your heart as well?"

He hesitated. "Have you not heard, dear Kate, that my heart is cold, that I am an utter rogue, and that I will only marry when my father has either blackmailed me into it, or is on his deathbed and gasping out his last dying breath?"

"Is that what they say about you?" Kate gasped, genuinely appalled.

"That is what the mothers who have set their caps for me as the husband of their daughters say, repeatedly. No mother, apparently, accepts the rejection of her daughter with dignity and grace. My reputation apparently is so black that no woman is safe alone with me." His golden eyes held hers. "Do I frighten you, Kate?"

"No." Kate's pulse throbbed. "You could not possibly frighten me. You can only intrigue me."

He reached for her. "And you intrigue me. You have intrigued me from the moment I first laid eyes upon you. You are different from them all. But then, you know that, and you are proud of it, and that, perhaps, is the most wondrous thing about you."

Kate's heart felt as if it were expanding to impossible proportions. "You shall soon embarrass me, good sir," she whispered.

"I don't think so. I have missed you, Kate. I have thought of little else but you since we met." His gaze held hers, darkening now with startling rapidity.

Kate's heart soared with joy. "I have also missed you, my lord," she whispered, "And I, too, shamelessly, have thought of little else."

He stared. A scant instant later he pulled her into his arms, his mouth on hers. Kate returned his kiss with one of her own. She felt him tense and knew she had crossed the line, becoming impossibly bold. But then he pulled her closer, wrapping his arms around her, bending her over backward, all hesitation gone. Kate's lips parted; her fingers dug into his strong shoulders. The kiss lasted forever; but when it was over, it felt as if it had lasted mere seconds.

He dropped her arms, eyes wide, stepping away from her.

Kate stared at him with real shock, her heart beating so thunderously she thought they could both hear it. Now, for the first time in her life, she understood desire. "Oh, God." She did not realize she had spoken aloud until it was too late, and she pressed two fingertips to her mouth.

He stared. And finally he said, "No woman has ever affected me as you have."

She wet her lips. "Meaning what?"

His stare remained; it was unrelenting. "You haunt me, Kate, ceaselessly, day and night, night and day. My journey abroad felt endless because I yearned for you." He paused then said, "We should not be alone together again."

"No!" Her cry was sharp, startled.

Edward stared. "Do you know how dangerous it is for us to be alone together? The gossips already blacken me, and you as well. Should we be caught in such a compromising position, you would be truly ruined, my dear."

Then marry me, Kate thought, but she said no such thing. "I don't care about the gossips. I care about you."

He was motionless. "You are a woman without guile—a woman of vast courage. I care about you, too, Kate. Still, our emotions are running wild. They might run away with us. We must exercise caution."

"Why? What good is caution? Does that bring joy, love, happiness?"

His eyes were unblinking, and filled with a serious light. "Should we live life fettered by the likes of Lady Bensonhurst?" Kate cried. "If we should live our lives, always caring what others think of us, pray tell me how one finds happiness, not misery?" She stared, imploring. "I have found happiness with you, my lord. Do not ask me to throw it away because of a few bitter, jealous old ladies with wagging tongues who delight in causing trouble."

He reached for her and pulled her close, embracing her without kissing her. He held her for a long moment. "I do not want to hurt you," he said.

Kate pulled back so she could see his face. "And how would you hurt me, my lord?"

"My father plans for me to marry some proper English miss. He has a list of young ladies with impeccable lineage, huge fortunes, and overly significant titles. I am a hair's breadth away from falling in love with you, Kate. Maybe I am already in love with you." His hand raked through his hair. "That would be a terrible mistake. It would be a mistake for us both."

Kate drew away. "Love, if it is true, if it is brave, if it is strong, is never a mistake."

"You are too romantic," he said.

"Yes, I am. And will you always obey your father?" Kate returned unsteadily.

"I am his heir. I have a duty to him, to the earldom," Edward said flatly.

Kate remained motionless. Despair mingled with joy. He wanted her, perhaps he even loved her, as she did him, but he was honor-bound to obey his father, to marry some proper Englishwoman with an ancient title and a fortune. How could he even conceive of such a thing if he was falling in love with her?

Then Kate reminded herself of the power of true love, of the destiny of two fated souls. She had loved him from the moment she had seen him, that day at Brighton, and she knew he loved her, too, as passionately—it was there in his eyes, even now. Surely one very old man, powerful as he was, would not stand in their way. True love, Kate knew, would always prevail. "I will not tell you good-bye when we have only just begun."

He smiled slightly. "Did I speak of good-byes? I am not capable of saying good-bye to you, Kate. Perhaps that is what so frightens me."

"It does not frighten me," Kate returned softly, exhilarated yet again.

His eyes darkened and he pulled her into his arms another time. This kiss was reckless, so much so that they fell to their knees in the grass, where they remained locked in an embrace until a cloud passing overhead blocked out the sun and brought them back to their senses.

And later, that night, when Kate lay in bed, staring at the ceiling of her room, listening to the sounds of lovemaking coming from the adjacent bedchamber where Lady Cecilia was allowing Lord Howard certain liberties, she thought about Edward, his sense of duty, and their blossoming love—which they only dared to claim. Edward's father might disapprove of her, but that was not going to stop her from seizing her dreams. Kate had no doubts. A true love such as theirs was far more powerful than a seventy-year-old man who should have died well over a decade ago.

Kate fell asleep, a smile upon her face, dreaming of Edward and the future that belonged to them.

Seventeen

SHE SAW THE THREE OF THEM, ANNE AND EDWARD AND KATE.

Jill tossed restlessly as the sights and sounds of a dinner party became more vivid, more clear, finally coming into sharp focus. She knew she was asleep, and dreaming—and she did not want to dream. Tension kept her body stiff and rigid even as she slept.

But it was only a dinner party, she managed to think. A long table was covered in a blinding white tablecloth, crystal stemware, and gold flatware, with beautiful gold-rimmed plates. Overhead were three or four huge crystal chandeliers, illuminating the room, causing the glasses to catch the light. Several dozen ladies and gentlemen were present, all resplendently dressed for evening, the men in black dinner jackets, the ladies in bare gowns of silk, taffeta, chiffon, in a riot of rainbow colors. Gems glittered upon swanlike throats, dangled from delicate earlobes, winked from graceful fingers. Laughter mingled with the quieter tones of pleasant conversation and the clinking of flutes and wineglasses.

Kate was astonishing in her beauty. Her bronze lace gown daringly bared all of her shoulders and a great deal of her chest. Her curly hair was for the moment tamed, swept back and up on top of her head and held there with diamond pins in the shape of butterflies. A gold locket was around her neck. Jill recognized it immediately and her tension, and her expectation of dread, grew. She knew there would be two exquisite portraits inside, one of Kate, the other of Anne.

Edward was seated across from Kate, beside Anne. In his tuxedo and white shirtfront, he was outstanding—impossibly debonair, elegant, utterly handsome. He was smiling, his gaze on Kate.

Jill could not see Anne clearly. Her gown was a soft blue, perhaps. Her dark hair was, she thought, curled and hanging loose. But her face refused to come into focus. Beside Edward, Anne somehow vanished among the other guests, as if plain and nondescript, as if she were only a shadow of herself.

Edward caught Kate's eye, lifting his flute ever so slightly in a silent salute, to her, for her, to them.

Kate hid her smile, casting her eyes down.

Anne watched them both.

Jill turned over onto her back, wanting to wake up. She did not want to know what might happen next. Kate was happy, Edward was happy, it was too good to be true . . .

The gardens at night, rich with the scent of hyacinth, freesia, lilies, and tuberose. A star-studded night. The guests were strolling outside. Inside, a small string orchestra played. Jill had never heard a harp before, but she recognized its melodious notes now. The pleasant harmony drifted on the night air. Anne, Edward, Kate. The trio was standing by a stone balustrade, not far from a water fountain. Edward said something amusing. Kate's laughter was low, husky, Anne's startling in its high, unusual pitch.

I must wake up, now, before something terrible happens, Jill thought, her fingers digging into the bed beneath her. It was cold, wet.

Why was it cold and wet?

Why was she so cold? Freezing cold, in fact?

Jill's fear grew, she froze.

Anne excused herself.

Jill felt as if she were there. She could not move. She watched Anne turning, leaving the terrace, moving with a grace she must have been schooled in since a child, wanting to see her face—yet not wanting to. Yet Jill could not envision her expression. Anne's small back was to her. Was she dismayed? Hurt? Angry? Or at this point in time, did she not

even care about the love affair unfolding before her very
eyes?

Was she happy for Kate?

Kate and Edward watched her go. Then Edward touched
Kate's bare shoulder. She turned to him, face uplifted, eyes
soft with love.

A stone wall reared itself up in front of Jill.

No! She tried to shout, to scream, the wall so close that she
could touch it, push at it, desperately, but it did no good, it
would not move. It was cold and rough beneath her fingertips.

No! Jill wanted to wake up. She wanted to wake up now,
before she saw something she did not wish to see—not ever
again.

The stone wall loomed over her. Jill tried to push it away
with all of her strength, the effort costing her dearly, hurting
her hands, her shoulders, her back. Sweat began to trickle
down her body, down her temples, interfering with her
vision. No! As she pushed again, the wall seemed to be moving toward her, leaning in over her, closing in upon her . . .

Kate's face flashed before her eyes. Alight with love and
laughter, the locket on the velvet ribbon about her neck.

And in the next instant, the image changed. Kate's face
was stricken with fear. Her porcelain skin was streaked with
tears and dirt. Her eyes were wide, imploring, filled with desperation, and she was reaching out, reaching out, something
in her hand . . .

Jill sat up with a cry.

For one instant, she did not know where she was, still
caught up in the dream, Kate's face in front of her, strained
with fear, her hand extended toward her.

Jill clutched the ground. And only then did the dream vanish, as Jill's fingers dug into cold, wet dirt.

She inhaled, in that shocking instant realizing that she sat
outside, in the dirt and grass, as dawn's gray light crept over
the night. Jill glanced wildly around.

A mist was swirling over the grounds, but she could just
make out the stone walls of the house, perhaps fifty yards
from where she sat. She had wandered outside in her sleep!

Jill looked down at herself in amazement. She was wearing a T-shirt and sweatpants. Her nightclothes were soaking wet and streaked with dirt. She realized she was just as wet, and freezing cold. Shivering, Jill slowly got up, pushing her hair out of her face.

Her teeth began to chatter. She had never walked in her sleep before. She did not know what to think.

Hugging herself—for it was forty degrees or so out and she was barefoot and hardly dressed—Jill ran back toward the house. As she did so, the day grew even lighter. A pink blush stained the mist, the sky. Glancing toward the sea, she could make out the glowing red sun rising over the horizon.

Jill was still dazed as she crossed the terrace that let onto what Alex called "the music room." In Kate's time, he had said, the company would spend an hour or so after supper in the music room, allowing various young ladies to play the piano or the harp and sing for everyone. Jill found the French doors wide open. Was this, then, how she had come outside last night?

And for just how long had she been outside? she wondered wildly. She had no recollection of leaving her bed, much less her room or the house.

Jill paused in the music room. Both the grand piano and a harp remained in it, the harp removed to a corner by a pair of windows, the piano in a central location. Shivering, she crossed her arms more tightly around herself, her befuddled mind now recalling that she had dreamed not just about Kate, but about Edward and Anne, as well. She had been afraid as the dream unfolded, but nothing had really happened in the dream, it had merely been some kind of dinner party, with Kate and Edward having eyes only for one another. It had been so vivid, so real, and they had clearly been in love.

Jill was still disoriented and confused. Why hadn't she dreamed of Edward being a cold and cunning playboy, out to use Kate? Unfortunately, he had been rather likable, but it had only been a dream.

Suddenly Jill remembered the last, frightening part of her dream. Kate had been frantically, desperately reaching out, toward someone, with something in her hand. Had she been trying to give something to someone? If so, who? And what had she been holding?

Then Jill recalled the stone walls. Her stomach tightened and lurched, sickeningly, and Jill was afraid she might throw up.

She waited a moment for her lurching stomach to subside, and then she turned and closed the terrace doors. As she did so, she caught a glimpse of her reflection in a gold-framed mirror that hung above a pedestal table against one flocked wall. Jill froze.

Then, trembling, slowly, she looked at her reflection again.

And for a blinding instant, she saw Kate.

Not as she had been at the dinner party in her evening gown, but as she had been in the tower, her face pale and dirty, her hair tangled in knots, swirling around her face.

Jill's heart began to pound.

Jill walked slowly to the mirror, pausing a foot or so in front of it, afraid to look at herself again.

But she did. Her face was as white as a new sheet. But dirt streaked it. Her hair was a riot of tangles, cascading about her face. Her eyes were huge, and in this light, they appeared black. And because her skin was so pale, her mole stood out darkly on her face.

She looked exactly like Kate. Fair, curly-haired, sensuous, terrified. Fear seized Jill. Suddenly she whirled to flee.

Alex gripped her shoulders. "Jesus Christ! What the hell happened to you?"

Jill stood in her bathroom wrapped up in the thick terry robe, hugging herself, staring at her pale face in the mirror. She had just gotten out of the shower and steam filled the bathroom, clouding the mirror. She was frightened. She had never walked in her sleep before. What was happening to her?

She did not move. She did not want to leave the sanctuary of the steamy bathroom. Alex was in her bedroom. She could hear him speaking to someone—either he was on the phone or he was talking to a housemaid.

But she couldn't remain in the bathroom forever. If only

her mind would stop spinning, racing, if only she could shake off the crystal-clear images of that last, horrible dream.

Jill left the bathroom. Alex had been pacing; he paused in midstride. "Come. Sit by the fire. Before you catch pneumonia."

She glanced at him as he pulled a huge armchair forward. She went and sat down in it. The upholstered chair dwarfed her. It was easier to obey than not.

Jill wanted to stop thinking, just for a while. But she couldn't. What if she were losing the last of her marbles?

Alex pulled an ottoman in a paisley silk fabric over and sat down beside her. Jill watched the dancing fire. "Jill." He took her hands in his. Jill was forced to meet his gaze. "You will become deathly ill if you keep this up. This has to stop."

She stared at him. "I don't know what happened," she finally said. "I was walking in my sleep. Can you imagine?" Her light tone was high and forced.

"Is this a habit of yours?"

"No." Jill felt herself losing her grip. She was ready to burst into tears. "I've never walked in my sleep before. I'm scared."

"You don't have to be scared," he said calmly. "As soon as you're dressed and ready we'll drive back to London. I want you to go to my doctor. He's a great guy. The old Marcus Welby type. He'll check you out and give you something to calm you down, help you sleep. You need a few days of rest, Jill. No more hunting down Kate." He smiled at her, his eyes warm.

Jill stared at him, her temples starting to pound. He was giving orders. He was telling her to quit her search for the truth. Why? "Alex, I'm so close, I can feel it. There's something on my mind, some clue I've overlooked, and I know it's going to come to me—"

"Didn't you hear a word I said?" He was incredulous.

She hesitated. A knock on the door interrupted them. Alex stood, opening it. A young maid entered, followed by another girl, the two of them carrying trays loaded with coffee, tea, muffins, fruits, and several covered plates. Jill smelled eggs and bacon and steaming hot porridge laced with cinnamon. She had no appetite.

"Sir? I brought enough fer two. Can I make the table, then, fer you both?" No more than sixteen, she smiled at him.

"Yes, please, Rose, that would be very nice."

Rose and her friend were very efficient. A moment later they left, closing the door behind them. Jill stared at the heavily laden table without even seeing it.

"What aren't you telling me?" Alex asked, pausing before her.

She looked up. "I dreamed about her again, but this time, she was with Edward and Anne."

"And that's it?"

"No, that's not it!" Jill cried. She began to shiver. She was so cold. The hot, endless shower hadn't been able to chase away the chill within her bones, and Jill knew why—it was because the chill was in her heart, not her body. "It was so vivid, so real, Alex, it was as if I were there! I could see everyone so clearly, and Edward and Kate were in love." Jill gazed at Alex, but she saw Edward's handsome, aristocratic countenance instead. Alight with love and happiness. "He didn't kill her. He was head over heels in love with her."

Alex was silent.

"I couldn't see Anne," Jill said, standing. "She was there, but so out of focus, her image was not clear. I could not tell what her expression, her feelings, were. Kate and Edward were happy, but Anne was an enigma."

"Jill. It was only a dream." He slid his arm around her waist.

"It was too real to only be a dream," Jill cried. She finally focused on him. "I'm losing it, aren't I? I'm going crazy. It's Kate. She's around, and she's haunting me. Because she wants me to deliver justice."

"You're not going crazy." Alex was firm. He cupped her shoulders. "In the past five weeks you've been through hell, Jill. *It was only a dream.* You've been living and breathing Kate's life. Why wouldn't you dream about Kate and Edward? I think it's pretty natural, and I think you're very romantic, and you would dream about them being in love and happy—I'm sure they were, for a while. And it makes complete sense that you would not dream as vividly about Anne—because Anne doesn't interest you, and in this quest of yours, you haven't learned anything about her, yet." He smiled, but it was fleeting. "Kate is dead, Jill, she's not here, haunting you."

Jill stared at him. She did not smile back. "I want to believe you. I do. But I don't. I can't."

Jill just looked at him. He didn't understand. How could he? He wasn't the one who had to find out the truth about Kate. He wasn't the one with the weird dreams. He wasn't the one who was completely alone in the world.

Alex slid his arm around her and guided her to the table. "I have a great idea. Why don't you take a long weekend on the coast somewhere? There are some very pleasant resorts scattered about this country, you know. Maybe I can even swing some more time for myself, and I'll go with you."

Their eyes held. Jill tried, desperately, to search their depths, but she could not read him. "Let's face the fact that you want me to go home. To *rest*," she said.

He shifted. "That's right. And what is suspicious about that? If I care about you, I don't want to see you hurting yourself."

"Your family covered up Kate's death," Jill said. "*Your* family, Alex."

"There is no proof," he said flatly. "You're clinging to dreams, Jill, because you're hurt and alone and desperate for a family of your own."

"And if I find proof?"

"If you find proof," Alex said evenly, "then I'd like to see it."

"You'd be the first," she returned, turning away. Her tote was on another chair, not far from the bed. Jill sat down, digging inside. She extracted the wedding photo of her parents, the one of Jack and Shirley surrounded by the best man and maid of honor, Shirley's parents behind them, alongside Peter. Suddenly Jill's vision blurred.

Sweet dreams, pumpkin.

Good night, dear.

Jill felt terribly alone. What she wouldn't give for one moment in her mother's or her father's arms.

"What's that?" Alex asked, wandering over.

Jill handed him the photograph. "My parents, the best man and maid of honor, my maternal grandparents, and Peter."

Alex's eyes widened and he stared.

"What is it?" Jill asked sharply, but as she spoke, the dream she'd had flashed through her mind, Edward smiling at Kate, that silent salute with the flute, Edward . . .

"Nothing," Alex said, shoving the photo back at her.

Jill stood, staring down at the photograph, her eyes on Peter. "Oh, my God," she inhaled. "Now I know why he looks so familiar. My grandfather is almost sixty here—and he looks like an exact older version of Edward in that portrait at Uxbridge Hall—doesn't he?" she cried. And it was a challenge.

Alex met her gaze. He seemed reluctant. "Yeah," he finally said.

December 1, 1907

Dear Diary,

I know I have not written in several months, but so much has happened that I hardly know where to begin! I miss Kate so much I hardly know what to do with myself—yet, in some unfathomable way, I am relieved that she has gone home. She departed for New York in great haste, so much so that I hardly know what happened. But Mother, of course, is so very pleased that she is gone. I think Mother knows about Kate's affair— but I am jumping ahead of myself.

How odd it is. I remember, before Kate left, how we would go to all the parties and fêtes together, how no one ever noticed me, how they all remarked on Kate— the men and the women, even though I am as great an heiress as she, and of course, I come from an ancient and noble lineage. How different it is with Kate gone. Now, when I go to a dinner party or a ball or even shopping on Bond Street, I am noticed instantly. Gentlemen cross the street in order to bow over my hand.

Ladies extend more invitations than ever, so many I cannot possibly accept them all. Mother says Kate was a terribly negative influence in my life, preventing me from numerous opportunities. I am beginning to believe that she is right.

I must take a great big breath and calm myself. That is easier said than done! One hardly knows what to do when one suddenly becomes en vogue! And now, smiling, I do use dear Kate's fondest expression. Ah, Kate. I must write her and tell her how popular I have become—without ever telling her the truth, of course.

I am even beginning to think that I might marry not just for position, but for love.

I can almost hear Kate applauding me now for my bold thinking. How pleased she would be for me. Yet thinking about Kate saddens me, too. The past few months were the most wonderful of my life. Kate was— is—the best friend I shall ever have. Sometimes I miss her so that I almost weep. But then I think about my popularity now that she is gone, and the sorrow diminishes. Mother keeps reminding me that if Kate were still here, it would drive my most respectable and pre-eminent suitors away.

That is why it is best that Kate has gone home. If I knew about her love affair (which she denied), then others undoubtedly suspected, as well. I am sure that Mother guessed. Kate is so headstrong. She refused to listen to my words of caution, and every time she stole out of my window to meet her lover, I envisioned the worst. Kate swore to me that their every rendezvous remained chaste. I hardly believe that. I know Kate too well. How often did Kate not tell me that one must live life in the present, instead of waiting for a future time that might never come?

I am haunted by her love affair. I think about it constantly, Kate in the arms of some faceless stranger. (For she refused to reveal his identity to me.) I admit, I admire her daring. I could never slip out at night to meet my paramour—if I had one—much less climb down from a second-story window to do so! I also admit that a part of myself is filled with envy. Imagine those heated nights, spent in a lover's strong arms! I have never been kissed and I wonder, continually, what it must be like.

I do wonder who this paragon of men is, to have so well stolen my dear friend's heart. I have concluded that he is married, and the worst of rogues. Because if he were not, he would court Kate openly. Either that, or his lineage is so ancient, so impeccable, that he could never consider Kate as a bride.

And, writing of paragons, I must come to the most exciting part of my tale. I have met a man. Dear Diary, he is the most charming, handsome, clever gentleman, a man who outshines all his peers. When he walks into the room, I can see no one else—it is as if he stands there alone. Actually, I first met him at Lord Willow's box in Swinton last summer. His name is Edward Sheldon, and he is the earl of Collinsworth's heir. I am falling in love, dearest Diary!

Indeed, I do think I have heard several dowagers discussing my prospects at several recent gatherings— and Lord Braxton's name was mentioned along with mine! I have already hinted of my interest to Papa. Oh, to recall the look in his eyes! And I have actually heard Mother and Lady Cecilia scheming over the union.

He is not courting me. But then, he has not courted anyone. The gossips say he is a rogue, with no intention of ever settling down, at least, not until the earl himself is dead. But then there are other rumors too, that his heart is taken, but by some inferior type, perhaps a French actress, who can never aspire to more than being his mistress, and that is why he is so reticent, why he seems to be bored with all the available young ladies of the ton, why he is forever so aloof and elusive.

I know that such a man could never love a French tart. Briefly, at Swinton Hall, I thought he might be interested in Kate. I must admit, I was somewhat taken by him even then, but last summer, with Kate beside me, outshining me, I was a true wallflower—and hardly confident enough to even speak with him. How that has changed. Still, I do confess, I was jealous when I saw his flirtation with Kate. But whatever interest he might have had for her, or she for him, it was either in my imagination or they both found other, newer pursuits. I have seen them in the same room many times since that week at Swinton Hall. They never even look at one another—if they did have a flirtation, it ended when our week in the country did.

I am glad. I love Kate, truly, and I want her to marry well (she should find an American husband, from among the nouveau riche), but I am going to marry Lord Braxton. I love him even now, as I write to you, dear Diary, and I shall be his wife, I shall bear his children, I shall manage his homes and estates. And one day, I shall be the countess of Collinsworth. This I have promised myself. I have no doubts.

Tomorrow Mother is allowing me to attend a small Christmas party. Edward shall also be there. I cannot wait.

Eighteen

JILL LET HERSELF INTO THE FLAT, HOLDING THE DOOR AJAR with her hip, her hands full with her small duffel bag and tote. She turned to watch Alex drive away in his sleek silver monster. She wanted to wave, but she couldn't. She smiled instead but was certain he had not seen her.

She entered the house. The flat felt like home. It was cozy and inviting and she was so glad to be back. Yorkshire had not been what she had expected. Jill shivered, thinking of all she had learned.

And sitting there on the stairs facing her was Lady Eleanor, licking one of her velvety paws.

Jill stepped inside, putting her bags down, letting the front door slam shut. "Hi, Lady E.," she said quietly.

The cat stopped bathing itself and meowed at her.

Jill walked over to the stairs and sat down beside the Siamese. She was aware of being very alone—and she had not felt that way during the weekend. But then, she had not been alone in Yorkshire. She'd had Alex as a companion—and as a lover for that one single night.

Jill shook herself free of such unwelcome thoughts. Lady E. had not leaped away. Jill touched her soft fur. The cat began to purr and Jill continued to caress her back.

She was aware of being exhausted, and she thought longingly of crawling into bed, even though it was only one in the afternoon. But she was afraid to sleep because she was afraid to dream—and what if she walked in her sleep again, as she had done last night? Somehow, the idea was more than frightening, it was terrifying.

"What's happening to me, Lady E.?" Jill whispered. She couldn't stop thinking about Kate, but now she was also haunted by someone who was very much alive. If only she hadn't slept with Alex, if only she could trust him completely.

Jill dialed up her neighbor, determined to concentrate on solving the mystery of Kate and not get sidetracked by personal feelings she hadn't ever wanted in the first place. "How was Yorkshire?" Lucinda asked after they had exchanged greetings.

"I have found out so much," Jill said. Immediately, her temples began to throb. "Lucinda, do you know of a handwriting expert who could compare signatures for me? Quickly?"

"Actually, I do. Having worked at so many museums, we've often used handwriting experts to authenticate works of art, old letters, and other artifacts of that nature." Lucinda gave her the name and telephone number of an Arthur Kingston, whose office suite was in Cheapside. "Why do you need a handwriting expert, Jill?"

Jill told her about the hospital records, the birth certificate, and the receipt signed by Jonathan Barclay.

"Well," Lucinda said slowly. "You most certainly have come up with some interesting clues. What did you think of Stainesmore?"

"I think it's lovely," Jill said. "Lucinda. We found Kate's grave."

There was a brief pause, in which Jill felt Lucinda's surprise. "You what?!"

Jill told her about the small, barely noticeable headstone and the engraved date. "Can you believe it?"

"Actually, I am stunned," Lucinda replied. "I hardly know what to think." She lapsed into silence and Jill knew she was thinking about the effort and risk someone had taken to bury Kate—and the fact that that someone had known she was dead, where her body was, and the day she died. "And to think the authorities never knew."

"Was Hal in love with Kate, Lucinda?"

Lucinda made a small sound of surprise. "I don't know, my dear. Wouldn't that have been rather, er, bizarre?"

"It would have been more than bizarre, it would have been an obsession." Jill told Lucinda about the portrait in the attic, and Hal having discovered it when he was thirteen. Hal's odd interest in Kate—his obsession—had begun then, that summer. She was certain of it. And Alex must have also known. Hadn't he said, more than once, that he and Hal had been very close as boys?

"What a fabulous discovery!" Lucinda cried excitedly.

"I think so." Jill sighed. "I still need some kind of proof that Kate is my great-grandmother. But if those signatures match up, then Edward Collinsworth was the father of her child."

Lucinda was absolutely silent.

"Lucinda? Are you still there?"

"Are you certain, Jill?"

"Yeah." Jill was about to elaborate when she heard a click on her phone. "Lucinda, can we talk later? I have another call."

"Of course, dear," Lucinda said.

Jill was about to depress the hook. "Lucinda, are you friendly with the Sheldons?"

"I beg your pardon?"

"I saw—or I think I saw—one of their cars out front a few minutes ago. No one buzzed me—but I was wondering if someone stopped in on you."

"Dear, I adore that family—but I am merely a paid employee. I would hardly receive a social call from the earl."

Jill thanked her, saying good-bye. And the instant she hung up the phone, having lost her other caller, something clicked in her mind. Jill froze. She hadn't asked Lucinda if William had dropped by. She hadn't been that specific. She had been asking about Lucinda's relationship with the entire family.

Jill would bet her last dime that Lucinda had just had a visit from the earl. What she couldn't figure out was, why?

Jill awoke, startled from a deep sleep by a noise she could not identify. For one moment she was disoriented and confused, and then, squinting through the darkness, she realized she had fallen asleep on the sofa in the parlor and it was already dark.

A cat yowled.

Jill sat up, unbearably groggy, reaching for the lamp on the table beside the couch. She missed and the next thing she knew, she heard the lamp crashing to the floor.

Jill cursed, because the lamp was porcelain and an antique. She wondered what time it was and if one of her cats had cried out in the backyard. A neighbor had a German shepherd puppy. Lucinda had told her that he'd gotten off his chain and out of his yard twice during the weekend while Jill was away, causing the cats no small amount of distress. Sir John had been treed, and had refused to come down for hours.

Groping, Jill found her way past the coffee table and armchair to the light switch on the wall by the front door. She flicked it and the entry was flooded with light. She immediately saw that the lamp had not been broken. She was relieved; it would have been nearly impossible to replace.

She looked at her watch. It was half past eight in the evening. She did not remember lying down, much less falling asleep. Had she slept all afternoon? Suddenly she was famished, and dialed out for a pizza.

Immediately she thought about Kate. At least she hadn't dreamed, thank God.

Something crashed outside in the backyard.

Jill hurried through the parlor, not pausing to right the lamp. In the kitchen she flicked on more lights, stepping out onto the back stoop. The backyard was only illuminated in the vicinity of the stoop, for there were no outdoor lights in the garden. When her neighbors were at home, their lights would shine brightly in the farthest corners of the yard. But tonight, apparently, they were out, because the two houses facing her garden were utterly dark.

"Lady E.! Sir John! Psst, psst!" Jill called, still fighting the deep grogginess she was afflicted with.

She scanned the yard, but saw no dog, and neither cat. Well, the cats could undoubtedly take care of themselves, and she did not have a clue as to what had fallen over, but she'd worry about it tomorrow in the light of another day.

A strange crying sound seemed to drift through the house.

Jill had just opened up a can of Coke and she froze. For a moment, she thought she was hearing a woman's weeping—and the first woman she thought of was Kate.

But the sound was so faint. Jill put the Coke down, straining to hear. Then she heard it again. A soft, pitiful crying.

Kate was dead. And Jill might believe in ghosts—sort of—but she had never seen one, nor did she want to. Her skin crawled. Anxiously, she glanced around the kitchen and at the night-blackened windows.

She told herself that she wasn't hearing anything. It was her imagination.

But the pervasive crying seemed to linger.

Her heart began to thud. Sweat dampened her skin. Jill told herself not to be an idiot. A television was probably on next door—never mind that she had not heard it or any appliance or even voices from next door since she had taken up residence in the flat. She walked out of the kitchen. As she did so, she heard nothing, but when she stopped in the center of the parlor, her footsteps no longer softly sounding, she heard the noise again.

Her gaze shot to the stairs. Was it coming from upstairs?

Shit, Jill thought. The upstairs was cast in blackness, and she did not want to go up.

The light switch was on the landing above.

The crying—more like a mewling—continued.

It seemed very real.

I'm a coward, Jill thought. She looked around, for an object with which to defend herself, then decided, if she was about to confront a ghost, nothing would help. She started cautiously toward the stairs. She went up them slowly. On the landing she paused, in utter darkness, the moaning now distinct.

It seemed to be coming from her bedroom, by God.

Jill hit the light. It flooded the hall. Was it the cat?

No longer afraid of ghosts, Jill rushed into the bedroom,

turning on the lights, glancing around. The pitiful sound came from under the bed.

Jill got down on all fours, her pulse pounding. "John? John?" She crept forward. She did not understand. Sir John never came into any room when she was present, and he had not set foot in this bedroom while she was in it, either. But now she saw him crouching beneath the bed, mewling, his gaze wide and fixated on her.

"Come here, sweetie," Jill called. "What's wrong, darling?" She knew better than to reach out to him.

The cat stopped crying. It stared at her, its expression unbelievably human—incredibly distraught.

The hairs rose up on every inch of Jill's body just as the knocker on the front door sounded. Jill jumped, scared out of her wits. Then she told herself it was probably the pizza. She glanced back at the bottom of the bed. What was wrong with Sir John?

The knocker sounded again, more insistently. Jill hurried from the room, stumbling downstairs. She had the sense to pause in the entry. "Who is it?"

"Pizza."

Relieved, yet still very distressed with the cat's behavior, Jill opened the door. A chubby freckle-faced boy held the box toward her with one hand, and with the other, he pointed—to his left. "Miss," he said.

Jill looked in the direction he was pointing.

"You have a dead cat on your porch, miss," he said.

As he spoke, Jill saw the decapitated cat, lying in a pool of bright red blood.

As the primal scream started to form deep inside her chest, she realized it was Lady E.

Jill screamed.

Nineteen

JILL FLED INTO THE HOUSE, RAN BLINDLY INTO THE GUEST POW-
der room, where she promptly threw up.

"Miss! You have to pay for the pizza!"

Jill clutched the toilet bowl, waves of dizziness assailing
her, Lady E.'s headless, bloody body engraved on her mind.
The delivery boy continued to shout at her. Jill could not
focus on what he was saying. *Lady E. was dead.*

She retched again, but dryly.

The delivery boy was banging on the door now.

Jill turned and staggered out of the bathroom. What
should she do? She was mindless with shock and confusion.

Suddenly she ran across the parlor and into the kitchen.
Oh, God! Where was her tote with her Filofax?

Jill rushed back into the parlor, saw her tote by the door
where she had left her duffel bag. As she ran to it, she saw
through the window that the boy with her pizza was leaving,
already on the sidewalk, about to climb into his Renault. Jill
reached for the tote as another wave of dizziness swept over
her. Lady E. was dead. Really, truly, brutally dead.

Someone had *beheaded* her.

Where was the damn Filofax? Her hands shaking, Jill
threw tissues, a pen, her lipstick and mirror, a tour guide of
Britain, and her relatively new black Ray•Ban sunglasses
violently from the bag. They scattered across the floor. A few
old business cards followed. More tissues, a map. She finally
seized the Filofax. The closest phone was in the parlor. Jill

ran to it, opening the book as she did so, P . . . Preston. She dialed and prayed.

Alex picked up instantly—and she had called him on his private line at his office. "Preston."

"Alex, she's dead, someone cut off her head!" Jill choked.

"Jesus, Jill! Who's dead?"

"Lady E.!" In spite of the fact that Jill's mind did not seem to be functioning, she realized what Alex was thinking. "One of the Siamese cats. They cut off her head, left her on the porch, oh, God, I'm going to be sick again." Jill dropped the phone and ran back to the powder room, only to retch violently and dryly again.

When the heaves had passed, she was on her knees, and she pressed her cheek against the side of the sink's medicine cabinet. Tears began to flow freely down her face. She gasped, trying not to cry, but she failed. And then she thought of Sir John, upstairs, hiding under her bed, crying so pitifully. Now she understood. He had been terrorized—and was now mourning the death of his mate.

Jill froze. The comprehension was brutal, searing—terrifying. A noise in the garden had awoken her from her nap in the first place. That, followed by a cat's yowl and a crash. Oh, dear God.

Jill managed to stand upright. She was shaking uncontrollably.

Someone had caught Lady E. and killed her while Jill was asleep—or just after she had woken up—right there by the house.

What if that someone was still lurking outside?

Jill ran to the front door and bolted it. Panting, she froze, straining to hear anything—anyone. To her dismay, she had left the phone off the hook, and now she could hear it buzzing loudly. She remained motionless, attempting to filter out that sound. She did not think she could hear Sir John crying upstairs. Her heart twisted painfully whenever she thought about him.

Had he stopped mewling—or was the damned telephone interfering with her ability to hear?

Pain stabbed through her again. Poor Lady E. How could

someone so grossly murder the lovely, elegant, personable cat?

The tears poured down her face. Why had someone done this? Why?

And then Jill knew why. It had not been a prank. Oh, no.

Jill wet her lips and slammed off the entryway lights. The downstairs was immediately cast in shadows and darkness, but the upstairs remained lit. Jill did not dare go up those stairs. It occurred to her that Lady E.'s murderer might have stolen into the house—if he or she had wanted to—while she was upstairs with Sir John—or downstairs with the pizza boy.

Don't be afraid, Jill told herself, inhaling raggedly. There's no reason the cat's killer would come inside.

Her heart was pounding like a heavy drum inside of her breast. Fear almost immobilized her. Jill started very slowly across the parlor, pausing every few seconds to listen for the sound of an intruder, hiding inside or outside of the house. She only heard the sound of her own labored breathing and the goddamned phone.

Before she entered the kitchen she peeked inside, her back flat to the adjacent wall. It appeared to be empty. Jill slammed off the lights, ran across it, closed the back door—which had been ajar. Oh, God! As she locked both the push button on the knob and then slid the small bolt home, she realized the two locks looked silly and incapable of deterring even the least experienced of burglars.

What had Alex said? He had said he could pick the front locks with his eyes closed.

And Jill heard the screech of tires and the roar of his monster's engine even from the kitchen, where she stood, forgetting to breathe. She did not move.

Lady E. was a warning. Jill was certain of it. Who had delivered that warning?

Someone who did not want her identifying Kate's murderer. A Sheldon—or even Alex Preston.

"Jill! Jill!" Alex was knocking loudly, repeatedly, on the front door. "Jesus!"

Jill began to shake again. Alex was very loyal to the Sheldons, but he would never go so far. He was not a nut, and he had not murdered Lady E. He had been in his office.

But what about call forwarding?

"Jill! Are you okay? God damn it!" he exploded from outside.

Jill did not move. For all she knew, he could have been outside with his cell phone, taking her call moments ago.

Or he could have had someone else do his dirty work for him.

Glass exploded, shattering.

Jill cried out.

Suddenly Alex was racing through the house, lights flooding it as he hit switch after switch. He halted in his tracks when he saw Jill, who remained standing frozen in the kitchen, her back to the door she had locked only moments ago.

"Thank God you're okay!" He strode to her.

His face was a mask of concern. But she stepped away from him, ducking out of his reach.

His eyes widened. "Jill?"

She tried, desperately, to think clearly—to get a grip on her hysteria and fear. But her emotions were out of control. Jill felt as if she were approaching the very worst downhill descent on a roller coaster. "Someone killed the cat!"

"I know. Jill. It's okay," he soothed.

She couldn't back up again—her spine was pressed against the door, the tiny bolt digging painfully into one shoulder blade. "It's not okay. Lady E. is dead. Who killed her?"

"How the hell would I know?"

She just stared at him, her mind going round and round in spinning circles, with Lady E.'s bloody image the heart of it all.

"You're shaking like a leaf." He stepped toward her, reaching out for her.

Jill stepped away. "It wasn't a prank."

His eyes widened.

"It was a warning."

"A warning," Alex repeated, as if he did not understand English.

Jill nodded, and she started to cry.

Suddenly he wrapped his arms around her and pulled her into his embrace. "You're shaking. You're stiff as a board. Honey. It was a prank."

"You're one of them," she wanted to say, but she didn't, because she was weeping, all over his pale blue button-down shirt and red checked tie.

One of his big hands stroked through her hair, over and down the back of her head. "Don't cry. Don't you know that's the one thing us big machos can't handle?"

She smiled against his chest.

He held her more tightly. "Oh, shit. This is out of hand," he muttered—or she thought that was what he said.

Jill hoped she hadn't heard him say that. Maybe she had misunderstood his meaning. Maybe he had meant he couldn't deal with her tears. In any case, she was being paranoid to think that he had anything to do with the cat's death, to think that he might know who had a hand in it. Alex might be protective of his family, but he was not a "sicko." Only someone with the lack of morals of a sociopath would decapitate a beloved pet—or any animal, for that matter.

He felt safe now, when the night felt terrifying.

His hands stilled, now on her shoulders.

Jill finally, slowly, looked up, into his eyes.

Their gazes locked.

"Do you know who killed the cat?" Jill heard herself say very calmly now. But the calm was superficial. She remained sick inside of herself.

He stiffened, releasing her. "Let's talk."

Jill nodded. She went to the kitchen table and sat down. Alex went to the counter, opening up cabinets. "I have no booze," she said.

"Great." He opened the refrigerator, scanned its contents, closed it. "You need help here, kiddo. Now I see why you're so thin."

"He took my pizza." Jill wasn't hungry, but she heard how dull her tone was.

He came and sat down, pulling his chair close to hers. "Did you call the police?"

"No."

"I'll call."

She seized his wrist. "Why?"

"So the kid who did this gets his due," Alex said with anger flaring in his eyes.

Jill looked at him.

He stared back.

"Someone wants me to go home," Jill said flatly. "Because of Kate—and you know it, too."

He studied her. "I don't know if I buy that," he said, his tone even. He turned away, but not before Jill saw the anger in his expression.

Was he furious because someone had done this to her? Or because someone in his family had something to do with it and she had correctly guessed so? Jill stared. She could not decide.

Alex did not have to do his own dirty work. He was loaded.

Jill closed her eyes briefly, wishing she'd not had that thought—again.

If he was involved in any way, then he was an utter sociopath.

"Let me make a few calls," Alex said. "I'll have someone come over and clean up, I'll have some scotch delivered, and some food, too. You want a Valium?"

She didn't answer, thinking that she was afraid not to have her wits about her.

"That doctor I mentioned. I can call him right now and—"

"No."

"Okay." He smiled at her, but his gaze was searching. "Hey. You are one helluva tough gal." He touched her cheek briefly with his fingertips.

His touch was comforting. Jill stood, confused. "I don't want to stay the night here alone," she said cautiously.

"Of course not. I'll stay. On the couch," he added, returning her stare.

Jill nodded. "Lady E." She stopped, fighting her sudden loss of composure. "We had become friends."

"I know," he said softly. "I know."

*   *   *

Jill had changed into sweats and thick white socks. As she combed her hair, which was damp from a shower, she stared at her reflection in the mirror. She was utterly devoid of color, except for her hair, which appeared a dark red, and her mole, which stood out against her pale skin. Jill's hand stilled. She felt as if she were looking at another version of Kate Gallagher.

She felt as if she were looking at her twin.

She laid the comb down. A few minutes ago she had heard Alex speaking with someone downstairs—perhaps a delivery boy or whoever he had called to clean up the porch.

Jill's knees buckled and she gripped the small sink for support. She had to tell Allen Barrows about his cat. And she had to ask him what he wanted to do with her. The prospect was unpleasant.

Sir John remained beneath her bed, crouching and watchful. Jill wanted to pick him up and hug him, but she was afraid she would chase him away.

Jill left the bathroom, making little noise in her thick wool socks. She checked on Sir John, who stared unblinkingly at her, and left the bedroom. The downstairs was cast in silence—Jill wondered if Alex had fallen asleep on the couch before offering her a scotch. She was about to take one step down those stairs, her hand on the smooth wooden banister, when she suddenly heard his voice. He was talking in very low tones, so she could not hear what he was saying, but he was extremely angry.

Jill stiffened, straining to hear. Now there was only silence.

Who was he talking to? And why was he angry?

Her pulse began to pound. Jill stepped down the stairs, one at a time, careful not to make a sound. On the bottom landing, she froze. He was, she thought, in the kitchen, on his cell phone.

Why hadn't he used her telephone?

"I'm warning you," Alex suddenly ground out. "You've fucked up big-time." There was a pause. And Alex said, his tone hard and angry and mocking, "Right."

Jill's heart slammed against her breastbone with sickening force. She clutched the wall for support, waiting for him to speak again. An endless minute or two passed. She finally concluded that he had hung up.

Surely "You've fucked up big-time" did not mean what it seemed to mean. It could mean anything. He could be on the phone with a business associate, they could be discussing a deal. She should not conclude that he was angry with his henchman, for messing up Lady E.'s murder.

There was another explanation for the call. There had to be.

Alex was not a killer.

"Jill?" He suddenly came striding into the parlor.

Jill rearranged her face and stepped around the corner of the entry, into the parlor, facing him. Her smile felt like a plaster cast.

"Now what? You're looking at me like I'm a serial killer." His smile vanished. "You don't think I had something to do with the cat?"

Jill shook her head vehemently. "No. I don't. I just came down to say good night. I'm really tired. Thanks for coming over." She hesitated. "I'm fine now. You don't have to stay."

His gaze was searching. "I'm staying. I don't want you here alone." He hesitated. "How about a drink?"

She finally dared to meet his vivid blue gaze. She no longer wanted him to stay—but on the other hand, she dreaded—was terrified—to be alone. Jill shook her head, biting her lip, tears forming in her eyes. "No. That's okay."

He came swiftly to her, pulling her into his arms. "Everything will work out, Jill. Trust me. Please."

She met his brilliant gaze, her body stiff and resistant against his. "I want to," she whispered. "I really do." It was the truth.

His hand has slipped to her nape, under her wet hair. "Then just do it. I would never hurt you. You know how I feel about you."

She found it hard to breathe, and she wanted to back away, but she did not. Her eyes searched his. "No. I don't."

His jaw flexed. His hand, on the nape of her neck, seemed

to tighten. An image of Lady E.'s decapitated, bloody body flashed through Jill's mind. And suddenly he was leaning over her, and his mouth touched hers.

The image of the dead cat vanished.

His lips were soft, barely there, uncertain. Jill forgot to breathe.

And then his mouth came down without hesitation, firmly, on hers. His hands closed on her shoulders. Jill's mouth parted and they stood there, for a long time, kissing with growing abandon and urgency, with mutual need.

Jill did not know who ended the kiss. But suddenly they were apart, staring at one another, breathing unevenly, both of them equally surprised. And then Alex glanced past her, toward the stairs.

Jill understood.

Then a sharp recollection of the bloody, headless Lady E. swept the sudden need away. She needed comfort, but she did not dare. "I can't. Not tonight."

"I understand." His smile was slight, forced.

Jill felt like crying again. "Good night," she managed. And she watched him walk back into the kitchen, where he was undoubtedly pouring himself a drink.

Jill turned and went upstairs.

The next morning, she found Alex hunched over the Libretto. It was just past seven, and the aroma of freshly made coffee filled the kitchen, as did bright morning sunlight. The day promised to be devoid of fog or rain.

Jill studied him from behind. He was so engrossed in whatever it was that he was doing that he had not heard her enter the room. He hit a few keys. "Good morning," Jill finally said.

He jumped, turning. "Scared me." His smile disappeared as his gaze searched her face. "How'd you sleep?"

"Nightmares." Jill went over to the coffeemaker and poured herself a mug. Her dreams had been terrifying, all of them about some faceless man with a bloody ax chasing her and Lady E. She didn't want to talk about it—she didn't want to think about it. She was exhausted. "You're pretty handy to

have around. A Sir Galahad who also makes fresh coffee."
She saluted him with the mug.

"Some of us bachelors can even fry eggs," Alex said,
smiling slightly. But his gaze was too direct, and Jill turned
away so he couldn't read her. "I've got a nine o'clock meeting so I have to run shortly. How are you doing?"

"Okay." A lie. She felt like death warmed over, and she
couldn't stop thinking about the length someone had gone to
in order to scare her away. Jill hesitated. "So who killed the
cat? Thomas? Lauren? Your uncle?"

"You don't mince words." He powered off and closed the
small, silver-gray lid. When he met her gaze, his face was
strained.

Jill wondered what had been on his screen—what it was
that he did not want her to see.

He slipped on his suit jacket. "It's nice to see a hint of
color in your cheeks, Jill." His words were not at all in keeping with his tone, which was slightly cool.

She stared. This would be so much easier, she thought, if
they hadn't slept together, if they hadn't even kissed last
night. Or if he hadn't spent the night on her couch, offering
some degree of both comfort and protection. "I want to talk."

He set his briefcase down on the table. "Obviously."

Jill leaned her hip against the counter, bracing her body.
"Alex. You're a smart man. Let's not play games. What happened last night was not a prank. This is a good neighborhood. There's no crime here."

He was silent.

"I'm upsetting the Sheldon applecart, aren't I?"

"No one in my family is capable of that kind of brutality,"
he said, his face stiff with tension. "And I disagree with you.
I think this was a prank. There's always some crime in every
neighborhood, Jill."

She felt ill at the prospect of baiting him. There was no
choice. "Then why didn't you call the police?"

"I already did. Someone came by last night, and I gave my
statement; a detective will be by today to take yours."

She'd lost that round. "I hope you're right," she finally
said.

"I know I'm right." He fisted his hands on his hips. "Jill, you are a wreck. Here." He reached into his breast pocket and handed her a business card. "Go see Dr. McFee. He's the kind of doctor who will take one look at you and then he'll sit you down and talk to you the way a father would. You need to shut down, Jill. You can't see clearly; you can't think clearly."

"You want me to quit now? When I'm so close to finding out the truth about Kate—and your family?" Jill was angry. "This isn't the first time you've gotten on my case—and we both know why."

"God damn it!" he exploded. "There's no conspiracy here, and what happened to Kate ninety years ago is a done deal. You can't bring her back. If she was killed, you can't prosecute her murderer. Let it go before you make yourself—and everyone—insane!"

Jill was shocked by his loss of control. "I can't. I need to know what happened to Kate. I think I already do know." She didn't hesitate. "Edward killed her because she stood in the way of his marriage to Anne." Her heart thumped painfully as she spoke. In her dreams, Edward had seemed to be in love—and not a killer. But those were only her dreams. She had to rely on logic now, not fantasy. Jill had seen too many portraits and likenesses of Edward to count, she'd read the letters and directives that he'd written to his staff and family, and there was little question that he had been a hard, cold man.

Alex stared at her and finally shook his head. "No one," he said harshly, "is better at leaping to conclusions than you."

"Kate needs me." Jill said, defensive and grim.

"Kate is *dead,* Jill."

Jill started. Sometimes that was a fact she seemed to forget. But Kate did need her. Jill suddenly closed her eyes and saw Kate in the tower, bloody and terrified, reaching out. And suddenly it was so obvious that Kate was reaching out to her, Jill.

"She expects me to help her, to solve this," Jill said, opening her eyes.

His regard was unblinking. "You should go home. Coming back to London was a mistake."

His words took her by surprise, like a blindside, and worse. It was like being stabbed in the back with a knife.

"And I didn't mean it the way you're taking it," he said angrily.

Jill shook her head. "I can't go home. Not now—not until this is over."

They stared at one another.

"Okay," Alex finally said, his face and tone grim. "I have to go, Jill." He glanced at his watch. "I'll call you later to see how you are. Think about calling this doctor. He'll not only fit you in at the drop of a hat, you can tell him everything. At the least, maybe he'll give you something to help you sleep."

Jill nodded just to appease him. She did not want to deal with that issue now.

He had picked up his briefcase. He suddenly strode to her and kissed her cheek before walking out of the kitchen.

The feeling of his lips lingered, as did the spicy, woodsy scent of his aftershave. Jill walked as far as she could toward the parlor, and glimpsed him exiting the front door. She turned away, a heavy depressive weight settling over. Or was it dread?

Jill sat down at the table, glancing briefly at the card he'd given her without really reading it. She could hear his Lamborghini roaring to life outside.

Something terrible had happened to Kate, and now, ninety years later, she was being warned in no uncertain terms to back off. Jill inhaled, stricken with the feeling she'd had at Stainesmore, that something terrible might happen to her next.

Because so much was at stake.

Jill flinched at the sound of Kate's voice, there in her mind, so loud and clear it was as if she were standing in the room with her, speaking aloud. Something caught her eye. Jill looked up, chills breaking out all over her body, and she turned.

Kate stood by the back door, staring at Jill.

Jill's pulse exploded, going sky high. She shook her head to clear it, blinking. And when she opened her eyes, Kate was gone.

APRIL 27, 1908

"Is he here? Is he here?" Kate cried, lifting her skirts and flying across her bedchamber. She leaned toward the window, her huge swollen belly in the way, making it difficult for her to get as close as she wished, in order to gaze down at the front yard and drive.

"Madam," the housekeeper said from behind her. "Please. Do not so exert yourself with the child due in two weeks."

Kate ignored her, for there was no mistaking the coach that had turned into the pebbled drive of Coke's Way. "It's Edward!" she cried, overcome with excitement. She turned and dashed past the ever-dour Miss Bennett, and out the door.

He had promised that nothing would keep him away from their child's birth. But his father had fallen ill while in the south of France and he had summoned Edward to his side—well over two months ago. Kate had not let on that she was despondent. She had encouraged him to go. She understood Edward's duty to his father. Until she had come into his life, he had firmly believed in duty and honor. Now he was torn.

The earl was approaching seventy years of age. Edward had not wanted to obey the summons, leaving Kate in her condition for even a minute—much less several months. But Kate was afraid the earl might die. While that would solve their problems—for then they could instantly wed—she had imagined the guilt that would fester should Edward refuse to go to his father's side, should he die. Kate knew Edward would never forgive himself.

Kate hurried downstairs, out of breath, for the baby inside her womb demanded so much from her. She heard the carriage door slam as she opened the front door of the small cottage where she had been staying for six achingly long, terribly lonely months.

Kate had never understood loneliness before. And the fear had begun—the fear every woman faces when it is time to give birth. One night, well past the midnight hour, she had picked up a quill and penned a will in the horrific case that she and her child might not survive the upcoming ordeal.

Edward was striding up the brick walk. He saw her and faltered.

"Edward," she whispered, clinging to the door, her knees going weak, her heart pounding far too rapidly for comfort.

"Oh, God, Kate!" Edward ran forward, and the next thing she knew, she was in his arms, and their mouths were fused and nothing had ever been so right.

He tore his lips from hers. "How I have missed you—how beautiful you are!" Only to kiss her cheek, her forehead, the tip of her nose, and then claim her mouth again.

This time Kate pulled back. "I did not think you would return in time!"

His eyes darkened as he clasped her hands to his chest. "Nothing could keep me away—not even the subterfuge of an old, rotten man."

Kate froze. Once, before she had appeared in his life, he had respected and even been fond of his father. No longer. "Darling?"

He forced a smile. "I am sorry. Come. Let's go inside, we have so much to discuss, it's been so very long."

They entered the house. Miss Bennett stood in the entry and she nodded at Edward. "My lord," she said, coming forward to take his hat and gloves. "How was your journey?"

"Very well, thank you, Miss Bennett." His smile was brief, and even as he spoke to her again, his warm gaze was on Kate. He stared at her big belly. "Please give us a few moments of privacy." He smiled at Kate. He could not take his eyes from her, she thought, not even for a moment. How it warmed her.

She felt herself blushing. Miss Bennett disappeared as Edward pulled her into the parlor—and into his arms. They kissed for an endlessly long time.

"I am shameless," Kate whispered. "I am thinking of what it would be like to go upstairs."

He stared at her, at once incredulous and horrified. "You are about to have a child!"

"I know." Kate cast down her eyes.

Edward finally settled himself in a large armchair. Kate brought him a glass of brandy. "What subterfuge did you speak of?" she asked with dread.

Edward drank. "My father lied. He was not ill. He sent for me only to keep us apart. I have told him about the child, Kate—and even that has not swayed him. He still refuses to permit us to marry."

Kate nodded, sitting on the sofa, her hands clasped in her lap. She was not surprised. Six months ago, she had been devastated when the earl had refused to allow Edward to marry her. She had even approached the earl herself—only to find herself subjected to such condescension and disrespect that it was one of the singularly most disheartening experiences of her life. "It doesn't matter. I met Collinsworth once, do you not remember?" To this day, Edward did not know that she had actually raised the subject of their suit, merely that they had been introduced. "I do know the kind of man he is. He will never change his mind about me. Indeed, I do think this is as much a war between you and him as it is about his finding me far too inferior to be a wife for you."

Edward stood, reached her with two strides, and dropped to his knees, taking both of her hands. He leaned forward, his cheek against her belly, closing his eyes. Then he looked up at her. "I no longer care that he shall disown me. Let my brother inherit the bloody earldom! I have you. I have decided. We shall marry immediately, and that is that." He smiled at her.

Kate stared in disbelief. She was trembling. "Oh, Edward," she began. Her love for him knew no bounds. She knew what soul-searching this had cost him.

"We will hardly be lacking, Kate. Thank God for your fortune." He smiled, but it was grim. "Perhaps we should even move to America?"

"Edward," Kate said, her tone uneven, tears filling her eyes. "Do you remember the very first time you gave me that grand tour of Uxbridge Hall?" She smiled through her tears.

"Why are you crying?" he asked with apparent dread. "I am going to marry you, Kate."

The tears tasted salty on her lips. "Darling. You told me about the house and its history. You told me about the earldom—which would one day be yours. You were such a proud peacock. You told me tales about your brothers, about all the mischief the three of you caused as children. You even spoke fondly of your father, dear—you spoke of his votes in the Lords in favor of the child labor laws. And then you told me about some of the family's holdings—the mines in Cornwall, for example, and the new shafts you were installing. The increased ventilation, you said, would save a dozen lives every year! You were so excited about those shafts! And then you spoke of the responsibility you had to your people. You called them 'your people,' Edward, as if you were a prince and this, your kingdom. Your eyes glowed as you talked of the possibilities of this new century—and how the time had come to take the earldom and modernize it. I was already in love with you, but that day, when I realized how you felt about your heritage, your responsibilities, your obligations, that day my love became irrevocable. I was so proud of you."

He remained kneeling at her feet. His eyes were almost black. "I do not like what you are saying."

"Your brother, Henry, is a rake," Kate cried tersely.

"Then the earldom shall remain as it is—and Henry can do as he will with it."

"He will gamble away every penny and every pound he can lay his hands upon!"

Edward shrugged—as if he did not care. Kate knew he cared.

"I cannot marry you, Edward." She stared and their gazes locked. Tears slid down her cheeks.

He was stricken.

"Please understand," Kate whispered. "I cannot take your life away from you."

"You are my life. I will not give you up." Edward was savage.

"I have never said you should give me up, because I cannot give you up." She slid her hand into his hair, threading her fingertips through the thick, dark strands. "If we married, one day, you would hate me for what I have stolen from you. Your birthright."

"No." His mouth was twisted, grim.

She wet her lips. "Then how about this? I could not live with myself, knowing what I had taken from you."

"Oh, God." Edward sat beside her, taking her into his arms. "Only you, Kate, would deny me, only you would have the courage and love to do so."

"Yes. It is because I love you so much." She refused to weep. But she could not stop the tears from streaming down her cheeks.

"Don't cry. You know I will not marry anyone else. You shall give me my heir, dear."

Kate looked at him. She intended to give him his heir, but she was not deluded. That old bastard could disinherit Edward if he did not marry elsewhere, and Kate knew it. What if their time together was limited? No! She would fight for her love—for their future. And as terrible as it was, maybe God would smile upon them, and the earl would pass away, leaving Edward the earl—and free to marry as he chose.

"Yes," she said, holding his face in her hands. "I shall give you your heir, perhaps sooner than we think."

He blinked.

"The doctor says I should deliver anytime now, dear."

"Oh, I am so pleased—and so terrified," Edward cried, embracing her.

And as she held him, she prayed that their child would be a son. It was, perhaps, their only hope.

Twenty

JILL HAD JUST STEPPED OUT OF THE HOUSE AND WAS LOCKING the front door when a tan Mercedes sedan halted in front of her gate at the curb. She recognized the vehicle immediately. She was on her way to see the handwriting analyst, Arthur Kingston, but now she approached the street slowly. A chauffeur in a dark cap remained inside the car as Thomas alighted and smiled at her.

Jill halted in her tracks and stared, unable to smile at him. Why was he there? What could he possibly want?

"Hello, Jill. How are you? Alex rang me last night and told me what happened to Mr. Barrows's cat." His expression seemed genuinely concerned.

"Hi." Jill could not return his brief smile. Had Alex been shouting at Thomas last night on his cell phone? Was Thomas the one responsible for the murder of Lady E.?

As upsetting as the notion was, it was also a relief because that would make Alex innocent of the crime. Unless he had known about it.

"I would have phoned, but Alex said you were already asleep."

"Thank you. I'm a bit better today. What a terrible prank." She started down the walk, Thomas falling into step beside her.

"Have you spoken to the police?" Thomas asked. He glanced around. "This is a nice neighborhood. Whoever was responsible deserves to be punished."

"A detective stopped by earlier." Jill wasn't about to tell Thomas anything. They paused by the Mercedes. "To what do I owe the honor of this visit?" Jill asked.

"I called this morning but I couldn't get through. Your machine didn't pick up. I thought you might like to have lunch."

Jill blinked at him. "I can't," she finally said. "I have an appointment." She forced a smile, wondering what he wanted. "I'll take a rain check," she lied.

He seemed to accept that. "Where are you off to? I'll give you a lift." He smiled.

"You don't have to bother. I can take the underground."

"Don't tell me you have already become fond of the tube?" His smile widened. "Come, Jill. It's my pleasure. It's the least I can do, considering what you went through last night."

"I like your subway system," Jill said. "I'm a straphanger—remember?"

He stared at her.

Jill smiled. She did not want him to know where she was going or, more important, why. On the other hand, Alex had probably told him every single detail of their trip to Staines-more. That notion upset her greatly.

A flicker of annoyance finally crossed Thomas's features. "Actually, I want to speak with you, and I'd prefer we weren't standing on the street."

Jill tensed. "That's okay."

"I spoke with Alex recently." His regard was direct. "He told me about your trip to Stainesmore."

Jill's pulse rate increased. She had been right. "What did he say?"

"He says you are more convinced than ever that you are Kate Gallagher's great-granddaughter." Thomas smiled, amused. "Of course, you don't have any proof."

"I am certain we're related. Just like I'm certain she was murdered."

"That's a terribly wild accusation," Thomas said calmly.

She folded her arms. "I'm sorry, Thomas, if my search for

the truth about Kate's disappearance, if my wild accusations, are disturbing to you and your family."

He regarded her and finally said, "Is there a reason you want to muddy my family's name?"

"So you understand that your family was involved in the tragedy?"

"I understand that my grandmother and Kate were best friends."

He either knew nothing, or he was a fantastic actor. "Kate was Edward's mistress, Thomas. She had his bastard son."

"That's absurd!" A flush covered his cheeks. Jill had wondered when he would lose his composure. "My grandfather probably kept a mistress or two—most men did back then—but I doubt he was having an affair with his wife's best friend. I did not know him, of course, but I know of him. He was a great man, with a vision, and he ran the earldom admirably. It's ludicrous to think he would have become involved with this Kate Gallagher of yours."

Jill did not respond. She wasn't going to tell him that Edward had been involved with Kate well before his marriage to Anne and that she was certain of it. Nor was she going to tell him that Edward was her number one murder suspect. "Is this why you came to see me? To discuss Kate Gallagher?"

Thomas's eyes widened abruptly. "Actually, Alex suggested that I make you an offer. Whatever you might unearth about Kate Gallagher, I'm open to the possibility that it might be damaging to our family name. I'd like to avoid the circumstance. So I'm offering you two million U.S. dollars, Jill, in cash." He smiled at her.

Jill froze. She could barely understand what was happening. Her mind had gone numb. "What?"

"Forget about Kate Gallagher and go home. She's been deceased a very long time. I'll wire the money into the account of your choosing." He smiled at her again.

He wanted to pay her off. Pay her off, shut her up, send her home. "Did you kill the cat?" she heard herself whisper.

His eyes widened. "I beg your pardon?"

"Did you kill Lady E.?!" Jill cried, as a new and devastating comprehension seared her brain. Thomas had said, *"Alex suggested I make you an offer."* Had he?

"Lady E.? Is that the cat?"

"You damn well know it's the cat, don't you!" Jill accused, fists clenched, her heart pounding with deafening force. Alex wanted her paid off? This could not be happening.

"Let me correct you, Jill, on several points." Thomas was angry, and his voice had become as hard as his eyes. "My family does not stoop to such hideous devices as beheading pets. We have no need to lower ourselves in such a way. And my grandfather was a great man. He hardly slept with his wife's best friend. I suggest you keep your views to yourself."

And Jill was shaking. "I don't want your money." She had to be clear, she had to make sure she hadn't misunderstood—surely she had misheard! "Alex suggested that you pay me off?"

"Yes. Alex is unquestionably loyal to me and mine, and never mistake that," Thomas said coldly. He leaned closer. "Do not misjudge him. He wants this finished as much as I do. How much would it cost me for you to end this investigation of yours and go home?"

Jill could not answer. *Of course this is what Alex, brilliant, clever Alex, would suggest and advise.*

How could she have ever thought to trust him? He was a total liar—stabbing her in the back, not once but many times. But this, then, would be the very last time. KC had been right.

Jill was sick to her stomach.

"I don't want your money," she finally said, numbly. "I want the truth—and I want justice."

"Justice," Thomas echoed, as if he'd never heard the word.

Jill turned and hurried down the block, unable to see where she was going, almost running—she had to get away from him—far away—from them all. And it was only when she reached the corner that she realized she was crying and that was why she could not see.

*   *   *

Jill sat alone at a table in a small, dark pub on the corner of a street in Soho, the name of which she could not remember. She had just consumed her third pint of ale. She had hated ale for her entire adult life, but now, she supposed, she was starting to become fond of it.

Alex was not to be trusted. KC was right.

He was a traitor, to her, to her cause. He was not her friend. He wanted her paid off, shut up, sent home.

Jill leaned her head upon her arms on the scarred, dark wood table. How could her heart hurt her like this? Alex meant nothing to her, nothing. She had to focus on that.

Jill smiled sadly, the silky texture of her shirt against her mouth. *Pay her off, send her home.* Is that what Alex had said? Is that how he had said it? Tears burned the closed lids of her eyes. And to think she had thought them to be friends, and had been on the verge of falling in love with him.

Abruptly Jill sat up ramrod-straight, wiping her eyes, grim. Her pulse raced. That last thought had come out of nowhere, and she didn't like it, not one bit.

Jill refused to dwell on it. She was overtired and very frightened and so terribly alone. She could not think clearly. It was as simple as that.

Good night, pumpkin.

Jill inhaled, her father's melodious tenor so strong and clear in her mind. She gripped her elbows more tightly, trying to envision her parents and find comfort in the memory, but somehow failing. Instead, Alex's face loomed in her mind. It was ugly.

Jill wished they had never met. But wishing desperately to undo the past would not solve anything. It would not bring justice, it would not reveal the truth. It would not change history, giving Kate a happily-ever-after ending to her life.

Jill flagged down a heavyset waitress, signaling for another pint. The handwriting samples had not matched. Edward Sheldon and Jonathan Barclay were not one and the same man.

She looked up at the clock on the wall by the bar, which

was filled with an after-work crowd of drinkers. It was six o'clock. She'd been at the pub for almost two hours—she'd walked aimlessly through London after leaving Kingston's suite, filled with disappointment that the handwriting samples had not matched.

Jill almost felt like throwing in the towel. Hadn't Alex said no one was better at leaping to conclusions than she was? Perhaps Kate wasn't her great-grandmother after all. Maybe Edward hadn't been her lover. Maybe Kate had disappeared of her own free will, for reasons she, Jill, would never discover. Perhaps, she, Jill, had been making up a fantasy she was determined to believe.

Maybe she should give up and go home.

Jill straightened grimly. She wasn't a quitter. She had never been a quitter for a single day in her life.

A gauntlet had been thrown—not once, but twice. Lady E.'s murder had been one warning, and then Thomas had tried to pay her off with two million dollars so she'd go home. Wasn't that reason enough to stay? She was making the Sheldons very uncomfortable, that much was clear.

She needed a new lead. There were so many pieces to this particular puzzle, but there was one Jill had thus far overlooked.

Marisa had to know about Hal's obsession with Kate.

Marisa just might have the answers Jill was looking for.

Jill saw four sedans and one limousine parked in the Sheldons' driveway and she hesitated. She had called Marisa's home only to learn from a housekeeper that she was at the Sheldons' for the evening. Jill estimated that there were at least eight guests present; she had assumed Marisa would be at the Sheldons' alone.

But it was too late to turn back. The taxi she had just stepped out of had driven away. Now Jill almost wished that the security guard had turned her away instead of recognizing her and waving her through a moment ago. It was crass to crash a party, period. Undoubtedly she was going to be tossed out on her ear.

Jill shivered, because the night air was cool and she was

wearing a jersey tank top under a cardigan and a matching knee-length skirt. She was about to turn and walk back out onto the road when Kate's image flashed in her mind. Her eyes were wide and filled with urgency.

Someone had killed Kate. Hal had probably known who the murderer was, given his obsession with her and her life. Marisa would probably know, as well. Jill turned back around and hurried to the front door before she could think twice about it.

The moment the butler opened the front door and Jill was admitted into the foyer, her courage failed her again. She could see into the living room where she had first met the Sheldons, and perhaps forty ladies and men had congregated there, the women in beautiful designer cocktail dresses or equally stunning skirted suits, the men in business attire. Most of the women wore diamonds, emeralds, or sapphires. Many guests held delicate flutes of champagne, and waiters in white jackets were passing silver trays containing hors d'oeuvres. Jill glimpsed caviar and toast points.

She did not belong there. She never had, but especially not now, not tonight.

And then she saw him.

Jill froze as a servant she recognized asked her for her cardigan, mistaking her for another guest.

His back was to her. He was speaking with a mixed group, and a tall, willowy blond in a mismatched print silk dress that screamed Ungaro was by his side.

Jill's eyes widened. The blond was touching his arm. Surely she was not his date?

"Miss Gallagher?"

Jill started, meeting the servant's benign gaze. "I was hoping to speak with Marisa Sutcliffe," she managed, still stunned and aware of herself trembling.

The servant seemed to realize that she was not a guest after all, and he seemed taken aback.

Oh, God, Jill thought, because at that moment, Margaret entered the foyer, stunning in a tuxedo pants suit with a starburst diamond-and-pearl pin on one satin lapel. The pearl was half the size of Jill's palm. "I had better go," Jill mumbled, turning to flee. She felt off-balance as she did so and she thought, I must be drunk. Now she only wanted to leave.

"Miss Gallagher." Margaret's surprised exclamation halted Jill. Slowly she turned. Her cheeks felt like twin balls of fire.

"Countess."

For one moment, the two women stared at one another with equal surprise. Then Margaret rallied and smiled. "How nice that you could come. I hadn't realized you were a supporter of Mr. Blair. Please, do help yourself to the champagne. Or a proper drink, if you prefer."

Margaret thought she was an invited guest and apparently this was some kind of political get-together. Jill spotted the prime minister across the room, holding court with a mixed group of guests.

Jill returned her attention to the countess. She admired her, for she was too polite to send her on her way as any other woman might have done. "Lady Collinsworth, I wasn't invited."

Margaret's eyes widened.

"I was hoping for a word with Marisa," Jill said hoarsely, wishing she were anywhere but there, in the Sheldons' foyer with the countess. And then she looked past Margaret's shoulder. At that precise moment, Alex noticed her. His eyes widened remarkably.

And the blond, who reminded Jill of Jerry Hall, was clinging to his arm.

"I see," Margaret said, in a tone of voice that indicated the opposite case was true. "Oh. Well, do come in, as you are here, and I am certain that Marisa will speak with you." She seemed confused.

But Alex was excusing himself and now he entered the foyer. "Aunt, you look beautiful," he said, kissing her cheek.

Jill watched them closely. Margaret's smile was instant, and it was the kind of smile a mother reserved for one of her sons. "Thank you, dear," she said softly. "Here." She straightened his tie, a brilliant black-and-white abstract print. "Miss Gallagher wishes to speak with Marisa, Alex. I've asked her to come in and join us for a glass of champagne."

Alex looked at Jill, his expression oddly blank. Jill felt, rather than saw, his unspoken reprimand. Even so, Thomas's words echoed in her mind . . . *He suggested I make you an offer . . . how much would it cost me?* And an image of the bloodied body of the dead Lady E. filled Jill's mind.

Margaret smiled at them both, then looked from one to the other, a question in her eyes, before she walked away to join her guests.

"Why are you here? Are you all right?"

Jill managed a smile. It felt horribly strained. "I didn't know there was a party." Don't let Alex guess you suspect anything, she told herself. She glanced past him. The blond had come to the salon's doorway and was staring at them, not with hostility, but with curiosity. And Jill finally saw Marisa in the crowd, stunning in a black-and-white, lace-trimmed Valentino dress.

Alex followed her gaze. He made no comment on the other woman's identity. "My aunt said you're looking for Marisa. Why?"

Jill's mind raced. Alex was smart. Too smart. She would resort to the truth whenever possible. "She probably knows about Hal's obsession with Kate." She tried to keep her tone light. But it was very hard to do, because there was this odd hurting in her chest—a hurt that had as much to do with what Thomas had told her that morning as it did with Alex's date. And Jill knew she should not care that he was dating a beautiful blond who looked like a young Jerry Hall.

"Jill, this isn't the time or the place."

Jill met his gaze. "There's never a good time or a place, is there, Alex, when it comes to life? In fact, wasn't it you who said life isn't fair?"

He was taken aback. "Hey." He touched her shoulder. "What's wrong?"

She pulled away before she lost control of herself. "Nothing." A quick glance told her that Marisa, who stood by Lauren, had seen her, too. "I think I will have that glass of champagne."

Alex gripped her elbow. Jill thought he meant to steer her away from the guests and back to the front door, but he guided her toward the living room, instead. "Don't overstay your welcome," he said softly. Then, "Have you been drinking, Jill?"

Before Jill could answer, Thomas materialized, walking toward them, his expression set in stone and impossible to read. "Hello, Jill." He was cool.

"Hello." She was cool.

"I wasn't aware that Alex had invited you to our fundraiser," Thomas said. "You never said a word."

Jill looked at Alex.

Alex smiled slightly. "Come on." He continued to hold her elbow, and he propelled her past Thomas. Jill could feel his eyes on her back. They did not feel kind and she shivered involuntarily. Nor could she understand Alex's behavior now. He was acting like an ally.

But he was not an ally. She would not misjudge him again.

The blond smiled at them as they approached. Jill managed a smile in return.

"Lindsay, this is Jill Gallagher. Jill, Lindsay Bartlett."

Jill nodded politely.

Alex signaled to a passing waiter, and in a moment the three of them had flutes of Krug in their hands.

The champagne was the best Jill had ever tasted. "So have you two known each other for very long?" she asked Lindsay. The moment the spontaneous question was out of her mouth she felt Alex's eyes upon her, and wished she'd never spoken.

"Actually, only a month or two. You were dating Alex's cousin, weren't you?" Lindsay asked, but not with rancor or pettiness.

"Yes." Jill decided to enjoy the champagne. But it now tasted like liquid lead. Jill couldn't stop herself from wondering if they were sleeping together.

Then Jill realized how errant her thoughts were. It was not her business, she did not care, he was a traitor. She quaffed her drink.

"It's so sad, what happened, and I'm so sorry," Lindsay said softly.

Jill looked at her and realized that she was sincere, intelligent, and that she might have liked her given different circumstances. "Thanks." She whipped another flute off of a passing tray. "Excuse me." She failed utterly in her attempt to smile as she quickly walked away from them.

Marisa was facing her expectantly.

Jill faltered. Marisa was with a crowd that included Lauren. Jill noticed Hal's sister now for the first time, clad in simple and elegant black. Marisa stepped away from the group, her eyes on Jill. The two women paused, face-to-face.

"You wish to speak with me?" Marisa asked tersely.

"Yes. It's important. Could we step outside?"

Marisa was startled. She hesitated and then she gestured for Jill to lead the way.

Jill pushed open the terrace doors. She crossed it. When she turned, she saw into the brilliantly lit room behind Marisa, where guests were turning to look their way.

"We are creating a stir," Marisa said worriedly, glancing over her shoulder. "This evening is difficult enough as it is, but it could not be postponed."

"I'll be brief."

Marisa's nostrils were pinched and reddening. "I wasn't going to come at all, but I am a big supporter of Mr. Blair's—as was Hal."

Jill stiffened.

Tears filled Marisa's eyes.

Jill's heart went out to the other woman. "I'm so sorry, Marisa."

"What is it that you want to ask me?"

Jill looked away, wished she had more champagne, then realized she held a full glass in her hand. She took a draft. "He loved Kate, didn't he?"

Marisa, already the color of porcelain, paled.

"Please, Marisa, please."

"How can somebody love a dead woman?" Marisa whispered.

"Hal was obsessed with her. Wasn't he?"

Suddenly Marisa was angry. She crossed her arms beneath her breasts, striding across the terrace, and another moment passed before she spoke, her back to Jill. "He didn't love her. It was like some teenaged boy with a crush on a pinup."

Jill felt sorry for her. "Was that the way it really was?"

Marisa whirled. "Yes! He admired her the way a man admires Marilyn Monroe."

Jill's eyes widened. "And they were both killed, weren't they, because of the men they loved?"

Marisa gazed at her darkly. "I have no idea what you're talking about."

Maybe she didn't. "Did Hal know the truth about Kate? Did he know the truth about me?"

Marisa continued to hug herself. She was shivering, but then, it was nippy out, and her dress was sleeveless. "You look like her," she finally said. "I saw that in the church." A tear slipped down her cheek. Her jaw tightened. "He knew who you were. He was so excited he called me soon after he met you," she said, her voice breaking. "He went to New York as much to look for you as he did to run away from me."

"I see," Jill said. She felt dizzy. "He tracked me down." She reached out to hold the railing of the terrace. The iron felt wet, clammy, beneath her hand.

"I hated her!" Marisa cried abruptly.

Jill froze. "Kate?"

Crying now, Marisa nodded. "Her ghost stood between us, always. How could I compete with a ghost? Hal thought she was perfection. He was obsessed. He claimed he wasn't, but he was lying to himself."

"I understand," Jill whispered. She wanted to comfort her, but did not know how. "Did Hal tell you who killed Kate?"

She stared, blue eyes wide. "No. He did not." She glanced over her shoulder again. "I'm frozen. I have to go back inside." She did not wait for Jill's response, hurrying away.

Jill stared, first after Marisa, and then across the terrace, into the night. One thing was clear. Marisa knew about Kate. And Jill would bet her last dime that both Hal and Marisa knew who murdered her.

Jill wasn't certain how long she stood there, outside on the terrace, when she became aware of a shadow passing through the terrace doors. She watched Alex approaching.

"Are you okay, Jill?" Alex asked.

She met his probing, extremely intense blue eyes. "I'm fine." Her smile was brittle and she knew it.

"Lindsay. . ." Alex began.

"I don't care about Lindsay," Jill said, striding past him and lying through her teeth.

He caught up with her. "You're jealous."

Jill refused to answer.

"She is not my date. She happens to be a friend of Lauren's."

Jill shrugged as she entered the living room. Heads turned her—their—way.

Alex caught her arm, halting her in her tracks. "What did Marisa say?"

As if she would tell him anything, Jill thought angrily. "She said that Hal knew the truth about Kate."

Alex stared.

Jill seized another glass of champagne.

"Don't you think you should slow down on that champagne?"

She gave him a cold look. "So you want Thomas to pay me off."

He started, eyes wide, head coming up.

"No rebuttal?" She was scathing and she knew it.

"Hold on. You are jumping to conclusions, Jill, and that's not fair."

"Life isn't fair. For the umpteenth time."

"I don't want to see this family torn apart by an old scandal that has little if any bearing upon the present," Alex said slowly, removing the flute from her fingertips.

Jill turned and took another flute from a passing waiter. "If my great-grandmother was murdered, it has a bearing on the present," Jill said. From the corner of her eye, she saw several guests straining to overhear her conversation with Alex. One of them was Lauren.

"Whoever did it can hardly be executed or serve a life

term," Alex said with caution in his tone. "Could you lower your voice, please?"

"You're a very smart man, Alex. But you must think me a fool." Jill ignored his command.

"I think you're one brainy lady, actually," Alex said, eyeing her. "And I also think you want to fight with me. But I won't allow it." He took her hand, either to guide her or drag her out of the living room.

Jill braced herself, refusing to budge. "Kate died—and her son got nothing. Her son . . . my grandfather. What happened to Peter? And where did her fortune go?"

Alex stared at her.

"Someone stole it, didn't they?" Jill cried heatedly.

"No one stole anything! Is that what you want—your share of her fortune?" Alex asked harshly.

Jill scoffed. "You know what I want. The truth! Edward killed my great-grandmother—which means a blue-blooded Sheldon was a cold-blooded murderer and it's been covered up by this family for ninety years!" Jill cried.

"Lower your voice," Alex snapped. "That's a wild accusation and you know it."

"Did you," Jill said, uncaring of the fact that theirs was the only conversation in the room and that heads were turned their way, "or did you not tell Thomas to pay me off so I'd shut up and go away?"

Alex's facial muscles tightened. Jill thought he would deny it. He did not. "I did."

"I see," Jill said. Now she knew she would throw up.

His hand was on hers again, but this time, his grip was painful. "You've overstayed your welcome, Jill," he began roughly.

Jill saw Lauren coming. She tried to shake him off and failed. He walked her into the foyer, where Lauren caught up with them, rounding in on them and blocking their way. "What is she saying?" she cried, her face utterly white, making her coral lipstick stand out starkly against her skin.

"I'll handle this," Alex said firmly. "I'm taking Jill home."

"No, you're not." Jill broke free of his grasp. "You're busy with Miss Jerry Hall. I'll get a cab."

"Jill." Lauren's gaze was wide, wild. "What are you saying? That my grandfather murdered someone? Are you insane?!"

"Your grandfather, Edward, was my great-grandmother's lover," Jill said harshly. "Kate Gallagher was Edward Sheldon's mistress and she had his child—and he killed her—in cold blood!"

Lauren gasped. "I don't believe that. You are insane! What do you want from us? Why are you doing this?"

Jill faltered, because Thomas reached them, his face flushed, his eyes blazing.

"Those accusations are highly irresponsible. We will not be blackmailed, Miss Gallagher. Not only will we not be blackmailed, I will not have my family's reputation muddied like this. You are slandering the good Sheldon name."

Jill did not move, incapable of doing so in the face of Thomas's fury.

Thomas seemed to recover some of his composure. He straightened. His smile was a mere curling of his mouth. "Get her out of here, Alex. And meanwhile, my lawyers will be contacting her in the morning."

Alex grabbed Jill's arm.

Lawyers, Jill managed to think. Did that mean he was suing her for slander?

"You are lying," Lauren cried.

"No." Jill shook her head. "Kate didn't disappear. She died. I found the grave. She died seven months after having Edward's child. And shortly after she died—eight months later, in fact—Edward married your great-grandmother. What your family has done disgusts me," Jill cried back.

"Jill." Alex's tone was like the lash of a whip. "I'm taking you home. You're angry, you're confused, and you can't possibly think clearly under the circumstances. Let's go. You've already made enough of a scene, and tomorrow you can formally apologize to the family before Thomas sues your ass."

"Let me go," Jill said.

And then, with her peripheral vision, she saw a shape clad entirely in black, with a huge diamond-and-pearl pin, slowly collapsing toward the floor.

Jill stumbled, pulling against Alex, turning in time to see William and Thomas supporting the nearly prone figure of Margaret.

The silver monster halted at the curb in front of Jill's flat. Jill remained huddled on her side of the car, staring straight ahead, hating herself. Not for her quest for the truth about Kate, not for her need for justice, but for bringing more pain and maybe even ill health to a woman as gracious and innocent of wrongdoing as Margaret Sheldon was.

Alex had not said a word to her in the entire twenty minutes since they had left the house. In fact, he had not even glanced at her a single time.

She had never seen him so angry. And now the tables were turned. She was angry with him but she felt horrible for behaving like such a low-class cretin with his family. They certainly had every reason to despise her and think her a threat. Why had she let her tongue loose like that? It had been so foolish. Now she might never uncover the truth, because whoever wanted to stop her knew her agenda. And worse, what if Thomas really sued her? She didn't have a penny to her name with which to defend herself.

"We're here," Alex finally said, turning off the ignition.

Jill tensed and dared to look at him. Why had he turned off the car? Did he think to come in? All of her suspicions about him—all of KC's warnings—rose to the forefront of her mind. "I am sorry," she said quickly. "I will apologize. Thanks for the ride." She shoved open the door and leaped out of the car.

He did not return her gaze. "We'll discuss everything in the morning."

"Yeah." Jill could not believe he would not even look at her. She should not care. She did not care. She slammed the door closed and stepped away from the sports car.

The Lamborghini's engine came to life, and it pulled

away from the curb. If Alex looked back, even once, in his rearview mirror, Jill did not see.

Jill watched the car's taillights disappear around the corner. She was hugging herself. "I don't care." Good riddance, she added silently.

Then she looked toward her flat. She hadn't thought to turn any lights on because she'd left well before noon. The house was utterly black, cast in shadows and darkness. It somehow appeared squat, almost ugly. An image of Lady E., dead, not alive, flashed through her mind. Jill stared at her flat, shivering.

The house seemed so cold. It was no longer charming and quaint, it had changed, as if it had taken on a life of its own. Jill shivered again, thinking that it appeared different, strange—almost ghastly, almost menacing.

Jill dreaded going inside.

She told herself that she was drunk and her imagination was running away with her. Which was very natural, considering that she was obsessed with a ninety-year-old murder—and that Lady E. had been killed just last night.

She glanced at the adjacent flat, where Lucinda lived. All of the lights were on, giving the house a warm, incandescent glow. Lucinda's flat appeared friendly, inviting, benign. Jill started up her brick path.

Lucinda opened the door immediately, smiling. "Hello, Jill." Then her expression fell.

"Is something wrong?" Jill asked, dread churning in her stomach, already knowing that something was terribly wrong.

"Janet Witcombe is dead."

Their gazes locked. Jill could not believe her ears, and for one moment, she pictured the kind old lady crumpled on some clinical floor, her features distorted and grotesque in death. "What happened?" she breathed.

"She died this morning. A blow to the head. Apparently she fell," Lucinda said, wringing her hands. "Oh, do come in, Jill. What am I doing, making you stand outside on such a cool night—and you without even a coat!"

Jill stepped into Lucinda's cheerful foyer. "So it was an

accident," she said slowly. "Janet was very old. She was well into her eighties."

"I think she was eighty, just," Lucinda said. "Shall I make us some tea?"

Jill didn't answer. Old people fell down and died every day. It was hardly unusual. Then why was she so . . . upset? So . . . uneasy?

Had it been an accident?

"Jill? What is wrong? You're so pale."

"I've had a bit too much to drink," Jill said, shaking her head, hoping to clear it. But she couldn't. Her senses were screaming a warning at her, one she didn't want to identify. "Janet seemed awfully healthy and spry for an elderly woman."

Lucinda blinked, her blue eyes behind her oversized tortoiseshell frames widening. "You don't think?" She gasped. "Jill, Janet *fell*. It's as simple as that."

"Lucinda, I'm exhausted, I think I'll just go back to my flat."

"Are you certain you won't stay for some tea? You seem distraught."

Jill declined, wanting to go home, to be alone, to try to think. On Lucinda's porch she paused, once again staring toward her house, the hairs on her nape rising. "Oh, don't be a fool," she snapped aloud. No one had murdered Janet Witcombe because of her recollections of a thirty-year-old conversation about a woman who had disappeared ninety years ago. And whoever had killed Lady E. was undoubtedly at the Sheldons' right now. Besides, she had to feed Sir John.

Jill started purposefully back to her flat. She seemed to have trouble fitting her keys in the front lock much less opening it. Jill realized that her hands were trembling.

Alex had given her the name of a doctor. Maybe she needed to go. She didn't know how much longer her body could stand up to such emotional distress.

She finally got the door open and found herself breathless from the effort it had cost her. Jill turned on the lights.

And she froze.

Her flat had been ransacked. Drawers were overturned on

the floor, their contents spilled everywhere, the pillows that had been on the sofa were slit open, its cushions were scattered about the room, and the doors of the armoire swung wildly ajar.

Jill staggered backward, taking in the extent of the mess, crying out.

And then her gaze veered back to the armoire—to the wide open doors. *They were swinging.*

Whoever had done this, had done it recently.

Jill turned and ran.

Twenty-One

KATE LEANED FORWARD, FILLED WITH EXCITEMENT, HARDLY able to contain herself. Bensonhurst had appeared ahead of her, in the cul-de-sac at the end of the block. Her carriage, drawn by two bay mares, moved swiftly toward the stone mansion with its Gothic spires and neo-classical columns. Kate sat back against the velvet squabs of her seat, clasping her gloved hands together, beaming. It had been so very long since she had seen Anne and she could hardly wait!

The carriage halted in the paved drive in front of the house. Kate could not wait for her footman to open the door, and pushed it herself. As she stepped down, he appeared to help her to the ground. Kate was rounder now, having given birth to her son just four months ago. She had become, she thought ruefully, a plump matron. Edward had told her just last night that her curves were delightful.

She did not blush, thinking about the passion they had found once again after so many months without. But her pulse raced and she was impatient to be in his arms yet again. And he had only left her a few hours ago. Already she missed him—almost desperately.

She loved him so much that sometimes she was afraid, no, terrified, that some terrible tragedy would befall him. That he would walk out of her door, only to be hit by an oncoming coach, ending his life—and ending their love. Kate had decided months ago that her fears were the result of his unyielding father. The earl had not changed his tune about them; even now, Kate knew he concocted schemes to drive them apart.

Kate walked past both a coach and a spanking new Packard motorcar, shaking herself free of her morbid thoughts, thinking about Anne again, and how delightful their reunion would be. Her knock was received by the butler, whom she recalled very well and smiled broadly at. "Hullo, Jenson."

"Miss Gallagher!" The short, bald butler beamed back at her. "I must say, it is so good to have you back!"

"It is wonderful to be back," Kate said, suddenly teary-eyed. In that instant, so many memories flooded her—the very first time she had met Anne, at Brighton on the promenade—which was also the first time she and Edward had laid eyes upon one another. Their come-out ball, the horse races at Newmarket, and the week at Swinton Hall. Overcome, and suddenly realizing how entwined her and Edward's romance had been with her life with Anne, she glanced around at the entryway, noting that nothing had changed. "Ah, one of my favorite paintings," she said, moving to stand in front of a Rembrandt oil of a mother and child. Then she turned. "Is my dearest friend in the entire world at home?"

"I will tell Lady Anne that you are here," Jenson said. "Would you care to wait in the salon?"

"I can find my way." Kate smiled as he left and she wandered into the salon with its pink walls and pale beige ceilings.

"Well, this is a surprise."

Kate tensed at the sound of Lady Bensonhurst's not particularly pleasant voice. "Hullo, my lady. How nice to see you again." Kate did not smile either.

Lady Bensonhurst did not enter the salon. Her gaze slid over Kate, lingering on the fullness of her breasts and the more pronounced curves of her hips and abdomen. Kate had the terrible inkling that Lady Bensonhurst knew she had a child. But that was not possible. No one knew other than the two simpleton maids, Miss Bennett, Edward, and of course, his father. And Anne. She had written Anne in the winter out of sheer desperation, loneliness, and fear.

"I thought you had gone back to New York," Lady Bensonhurst said flatly.

"I did. But I have returned to London. Truly, I have become quite the Anglophile."

"I see." She refused to smile. "You are losing that stunning figure, my dear."

"Too much rich food, I fear." Kate also refused to smile.

"Hmm. My daughter is not at home—" she began.

Anne appeared, moving swiftly down the corridor. "Kate!" Her face lit up.

"Anne!" Kate smiled as her dear friend continued forward. She expected an embrace. To her surprise, Anne held out both arms, but clasped her hands instead and kissed her cheek.

"How wonderful that you are here," Anne said.

Kate looked at her, oddly taken aback. Anne had changed, and it was difficult to put her finger on it—she was more assured, less meek of manner, more gracious—and more aloof. Anne had dropped her hands. Kate clasped them to her skirts. "I have missed you so, my dear," she said. "You look wonderful, Anne." And it was the truth. She was prettier than ever. Her fair skin glowed.

Anne smiled, a slight blush covering her cheeks. "We have much to talk about." Her gaze also took in Kate's weight gain. Anne turned. "Mother, if you do not mind?"

Lady Bensonhurst finally smiled, and it was strained. "Do recall, Anne, that we must attend the dinner party tonight at Uxbridge Hall and you must soon dress." She nodded at Kate and walked away, her full skirts billowing.

Kate had stiffened. She could not help but be peeved, even dismayed, and perhaps envious, for she had not been invited to dine at Collinsworth's—and she never would be. She wondered if Edward would be present at the dinner party.

"So tell me how you are?" Anne asked, low, as they sat down side by side on a velvet settee.

Kate dismissed her touch of jealousy as ridiculous. She touched Anne's hand. "I am so happy, my dear, you have no idea."

"I received your last letter. I am so glad you delivered the child safely, Kate. How do you feel? And how is the babe? Will I ever see him?" Anne's voice had dropped to a whisper.

Kate beamed. "He is a bundle of joy. Oh, Anne. I am two times in love—with our son and his father." Tears filled her eyes. "I think I am the luckiest woman on this earth."

Anne stared. "But he does not marry you, Kate," she finally said, low. "I have worried about you, dear. He should have married you some time ago."

Kate shook her head. "Anne, we have not truly shared our thoughts or feelings in almost a year. He asked me to marry him. In fact, he decided to go against his father and was prepared to be disowned. I would not let him do such a thing."

Anne's eyes were wide. "I wish you would tell me who this paragon of men is! I do admit I have wracked my mind, time and again, trying to discover who he could possibly be."

Kate hesitated, almost blurting out the truth, and truly wanting to do so. But the moment of recklessness passed and she patted her hand. "One day, you shall learn the truth. But for now, because our situation is so delicate, it is best that we keep his identity a secret. I do fear what his father would do to us if we revealed our affair to the public. I dare not tell you who he is."

"So what will you do? He wants to marry, and you have your fortune, but now you will not marry him?" Her brows slashed together.

"One day he would come to despise me for taking away his family and his heritage." Kate sighed. "I do know how terrible this sounds, but his father is very old." Kate winced just hearing how her words sounded. She was the last person in the world to wish someone dead. If only Collinsworth were not such a stubborn, manipulative, and callous old man.

But Anne was calm. "So you wait for him to die. Well, that would be splendid! Your paragon could have his title and you."

"It does sound so cold and calculating. If only his father were not so set against us," Kate said, feeling a deep despair. She quickly shoved it aside, because she wanted to enjoy her reunion with Anne and because she believed in true love.

Their love would win out in the end, and it was a precious belief that she'd clung to during the entire past year.

At that precise moment, Jenson appeared with a maid, the latter wheeling in a trolley filled with scones, cakes, and tea. "Oh, thank you, Jenson," Kate cried. "How did you guess that I am ravenous today?"

He was smiling from ear to ear. "You always had a hearty appetite, Miss Gallagher. Do see. I have brought you your favorite—raspberry tarts and green tea."

A few moments later, the servants were gone. "So how have you been, Anne? What delicious news do you wish to share with me?" Kate asked eagerly.

"Kate, you cannot imagine how wonderful this past year has been. I am quite popular now—I can hardly believe it. I mean, I do know my fortune is very enticing, but still, it is so nice to be all the rage. I can hardly believe that two years ago when we first met I was so shy and retiring and so utterly lacking in confidence."

Kate smiled because Anne's eyes were wide, her cheeks flushed, and she had never been more animated or prettier. "You have grown up, my dear. I am so happy for you."

"Father has been deluged with offers for my hand," Anne said excitedly. "I have had a dozen serious suitors in the past half year. Is it not unbelievable?"

"Actually, it is very believable, for you are one of the loveliest people I know. Anne, I want you to find love, not just a husband." Kate hugged her impulsively. Anne did not pull away, but she did not return the embrace. Kate stared, somewhat perturbed.

Anne smiled, eyes lowered. "Oh, but I have."

"I beg your pardon?" Kate was not quite sure that she had heard correctly.

Anne faced her, eyes aglow, clasping both of her hands tightly. "I am in love, Kate, with the most wondrous man, a man of elegance, charm, and astounding good looks! Indeed, he is one of the premier bachelors in this land, and our families have already agreed upon this match!"

"Oh, Anne—why didn't you tell me this immediately!" Kate cried in delight.

Anne shrugged, her smile secretive. "Sometimes the best must come last."

"Oh, do not tease and torment me now! Who is this knight in shining armor whom you shall wed?"

Anne laughed. "Oh, he is a knight, Kate, in fact, I am sure you will think so too, for you met him last year. It is Lord Braxton, Collinsworth's heir."

Kate gasped. Her heart dropped like a rock, with sickening force.

And somehow a part of her knew that it was the beginning of the end.

Jill's first impulse was to flee. Instead, she slammed the light switch, turning off the lights. Darkness bathed her.

Oh, God. Was the intruder still inside? Should she call the police? Was Sir John all right?

Jill dared not breathe. She strained to hear, and had a pin dropped, she would have heard it. The house was devastatingly silent.

Frighteningly silent.

She had to find Sir John. She was afraid he had befallen the same fate as Lady E. But her courage was failing her—her back remained pressed to the wall by the front door. Her knees felt strange, weak.

Jill reached behind her and slowly groped for the knob. When she had found it, she turned it, then pushed the door and ran outside and all the way back to Lucinda's. She pounded on the other woman's front door.

"Jill?" Lucinda appeared almost immediately. "Dear, what is it? What has happened?"

As Jill spoke, her teeth chattered. "Someone has ransacked my flat." Alex's image flashed through her mind. Had he gone home—or had he parked the Lamborghini a few blocks away and come back to do his damage?

She shook her head to clear it. Was she a fool? Whoever had ransacked her flat had done so while she was with Alex—no single person could have made such a wreck in a mere few minutes.

She was relieved, but only for a second. Alex could hire a

henchman, as could Thomas or William or anyone else. Any-one in the family could have had their hand in this.

"Come inside, Jill," Lucinda was saying with real worry. She took her arm and pulled her into the house. "Are you certain that the flat was actually ransacked?" She locked her door behind them.

"Lucinda. Everything has been turned upside down in the parlor. Pillows were slit," Jill cried tersely.

"Oh, dear. But—in this neighborhood?!"

Jill walked past her and sat down on the sofa, holding her head in her hands. "It's one of them. Someone in the Collinsworth family. Someone who thinks I want a part of their fortune. Or someone who doesn't want me blabbing to the world what I know about Kate and Edward."

"Jill, I don't think anyone in the family would ever behave in such a way. Maybe you should ring up the police, Jill."

Jill grimaced, reaching for the phone, watching her hand shaking. But she did not pick it up. Instead, she said slowly, "What will the police do? They'll hear my story and write me off as some Looney Tune." Jill regarded Lucinda, suddenly shaken all over again. The police would hear her talking about her murdered great-grandmother and laugh in her face. They would think her a nutcase. And she could easily imagine how convincing and sincere William and Thomas would appear to be if the police dared to question them. "The Sheldons are respected members of this community—I'll be the one who comes out of this blackened, not them."

"Jill, I am certain the family had nothing to do with this. Collinsworth is a pillar of the community. Did you know that the various earls were all preeminent men? Leaders and law-makers and such? It is almost a tradition; the community expects leadership and altruism from the earls of Collinsworth."

"No, I did not know any of that." Jill continued to shake, and to stop the tremors, she hugged herself, trying to breathe deeply. It was impossible. "Was Edward Sheldon a leader and a lawmaker, too?"

Lucinda's eyes brightened. "Actually, my dear, he spent his lifetime modernizing the estates. He brought the earldom into the twentieth century. He was also a major supporter of labor reform."

Jill felt like pulling out her hair. "He doesn't sound like the kind of man who would murder his mistress," she said. "But appearances are deceiving."

"Jill, Edward would have *never* murdered anyone," Lucinda said firmly. "I think you should notify the police. Maybe we should ring up Mr. Preston as well."

"No! He's the last person I want to call," Jill cried sharply. She took a deep, ragged breath. "There's no point in calling the police. Trust me on this one." Jill started to tremble uncontrollably all over again.

"Oh, Jill, first the cat, now this. This is so terrible!" Lucinda stared at her. "And Mr. Preston is a gentleman. Surely you don't think *he* had anything to do with this?"

Jill stared, feeling near-hysterical tears rapidly rising to the surface. She fought to swallow them. "I don't know what to think. I trusted him. I . . . I liked him. I don't know what to think." Tears slid down her face. "I can't trust anyone!"

"You poor dear." Lucinda came and sat beside her, putting her arm around her. "I am going to make you some sandwiches and tea. You need to eat, it will make you feel better. In fact, I'll spike the tea with some brandy. That will do the trick."

Jill didn't hear her. What if something terrible had happened to Sir John?

Suddenly she could see Kate in the tower, begging for her life, reduced to tears, terror, and desperation.

Something terrible had happened to Kate . . . what if she, Jill, had been home earlier? What would the intruder have done?

Jill was on her feet.

"Jill?" Lucinda asked, bewildered.

"I need to find Sir John. Lucinda—do you have any weapons in the house?"

Lucinda blinked. "I have some Mace."

"Mace," Jill said, a bubble of frightened laughter erupting from her chest. "How about a flashlight?"

Lucinda nodded and disappeared into the kitchen.

Jill's knees seemed to knock together. She was a coward—but she had to go look for Sir John anyway. No matter how frightened she was.

And suddenly Jill realized, knew, and felt just how frightened Kate had been, a prisoner at the mercy of a madman, with her life at stake.

She stood and walked to an oval mirror in the entryway. For one instant, Jill could not believe that she was looking at herself.

She was ghastly white. Her face seemed narrow and pinched with strain and fatigue. Her hair was an uncombed riot of tangles around her face. But what was truly the most frightening was the wild, panicked look in her eyes.

It was a look she had seen before. It was the exact same look Kate had in her dreams.

Lucinda returned, handing Jill the Mace, holding the flashlight. "If you're going back over there, I'm coming with you," she announced.

Jill's heart turned over with real gratitude. "Thank you," she whispered.

They crossed between the two houses in darkness. Lucinda held a flashlight, but she kept it low, shining it only directly upon the ground in front of them. Jill told herself not to be nervous—the intruder was, by now, gone. And although she had every reason to feel dread, she kept telling herself that she was not going to find Sir John bloody and headless. It was a mantra.

The three steps leading to the front porch creaked as they went up them. The groaning wood sounded so loud in the quiet of the night. Where were the crickets? Jill wondered. The street cars? How come the neighborhood was suddenly so deserted? She glanced uneasily around but saw nothing and no one. She felt breathless.

They paused before the front door. Jill gestured at Lucinda, who understood, and she swept the front porch with the flashlight. There was no headless cat anywhere in sight, thank God.

Jill dared to breathe. She slowly opened the front door,

her heart slamming, almost expecting someone to jump out at her, and she turned on the lights.

"Oh, dear," Lucinda said quietly, taking in the mess in the parlor.

Feeling slightly braver because she was not alone, Jill crossed the parlor and entered the kitchen, turning on every possible light as she did so. The kitchen was empty, but it, too, had been ransacked. The cupboards above and below the kitchen counters were open and various items were scattered everywhere, from bags of coffee to containers of ketchup and mustard to salt shakers, cereal boxes, and frozen bagels. Broken plates, saucers, and cups were shattered on the linoleum floor. Even her refrigerator door was open.

The floor creaked behind her. Jill whirled, but it was only Lucinda. Her heart thundered at a frightening rate. Jill whispered, "Can I borrow that light?"

Lucinda handed it to her, her expression grim, and Jill went out the back door. She called for the cat loudly, hoping if the intruder was around, her cries would encourage him to flee. A few minutes later she ducked back inside, the house suddenly inviting compared to the dark shadowy gardens outside. When she rejoined Lucinda in the kitchen by the back door, she had failed to find the cat.

"Maybe he's upstairs," Lucinda suggested.

"I hope so." Jill closed the refrigerator as she walked past it, avoiding stepping on shards of glass and porcelain. Her pulse seemed to be slowing—but it was hardly normal yet. "Well, at least we can be pretty certain that whoever was here is long since gone." The fear had lessened, but she remained ill at ease. Whoever had done this had been angry. Why else sweep the china to the floor?

"Yes," Lucinda said, her tone tight.

Jill glanced at her and immediately felt sorry for the older woman. "Lucinda, you don't have to do this. I'm okay. I was shaken up, but I'm fine now." It was an utter lie.

"That's all right, dear. I don't think you should be alone right now." Lucinda seemed pale. Her eyes were wide behind her tortoiseshell frames.

Jill led the way as they went upstairs, calling loudly for Sir

John now. Five minutes later they stood in the upstairs hallway, at a loss. "He's gone," Jill said. "He has disappeared."

"Undoubtedly he is fine." Lucinda patted her arm but she was not smiling. "He probably was frightened by the intruder. You know how he is. He's hiding somewhere."

Jill looked at her, saw the doubt reflected in her eyes. "I hope so."

"I think you should sleep on my sofa, dear," Lucinda said, glancing nervously around.

"Thank you," Jill did not hesitate.

They went downstairs. Jill locked the house, leaving on two lights, before they left it together. As they crossed between the two flats, Lucinda asked her what she intended to do next.

"I don't know." Jill was terse, glancing over her shoulder not once but three times. No one was lurking about. No one was following them. "But the prospect of staying here doesn't thrill me." That was one of the greatest understatements of her life. "Maybe I'll go back to Yorkshire for a few days." An image of Kate and the tower overcame her with stunning force. Jill's stride slowed. She thought about the photographs she had found at Coke's Way. Hal had been drawn to the ruined manor for a reason. Were the answers there?

Jill was certain of one thing now. KC was right. Somehow, across the span of a century, Kate was desperately reaching out to her, Jill. Kate wanted her to find out the truth. A truth that others were determined to hide. And that truth was in the northern countryside.

"Do you expect to rest in the country—or to continue your search for clues about Kate's death?" Lucinda cut into her thoughts.

It took Jill a moment to comprehend her question, for she was already back at Coke's Way, already back at the tower. She had to reorient herself to the present, away from both the future and the past. "To continue my search," Jill said. "I need hard evidence, Lucinda, I need real, solid proof that Kate is my great-grandmother, that Edward fathered my grandfather, that he killed Kate." She hesitated. "And if he did not kill her, then I want to find out who did."

"And you think those answers are in Yorkshire?" Lucinda asked, pushing open her own front door.

Jill realized she had not locked it when they had left to go search for the cat at Jill's flat. "I feel it in my bones. I didn't get to play sleuth up there the way I wanted to. I hardly got a chance to search Stainesmore or Coke's Way. The staff knows me now. If I'm very bold, I'll bet I can talk my way in as an invited guest."

Lucinda nodded. "Let me make you those sandwiches, Jill." She hesitated. "Jill? I wouldn't mind making the trip with you. I can probably take a few days off. I would love to see that portrait of Kate."

Jill's eyes widened. "That would be great! I could use the company. Should we drive?"

"Unfortunately my Honda will never make the trip."

"I can rent a car," Jill replied eagerly. "In fact, I'll do so tomorrow."

How far would someone go, Jill wondered, pushing a Hoover vacuum back and forth in the parlor, to scare her away from Kate Gallagher?

It was a frightening question—one that had kept her up all night.

And she was scared. Things had gone too far. First Lady E., then the intruder. Jill didn't think he'd been looking for anything. Jill thought he'd merely wanted to terrorize her—and he had succeeded. Even now, she had a knot in her stomach that would not ease.

She sighed grimly, her back starting to ache. She wanted to finish cleaning the mess from last night so she could rent a car for the trip north. She'd been housecleaning since early that morning—it was almost noon—and this was not her favorite chore. Jill was about to quit when she sensed a presence behind her—when she sensed that she was being watched.

In that instant, her heart lurched hard and she froze. Then

she turned, gripping the Hoover's tube and preparing to use it as a weapon. Her gaze fell upon Margaret Sheldon, standing on the threshold of the parlor—the very last person she expected to see.

Jill recovered and turned off the vacuum. She approached the other woman slowly. Margaret looked every bit like royalty in a pale blue spring suit that cried Yves Saint Laurent and a smart off-white hat. "Lady Collinsworth. You startled me." Recalling how crass she had been to crash her party last night and mouth off, Jill winced. She was afraid to find out why Margaret had dropped by.

Margaret did not move. "I apologize. You did not hear your knocker." She stared, unsmiling.

Jill tensed. In that moment, she knew this was no ordinary social call. "I owe you a huge apology," she began.

"No." Margaret raised her hand, where a huge emerald sat. Her smile was forced, tremulous. "Miss Gallagher, I don't know what you want, or why you're doing what you're doing, but I am asking you to stay away from my family."

Jill flinched.

"Hal is dead. You have no idea what that has cost me." A tear slid down her face—which was set in a mask of controlled anger and equally controlled grief.

"I'm sorry."

"No!" Margaret trembled. "I know that you and Alex motored up to Stainesmore for the weekend. I want you to stay away from him. Please. You've done enough as it is. Stay away from all of us." She was frighteningly white.

Jill did not know what to say. She had never felt so rotten. "It's not what you're thinking. There's nothing between Alex and myself."

"Hal isn't even cold in his grave." She reached into her pale blue alligator bag and produced a silk handkerchief. "I must be frank. I believe you're taking advantage of him. I'm not quite sure what it is that you want—from him, from us all."

"I've never taken advantage of anybody," Jill said hoarsely.

Margaret did not seem to hear her. "I heard what you were saying last night in my home. How could you? I was kind enough to invite you in—and you accuse my father-in-law of . . . of . . . I can't even repeat it!" she cried.

Jill could not feel worse. Margaret was beginning to cry and Jill felt sorry for her and was close to hating herself. She knew her grief over the loss of Hal remained as strong as ever. Jill told herself to listen to the other woman, to walk away. Instead, she said, "Someone killed Kate Gallagher, Lady Collinsworth. There was never any justice. Don't you care?"

Margaret sat down abruptly, her hand on her bosom, as if her heart was bothering her.

Alarmed, Jill knelt before her. "Are you okay?"

"No." She looked up, breathing heavily. "Frankly, I don't know what you are talking about. I know nothing about this Kate Gallagher, and whatever did happen, why, that was almost a century ago! Maybe, for some reason, you want to hurt all of us. Is that what you are about? Do you want to hurt my family?"

"No. I'm not trying to hurt you." Jill stood. "Let me get you some water." She rushed off into the kitchen, wondering what she would do if Margaret fainted on her sofa. When she returned, handing the countess a glass of ice water, Margaret opened her eyes and took a sip. "I'm sorry," Jill whispered. "Just stay calm. I didn't mean to upset you."

But Margaret shook her head. "My father-in-law was an honorable man. He was a fine man, a strong man, a man with ethics. He did not have a mistress, Miss Gallagher. I knew him."

Jill stared. "But he died in '45. You must have been a child."

"Yes, I was a child—I was ten or so when he died, but our families were close. He was a great man."

"He had an affair with Kate, before he was even engaged to Anne."

Margaret looked up, directly at Jill, her face stiff with

tension. "Do you have a price? Is that what this about? What is happening is intolerable to me. I will write you a check," she said. "Name your amount, Miss Gallagher, and then leave us be."

Jill straightened, frozen inside. Alex, Thomas, and now the countess . . . Her mind raced and she immediately dismissed her suspicion that Margaret was in any way involved with the threats recently made against her. It was impossible. She finally said, "This isn't about money. This is about a murder, this is about the truth."

Margaret stood. "I don't understand," she said. "What will you do if you find out the truth? Write a book?"

"I haven't thought about it."

Margaret regarded her with skepticism. "Don't do this," she said. "Hal wouldn't want you to do this."

Jill stared. It was a terribly low blow—it was a direct hit.

Jill paused before sliding out of her rental car, a blue four-door Toyota. Alex was standing on the street in front of Lucinda's gate, speaking to the other woman. His back was to her—he had yet to see her.

Jill slammed the door and locked it, aware of the mad pounding of her heart. She did not want to see him. And what were they talking about?

She trusted Lucinda and knew she would not say a word about their plans to depart for Yorkshire tomorrow morning. But what if she told him about what had happened last night at her flat? Doing so because she believed that telling Alex could only be helpful to Jill?

At that moment, he turned. Their gazes locked.

Jill did not move. As they stared at one another, she recalled everything she wished had never happened—the way he'd held her at Kate's grave, the way he handled the Lamborghini with his strong hands, the way he handled everything—decisively and effectively. She recalled their single night of passion, and his sleeping on her couch the night Lady E. had been murdered.

Jill closed her eyes, in that moment wishing, desperately, that someone or something could give her the answers she wanted—not the answers she was afraid she had already found.

She reminded herself that she must not, for a minute, forget that he wanted her paid off. That was a fact that he had admitted to.

Alex said something to Lucinda and started purposefully toward Jill. His gaze was searching. "Hi."

Jill nodded, trying to be cool, composed. Undoubtedly he could hear her deafening heartbeat. He had been furious with her last night; today, he seemed to be his usual self.

"Lucinda told me what happened last night." His tone was sharp. "Why didn't you call me? Why didn't you call the police?"

Jill wet her lips. "It crossed my mind," she said slowly, "but it also crossed my mind that you or someone in your family was giving me another warning."

He stiffened. For a long moment he did not speak. "Let's go inside. I want to talk to you about everything."

"I think it was another warning, like poor Lady E." Jill's chin tilted up defensively.

Alex just stared at her. His eyes seemed very dark. "I hope that is not the case," he finally said.

"Do you?" Jill asked, wondering if he was becoming angry, and if so, why? He was controlling his expression and she was finding it difficult to read.

His face had tightened. "Yes, damn it, I do."

Jill shrugged. If only he were being absolutely honest with her. And out of the corner of her eye she saw movement on the porch. She turned, gasping, as Sir John settled himself by the front door, staring at her. "Sir John!" she cried, almost in disbelief.

She flung open her gate and rushed up the stone path, then slowed as she approached the front steps of the porch so she would not frighten him away. But Sir John did not move. Jill had never been happier to see anything or anyone. She sat down on one of the steps. "You're okay," she whispered, overcome with dazed relief.

To her amazement, he got up and came over to her, pressing his sleek, silvery body against her arm.

Immediately Jill ran her hand over his back. He arched beneath it. "You're really okay," she whispered again, tears blurring her vision.

She pulled the cat into her arms, hugging him, expecting him to protest. He did. With a soft sound he leaped away, but then sat down a few feet from her, delicately cleaning the fur by her shoulder.

As Jill wiped her eyes with her fingertips, she became aware of a shadow falling over her. She knew it belonged to Alex. She looked up.

He looked down. Then he extended his hand to her.

Jill stared at it. It was a broad hand with long, capable fingers; it was a strong hand. The symbolism was overwhelming. Jill hesitated.

"Jill."

Jill put her hand in his and he pulled her to her feet. She tried to break free of him, but his grip on her hand tightened, and the next thing she knew, he had pulled her hard against his body, wrapping his arms around her, crushing her to him. "I would never let anything happen to you," he said harshly in her ear. "I don't like this, Jill. I don't like what's happening to you—to us."

Jill was stiff as a board. She felt like she belonged there, in his arms, against his chest, thigh to thigh and heart to heart. Had Hal ever felt like this? Jill did not think so; she could not remember. Her body began to soften against his in spite of her doubts. Oh, God, she thought helplessly, what am I doing? What should I do? "There is no us," she whispered.

"No?" he asked, looking down at her, holding her gaze.

"No," she returned, as firmly as possible.

"Then what was that night about?"

He did not have to elaborate. Jill stepped back from him. "That was about sex."

His nostrils flared. "Right," he said, the one word heavy with disbelief and sarcasm.

"What are you doing here?" Jill asked.

He gripped her shoulders so their gazes could meet again. "I told you last night we'd talk today. Thank God I came over. You weren't going to call me, were you?"

"No."

She glimpsed anger again, flitting through his eyes. "Maybe you were right, not to call the police," he said. His gaze was intense. "But you should have called me."

Jill's temples began a slow, dull throbbing. In his presence, like this, she was torn. And in that moment, she had to face what she didn't want to face—a part of her was glad that he was there, just as a part of her had been glad that he had stayed the night Lady E. was murdered. "I'm scared," she said unthinkingly. And it was too late to take it back.

"I know." He touched her face. "Trust me. I won't let anything happen to you."

An image of Lady E.'s headless, bloody body came to mind, followed by an image of her ransacked flat. Alex's eyes were so blue, the color of a clear country sky, and filled with sincerity. Jill thought about Kate, desperate and terrified, begging for her life. And suddenly she remembered how Hal had felt as he lay dying in her arms, his life ebbing rapidly away, before her very eyes, with herself helpless to prevent it.

Jill closed her eyes. In that moment, she needed his strength and she knew it—but she didn't want to need him. Especially because he might be an illusion. But he was so goddamn strong. "Alex, I'm so confused," she whispered.

"I know." He pulled her back, into his arms, against his chest. He spoke to the top of her head. "Promise me, Jill, if something like this ever happens again, I'll be the first to know," he said.

"All right," she said, not quite sure whether she meant it or not, her cheek against his shirt and jacket, her heart beating against his. Would it be so bad, she wondered, to find comfort with him again? Even if it was fleeting, even it if was brief?

He stroked her hair. "You made me so angry last night. I regret it now. I'm sorry, Jill, really sorry. But I don't want my aunt and uncle hurt any more. How can I convince you to let this suspicion of yours about Edward go?"

She tensed again, afraid he was manipulating her, but his arms tightened around her and she closed her eyes, succumbing to his embrace. "I have to know who killed Kate."

"I know you do." He seemed to kiss her ear. Tiny jolts of pleasure shot through Jill. "I want to know, too. But they don't need to know. The tabloids don't need to know. And you're making yourself ill. Jill—I think you should make an appointment with Dr. McFee."

She finally looked up at him, trembling—but not with fear. "I'll think about it."

"Good." His gaze held hers. "You are so beautiful," he whispered.

Jill's heart slammed to a halt. When it resumed its beat it did so slowly, firmly, resonating in her chest. Her gaze was riveted to Alex's. And she recognized the look in his eyes.

Worse, she recognized the feeling in her own body, the urgent vibration of need. This could be a huge mistake, she thought. But she was now the first to admit to herself that, in spite of her fears, her doubts, and her suspicions, she was insanely attracted to him, enough so to throw caution to the winds. And right now, it did not seem possible that he'd had a hand in the threats against her, not in any way. Of course, how could she think clearly when his chest was crushing her breasts, his thighs molding her thighs? They had started something at Stainesmore that she had to continue. What if she could trust him? What if this was a beginning for them? She would never know if she did not take a risk.

Her hands slipped to his waist. It was hard and tight.

He kissed her. Interrupting her thoughts, framing her face with both hands. Jill had almost forgotten how exquisite kissing him was. Almost, but not quite.

The kiss became hungrier. There was only his mouth and hers, his body and hers.

She did not move, because she could not move. Eternity passed.

Jill's hands slid into the thick, short hair at his nape. There was one place she wanted to be. And that was in his bed, beneath him, thighs spread, with him deep inside of her.

She wasn't sure she had ever wanted anyone this way before.

Alex. Tall, lean, dark, cashmere sweaters and faded, tight jeans.

He was bending her over backward, his mouth demanding now, his tongue searching. One of his thighs had pushed between hers. She rode him.

Jill's hands moved to his shoulders, but not to push him away. To hold him more tightly.

He broke the kiss. "Christ."

"Let's go upstairs," Jill said hoarsely. "And we'll worry about tomorrow then."

Jill was aware of him following her up the stairs, and she felt his gaze on her back. Her heart had the cadence of a jungle drum. Every nerve ending in her body was firing off neurons and transmitters in a rapid, mindless succession. She was beginning to feel dazed, and she couldn't help thinking, perhaps foolishly, that she had missed him, and badly.

In her doorway she hesitated, the bed looming before her in the room, acutely aware of him behind her. She was shaking. Without warning, his hands gripped her waist, turning her abruptly around, his mouth coming down hard on hers.

Jill couldn't wait either, and she met his tongue, wrapping her legs around his hips. He thrust into her and pressed her against the wall. His erection—hot, hard, huge, straining his jeans—ground against her crotch. Jill clutched his shoulders, kissing him back, moving her hips against him.

He tore his mouth from hers, kissed and bit her jaw, her throat. Jill cried out.

He suddenly set her on her feet again, lifting her sweater up over her bra, and lifting the bra up too. His tongue slashed over her nipple. He palmed her. Hard, between her legs, where she felt damp with urgency.

Jill heard herself moan again, with abandon—she could hardly breathe—she was going to come. She reached for him, grabbed the bulge of his rock-hard penis. "Alex."

But he was already pulling her jeans down her hips. He cupped her sex again, inserting a finger there.

An instant later they were on the floor. Alex kicked off his jeans and drove into her; Jill wrapped her legs around his waist and encouraged him to push faster, harder. He strained over her and began to whisper into her ear. Shock seized Jill, and she exploded.

He slid out, still fully distended, and rubbed the ripe tip of his penis over her wet pubis. Instantly Jill tightened. Their eyes met. In spite of his strained expression, he smiled briefly at her. "One more time," he said roughly.

Jill leaned up on her elbows and nuzzled the length of his erection. Then, heart rioting, body aching, she slowly sucked him into her mouth—every possible inch.

He gasped her name, gripping her head, surging forward. And abruptly he moved away, pulling her thighs over his shoulders, going down on her, his tongue everywhere. Just as Jill knew she could no longer stand it, he reared up and thrust deep, hard and slick, wet, raging heat.

They came together in one stunning, blinding moment.

They lay still, unmoving, on the floor, except for their pounding, racing heartbeats. As the tension began to drain away from her body, Jill listened to his breathing as it slowed and evened, running her hands over his leather jacket. She still had her sweater and bra on, too—twisted up over her breasts.

Oh, my God. Her only coherent thoughts.

He kissed her on the lips, met her eyes, and sat up. Jill met his gaze, which was unflinching, also sitting up. Was there a question in his eyes? Was there regret?

Reality hovered over them. "Not now," Jill whispered, speaking her thoughts aloud. Jill bit her lip, then tore sweater and bra up over her head and flung them aside.

He didn't smile. His blue gaze drifted over her, slowly, until Jill felt a blush staining her skin.

"I want to stay the night."

Jill could hardly speak. She nodded.

He smiled. And he removed his jacket, his sweater, his socks.

Jill woke up alone.

Her small travel alarm clock buzzed insistently, annoyingly. She wanted to go back to sleep, she was exhausted—but then, instantly, her mind flooded with memories of

Alex's lovemaking and she was wide awake. She did not move, recalling the touch of his hands, his fingers; the taste of his mouth, his tongue; the powerful, consummate feel of him inside of her; the way he'd lowered himself between her legs to lick her senseless. She thought about how he'd tasted inside of her mouth. They had not slept very much last night.

Jill groped for the clock and turned it off. She recalled setting it now because Alex had said he had a breakfast meeting at the Dorchester at eight. It was seven.

And she and Lucinda were to leave for Yorkshire at nine.

Jill sat up. His side of the bed was mussed, his pillow indented. Her bedroom door was open, as was the door to the bathroom across the hall. He was not in the bathroom, either. She wondered, with a sinking heart, if Alex had left without saying good-bye.

But wouldn't that be for the best?

She gripped the mattress grimly. She had thought the sex she'd had with Hal to be unsurpassable. She had been wrong.

Jill was unhappy. She got up, stepping into a pair of jeans and pulling on a white T-shirt. She had loved Hal, even if it had been one-sided and a mistake. She did not love Alex. She did not know how they had achieved such passion last night.

Maybe it was due to the bizarre circumstances she found herself in, she decided. Maybe the fear and treachery surrounding her had made their lovemaking that much more intense.

She paused before the mirror above the bedroom bureau, her hand pressed against her swollen lips, her eyes growing moist. She had regrets. Her fears—and suspicions—were not really allayed. She had to consider everyone related to the family a suspect. But worse than that, she wanted to be with him, again. "Oh, God. What am I going to do?" she asked herself in the mirror.

The answer came immediately. *Find the truth.* Kate's voice, there in her mind, so frighteningly loud and clear.

Jill glanced around, but Kate was nowhere to be seen— thank God. She was grim, uneasy. When she found the truth, she would also know the truth about Alex. She prayed that he had not been involved in anything more than wanting her paid off.

Jill heard a noise downstairs. She hesitated. If he had left, without even a good-bye, it would be both a disappointment and a relief. If he was downstairs, a part of her would be pleased—while another part of her would be dismayed. Jill realized she was stuck between a rock and a hard place. She walked slowly downstairs, barefoot.

He was in the kitchen, on his cell phone. And the coffeemaker was brewing up a pot of fresh coffee. Its sweet, thick aroma filled the room.

He saw her and halted in midsentence. Their gazes locked.

Jill was tongue-tied, like a fifteen-year-old after the first time.

Except that she wasn't fifteen, and someone had killed Lady E. and ransacked her home and that someone had to be a Sheldon.

Alex smiled at her, and said, "Okay. Thanks. Bye." He flipped the phone closed. His eyes were warm.

"Good morning," Jill said cautiously.

He continued to smile. "Good morning."

He was staring. She crossed over to the counter and poured coffee into the two mugs, her back to him. "I haven't forgotten that you make a great brew." She wanted to smile back at him, but she was sane again, and her mind would not let her.

He said, softly, "I hope that's not all that you remember."

She felt her cheeks heat as she turned around to face him. "Last night was great." Her tone was so calm. She did not know how she remained so composed. And her words were a vast understatement.

His gaze remained steady on hers. But his smile faded. "Yeah. You okay?"

Jill glanced away. "Yeah."

One of the most awkward silences in Jill's life settled abruptly between them. Jill could hear a neighbor's dog barking, a car on the street outside, and water dripping in the kitchen sink. Finally he said, "I have to run. I forgot an important file at the office, otherwise I'd have time to have coffee with you."

"That's okay," Jill said, clutching the hot mug in both hands. Stupidly, she was disappointed. Yet a part of her needed him to leave. So she could figure out what to do now—about him—about them.

He walked to her, paused. A moment passed in which he said nothing, in which he only scrutinized her. "I'll call you later," he finally said, sliding his thumb over her jaw.

Chills swept over Jill. How easily he could arouse her. In response, she pulled away.

"Jill?"

"Okay," Jill said. Not telling him that she would not be home later—that she would be in Yorkshire, at Stainesmore.

He kissed her cheek, unsmiling now and even grim and maybe even hurt, and strode from the kitchen. Jill watched him go.

When he had left, the front door slamming behind him, Jill slowly sat down. Talk about a no-win situation, she thought miserably.

But there was no point in dwelling on what had happened. It had happened, and she would have to face the consequences, whatever they might be. And if she could stop thinking about Alex, she would, but right now, he was a strong presence in her mind.

Jill went upstairs with her coffee to shower, dress, and pack. At eight forty-five she was ready, and she carried her duffel outside to her rental car.

She had just opened the trunk and was heaving the duffel in when Lucinda appeared with her own overnighter. They exchanged greetings and Jill took the other woman's bag from her and deposited it in the trunk, slamming it closed.

"Shall I drive us out of the city?" Lucinda asked. "Or would you rather? I am very good at giving directions." Lucinda smiled.

Jill glanced at the older woman. She felt obligated to do as much of the driving as possible because of their age differences. "Why don't I drive for the first two hours or so and then we'll switch?"

"Thank you, dear," Lucinda said cheerfully, getting into her side of the Toyota. "I'm not the best driver in heavy traffic, you know."

Jill climbed in. A moment later they were on A40, traveling at a good forty miles an hour. The traffic was moderate. Jill thought that that, along with the fact that it was a clear day, was a very good sign.

Alex pushed his way into her mind. She tried to shove him out, and failed.

"There's a light up ahead," Lucinda remarked.

Jill had noticed the roundabout where several vehicles had stopped ahead of them, allowing cross traffic to proceed through, and was already touching the brake. To her initial surprise, the Toyota did not slow.

She stepped on the brake again, more firmly—but the Toyota continued to cruise along at forty-three miles an hour.

Jill pumped the brake, realizing in that single moment of horror that they had no brakes. *Their brakes had failed.*

It was déjà vu. *They were speeding along—the huge tree looming before them—a scant instant before that heartstopping, violent, terrifying moment of impact.*

"Jill?! Slow down!" Lucinda cried as they careened toward the cars halted in front of them at the busy intersection.

"I can't!" Jill shouted, pumping the damn brake frantically, sweat breaking out all over her body. "The brakes don't work!"

A red car was only yards away, in front of them. The Toyota raced on. The red car bumper looming before them. It was seconds until impact . . .

Lucinda screamed.

Part Four

Judgment

Twenty-Two

SHE WAS ILL. KATE HELD HERSELF, AFRAID TO SUCCUMB TO nausea, as her carriage careened down the street.

But they were not going fast enough. Kate rapped on the back of the coachman's seat with her gloved fist. "Faster, Howard," she demanded. "Faster!" The two bays were already whipped into a canter.

"Yes, m'lady."

Kate told herself to breathe deeply. There must be a mistake, she thought, bouncing on the velvet squabs of the seat.

Abruptly she closed her eyes, which were filling with tears. Hadn't she known that one day Edward would be forced to wed someone else? As easily as his wicked old father had threatened him with disinheritance if he married her, Kate, he could do the same if he did not marry the bride of Collinsworth's choice.

But dear, dear God, Anne? Edward was to marry Anne? Her very best friend in the world?

Tears slipped down Kate's cheeks. Pain pierced through her breast. There had to be a mistake—a vast and monumental mistake.

She opened her eyes and dabbed at them with her gloved fingertips. Two images vied for her attention in her mind's eye. One was Edward's striking face, his eyes soft with the love he felt for her. The other was Anne's face, her eyes glowing, her expression animated—and never prettier. Anne was in love with Edward.

Kate pressed her hands to her mouth to cut off a cry. This was terrible! And why hadn't Edward told her of this? Had he decided, finally, to capitulate to his father? No! That was impossible. Kate reminded herself of their interlude just hours earlier that day, the passion and love that they had shared. Undoubtedly he hoped to spare her feelings, Kate thought.

Kate had been so upset when Anne had told her about the engagement that she had not even been able to ask the questions that now gnawed at her. Had Edward been courting her? Kate did not believe it, but Collinsworth was very powerful and who knew what he might hold over Edward's head? And now she was trying to recall if she had seen an engagement ring upon Anne's hand. She did not think so.

The carriage was slowing. Kate was overcome with fury, and she was about to bang on the coachman's partition and scream at him, demanding to know why he dared to slow down, when she realized that they were turning into the drive of Uxbridge Hall. Her heart now lurched hard. And she was afraid.

She had only been to Edward's ancestral home once, when he had brought her there after a ride in the park to give her his "grand" tour. Shortly afterward the earl had denied Edward permission to court her, much less marry her, and their affair had turned into a secret liaison. It hurt Kate's heart to be faced with the huge and imposing stone mansion now. She could not help but think about how she would never be welcome there, not unless one day, soon, Collinsworth died so she and Edward might wed.

What is happening to me, Kate whispered, aghast, that I am waiting for an old man to die? *Oh, God, what is happening to me?*

"Miss?" A servant was opening the carriage door.

Kate came to and slid her hand in the servant's, allowing him to help her down.

"May I help you?" one of two footmen asked her at the front door.

Kate's hand was trembling as she took one of her calling cards from her purse. She remained dazed, but she needed all of her mental acuity now and she knew it. "Is Lord Braxton at home?"

"I will make certain he receives your card," the footman said, taking the small, printed piece of parchment from her.

"Is he at home?" Kate asked very firmly.

The footman's eyes flickered. "I do not believe so. I will give him your card, Miss Gallagher. I am certain he will return your call."

Kate did the unthinkable. She walked right past the servant and into the Hall's marble-floored foyer. "Please tell Lord Braxton I must have a word with him now. It is of the utmost importance."

The liveried footman stared at her, eyes wide. Kate knew her breach of etiquette was severe. She could not care.

"Very well," he began, when a sharp, patrician female voice called, "Fordham. What is going on there?"

Kate trembled as the countess of Collinsworth entered the foyer, her organza skirts billowing about her.

"Miss Gallagher has called upon the viscount," the footman began.

The countess was a beautiful, elegant, very wealthy, and very haughty woman. Kate had been introduced to her just once, and had been immediately and obviously dismissed as unimportant. Now the countess stared at her with dark, penetrating eyes. And although her eyes were brown, her hair was blond. It was a startling contrast.

"We have met, my lady," Kate curtsied. "Please forgive me my insolence but I must see your son."

The countess stared. Her head was held at what Kate thought to be an impossibly high angle. Finally she nodded at the footman. "Send for his lordship. But do give us five minutes, Fordham," she called after him as he went upstairs. "Come with me." It was a command.

Kate obeyed, following her down the corridor and into a room where a grand piano sat in the center, next to that a harpsichord, with chairs arranged in a semicircle around the instruments. The rest of the room was comfortably furnished with seating areas and card tables. The countess moved to one arrangement, a gold velvet sofa and two brocade chairs, and gestured for Kate to sit down in a chair.

Kate did not want to sit. But she did. She steeled herself for a lecture on her manners, at best. For she could only assume that if Collinsworth knew about her and Edward, then his wife did, as well.

"You have tremendous courage, coming here, as you have." The countess stared down at her.

Kate wet her lips. "I did not feel that I had a choice."

"Everyone has choices, Miss Gallagher," the countess said, sitting down on the sofa and gracefully arranging her bronze skirts. A huge emerald ring sparkled on her right hand, a matching necklace glinted on her chest. "And you have chosen to pursue my son."

Kate did not know how to respond. "Actually, my lady, and I mean no disrespect, but he pursued me, it was not the other way around."

"I understand that you have a nice fortune." Her eyes were piercing.

"I do. A very substantial one," Kate said.

The countess nodded. "I do believe my husband made some inquiries—hiring runners and the sort. That is to your benefit, you know."

Kate blinked. She was expecting an assault, but the last declaration was not an attack. "I do not seek Edward's fortune, obviously."

"I have no wish to address the issue of what you seek. I only wish to advise you that my husband will never allow the match, he has other plans for our son, and it would be best for both you and Edward to realize that and part now, before it becomes increasingly awkward to do so."

It was on the tip of Kate's tongue to tell her that it was already awkward—not just because they loved one another, but because of the child. Kate did not think that the countess knew about Peter. "I am aware of what you and the earl wish," Kate finally said.

The countess's regard was unwavering. She was an intimidating woman—Kate did not like their being adversaries. Finally she stood. "I only wish for Edward to take his rightful place in society—and be happy." Her smile was faint, her gaze remained piercing. "That is every mother's wish, is it not?"

Kate slowly got to her feet. "Yes." Her heart drummed. "Yes, it is." Was there a double entendre in her words? Did the countess know about little Peter after all?

"Please do not make this far more difficult than it need be," the countess said simply. "For everyone's sake."

The door opened. Kate whirled. Edward stood there, eyes wide and disbelieving, upon them both. And then his gaze held hers.

"Edward," Kate whispered, her heart twisting impossibly with the extent of her love. She knew that there was an explanation for this terrible misunderstanding. There had to be. He could not have betrayed her by becoming engaged to Anne behind her back.

His gaze went to his mother. "Madame! What is going on here, may I ask?"

The countess was not perturbed. She approached her son. "You have a caller. Please do not forget that our guests arrive tonight at seven." She kissed his cheek and left them alone, closing the door quietly behind them.

Kate stared at Edward, feeling every ounce of the huge, crushing weight of fear. She could not speak.

As he came swiftly to her, concern covered his features, entered his eyes. "Kate? What is it? What is wrong? Oh, God! Has something happened to Peter?" He gripped her shoulders in his.

She wet her lips. It was hard to clear her throat so she might speak. "He is fine. Our son is fine." As she looked up at him, her vision blurred.

"Thank God." Suddenly he stared. "How could you come here? Like this? And what did my mother say to you?"

"She wants me to give you up," Kate whispered. "How convenient that would be."

Edward groaned. "I did not know she knew. She has never indicated that she did. I do not want to trouble her with our dilemma."

"I have just seen Anne."

He froze.

"Your fiancée!" She did not mean to be scathing, but the words formed themselves. "You do recall her, do you not?"

His eyes darkened. "She is hardly my fiancée!"

Kate stared, suspended between hope and futility. There was no mistaking that Edward was angry. "She said the two of you are to wed," she began slowly. "She said you are *engaged*, Edward."

"Kate! And you believed her?" He gripped both of her hands urgently. "I am *not* marrying her." Suddenly he took her in his arms. "It is you I love—you I intend to marry. I offered you marriage two months ago—or have you forgotten? My offer stands." His gaze locked with hers. It was hard, brilliant, intense.

He did not intend to marry Anne. Kate's knees buckled in relief. "And I cannot marry you if you shall lose everything," Kate whispered, clinging to his hands. "Anne thinks the two of you are going to wed, Edward. Are you engaged?"

His face tightened impossibly. His temples visibly throbbed. "I am well aware that Bensonhurst and Collinsworth have agreed on the union—but I have not. Dear God! I cannot tolerate the thought of marrying anyone but you—and especially not your best friend." He pulled away from her to pace with angry strides before confronting her again. "We are *not* engaged. Although I suppose my father and her family consider the union to be all but a fait accompli."

"Oh, God," she cried, trembling. "I could reconcile myself to being your mistress, Edward, I could, and to your having a wife, another life, for that is how shamelessly I love you, but not with Anne. Never with Anne. I confess, I was so afraid."

He came to her and embraced her, hard. "Do not worry about us, dear. Let me worry, let me plan. You are a mother now—you have our son to concern yourself with." He kissed her cheek tenderly.

Kate gazed up at him searchingly, and what she saw in his

eyes made her love him even more. "I am so worried about Anne. She is in love with you, Edward—of course, how can I blame her? I think I must tell Anne the truth. Before she sets her hopes even higher than they are—before she comes to love you as I do. I do not want her heart broken, Edward."

"No. You may do no such thing," Edward said harshly. "I forbid you, Kate, to speak of us to her. Do you hear me?"

He had never used such a tone with her before. Kate was stunned. Finally she said, "Yes. I hear you, Edward. You were very loud, and very clear."

"I apologize for my tone. But this is already so very complicated." Worry creased his brow. "It is not easy, doing battle almost daily with Collinsworth. But"—and his smile was grim—"he cannot force me to the altar."

"Oh, but he can force you to the altar. Haven't you realized that?" Kate looked up at him.

He became motionless. "No. He cannot. He will not. I prefer to lose everything—so if Collinsworth thinks to blackmail me again, he shall not succeed. I will walk away—mark my words, Kate—for good."

"Look at what I have done," Kate cried. "Father blackmailing son. Threats and anger and even hatred between the two of you . . . I can see it in your eyes! You hate him!" She was more than aghast. How had their love come to this?

He held her hard. "I would not change anything, because I have you."

Kate was not reassured. The immensity of their dilemma now struck her with brutal force. And suddenly she felt as if she were seeing the world for the very first time as it actually was—a place filled with cunning and manipulations, with fraud and deception, where the iron fist ruled over goodness and love, and she was more than afraid. Since she was a small child, she had believed in goodness and happy endings. She had believed in true love. Now, suddenly, shockingly, she was faced with the very real possibility that tragedy, not triumph, that power, not love, would decide their future, their lives.

Kate was terrified.

*   *   *

Jill slammed the shift into neutral, steering wildly to the right of the two stopped cars. Tires screeched and her front fender grazed the red wagon's rear bumper, the contact causing the Toyota to jump and sparks to fly. As the Toyota sped past the two standing cars, across the oncoming lane on a diagonal, Jill glimpsed the white, shocked reflection of one driver's face in her mirror.

Ahead of her, traffic was cruising in two directions through the intersection at a steady pace. There was no oncoming traffic because of the red light. Jill continued to frantically pump the brake but nothing happened—the Toyota was cruising now under its own momentum and a glance at her digital speedometer told her that the car had hardly slowed. Her hands were wet on the steering wheel. Jill inhaled. A blue sedan was entering the intersection from her right; Jill turned her wheel hard to the right to avoid hitting him head-on.

The Toyota whipped around in a three-hundred-sixty-degree arc. Lucinda screamed again.

Everything became a blur—the blue sedan, trees and road railings, the traffic lights, as the Toyota spun around dizzily. A telephone pole loomed ahead. Dark, almost black wood, closer and closer still. And Jill thought, *Oh, no, God, not again.*

The left front fender of the Toyota hit the pole and the car ricocheted into the metal railing on the other side of the road.

Jill's head was whipped back by the impact as her air bag inflated instantaneously. And suddenly everything was still.

Jill stared through her windshield, which was intact, at the dented gray metal railing, beyond which was a grassy knoll, a brick wall, and behind that, a pleasant little wood-shingled house. Her heart began to beat. She gulped in air. The Toyota had been badly crushed in the front end, having crashed directly into the railing. The front fender had collapsed into a wide V. The hood had popped open. Jill continued to grip the wheel, so hard that her hands and fingers, which were dripping wet with sweat, began to cramp. Jill began to shake.

It remained hard to breathe. She could not seem to get enough air.

All she could think was, *It had happened again.*

Hal's bloody image, as he told her he loved her, as he called her "Kate," as he died in her arms, assailed her.

Sirens sounded.

Jerking her out of the past. "Lucinda," Jill whispered. If anything happened to her, Jill would never forgive herself. "Lucinda!"

"Jill," the other woman said, one breathless word. Her skin had become grayish green, but her eyes met Jill's, her glasses having disappeared.

The sirens sounded louder.

"Are you all right?" Jill cried. She did not seem to be hurt, other than one bruise beneath her eye.

Lucinda did not answer. Jill watched her coloring turn even more of a ghastly green as her head lolled back and she became unconscious.

Terrified, Jill struggled with her seat belt and the air bag and staggered out of the car. From the corner of her eye she glimpsed two policemen alighting from their car just behind her, their lights flashing. "Officers!" she shouted, waving frantically. "There's an older woman in the front seat and she just passed out!"

Jill stood still, watching and stricken, as one of the officers picked up his radio and as the other one ran around to Lucinda's side of the car. The day, which was bright, dimmed and blurred. As if in a fog, or as if she were watching a television show with terrible reception, Jill watched the officer bending toward Lucinda, who remained inside the vehicle. Reality became distorted. Jill felt as if she were an observer, yet far away from the events actually taking place. Her knees slowly buckled and she sank into a heap on the ground.

Their brakes had failed. They had almost been killed.

Someone had almost killed them.

An ambulance sounded, its siren growing louder as it approached.

"Miss?"

Jill could not look up, hardly hearing the officer behind her. She hugged her shaking legs to, her breasts. She no longer believed in coincidence.

Lady E. was dead. Her flat had been ransacked. And now this.

Someone was responsible for her failed brakes. And whoever that someone was, he—or she—did not care if Jill died.

Or maybe he did care. Maybe he wanted her dead.

"Miss? Are you hurt?"

Jill finally looked up as the officer came to stand in front her. She continued to shake. The ambulance had slammed to a halt beside the police car. Jill watched numbly as paramedics leaped from the vehicle, rushing toward the wrecked Toyota, a stretcher in tow.

I'm going to be sick, she thought, suddenly seeing the paramedics racing toward her and Hal, not Lucinda trapped in the Toyota.

She struggled with herself and found the presence of mind to speak to the officer. "Is she all right?"

"I don't know. They're taking her out of the car now."

Jill got to her feet, no easy task, gripping the officer's arm without thinking about it, as Lucinda was laid on a stretcher, her neck in a brace. "Oh, God." The paramedics carried Lucinda on the stretcher toward the ambulance. Jill ran to them, stumbling. "How is she?"

"Nothing seems to be broken. Blood pressure's low, pulse is steady. Looks like she fainted; she's coming to."

Jill muffled her cry with her own hand, watching as Lucinda's eyes fluttered while she was being loaded into the back of the ambulance. "The neck brace?" she whispered.

"A precaution."

Jill covered her face with her hands and wept.

"Miss." It was the officer. "We're going to have to take you into Emergency, too."

Jill nodded, still covering her face with her hands. Lucinda was all right. Thank God.

And suddenly a blinding anger overwhelmed her.

Whoever had done this had to be stopped.

And she would not be stopped.

She realized she was staring at the officer, and her expression must have shown her rage, because he seemed taken aback.

Jill inhaled. She must not say anything that might have ramifications in front of the policeman. "The brakes didn't work."

The second officer stepped forward. "I know," he said grimly. "I took a look while the medics were removing your friend. The line was cut. You've been leaking fluid, miss."

Jill stared. As she had thought, this was deliberate. But who?

And suddenly she recalled Alex and Lucinda standing on the street in front of Lucinda's house yesterday afternoon. Alex, who had spent all of last night with her.

Alex, who could have crept out of her bed at any time while she was asleep.

Jill awoke to the sounds of a gull cawing. Soft, mist-laced sunlight was creeping into the large yellow and white bedroom where she had slept. As she blinked and found herself gazing at the four posters of her bed, the flocked walls and finally the gray morning sky outside, she stiffened. She had arrived late last night at Stainesmore in a state of fear and exhaustion, having taken a train from London and a taxi from York. After the accident, there had not been any way she could have driven up to the north. Making the police report had taken two full hours, and from there she had gone directly to the Paddington train station—ignoring Lucinda's vociferous protests. Lucinda had been fine, other than some bruises, and had been released from the hospital shortly after arriving there. Jill had refused to wait to depart London for even another day. She had been more than determined to get to the north—she had been afraid to stay in town.

Last night, at half past eleven when her taxi had dropped her at the house, the housekeeper had greeted her warmly, as if she were an old family friend or an expected guest, and Jill had been shown to her room immediately.

Jill lay still for another moment. Sleep had been blissful; a blessing. She had been so tired she had not dreamed, not about Kate and not about the fact that someone might want her dead.

Thinking about Alex hurt. It hurt so much.

God. She had slept with him.

Jill flung her hand over her eyes. She could think so much more clearly now, with the accident almost twenty-four hours behind her. Ah, but it was not an accident—it had been sabotage.

Lucinda had told Alex their plans, as it had turned out. Lucinda refused to even entertain the possibility that Alex might be behind the failed brakes or Lady E.'s death. Jill was grim. She supposed that Alex could have gone directly to Thomas with the information. Thomas might have been the one to cut her brake lines. Jill hoped so—but she did not think so.

Jill sat up. She had left a window open and the morning air was chilly. Goose bumps were raised on her arms. Feeling terribly grim, she got up and slammed the window closed.

How could this be happening?

First Hal, now Alex. She had loved Hal. At the time, he had seemed so perfect. Now she knew better. Now she didn't even understand why they had been together. He had deceived her, repeatedly, and she had only been a stand-in for his odd obsession with Kate.

Jill stared out at the mist-covered moors. Someone had tried to kill her and the odds favored Alex.

Jill washed and dressed quickly in jeans and boots. As she left her room, she could not help but glance at the closed door across from hers. Only a few days ago, Alex had stayed in that room. It felt like an eternity had passed since then. Worse, she almost expected the door to open and him to stroll out, smiling ever so slightly at her. Furious at herself, she shoved the image aside.

Trying not to glance repeatedly over her shoulder, but making sure no servant was about, she grabbed a cup of coffee from the buffet in the dining room and moved swiftly through the house and into the small study where she and Alex had previously gone over the estate ledgers.

Jill set her mug down on the worn desk, returned to the door, glanced into the hallway, and saw no one. She closed it, debated locking it, and decided against it. She turned on one small lamp, parted the curtains very slightly, and found herself staring at the cliffs and a short, distant stretch of the beach and the sea. Someone was walking on the beach, a small distant stick figure, and gulls wheeled overhead. Jill turned away from the stark yet breathtaking view, pulling the draperies closed. Her heart drumming, a dozen excuses forming on the tip of her tongue should someone intrude upon her, she went over to the shelves and took down the unwieldy ledger for the years of Kate's short life. She began reading each page, entry by entry. Every few minutes she would stop and cock her head, straining to hear if someone was approaching.

Jill could not relax. The task was endless, but her pulse kept up a swift, arrhythmic beat. She was hardly interested in the rents collected, salaries paid, taxes owed. But then she paused. Every single expense paid out was recorded. She was staring at kitchen records—the costs of groceries were itemized right down to four pounds of butter. *What if there was an expense referring to Kate's stay in the Yorke Infants' Hospital?*

Briefly exhilarated, Jill combed through the month of May. An hour later Jill was prepared to give up. There was no expenditure listed for mid-May of 1908 assigned to the hospital. She was glum. Perhaps this was a wild-goose chase after all.

Then Jill realized that she was staring at a page listing the monthly salary of employees for the month of December. Jill started to close the ledger, thinking to poke around Coke's Way, when the name Barclay leaped off of the page at her. She froze.

And bent closer over the volume, wide-eyed. She was looking at a list of Christmas bonuses—and one Jonathan Barclay had received ten pounds. Barclay, who had signed the receipt for Kate's stay in the hospital, had been an employee of the family's.

Trembling with excitement, Jill realized that next to every

employee was written a job description—housemaid, butler, etc. But his position in the household was not listed. Jill thought it odd.

But her pulse continued to pound with excitement. Barclay did exist—and there was no mistaking his connection to the family now!

Jill went back a year, scanning lines, looking for his name. It did not appear.

Then she returned to May of 1908. She found the entry she was looking for. A purchase had been made for Lord Braxton in the middle of the month for the amount of seven pounds five shillings—but unlike other purchases in the ledger, this one was not itemized. Did it matter? Kate had just given birth to Peter—and here was proof that Edward had been here, at Stainesmore, only miles away from the hospital.

She was getting closer and closer to the truth. And there was no doubt about it. The truth was in Yorkshire. She flipped backward. Her eyes widened when she found an entry for April 22. "Lord Braxton arrived at six P.M. with Mr. Barclay for a stay of indeterminate length."

"Oh, my God," Jill said, her pulse going wild. And she smiled. Here was the evidence she was looking for. Perhaps Barclay had been his butler or his valet, or even just a secretary. She might never know. But what she did know was that he worked for Edward—he had received a holiday bonus—and that both he and Edward had been in the country when Kate had given birth—when Barclay had paid and signed for her hospital bill.

Jill wished she had a copying machine. She hesitated, glancing around at the windows behind her—but the draperies remained closed. Jill could not help herself. She got up, went to them, parted them, and glanced outside. No one was peeking in and spying upon her. She tore the April twenty-second entry from the book, feeling horrible for doing so, and then she also took the entry that listed Barclay's bonus. She hurriedly folded both items, putting them in her jeans pocket, and closed the ledger, trembling slightly.

As soon as possible, in town, she would make copies of

everything and fax the pieces of the puzzle to Lucinda—with instructions that if anything happened to her, she should turn everything over to the press and the police.

She left the study, closing the door firmly behind her and pausing to listen to the house. She heard no sound of footsteps. No one, apparently, was aware of where she had been in the past hour or so. Relieved, Jill hurried back into the central wing.

Jill was poised to rush upstairs to her room. But the doors to the library were ajar. She faltered, her instincts going into overdrive. Apprehension seized her. But there was no reason for it. The house remained silent.

The hairs prickled on Jill's nape.

Her breath felt constricted in her chest.

Suddenly Jill approached the library slowly. No. It could not be. She froze in midstride.

And her gaze settled on a canary yellow cashmere sweater, lying on the arm of an upholstered chair.

Then her gaze slammed on the small gray Libretto, on the side table beside the couch.

Alex was here.

OCTOBER 5, 1908

"I am so glad you could come," Anne said with a smile. As it was unseasonably warm out, the two young women were strolling on the lawns surrounding the Fairchilds' house, where a birthday celebration for their youngest daughter was being held. Although it was late afternoon, the women were clad in their evening gowns, the gentlemen in their tails. At the moment, a game of croquet was in progress, both men and women playing. Other ladies and gentlemen clustered in groups, chatting and sipping champagne and tasting the hors d'oeuvres being passed about by white-coated waiters. Several children ran about, one chubby boy in particular chasing three little girls. In an hour or so the party would move inside, where an early supper would be served, followed by hours and hours of dancing.

"Thank you for inviting me," Kate said quietly. She

remained worried and depressed. Although she saw Edward every day, and he was as ardent and as tender as usual, she was aware of the gossip on the streets. For whenever she went out for a stroll or to do some shopping, she ran into ladies she knew. Everyone was talking about the impending engagement, and the fact that Edward's refusal to marry the perfect bride—as Anne was a premiere heiress—had to indicate that he was smitten with his latest mistress—whoever that might be.

Kate had ceased to go out. It had become too hurtful. She found it impossible to sleep at night, and she had lost her hearty appetite. She was afraid of the worst happening—she did not know what to do.

She had begun to hate the earl of Collinsworth.

"Kate! Why are you so glum? I have never seen you this way before. And every time I have sent you a note asking you to join me for a drive or tea, you have declined." Anne had halted and was staring at her. "Are you avoiding me? For that is almost what I must think."

Kate forced a smile. "Dear, I would never avoid you." But she had been avoiding her. She had been avoiding her best friend more than anyone else.

Kate was afraid she had glimpsed the handwriting on the wall. That she had glimpsed the future—Anne as Edward's wife. For who was she to think that the earl of Collinsworth could be defied and denied? He was one of the wealthiest and most powerful men in England. Only a very foolish woman would think to go up against his very will and emerge triumphant.

"Miss Gallagher! I had heard you were back, how good it is to see you again!" a very enthusiastic young male voice cried.

Kate turned to see a dashing red-haired man bowing before her. "Lord Weston, how nice to see you, too." She managed to smile.

He was beaming at her—then he saw Anne. He bowed to her as well, but returned his avid attention to Kate. "So how have you fared this past year?" he inquired eagerly.

Kate was about to respond, instead, she noticed Anne's

almost smug condescension toward Weston. She started. It was not just her expression, but the very way she now carried herself—as if she felt herself to be far above anyone else. It was not the Anne she knew so well and loved so dearly.

Weston turned to her. "You will dance with me tonight? You do know that when you returned to New York last year you broke my heart—severely."

"I am sure that you exaggerate, sir." Kate smiled more genuinely this time.

"I do not exaggerate. May I call on you sometime?" he asked with a grin.

Kate froze. She realized Anne continued to watch her with a small, fixed, odd smile, but that was not the cause of her surprise. Edward stood on the other side of the crowd, staring at her, Kate.

"I am afraid I have not been well of late," Kate said softly, her pulse quickening as it always did when he entered the same room as she. "But perhaps another time?"

His face fell. "I shall not give up, you know," he declared. He bowed to them both and left.

Kate did not look after him. Her gaze found Edward again instantly, and this time their gazes locked.

Very slightly, he smiled at her.

Kate's heart leaped. There was something in his eyes, she knew, a message for her alone, even though she could not decipher it at this distance. She smiled back.

And in that moment, her fears and worries vanished. She loved him so, and she could only think how lucky she was to have found a love like theirs, no matter that she might remain forever a mere mistress.

And then she became aware of Anne, standing at her side. As Edward turned away, she whirled to face her friend. Anne was staring after Edward out of wide, shocked eyes. Her eyes followed him as he disappeared into the crowd. It was only when he was no longer visible, having immersed himself among a group of gentlemen, that she turned and stared at Kate.

Her wide-eyed expression was one of disbelief—and perhaps of bitter accusation as well.

It was not pretty—and it made her eyes seem hard and cold, frighteningly so.

And then the expression was gone, replaced by a smile and, "Oh, look. There is Lady Winfrey. We have yet to say hello. Come, Kate, let us chat with her for a moment—she is always so amusing."

Kate's heart was pounding. Had she imagined what she thought she had just seen? Edward had forbidden her to tell Anne the truth. But Anne was about to guess—or was she? Kate wet her lips. A small voice inside of her warned her to hold her tongue. "Anne, wait."

Anne halted, slowly turning. There was something strange and masklike about her face. She might have been a perfectly painted porcelain doll.

Kate gripped her arm. "We must talk." She could no longer live with herself if she did not tell Anne the truth. She pulled her by the hand, making her way past the most crowded part of the lawn, until they stood beneath two shady elm trees, alone and out of earshot.

"What is this about?" Anne stepped back from her as Kate released her. Her tone was mild, unlike her stiff, set, pale face.

Kate swallowed, breathless and afraid. "I do not know how to begin."

Anne did not smile. Her gaze was unwavering. "You have something you wish to say to me. What could it possibly be?"

"Edward is my lover. Edward is the father of my child."

Anne stared. A silence ensued. To Kate, it was the most terrible silence she had ever endured. Then Anne smiled, a mere upward curving of her somewhat narrow mouth. "I do not believe you. You make fun."

"I love him—I have loved him ever since I first met him, well over a year and a half ago," Kate said hoarsely. "He loves me. He loves our son. Oh, Anne! I never dreamed you might fall in love with him, too! I have been avoiding you—for I have been heartsick!"

Anne continued to stare. But the waxlike smile was gone. A long moment passed. Her expression, although pinched, remained otherwise impossible to read. "No," she finally said. "No." She might have been refusing to purchase a bonnet—or refusing a dance.

"Anne, you are my dearest friend. I would never wish this circumstance on anyone, especially not you. But we are already involved. We plan to wed. I am the mother of his child," Kate cried. "Surely you realize that you must seek another bridegroom!"

"Stop!" Anne cried. Her eyes flashed. Her tone was high. "Stop now. Go no further. You have done enough."

Kate gasped.

"I think," Anne said, low and intense, her nostrils flaring, "that you do not wish me happiness."

"No!"

"I think you plot against me!"

Kate was so shocked she could not respond.

"It is agreed!" Anne cried, too loudly. "Contracts are being drawn. A date for the wedding shall soon be set. He is to be—he *will* be—my husband—and you cannot take this from me, Kate!" Her tone was shrill, warning.

"Anne—I am the mother of his son!" Kate began desperately.

But Anne, tears shimmering in her eyes, gave her a look charged with anger as she turned and rushed away.

Kate collapsed against the tree.

Twenty-Three

His door was ajar. He was not in his room, of that Jill was certain, but she had no idea where he was. The moment she had realized he was at the house, Jill had closeted herself in her room, trying to think, to be rational. Why had Alex followed her to Stainesmore? And he had followed her, of that there was no doubt. Was it because he had failed to hurt or even kill her when he had cut the brake lines to her rental car?

Had he followed her to stop her from discovering the truth—and if so, how far would he go?

Jill could not seem to think clearly. Even when she reminded herself of all the times Alex had been kind, and that anyone in the family could have killed Lady E. and sabotaged her brakes. It did not have to be Alex. Maybe he had come north to try to protect her from whoever was out there menacing her, stalking her.

Jill continued to peer past her cracked door at his slightly open one, shaking like a leaf. She had to find out whose side Alex was really on. Just because he wanted her paid off and shut up did not mean he was a killer. She needed to thoroughly search his possessions. Maybe retrieve his voice mail. If she could, she would even try to break into his Libretto, to see if he had copied the missing letters. But the Libretto was downstairs in the library. In a way, Jill was relieved.

Her pulse rioted; she was a jumble of nerves. Sneaking

into his room to ransack it was hardly her style. She could imagine his reaction if she was caught.

Jill took a gulp of air for courage and ran to his door. She pushed it slowly open. Her gaze swung around the room—taking in the made-up bed, the furniture, and, by God, the Libretto on the end table. She froze, staring at the small gray machine, unable to believe this stroke of luck—he had moved it from the library. She then noticed that the modem was hooked up to the jack on the wall, and a small black object lay on the floor by the end table where the mini-notebook sat.

Jill slipped into the room, closing the door behind her. If the modem was hooked up and he had taken the notebook upstairs, it was to send or receive E-mail—privately. Her mind raced. This was her chance—maybe her only one. But she needed a password, damn it.

Her pulse pounded so fiercely and disturbingly now that she could hardly breathe. Jill went to the Libretto, opened it, and powered on. As she waited for the tiny screen to light up, she knelt and inspected the small black object. It was a portable printer.

Her heart raced. Jill looked around, found his briefcase, and sure enough, there was a cable in it. She returned to the Libretto, and as she did, she happened to glance out the window. She was just in time to see Alex step into the pool, clad in what appeared to be a Speedo bikini, and begin to swim hard toward the other side.

Her heart careened. Hopefully he was taking a long swim. In any case, his doing a few laps was perfect for her—because now she could keep one eye on him.

Jill sat down on an ottoman. The screen was cuing her for a password. Jill gritted her teeth and thought hard. People used familiar words, words that held a significant meaning to them. Alex was clever, his wit dry. Jill tried all of the names of his family, backward as well as forward. Suddenly Jill froze. She punched in her own name—and expected to see the screen blossoming with Windows 98.

Nothing happened.

Her heart sank. She had been so certain—now she was at a loss.

Think! She gritted silently. Alex—the Collinsworth Group, Brooklyn, Princeton, cashmere, jeans, the Lamborghini ... .

Jill inhaled, and a second later was typing "Lamb."

Windows 98 filled the screen.

"Yes," she said savagely, glancing out of the window. He was cutting through the water with the sleek, precise strokes of a seasoned swimmer. Jill went to FIND. She typed in "Gallagher" and instructed the search to be in the C drive.

Jill was paralyzed as the screen blossomed with characters. To her shock and dismay, a series of Gallagher documents were listed in a single folder. Jill recalled that he had downloaded a few articles for her, naming them Anne's Wedding, but that was not what she was looking at now. The first four were each labeled "JGallagher.doc" with attached dates, and oh, God, the first date was April 13, 1999—the day after Hal's death.

Obviously she was JGallagher.

She inhaled, trembling. The last one was dated yesterday. There were also three "KGallagher.doc" documents.

Jill began to shake. Her mind had become numb and almost blank. It refused to function. She could only think, No.

This could not be happening.

She was not going to discover what she had dreaded discovering all along.

Kate's voice sounded, loud and clear, so much so that Jill shot to her feet, looking wildly around the room, expecting to see her. *"A nightmare come true ..."*

But Kate was not present—Kate was dead. Betrayed. And then Jill's vision blurred. It was a catalyst. For another moment she could not move. She found herself wishing, with all of her being, that this was not happening—that she was not seeing what was on his damned computer screen in front of her very eyes, the absolute and conclusive proof of his treachery.

He had kept files. He had files on her. He had files on Kate.

It remained hard to breathe, to move, to think. She could

not seem to think clearly—unfocused, scrambled images were competing in her mind—including Alex as he made love to her, including Alex as she had seen him in her kitchen the morning after they had spent the night together, telling her he had to go, he had a meeting, but asking her to see that doctor friend of his. Yeah. She was not the sicko. He was the sicko. Jill opened the first and oldest JGallagher document, her heart sinking, her hand shaking uncontrollably. It was a report.

She was stricken anew. The letterhead was the Periopolis Investigative Agency of New York City. Jill scanned the first paragraph and realized that she had been the subject of a thorough private investigation before Alex had ever met her—the day after Hal had died.

"Oh, you bastard," she whispered, knifelike pain stabbing through her chest.

Abruptly she stood. He was still swimming laps.

Jill reached for the cable. Her hands were shaking so badly that it took her a good minute to connect the printer to the laptop. She glanced wildly around. Paper. She needed paper.

There was sheaf on the table by the window. Jill ran over to it, watched Alex treading water. She ducked away from the window, afraid he might see her, and ran back to the printer, panting now. She shoved the paper in. She knew she didn't really need his report on her, but she hit the PRINT button. As the printer began to print out the report she stood, gazing out of the window. Alex was standing in the pool now, adjusting his goggles. Was he getting out?

"Damn!" She tore the two pages from the printer, opened up the next file on herself, her vision oddly blurred again. She hit PRINT again and stood, looking outside.

Alex was stretching, standing waist deep in the water.

"Oh, God," Jill whispered, squatting beside the printer. "Hurry, hurry up." Then she stiffened, her gaze taking in the name McFee. What the hell was this?

She shifted to read the Libretto's screen. It was a medical report, but the subject was DNA—DNA?!

Jill gripped the Libretto with both hands. ". . . no possibility that Jill Gallagher is not a relative. The DNA matches

taken from her hair sample and William's blood were conclusive . . ."

Jill sat back on her heels. For an instant, she was so
stunned she could not think.

Then it came. Edward was her great-grandfather.

Kate was her great-grandmother.

There was no elation, there was only absolute stunned
confusion.

And Alex would finish his laps at any moment.

Somehow Jill hit PRINT on the next JGallagher file, ran to
the window. He was hoisting himself out of the pool!

And as she turned to run back to the notebook, she
thought he looked up, at his window—at her.

"No," she gritted, tearing the next pages from the printer.
She opened the first KGallagher document. And she recognized it immediately.

It was the letter Kate had written to Anne that she and
Alex had discovered together on the desktop PC at the Fifth
Avenue apartment. Jill could not be surprised. But the extent
of her bitter dismay stunned her. He was more than a bastard.
There was no word in her vocabulary that would do justice to
what he was.

Jill canceled what she had done, opening the next letter.
She hit the PRINT command.

Her teeth were chattering. The room seemed oddly cold.
She was cold. Cold, sick, betrayed. As the printer began to
whir, she ran to the door, cracking it ever so slightly, and
peeked out. She saw no one. Oh, God! How long would it
take Alex to come upstairs?

Jill calculated she had mere minutes left before he would
discover her.

And then what?

The Land Rover was outside. The keys were left under the
rubber floor mat. She would use that to escape.

But she wanted both of the last two KGallagher documents. She knew she did not have time to get them.

The printer stopped. Jill tore the page from it and jammed
it into her jeans with the other pages that were already there.

She ran to the printer, yanking at the cable. She thought she could detect footsteps in the hall.

Jill glanced around his room as she unscrewed the printer cable. She ran, tossed it back into his briefcase, certain she heard footsteps now. Then her gaze took in the open Libretto and the printer with a stack of paper in the feeder. Jill slammed the Libretto closed, tore the paper from the printer, closed that, and, the sheaf in her hand, she ran to the door, peeking out. She could hear him coming up the stairs.

Jill dashed across the hall, into her room, slamming and locking the door behind her.

Alex walked directly into his bathroom, turning on the shower. He fooled with the temperature until the shower was so hot that the bathroom immediately began to fill with steam. He shed the thick terry robe and skimpy Speedo, stepped inside, closed his eyes, and let the hot water pummel him. It did not, could not, ease his tension.

Which was unbearable.

Perhaps ten minutes later, he turned off the water and stepped from the stall. He toweled off, refusing to regard his reflection in the bathroom mirror, unable to look himself in the eye. Naked, he walked into the bedroom, reaching for briefs that he'd left on the bed. As he stepped into them, he felt disturbed.

With the finely attuned instincts of a hunter, Alex froze, not reaching for his jeans. He listened carefully to the sounds of silence all around him.

But his room was not absolutely silent. The faucet in the shower was dripping. He'd left one window cracked, and the cord from the Venetian blinds behind the draperies was pinging against the wall.

Alex looked around his room. Neither of those sounds interested him.

And then he heard it, a soft, faint, barely-there whirring.

His gaze slammed to the Libretto, which was closed. An instant later he had reached his machine, and opened it, but it was off—and it did not whir, anyway.

His gaze fell on the portable Brother printer. The power light was ON.

His jaw flexed, hard. "God damn it," he said.

In her red anorak, Jill ran across the lawn toward the Land Rover. Panting, she reached the black utility vehicle, swinging open the door and reaching beneath the seat, where she'd seen Alex leave the keys. Her hand closed over them.

She was shaking, breathless, terrified. A chant was echoing in her mind . . . He was the one. He had to be the one. The letters, the files, the lies. How long had he known the truth—that she was Kate and Edward's great-granddaughter? She had to get away. She had to get away *now*.

Jill jammed the keys in the ignition, glancing backward over her shoulder, out of breath, her bangs in her eyes, expecting to see Alex flying down the front steps of the house at any second. She saw nothing, no one, behind her. The heavy front door remained solidly closed. The engine turned over, far too loudly. Jill prayed that Alex was still in the shower—she'd heard it running as she'd made her escape from her room—as she shifted into first and then second and took off down the drive, gravel spitting in the Rover's wake.

And just as she reached the end of the drive, a big tan Mercedes sedan pulled into it.

Jill wrenched the wheel hard to the left to avoid a collision, careening past the sedan. As she did so, she caught a glimpse of the driver and the passenger. Even though William wore some kind of cap, there was no mistaking who he was. The woman beside him in the front seat had her hair covered with a scarf—Margaret.

Jill turned onto the narrow coastal road, burning rubber, her heart wedged unpleasantly into a hard knot high up in her chest. William and Margaret, there in Stainesmore—it made no sense. Glancing repeatedly in her rearview mirror, Jill stepped on the accelerator. She gripped the leather-bound steering wheel with both hands, which were clammy and wet, her heart drumming in her chest, the Land Rover leaping over the road's bumps and ruts. It was only a matter of time until Alex discovered either the violation of his files or that she was gone.

Jill did not know what to do. She wanted to fax all of the documents stuffed into her anorak to Lucinda, but she was afraid to stop in the village, afraid those few precious minutes would enable Alex to catch up with her. The Land Rover careened down the hilly, twisting road. It was misting out and Jill tried—and failed—to find her wipers.

Periodically Jill could glimpse the choppy gray waters of the North Sea through the sparse trees on the left side of the road. She realized Coke's Way was not far ahead.

Grainy, grayish headstones pierced the fog, ahead of her, against a backdrop of slick wet grass and spiny trees.

The chapel! She could fax everything from the vicar's office.

Jill gunned the accelerator pedal. She raced down the road and swung the wheel wildly, turning far too abruptly across the oncoming lane into the drive of the chapel. She hit the brakes, the Rover spitting gravel. And even as she ran toward the old stone church, she was frantic, wondering if Alex was on the road behind her, if she was losing her small, precious head start.

Lights were on—a good sign. She thrust open the old, scarred wooden door, found herself standing in the nave. The chapel was filled with shadows because of the late afternoon and the rain that would start at any moment. "Vicar? Vicar Hewitt?" Her voice sounded high, raw, and panic-stricken even to her own ears.

He appeared out of the shadows at the far end of the nave. Slowly approaching. Jill could not make out his expression because of the gloom but suddenly she was paralyzed, because it flashed through her mind that he had been waiting for her. But no, that was impossible, she was losing her grip, completely.

"Miss Gallagher?"

"I need your help," Jill cried, twisting her hands and realizing with some odd, detached surprise that they were scratched. "I need to use your fax, and I need you to keep a lookout for me!" Tears slid down her cheeks.

"A lookout?" the vicar asked, pausing to stand before her.

"I'm being followed," Jill whispered. "I'm in trouble. Can I use your fax now?" She started past him, toward the small office behind the nave.

"Miss Gallagher. You are distressed. Let me take you to my home for some hot tea and you can explain to me what this is all about."

Jill shook her head, running now down the nave. "Maybe you could send these faxes for me." She could envision Alex behind the wheel of the Lamb, just moments away.

"I'm afraid you do not understand. I do not have a fax machine."

Jill stumbled and stared. It took her a full moment to comprehend what he was saying, and then, when she did, she heard the most awful sound she had ever heard in her life—a familiar, powerful roar—the sound of Alex's Lamborghini stopping in the drive outside of the chapel.

For an instant, Jill was paralyzed.

In the next instant, she looked up, met the vicar's dark eyes. "Don't tell him I'm here!" And she ran past him, down the nave, into his office, and out the back door.

The vicar did not move. A moment later the front door opened and Alex stepped inside, removing a pair of yellow-tinted sunglasses. It had begun to rain, and his distressed brown leather jacket was spotted with water.

"Good afternoon, Mr. Preston," the vicar said. He pointed. "She went that way."

Alex nodded.

Twenty-Four

THE LAST PLACE SHE WISHED TO BE WAS AT BENSONHURST.

Kate stood on the landing above the ballroom, staring down at the crowd. She had not seen or spoken to Anne since that horrendous occasion a week and a half ago at the Fairchilds'. In the interim, she had not been able to eat or sleep. She had spent most of her time with Peter, holding him to her breast, trying not to give in to her grief and despair and a terrible sense of impending doom.

Kate clutched the railing for support. She had nibbled on dry toast that morning, and now felt faint. She wished she had eaten something heartier. But she supposed there was a bright side—she had been able to squeeze into her most dramatic ball gown, a bare, black lace creation she had worn once before her pregnancy. She was making a statement. She knew she was beautiful and desirable, and tonight, no one would think otherwise.

She had dressed for Anne now that they were rivals.

The ballroom below was filled with guests; Kate was late. She saw Anne and her parents holding court in the very center of the huge room, Anne lovely in a pale pink taffeta gown. She was wearing, Kate realized, some of the Bensonhursts' most priceless jewels. Diamonds dangled from her ears, were roped about her throat. The jewelry was overpowering. Kate herself was wearing nothing but a locket on a black velvet ribbon. It was a very special locket, given to her by Anne at Christmas two years ago. In it were their two portraits. That holiday, they had sworn to be best friends forever.

Briefly, Kate's eyes blurred with tears as sadness overcame her. She had become overly emotional these past few days—every little thing, every recollection, every memory, every doubt, every fear, was enough to make her weep. How torn she was over her predicament. She did not want to be at odds with Anne, she did not want to fight with her for Edward's hand. She wanted everything to be set right; for things to be the way they had been before Kate had returned to London.

Then Kate realized that the earl of Collinsworth and his wife, the countess, stood beside Anne and her family and she stiffened. They had all seen her.

Kate slowly came down the stairs, refusing to tremble, her long, scalloped hem trailing after her. She wondered if Anne had told her secret—hers and Edward's—to the world. Everyone seemed to be staring at her, as if she were an uninvited guest—or a fallen woman. Kate neither faltered nor flinched. And she had been invited—before that fateful day in the Fairchilds' gardens.

Kate continued toward Anne, her parents, and the Sheldons, her head held impossibly high, her cheeks flaming, hoping against hope that Anne had not heartlessly destroyed her reputation. They were at a terrible impasse, but surely such a friendship meant something, still.

And where was Edward? Kate did not think he had arrived yet.

She had not breathed a word of what had transpired to Edward. She had not dared.

Kate felt more than ill. She felt as if she were on a terrible precipice, and that there was no way to step back, that there was no way to safety, to certainty. She had been living with an almost insane fear, a feeling that one small nudge and she would be hurtling downward, to her death. These past few days, she had been haunted by her fears and what could only be a frightful premonition—that something disastrous was about to occur. That her very worst nightmare would soon come true. That she was about to lose Edward, Peter, everything.

She had recently come into the habit of glancing over her shoulder, almost expecting to see Anne there, or someone, watching her, waiting for her. Kate was afraid she was unraveling; she was afraid she might be losing her mind.

She paused before Anne and her family. "Happy birthday," she said with her most gracious smile. Her pulse was pounding in her chest. Nerves beset her.

And Anne did not smile back. Anne stared at her as if she were a monster with two heads.

Oh, God, Kate thought, feeling so ill she might very well vomit there on the spot. But she continued to smile, and she kissed Anne's cheek. Anne said not a word. Her expression was frozen into a nearly expressionless mask. Her eyes, however, were filled with disdain.

Kate turned so abruptly that she lost her balance. Only to find Lady Bensonhurst staring at her with such censure that she realized, in the next heartbeat, that Anne's mother knew about everything. And the civil greeting Kate had been about to offer died unspoken on her lips. *Anne's mother knew— Anne had told her about Edward and Peter.*

A feeling of panic rushed over Kate.

She looked past her to the earl of Collinsworth and his wife. His cold hard stare was every bit as unwelcoming as Lady Bensonhurst's. The only person present who seemed to have any compassion was the countess; her smile was slight, but perceptible.

It hardly mattered. Kate had come out of pride. She had also come to stake out her territory, even if Anne would be the only one to know what she was about. And perhaps she had come hoping to find that an old friendship still lived. Now she managed a curtsy, muttered some greeting, she knew not what, and fled.

She needed air. Desperately.

As she rushed through the crowd she finally saw Edward, his gaze fixed upon her. But Kate could not stop. She was truly about to be sick. She ran past astounded guests and through the terrace doors onto the terrace behind the house.

In the corner, she hung over the railing, heaving dryly, miserably. The night could not be worse.

"Kate!"

Not now, she thought silently, desperately, clinging to the stone balustrade.

Edward's hands steadied her shoulders as she straightened. "You're ill! When did you become sick?"

Kate did not face him; he remained standing behind her. The moon was full in a starry night sky—a very unusual sight. "Very recently," she said with real and bitter irony.

He was silent. Then his hands tightened on her shoulders and he turned her around. "You have been acting strangely all week. Avoiding me, I think, as much as it is possible for a woman to avoid the man she shares a bed with. What aren't you telling me?"

Kate looked up at his beloved face, into his searching eyes, and almost blurted out everything.

Anne said, "Edward. Kate is ill, please do not embarrass her. Let me manage this, as this is a moment between women."

Kate looked past Edward and saw Anne behind him, her eyes overly bright, her expression extremely, severely, composed. And she was afraid, terribly afraid, to be alone with her.

For one moment, Edward did not move. Then he stepped aside. "Of course. I would never wish to embarrass a lady." He bowed and finally smiled at Anne, but stiffly, before striding away.

Kate almost called him back.

And Anne's face changed. "How dare you come here!" she cried, low. "How dare you set foot in my home!"

"Anne . . ." Kate began, shocked by her vehemence. She had expected bitterness, perhaps, and anger, but not fury, not rage.

"No! You must leave, this instant, before you humiliate me upon my birthday!" Anne's eyes were glittering unnaturally. Two spots of pink had appeared on her cheeks, perfect little round circles that might have been painted there. The effect was clownish.

Kate stepped backward. "Anne, I did not come here to humiliate you. In spite of everything, we are still friends, I do love you . . ."

"Then why did you come? To congratulate me because of my engagement to your lover?"

Kate flinched.

"Get out," Anne gritted, gloved fists clenched. "Get out and do not think to ever come back!"

Kate felt as if a stake had been stabbed through her heart. How could this be happening? How could Anne despise her so? For one moment Kate hesitated, seeking desperately the words that might mend an ancient friendship and end a bitter new rivalry, but no words came to her mind. Anne's angry, hostile gaze did not relent. Kate gave up. She lifted her skirts and rushed past Anne. She could not retreat fast enough.

As Jill ran out of the back door of the chapel, it began to rain. From the corner of her eye, she glimpsed the Land Rover sitting in the drive. Damn it! Vicar Hewitt could lie for her but Alex would know she was there anyway. A tight, frantic feeling seized her, interfering with her breathing, as she raced across the lawn behind the chapel.

She thought she heard him coming, behind her.

Jill had reached the stone wall that ran parallel to the road. She did not hesitate, but launched herself onto it, scrabbling over it, and jumping off of it to land on her hands and knees on the other side. Stones and the roots of trees dug into her hands. She thrust herself to her feet. She could not get enough air and she was covered with sweat.

Jill dared one quick glance over her shoulder, but it was pouring now, and she could not make out any sign of Alex approaching.

It didn't matter. She knew he was there. She could feel him coming after her.

Was this the way it had been for Kate? Had she run like this from Edward?

Suddenly Jill thought she heard the engine of a car.

She rushed to the side of the road, strained to hear, and at first heard only her thundering heartbeat and her raspy, tortured breathing. Then she heard it—louder now—there was no mistake about it. A car was driving in from the north—from the direction she herself had just come.

Jill turned abruptly, but didn't see Alex. Shaking like a leaf, she waited, until she saw the headlights piercing the gloom. She began waving her arms frantically, not daring to cry out. A small hatchback approached. Jill debated jumping in front of the car, but it was coming on at a good clip and she was afraid that, in the downpour, she might get run over. She jumped up and down, waving at it desperately, tears streaming down her face, praying that the car would stop, the driver would let her in, and take her to safety. The hatchback zoomed past her.

God! Jill didn't think twice. She raced across the road, her footsteps sounding terribly loud on the pavement, climbed the opposite stone wall, and found herself in the cemetery.

Coke's Way. She could hide there—it wasn't far.

Jill ran through the maze of headstones, through the fog steaming up from the ground, stumbling on the sodden earth and grass, dodging the shadows that were misshapen trees and bushes, flinging glances repeatedly over her shoulder. And then she heard him.

Jill turned, frozen, but now heard only the rain and the wind. She whirled, running—and the ground disappeared beneath her feet.

Jill fell.

Hard, into a wide hole in the ground.

She landed on her buttocks and her hands, and for one moment was stunned and out of breath. She had fallen into a deep pit or cavern. In the next instant, wet earth squishing through her fingers, a series of chills swept over her entire body. Realization struck. She had fallen into a grave.

Jill jumped to her feet, breathing harshly, loudly, afraid Alex would catch her now—and then what would he do? Fortunately, her eyes were level with the top of the grave—it wasn't as deep as she had feared. Fear and adrenaline gave Jill the kind of strength she'd never had before. She managed to hoist herself out of the grave while scrabbling up the dirt walls with her feet.

Once on solid ground, Jill lay flat on her stomach, panting and fighting for air. But she did not have time to lose. She got up—only to realize that she had been lying in the freshly overturned earth. Her gaze fell on the tiny, barely discernible headstone at the head of the grave.

She stared, for one moment stunned motionless. A second later she was on her knees, bending over the tiny, almost nonexistent slab of stone that marked Kate's grave.

Jill was paralyzed. *Kate's grave had been dug up.*

Someone had desecrated Kate's grave.

Or had it been desecration?

"Jill!"

Jill inhaled at the sound of Alex's shout.

"Jill! Jill! Where are you?!"

He was some distance away. Farther than she had thought—maybe across the road. But he was big and strong—he could cut the distance down between them to nothing within seconds.

"Jill!"

Jill ran. She left the cemetery, the manor with its two chimneys a dark, looming shadow ahead of her. Thunder boomed overhead. Jill faltered, finally collapsing against a gnarled tree, the rain beating down on her. She could hear Alex calling her again.

She started to cry. Had he been the one to destroy the grave? And why? Was it for more DNA? Or to find out the truth about how Kate had died?

Lightning split the sky, out in the sea.

She froze, realizing the way the lightning had lit up the dark sky. It had lit up the entire landscape—and she had practically been standing out in the open. Had Alex been able to see her? Suddenly Jill wished he would call her again—so she could discern where he was. But no shouts rang out now from the vicinity of the cemetery and the road. There was only the rumble of distant thunder, the drumbeat of rain, the howl of wind.

Lightning pierced the night sky again, thunder cracking directly overhead.

Jill saw him. An unmoving solid shape among the swaying, misshapen trees that marked the boundary between the manor and the cemetery. Jill turned and ran.

Like a sprinter, clods of dirt and mud flying up beneath her feet, finally reaching the overgrown grounds surrounding the manor and then the side of the house itself.

The house looked ruined, vacant, brooding. Jill debated hiding somewhere inside—but she was afraid of being trapped. Besides, wouldn't it be the first place Alex would look for her?

"Jill! It's me, Alex! Jill! Wait!"

Jill could not believe her ears, because it sounded as if Alex were only yards away from her, and whereas before he had been behind her, and to her left, now he sounded as if he were in front of her, and to her right. *But that was impossible. No one could circle around her so quickly.*

Jill didn't think twice. She ran past the house. Ahead was the dark, jagged outline of the tower.

"Jill! Stop!"

She could hide in the tower—or she could try to scramble down the cliffs to the beach.

There was no safe hiding place. Alex had seen her—he was going to catch up to her at any moment.

And Jill ran directly to the tower. Frantic, she bent, and within seconds, her hand closed over a huge, sharp rock. Jill straightened.

"Jill," Alex said, and he stepped through the gaping stone walls to face her.

OCTOBER 18, 1908

It was almost three o'clock. Kate paced the foyer of her home, wringing her hands, trying to tell herself that everything was all right, trying not to be afraid. But her temples throbbed with astounding pain—and nothing was right.

Edward had not come home last night, which meant he

had stayed very late at the birthday party, and that morning Kate had received a letter from Anne.

Pain stabbed through her head with such intensity that Kate cried out, seeking a chair. And when the pain had passed, she pulled the folded letter from the pocket of her cloak with shaking hands and reread it for the fourth time.

Dear Kate,

I owe you a tremendous apology. I have never behaved in such a manner before, as I did last night, and I am filled with regret. I can only say in my self-defense that my passions ran away with me, given the unusual circumstances which we find ourselves in.

Kate, I have spent the entire evening thinking about this terrible twist of fate. I believe that we must meet to discuss what we must do. Surely, as we are both reasonable women, and good friends, we can find a solution to our dilemma that is acceptable to all involved. I wish to pick you up at 3 o'clock. Please, meet with me, so we may lay this matter to rest once and for all.

Sincerely, Your Friend, Always, Anne

Kate stared at the neatly scripted letter. Something was very odd. But she could not say, precisely, what.

Her pulse raced. There was a noise behind her and she leaped to her feet, whirling, but no one was there. Kate licked her lips, which were dry. She could not understand her fears or herself. She no longer felt safe, not even in her own house. She had tried to tell herself that she was distraught, overtired, and that her imagination was running wild, that nothing was so vastly wrong, that no harm could come to her in her own home. But she could not soothe herself.

Kate paced, replacing the letter in her pocket, glancing nervously at the clock standing on the marble table. It was ten to three. Maybe what was so disturbing was that Anne not only wished to meet, but that she wished to pick her up as well. That made no sense. Where did Anne wish to go? Why not speak frankly in the privacy of Kate's home?

And the tone of the letter was at such odds with Anne's hateful words last night.

What if it was a trap?

Kate cut off her own cry with one of her gloved hands. She was becoming mad, to suspect a trap, and what kind of trap could it possibly be? Perhaps Anne had been up all night, as she herself had been, regretting everything. Perhaps she truly wished to find a solution to their dilemma. Kate had to believe that.

Kate wanted, desperately, to believe that.

"Madame." Peter's nurse came forward, the bundled-up baby in her arms. "We are ready." She failed to smile as she usually did. The Frenchwoman's eyes reflected concern and worry as they met Kate's.

"Let me hold him," Kate whispered, overcome with grief. It was overwhelming, as if she would never see her son again. But that was absurd. She would go out with Anne and be back by suppertime.

Tears interfering with her vision, Kate held Peter to her breast. She rocked him, watching his angelic face as he slept. Already she could see signs that he would look like his father. How happy that made her.

Kate finally gave the baby back to Madeline.

"Madame. How long shall we stay at the countess's?"

Kate looked at her. Was she doing the right thing in sending Peter to the countess? The urge had struck her almost violently, shortly after receiving Anne's letter. Peter would be safe in the Collinsworth home, in the countess's care. Of that, Kate had not a doubt. "Until I return," Kate swallowed. "I expect to be back at supper."

Kate really didn't know why she felt compelled to send Peter to his grandmother. She told herself that the countess would fall in love with him and change her mind about Kate and Edward's marriage. Perhaps the countess was their very last hope.

"Good day, then," Madeline said.

Impulsively Kate kissed her cheek, then did the same with

Peter. He woke up and smiled sleepily at her. His eyes were brilliantly blue.

Kate felt a surge of panic. But she waved them out, then stood in the doorway and watched their small carriage departing. Tears streamed down her face.

Kate found it hard to breathe as she faced the street, waiting for Anne. She heard the coach first. The Bensonhurst carriage rolled down the street, pausing before Kate's house. Kate inhaled, motionless, her heart careening inside her chest, wanting to turn tail and run the other way now that Anne had come. But she summoned up her courage, telling herself that she was a silly fool, and hurried from the house. They would solve this, then, once and for all.

A servant opened the carriage door for her. Kate faltered because Lady Bensonhurst was seated in the backseat beside Anne.

Kate hesitated, filled with dread.

"Do come in, Kate," Anne said, her voice odd and high and filled with shrill tension.

Kate almost refused; she almost turned and fled back to the safety of her own house. But she could not continue to live this way, made ill by panic and fear and frightened of her own shadow. Kate stepped up into the coach.

The door was closed.

Kate faced Anne's mother as the coach rolled away, expecting a severe, hateful tongue-lashing. To her surprise, Anne's mother was pale, sitting rigidly on the forward-facing backseat, clasping her hands tightly in her lap. She seemed anxious. She seemed afraid. She seemed to wish to be anywhere but there, in the carriage with Kate. And she avoided Kate's eyes.

"Very well." Anne's jaw flexed. She produced a small pistol from her handbag and pointed it at Kate.

Kate's heart stopped. In that moment, her entire life sped before her eyes—every single happy, bitter moment. "Anne!"

Anne did not smile. "Don't worry. I am not going to shoot you. Mother, tie her hands."

Kate was disbelieving as Lady Bensonhurst produced a

cord from behind her back. "Anne! You are mad! What do you think you are doing?" Kate cried.

"Do be quiet," Anne said. "I am abducting you, Kate. You see, you are now about to disappear, from my life, from Edward's life, forever."

Twenty-Five

IN SPITE OF BEING TRUSSED UP LIKE A FELON, HER HANDS AND ankles bound so tightly that they had lost sensation, becoming numb, Kate had finally fallen asleep out of sheer exhaustion. She was awoken by the sound of her locked carriage door being opened. A dismal twilight greeted her—followed by Anne's and Lady Bensonhurst's severe, strained expressions.

Kate stiffened, her gaze locking with Anne's. "Where are we?" They had been traveling since yesterday afternoon without a single stop—except to dismiss the coachman at a wayside inn. From that point on, Anne had driven the coach, and Lady Bensonhurst had chosen to sit with her. Kate had only been able to discern, before the window shades were drawn, that they were traveling north.

Anne smiled slightly. "Get out."

Kate's tension increased. She did not like Anne's superior smile. And the light in her eyes was so brilliant that it was unsettling. Her friend had become insane—there was no other explanation for her behavior. "Anne, I wish to talk to you," she began.

Anne raised the pistol. "Mother, untie her ankles so she can walk."

Lady Bensonhurst succeeded in doing what Kate had spent all night trying to do, without success; with one stroke of a small knife she cut through the cords that had left Kate's fingers bloody and in shreds. Immediately the circulation began to return to Kate's feet. The effect was painful, causing her to cry out.

Anne pulled the trigger on the gun. "I said get out, Kate."

Kate froze, biting her lip. "Surely our friendship must mean something to you," she implored.

Anne's face became set in a manner that was frightening. There was no mistaking her resolve or the depth of her anger.

Kate did not hesitate. She somehow stood, reeling, unable to use her hands to prevent herself from falling. Anne gripped her elbow and pulled her roughly down from the coach. Anne pushed her forward.

And Kate gasped. They were at Coke's Way. But the manor house that belonged to the Collinsworth family was locked up. There was no tenant there now. Edward had told her, fondly, that he would never let the place again. "What are we doing here?" Kate cried.

Anne pushed her another time. Her strength was inhuman now. "How stupid do you think I am, Kate? Do you think you could tell me about the child and that I would fail to learn every detail of your life from that point on?" Her laughter was low, brief. "Recently I discovered that Edward sent you here to have Peter. It is ironic, is it not? You shall disappear here, under his very nose—in a place he will never think to look for you. I have spent days deciding where to hide you!"

Kate refused to move forward, facing Anne. "I won't do this. Anne, can you not see that this is not the way for you to build a future with Edward? You cannot build a life with someone based on lies and even murder!" Kate began to tremble. She did not believe Anne intended for her to die. She refused to believe it. Anne would make her disappear, and dear God, Edward might think she had run away, but after Anne married Edward, she would let her go. Wouldn't she?

Kate knew there were ramifications to that scenario that she was not considering. But she could not consider them. They were far too terrifying.

"Lady Bensonhurst," Kate cried. Anne's mother stood by the coach, not looking at either of them—as if that might prevent her from seeing what was actually unfolding before her very eyes. "Please stop your daughter from committing what we all know to be a grave and dastardly crime!"

Lady Bensonhurst regarded Kate. She was as white as a sheet. Her features were pinched, her eyes wide, dark circles underneath. Kate wanted to see moral fortitude. What she saw was resignation.

"Go," Anne gritted, pushing Kate forward—but not toward the manor house.

Ahead was the tower.

Kate froze.

She had always hated the tower. She had never once gone inside. Edward had teased her about it. He had told her it was quaint and charming, all the guests at Coke's Way thought so. Kate began to shake—convulsively. "Please don't do this," she whispered, her teeth beginning to chatter.

Anne pushed her forward roughly again. The heavy wood door was open. Kate halted. She was not going to go inside—she could not. The tower, she knew, would be the death of her.

"Go in," Anne said, shoving her inside.

Inside, the tower was cold, damp, and airless. Kate could not see at first—her eyes had to adjust to the darkness. The roof was missing in places, and high up, far too high for her to reach or climb, sections of stone were also missing. Had those sections been lower, Kate realized desperately, she would be able to squeeze through and crawl out to freedom.

Freedom. Would she ever be free again?

"Where is Peter?" Anne's voice cut through the shadowy darkness, the frightening stillness, of the tower.

Kate whirled. "At home."

"You lie. I can see it in your eyes. I won't have that bastard competing with my son." Anne's eyes were wide and filled with determination. Her pupils seemed huge.

Kate was panting. She felt claustrophobic. "I don't like it here. Don't leave me here. I can't breathe!"

"Then you will die, won't you?—for lack of air," Anne said coolly. "Perhaps we can make an exchange. You—for Peter."

Kate stared. "How can you be so hateful? I loved you like

a sister. And I swear, if you touch Peter, you will pay for it! Edward will make certain of it! Anne, stop, think, *please*, consider what you are doing! Release me—and I swear, no one will ever know what has happened these past two days."

Anne stared back. "You are the insane one, Kate. To think to destroy my life, my dreams, my love. Never mind. I will find Peter, just the way I found out that you were here, and not in New York, during your pregnancy." Anne turned to go.

Kate's shaking increased. "Please untie me." She rushed after Anne and stumbled, falling to the ground on her bound hands and knees, where she choked on a sob. The immensity of her predicament, the hopelessness, finally seized her. Kate looked up. Anne stood in the doorway. Behind her was nothing but a dark, dusky sky and the grotesque shapes of trees left stunted and gnarled by too many storms to count. "Don't you remember Christmas two years ago?" She wept. "We were to be best friends forever. You gave me the locket."

Anne regarded her unblinkingly. "Of course I remember. That was before you betrayed me."

Kate remained on the ground. Their gazes locked. And then dizziness assailed Kate. She closed her eyes, trying to control herself, and she failed. Kate vomited.

It was not a short spasm, but one that seemed to go on and on endlessly. And when it was over, Kate wept, faced now with nightmare reality.

"Are you carrying another bastard, Kate?" Anne's cool, distant voice cut into Kate's misery and grief, into her sudden, utter futility, like the blade of a knife.

She was exhausted, beaten down, and, too late, wished so desperately that she had told Edward about her confrontations with Anne. "Yes," she whispered, not looking up. "Have mercy," she choked.

The door slammed closed. Kate heard the sound of a lock turning. She collapsed into a heap on the ground, the damp earth her mattress and her pillow.

"Please, Edward, please find me," she moaned. But she knew Anne was right. He would never think to look for her under his very nose.

*   *   *

Jill's heart was pounding with such force that she could not seem to breathe, that she felt faint. She backed up, away from Alex, gripping the rock that she held behind her back.

Alex stared at Jill, shining his penlight directly on her face. Jill couldn't see his expression; the light was blinding. Her heart dropped with sickening force. This was it, she knew. This was the very end of the line, the very last stop.

Images swept through her mind with stunning speed, a confusing kaleidoscope of scenes with her and Alex, as lovers, as friends, as adversaries.

Jill backed up again. A nightmare, she thought, come true.

"Jill." He lowered the light and suddenly she could see his eyes, pale and unnaturally bright in the darkness of the tower. "You're too brave for your own good, aren't you?"

Jill clenched the stone. There was no point in replying. She wondered if he would search her for the evidence she'd stolen from the Libretto before doing whatever it was that he had come to do.

"And too damn smart," he said grimly, and then he sighed. He started toward her.

"Alex, don't come any closer," she warned, trembling and backing up. Her spine hit the wall. Her frantic gaze darted past him—she could never get by him to run out of the tower.

He halted in midstride. "Jill. You didn't have to run away—even if you did steal my files. I want to explain. But not here, in the goddamn rain."

Jill fought to breathe, harshly and loudly. A line of sweat was creeping down the side of her temple, more sweat was pooling between her breasts. Outside, lightning lit up the sky and thunder cracked. "Where do you want to go, Alex? Out to the cliffs? So I can fall to my death? That would be damned convenient, wouldn't it?" She choked on her last words.

The penlight wavered, and briefly, she saw his eyes, which were wide. "Are you crazy? Has Kate Gallagher driven you insane? Jill, I'm trying to stop you from hurting yourself," he said vehemently.

Her gut reaction was that this was a trap. But it dawned on her that he did not seem to have a weapon. He was holding the penlight, nothing more. Jill shook off her confusion with an effort. "I can't believe I ever trusted you at all." Bitterness echoed between the tower's four stone walls.

He did not reply. A sudden silence fell there between them, hard, and because he'd raised his light again, Jill could not see his face, just the eerie dark shadow of his form. It was disconcerting, frightening. Pounding rain filled up the silence of the night.

"Jill," he started, when a car's engine sounded from outside. Alex turned his head. The engine was cut and it died. Jill froze, paralyzed. She could hit him with the rock now. His back was to her—this was her chance. Knock him out—maybe even kill him—and run like hell.

She could not move.

She could not lift the stone.

"Who the hell is that?" Alex asked abruptly.

A car door slammed.

"Your accomplice?" Jill suggested with sarcasm, but she was alarmed—because there had been alarm in his own tone.

"Step back," he ordered.

Jill didn't obey. A shining light wavered as the person holding it walked toward the manor. And an image of the Mercedes with William driving flashed through Jill's mind. Then she thought about Vicar Hewitt, just across the way. Maybe he had called the local police. Jill dared to hope, to pray.

He came toward her in a rush.

Jill flinched, her heart ceasing its frantic beat with sickening abruptness as he threw his arm around her, almost tackling her. Jill met his eyes, thought, This is it, he's going to strangle me, but he moved her back against the wall, turning off his own penlight. "Don't make a sound," he breathed in her ear.

His grip was like a vise. Shock and confusion reigned. Sweat streamed down Jill's body in rivers. Relief came. Alex was hiding her, not hurting her, but why? Who were they hiding from? And was Alex the good guy or the bad guy? And did the person outside know they were in the tower, and not in the house? What if that person was the police? Should she scream for help?

As if he understood her thoughts, he whispered, "Ssh," in her ear, the single hushed sound filled with warning. Their gazes locked. And Jill nodded.

If she was making a mistake, she would find out—sooner rather than later.

The minutes passed endlessly—a painful slice of eternity. And suddenly a large flashlight was shining into the interior of the tower, blinding them. "How quaint," a very familiar female voice said.

Jill jerked at the sound of Lucinda's voice. For one moment, she was stunned. And then she cried, "Lucinda, get help!"

"Mr. Preston, please stand back from Jill," was Lucinda's calm reply.

Jill did not understand. Alex continued to hold her against the wall, and he did not move. Then he shone his penlight toward Lucinda.

Her face was an expressionless mask.

And then Jill saw the large steel revolver in her hand. It was pointed at them both.

OCTOBER 23, 1908

She was going to die.

Kate lay curled up on the wet, cold ground, shivering, too weak to move. Three, four, five days had gone by since Anne had locked her in the tower. At first, Kate had kept track of the days by the rising and setting of the sun. At first, she had been hopeful. She had shouted for help until she could no longer speak, her throat left miserably raw and sore and dry. No one had heard her cries; no one had come to her aid. There was no way to get out of the tower; the front door remained securely locked. The hope had died.

The way she would die.

For Anne had left her to die, without food, without water.

A cramp seized Kate, not for the first time. She could barely clutch herself, her muscles were so weak. Kate moaned, rocking slightly, the pain unbearable. The spasm lasted much longer this time than before. Kate finally cried out.

And when the spasm had died, Kate felt the trickle of warm wet blood between her legs and tears slipped down her face. She clawed the wet earth beneath her, but it was not a pillow, and it could not give her any comfort.

She was losing Edward's child the way she was losing her life. How she missed him. Was he frantically searching for her? Or because she had left Peter with his mother, did he take that as a sign that she had abandoned him?

She would never see him again. The realization was brutal.

She would never see her son again. The realization was agonizing.

More silent, salty tears fell.

A click sounded loudly, penetrating the silence of the tower, the aching stillness, penetrating her thoughts.

Kate's lids lifted.

Her heart raced as she watched, disbelieving, the door to the tower slowly opening. She stiffened—expecting to see Anne.

But a big man in coarse clothes whom she did not know stood there, holding a bucket and a package, staring at her.

Water! He had to be bringing her water—maybe she would not die after all! Kate wanted to sit up. Desperately. But she did not have the strength to do more than lie there and watch him.

He set the bucket down by the door, then also set down a brown paper parcel.

Wait. Kate realized she hadn't spoken aloud, and she tried to wet her dry lips, to no avail. "Wait." But her cry was hoarse, low, and inaudible—a pitiful attempt at speech.

He turned and left.

The lock clicked again loudly in the door.

Kate's hopes plummeted. *He had left her to die.* She

wanted to scream, to shout after him, to pound the earth, to sob. But she did none of those things. She was too weak, she could not move. So she lay there, panting, fighting waves of nausea and pain.

And then she thought, but he had brought water. I will not die.

Kate fought for courage and resolve, for strength. And she began the endless, painful process of crawling forward, inch by painful inch, toward the water bucket. She had to stop repeatedly, panting badly, her heart thundering at an alarming rate, wondering if it might not give out on her. She was so weak. She had never been this weak before. It was frightening.

She finally reached the bucket. A cup floated in the water. Kate had never been so thirsty in her life—she had never wanted anything more. Her thirst gave her the strength to sit up and reach for the cup. Half of the water spilled down her chin and chest.

And then she stopped.

Her mind, functioning so oddly now, made a terrible deduction. She had been locked up in the tower for days, maybe even a week. What if he did not come back for another week? She must ration the water. Kate let the cup slip from her fingers, back into the pail, despondency settling over her like heavy chain mail.

She could smell food. The saliva increased in her mouth and she tore open the paper parcel. In it was stale bread and moldy cheese. Kate was not disappointed. It was a glorious sight. She tore into the bread, stuffing it into her mouth, and ripped off a piece of cheese, but in the end could only ingest a few bites. Then she collapsed, severely exhausted, incapable of further movement.

Night fell.

She slept.

When Kate opened her eyes, she thought—and hoped— she felt slightly better, and looking up through the holes in the roof, she saw a sky brilliant with stars and a crescent moon. Bitter sorrow washed over her and more tears fell as she thought about those she loved and missed desperately, whom she might never see again. She was too young to die, dear God.

Maybe, just maybe, she would live. If God blessed her with a miracle. But if she did not live, there was something she had to do.

Anne could not get away with this.

Kate slowly removed the locket from her neck. The task seemed endless, her fingers refusing to work adeptly, and when she was done, she had to rest for a few more moments. Then she began another long journey—crawling inch by inch to the nearest wall. Pausing many times to rest. Getting there took forever. It took more than fortitude, it took absolute determination. And when she was there, she was not through. Somehow she sat up, clawing her way up the stone. Her hands and fingers were numb and bloody.

And using the clasp, she began to engrave a message onto the stone.

A message for anyone who might find it and read it, anyone at all.

Twenty-Six

Is THIS A JOKE?" JILL ASKED SLOWLY, SICK WITH DREAD. FOR
she knew it was not. Lucinda's expression—and the gun she
held—told her that.

Alex's grip on her wrist tightened, a warning for her not to
speak.

"I don't like jokes, they are a waste of time and so very
American," Lucinda said with disdain. "Shame on you, Mr.
Preston," she added. "Allowing her to destroy the good
Collinsworth name."

Jill stared, incredulous but not disbelieving. "Lucinda—
what are you doing?" But she knew. Oh, God, she did. What
had Thomas said? That Lucinda was, perhaps, as loyal as any
Collinsworth? Lucinda, who had been director of Uxbridge
Hall for well over twenty years. Lucinda, who knew as much
about Kate and Anne and Edward as anyone.

Lucinda, who was her friend.

Or who had appeared to be her friend.

An accomplice was out there, Jill realized. Unless
Lucinda had not cared if she lived or died, someone else had
cut those brake lines. But was it Alex? Again, it crossed Jill's
mind that William was at the house. Either with Margaret—
or he had come with Lucinda and Jill had assumed his passenger to be his wife.

Lucinda did not smile. "I am doing what Mr. Preston has
failed to do, my dear. I am going to prevent you from
destroying the Collinsworth family," she said. "I have

devoted the last twenty-five years of my life to this family. I have devoted the past twenty-five years of my life to his lordship. What you are doing is intolerable—destroying a great man and his family—tainting their immortality." Her stare was hard. "Mr. Preston, I wish you were not here. But you are, and the greater good must prevail. Please move away from Jill."

Alex did not move. "Lucinda, Jill is not about to destroy anyone," Alex said quietly. "Why don't you give me the gun before someone gets hurt and you are guilty of a felonious crime?" His tone was firm and commanding. "We both know you did not cut the brake lines. This does not have to go any further than it already has. I think, with some persuasion and compromise, we can all walk away from this satisfied."

"She has gone too far, Mr. Preston," Lucinda said as flatly, standing as still as a statue. The gun in her hand did not waver, not even slightly, and that frightened Jill even more. "I had hoped you or Thomas would dissuade her from her quest, but neither of you did so. If I had guessed when I first met her that it would come to this, I would have never befriended her as I did." Lucinda blinked at Jill. "It was amazing, the first time I saw you, I felt as if I were seeing a ghost. I made the connection between you and Kate immediately. As I believe everyone did. And I thought, Thank God Anne is not here to see this day. She was probably turning over in her grave, my dear, knowing you were with her grandson, knowing you had come to town, knowing what you were about.

"I made a terribly erroneous assumption. I assumed you would learn that Kate was your great-grandmother—and she was, my dear—and that you would leave it at that. Her son, Peter, despised the family—Anne hated him, and Edward was never there. When he was eighteen he ran away to New York, giving up a small fortune as well as his entire heritage. I had no idea you would be so terribly stubborn."

"Lucinda, give me the gun," Alex said. "Jill doesn't want to destroy anyone."

Jill gripped Alex's wrist. "So Peter was raised by the family?"

"Not exactly. He spent his first few years at Stainesmore, with the best care, as Edward wished. As soon as he was old enough, he was sent off to Eton. He hardly suffered, except, of course, Anne would not allow him to set foot in any of her homes—including Uxbridge Hall and the house in Kensington Palace Gardens. But can you blame her?"

It was almost too much to absorb. "How do you know that Kate is my great-grandmother?" Lucinda had no DNA tests to go on.

Lucinda smiled. "Anne kept a journal. For the course of her entire life. It is very explicit. When Peter ran off, Edward's heart was broken all over again. How angry Anne was. Not that Peter was gone—that thrilled her—but that Edward was distressed. And he hired investigators to locate his son—against Anne's will. I am certain that Edward knew where Peter was, and I do believe he even tried to contact him several times." Lucinda shrugged. "But Peter wanted nothing to do with the family, not ever again."

Jill could not speak.

"Mr. Preston? Stand aside. I have no wish to hurt you."

Alex did not move. "Give me the gun," Alex said. He stepped toward her, hand outstretched.

She pointed the gun at him, causing Jill to cry out—suddenly terrified. Not for herself, but for Alex. "I suspect you are fond of her, Mr. Preston. But alas, that is of no avail. And in the end, I am quite certain you will come to the same conclusion."

"Lucinda," Jill said quickly, "give Alex the gun. I know you don't want to hurt anyone. There's been enough scandal and deception to last hundreds of years, hasn't there?"

"Any scandal that now ensues will be laid at my feet," Lucinda said flatly.

"You can't possibly want to martyr yourself—not over this," Jill cried.

"I am hoping William will be able to talk some sense into Mr. Preston."

"My uncle would never justify a murder. Lucinda, before you break the law, give me the gun." Alex took another step forward.

Lucinda whirled, pointing the gun at him—and he was only five or six yards from her. "Stop right there."

"Alex!" Jill cried, terrified that he would choose this moment to play the hero and prove himself to her.

But he froze. Smiling—and it was strained. "My uncle will not approve of this," he repeated. "You won't get away with this," he said quietly. "This is 1999—not 1909."

"Injustice is a fact of life. Is not Kate's death proof of that?" Lucinda replied.

Thump, thump, thump. Jill touched her heavy heart. "Was she murdered? Someone dug up her grave recently. Was that you? Did you think to hide the evidence?"

Lucinda's brows lifted in surprise. "I believe that was Mr. Preston."

Jill whirled to stare at Alex.

"Jill," Alex said. "I decided to exhume the body. But there was no body, no coffin, nothing. The grave was bogus. She was never buried there."

Jill was stunned. "I don't understand."

"That grave's a red herring, but for the life of me, I can't think why."

"Where is Kate?" Jill cried to Lucinda.

Lucinda did not bat an eye. "I don't know."

"Did Edward kill Kate?"

"No," Lucinda said firmly. "Edward did not kill Kate. He was in love with her. Don't you know that he was never the same man after she disappeared? He grieved until his very own death. Kate's ghost stood between them, between him and Anne, for his entire lifetime."

"Then . . . who?" Jill asked slowly. She felt ill. The best of friends . . . the worst of enemies. The hairs stood up all over her body and somehow she knew. "It was Anne." Suddenly she gasped. "Anne killed her—and out of guilt, or some other perverse emotion—she put that headstone there!"

"Who killed Kate, and why, is a secret, my dear, that has gone to the grave with Kate. And it will stay buried there—for all of our sakes. Please step aside, Mr. Preston. Although I am a very good shot, I have never shot another human being before, and I might very well hurt you, which I prefer not doing."

"I'm not moving," Alex said.

Jill felt real terror then.

"You underestimate me," Lucinda said. "You see, I cannot allow William to suffer any more than he already has."

Her words were not even finished when Alex leaped forward, at her. The gunshot sounded, a deafening blast, its sound magnified within the four stone walls of the tower.

"Alex," Jill screamed as he collapsed.

She was on her knees, bending over him, his face in her hands. His eyes were closed; in the darkness, his face had turned gray. And there it was, a bright red blossom on his shirt and Jill thought, Oh, God, not again! She pulled Alex into her arms. "Don't you dare die!"

"Jill, please stand up."

Jill froze at the sound of Lucinda's cold voice. She looked up.

Lucinda continued to point the gun at Jill. "I am sorry," she said. "I liked Mr. Preston."

Jill didn't think. She grabbed a handful of dirt and flung it with all of her might. Lucinda cried out in surprise, reflexively jerking backward. Jill launched herself at Lucinda, but Lucinda was a big, strong, outdoorsy woman, and it was like landing on a brick wall. She pushed Jill off as if she were a fly. Jill went sailing backward, landing on her back on the hard earthen floor. For an instant, she saw stars.

As her vision cleared, Lucinda loomed over her, her expression finally furious, aiming the gun at Jill's head.

The clarity was stunning. In that instant, Jill knew she had been a fool to ever doubt Alex. So many images and memories and hopes and dreams swirled through her mind that Jill felt a terrible and bitter regret that it would all end now, like this.

She was too young to die.

A shadow closed in on Lucinda from behind. Alex.

Jill must have made a sound of surprise, because Lucinda whirled as Alex charged her. He hit her like a battering ram. Lucinda was driven backward under the force of his assault, into the wall. They grappled for the gun and an instant later it went off, another deafening explosion.

They fell to the ground together.

"No!" Jill cried, on her feet. An instant later she pulled Alex off of Lucinda. He was a dead weight in her arms. Her terror was magnified.

"Alex," she whispered, cradling him.

His lashes fluttered and his eyes opened.

"Thank God," Jill cried, a sob.

"Lucinda," he said.

Jill jerked, her gaze slamming to the other woman, who lay on her back, eyes wide open and unseeing. A huge red hole was in the middle of her chest. "I think she's dead," Jill whispered, stunned.

She looked down at the man in her arms and saw his eyes were closed. "Don't you dare die," she shouted, and she kissed his head, hard.

"Wouldn't think of it," he said.

JANUARY 12, 1909

Water.

Kate was desperate.

No one had brought her water, or food, in days. It was as if she had been forgotten.

She was dying and she knew it. It was what Anne had wanted all along. So she could have Edward . . . Kate's thoughts veered wildly. What did Edward think? Had he searched for her? Was the countess taking care of Peter? Peter! There was such a stabbing pain in Kate's breast as she thought about her infant son, knowing she would never lay eyes on him again . . . and the smallest anger rose up inside of her, but it was weak and faint, as she was, and overshadowed by the fear of the specter of death.

Kate did not want to die.

She was only eighteen.

She wanted to live.

Anne. Her image was always there, haunting Kate, but not as she had once known her, shy and timid, afraid to be carefree, but as she was now, a cruel, cold-hearted monster. Anne, who had professed to love her forever, who had so foully betrayed her. Were Anne and Edward married? Kate had no idea how much time had elapsed since her imprisonment. Clearly Anne wanted her to die very, very slowly. But the other day, it had snowed.

Just a flurry, but the fat, wet snowflakes had drifted in through the holes in the roof, settling on the dark earth like white four-leaf clovers, mesmerizing Kate.

Kate wanted to sleep. She was so cold, so exhausted, so thirsty, but beyond hunger, and sleep beckoned, dangerously. She was afraid to fall asleep, afraid she might never wake up. Drifting with her wildly changing, kaleidoscope thoughts was so much easier, safer.

If only . . .

At times, Kate could see Edward so clearly, she felt that they were together, and if she had the strength to reach out, she would actually touch him. She saw him in his smoking jacket and slippers, in her sitting room, bouncing Peter on his knee. He was smiling at their son, and then he'd look up, across the room, at her. His smile changed. It warmed. The look he gave her was reserved exclusively for her, the look a man gives a woman he loves . . .

It was so vivid, so real. On some level, Kate knew she was hallucinating. She did not want her hallucinations to stop.

Anne appeared. Cold, hateful, evil.

Kate wanted her to go away. She wanted to be left alone with Edward and their son, she did not want to be confronted by the cold-hearted murderess.

Light. Bright, white, streaming through the roof of the tower.

Kate blinked in surprise. She had been so cold, so utterly exhausted. But suddenly she wasn't cold anymore, and she wasn't tired. The light wasn't just bright, it was warm, bathing the interior of the tower, bathing Kate. Where was the sunlight coming from in the midst of this gray dismal winter day? It was so bright, so clear, so pure. It was so . . . calming. Kate suddenly smiled.

Suddenly she was at peace.

Never had there been so much peace. So much light . . . and so much peace . . .

Click.

Kate was confused. The noise disturbed her, the light began to fade. Click.

She struggled for consciousness. The lock was turning, and the tower was once again wet and raw and cold. In fact, it was so dark with shadows that she could barely see. Kate clawed the damp earth, shivering uncontrollably now, watching as the door opened, watching as Anne stepped into the tower.

She had never thought to see Anne again. She wondered if she was dreaming. "Help me," she whispered, but then realized that she was so sick that she could not even speak, not even in the lowest, most inaudible of whispers. She could only speak in her mind.

"Hello, Kate." Anne came closer, until she was standing over Kate, peering down at her. "Are you still alive?"

Kate wet her lips. Or she tried to, but she could hardly make her tongue move to carry out the action. "Anne. *Please.*" She did not want to die. Not after all. She could not die! Edward and Peter needed her . . .

"You're still alive." Anne squatted, face-to-face with Kate. "You're not beautiful anymore, Kate. You're downright ugly."

How could Anne have become so hateful, so evil? "Help," Kate whispered—or she tried to.

"Edward thinks you left him. He thinks you ran off—with another man." Anne laughed. "Isn't that amusing?"

Kate squeezed her eyes shut, over sudden tears, suddenly realizing that she clutched the locket in her palm. It was her last hope. Maybe, if she gave it to Anne, Anne would be jolted out of her madness. Maybe she would remember their friendship. Maybe she would have mercy on her.

But Kate could not raise her arm to give the locket to Anne. She could not move her arm at all. The effort was monumental, and it made her break out in sweat.

"Where is Peter? Where is he? He disappeared, damn it, Kate. I want to know where he is!" Anne cried, rising to her full height and staring down at Kate.

Kate closed her eyes, shaking, giving up the struggle to hand Anne the locket. Peter. He was safe. And Anne would kill her after all. She was suddenly filled with determination. Her eyes opened. Her gaze locked with Anne's. She said, low but clear, "The countess."

Anne's eyes widened in shock. "You bitch! You clever, scheming bitch! You think to thwart me from the grave, do you not?" Anne paced, wringing her hands, furious.

Kate collapsed once again. Speaking had cost her dearly, she had nothing left to give.

"Edward and I have set our wedding date. For August. And I will not raise your brat," Anne spat.

Kate looked at her. And something odd happened. The gray shadows in the tower began to disperse as more bright, pure, brilliant light streamed inside. Anne became bathed in it. Kate watched her slowly disappearing, swallowed up by the tunnel of blinding light.

She smiled. She was floating, and at peace. Death was not, she realized, so very frightening. It was peaceful and calm.

Why had she been so afraid to die?

Anne stared down at her. "Why are you smiling? What is so amusing? What do you know that I don't?"

When Kate did not answer, but continued to smile, her eyes closed, Anne nudged her with the toe of one shoe. There was no response.

"I won't let you have the last laugh, and I won't raise your brat," Anne cried. She bent and grabbed Kate's hands, about to drag her, then she paused. She opened Kate's tightly clenched palm, which felt very cold, as if she were already dead. In it was the locket.

Anne recognized it immediately. Her instinct was to toss it aside. Instead, she paused, opening it, and saw the portraits of two so very young, so very naive, smiling girls—the best of friends.

Oddly shaken, she snapped it closed and slid it into her bodice, beneath the coat and dress she wore. Then she shoved any remorse—and regret—aside. Was Kate dead?

Anne knelt, placing her hand beneath Kate's nose. She seemed to be breathing, but barely.

She dragged her across the floor of the tower and outside. It continued to flurry.

Panting, Anne continued to drag her toward the manor, which was boarded up now. When she came around the side of the house, gasping for air, she finally paused, releasing Kate. If Kate wasn't dead yet, Anne decided, she would be, soon. In the daylight, Anne finally took a good look at her. Not only was she emaciated and ugly, she looked very much like a corpse. Edward would not think her beautiful and enchanting now.

The doors to the root cellar were open. Anne didn't hesitate. She pushed Kate's body over the edge, and heard her land with a thud on the earthen floor below.

She closed and padlocked the doors. Then she walked away from Coke's Way, across the street, to the chapel, where she'd left her carriage in the drive.

And deep in the root cellar, the darkness was complete.

January 15, 1909

Dear Diary,
It has been some time since I last wrote. I have just returned from another trip to Stainesmore. My last and final trip there, I suppose. For I surely will not allow Edward to go there when we are wed. The memories for us both would be far too awkward.

It is done. Kate is dead. I have seen so for myself.

Mother and I have never once discussed our secret. That is for the best, as there is not much to say. I do think Mother is in awe of me. But there is little I can do about that. I do not think she ever really believed I would become the next countess of Collinsworth. I had not a doubt.

The wedding is now scheduled for August. All of London is talking about the affair, labeling it the grandest union of our times. I am so excited. I can hardly wait.

Twenty-Seven

Jill cut the Lamborghini's engine but left the headlights on. They shone directly on the front door of Stainesmore and the huge, night-blackened windows of the ground floor. The entire stone mansion seemed to be cast in darkness, which was very odd—and very disturbing. At night, lights were always left on. Where was the staff? And wasn't William, and possibly Margaret, at home?

Alex sat beside her in the passenger seat, head back, eyes closed. It was close to midnight. Jill had never been more exhausted, but bed was the last thing on her mind. Lucinda was dead, and had been taken to the morgue in Scarborough. She had driven to Coke's Way in the Sheldons' Mercedes sedan, because the car was still there, parked in the driveway in front of the manor house. Alex's gunshot wound had been treated at the Scarborough Hospital. They'd both given statements to the local police.

She looked at him, dreading going inside. To her surprise, his eyes opened and he smiled very faintly at her. She had thought him soundly asleep.

He looked like hell. His face remained a ghastly hue of gray, there were dark circles under his eyes, not to mention a day's growth of beard. The upper right side of his torso was bandaged, his right arm was in a sling. There was dried blood all over his shirt and pants. "You look like a drug dealer," Jill said, hoping to lighten his mood. When what she really wanted to do was to pull him into her arms and weep. Not for herself, but for him.

He laughed. The sound was brief, but genuine. Then he sobered. "I feel like shit. Those painkillers suck."

Jill winced. "You were supposed to take two."

"I need to think," he said, staring now straight ahead at the front door of the house.

Jill wondered what awaited them inside.

Alex suddenly reached for the door with his left arm—he'd been shot in the right shoulder, and that arm was now useless—grunting, "Let's go."

Dread filled her. Jill killed the headlights and got out of the car, shutting both of their doors for them. All she could think of was the fact that William was inside of the house, probably alone. She felt certain that Lucinda had been his passenger, not Margaret, although perhaps she had not seen a third passenger in the car. But did that make him Lucinda's accomplice? She could hardly think straight.

"Let me help you," Jill said, taking Alex's left arm so he could lean on her as they approached the house.

"You didn't tell the cops about the cat, the ransacking, or the brakes."

Jill's heart began to thud. Slowly. Painfully. "No. I did not."

"You said Lucinda came after you because of your research into Kate's life, period."

"I know what I said," Jill replied, tense and strained. They paused at the front door, eyes locking. "Lucinda helped me at first. But when the ugliness started to emerge, she became unhinged. Insane."

"Shit," Alex cried.

"Oh, Alex, I'm sorry," Jill cried back. "This is all my fault!"

He flung her a look that was pained, angry, and resigned all at once and stepped inside his uncle's house.

The foyer was cast in absolute blackness. It had stopped raining hours ago, a few stars had managed to creep out from behind thick clouds, and shadows seemed to dance across the room. The huge entry was achingly silent. Jill's tension increased.

And with every painful beat of her heart, she prayed that William and Margaret were not involved in the threats made against her, in the assault on her life.

Alex cursed and pounded the wall switch, flooding the foyer with light.

Jill's eyes widened. William sat in one of the thronelike, velvet-backed chairs against the far wall, unmoving, his face absolutely ravaged with emotional distress.

"Uncle William."

William stared, and then he stood slowly, showing every one of his years, his hands shaking. "Lucinda. Where is she? Dear God, she's been gone so long!" And his gaze swung wildly from Alex to Jill and then to Alex again.

He was in love with her. Jill stared in shock at William, who was beginning to cry.

And suddenly she began to understand.

As Alex went to him, putting his good arm around him and begging him to sit back down, William lost all control and began to weep openly. Jill's mind raced. Margaret was so elegant, so beautiful, how could this be? But then, love was a strange and odd thing, wasn't it?

And then she thought about Edward and Kate. Was it the fate of the Collinsworth men to fall in love with women they could not marry?

"Uncle William, something terrible has happened," Alex said hoarsely.

He looked up. "She's dead, isn't she?"

Alex inhaled.

Jill realized then that William had not once asked after Alex's welfare. Like a metal stake, pain stabbed through her breast.

"Yes," Alex said slowly. "There was an accident. She had a gun. It went off." He closed his eyes tightly.

William covered his face with his hands and wept with the abandon of a child.

Jill tried to think. If William loved Lucinda, then he

would have never cut the brake lines to the rental car. Relief overcame her, and she darted forward, to pull Alex aside, to tell him that Lucinda's accomplice was not William, when William said, "I don't know how all of this has happened, dear God, I do not!"

Jill froze.

"William." Alex spoke as if with great difficulty, as if with great pain. "Please. Don't say anything. Not a word. You need a lawyer."

"Alex," Jill tried.

But William shook his head. "I've lost the woman I love. The woman I've loved for well over thirty years. We never meant to hurt anybody. We only wanted her to go home before she discovered the truth about my mother." He was pleading, plaintive, and looking now at Jill. "My mother told us the truth about what she did to Kate—she was dying and she couldn't bear the guilt. But Lucinda told me not to worry. She kept repeating that. She said she would manage everything!"

"Oh, my God," Alex cried, shocked, gripping both of William's hands so tightly that his knuckles turned white— while his face lost the little coloring it had. He was not supposed to use his right arm at all. "Please. Do not say a word. Do not confess. I beg you. I will see to it that you have the best defense team in the country."

But William was gazing at Jill. "I knew," he said heavily, "that the day Hal found you, we were all in trouble. What will you do?" he asked. "I am destroyed. Hal is dead. Lucinda . . ." He broke off, unable to continue, tears pouring down his face again.

"I'm sorry," Jill whispered. "I only wanted to know if Kate was my great-grandmother, and then I only wanted to know that she ran away to live happily ever after with her love. I had no idea Edward was her lover or that she was murdered. I'm sorry." Jill realized she was crying, too.

"I didn't want to hurt anyone," William whispered. "I thought your brakes would fail right in front of your flat." Suddenly he squeezed his eyes tightly shut, as tears streamed down his face. "I had no idea Lucinda would be in that car with you. I am so sorry."

Jill's heart stopped.

"William!" Alex cried, and it was a command.

But William wasn't listening to Alex, or even to anyone. He somehow stood up, standing unsteadily, swaying like a leaf. "There's a trust. My father kept a trust for Peter. He loved him, very much. I believe Kate's estate was settled privately, between my father and Kate's mother. The trust he set aside is for Peter and Peter's heirs, in perpetuity. It's yours, you know. Edward would have wanted you to have it." He inhaled raggedly. "I should have been forthright from the first. But Thomas told me you would go home. Lucinda said the same thing." He started to cry. "The trust is yours. Now will you go home?" he whispered.

That last question had been uttered with the bewilderment of a little boy. Jill nodded, aware of the tears spilling down her cheeks. She realized Alex was staring at her, and she wondered how much he hated her now, for this. When she could speak, she said, "Alex, there's a bottle of Xanax on my bed table. Why don't you take your uncle upstairs, give him two tablets, and put him to bed?"

Alex stared at her, every muscle in his face strained. He did not answer her, but walked past her to the closest room, a salon, where he picked up the telephone. But he did not dial. His eyes closed, his shoulders slumped.

Jill ran to him, taking the phone from him and slamming it down. "Who were you calling?"

He didn't face her. "The police."

Jill gritted her teeth as she pulled the phone right out of the wall. "Take William upstairs, give him those Xanax, and put him to bed," she panted. "Okay?"

He slowly turned, and their gazes met.

Jill stared back, watching as his gaze became questioning and then searching. "This is our secret," she said. "And I promise I won't tell."

In spite of her exhaustion, Jill could not sleep.

All she could think about was William and Lucinda having a thirty-year affair, and of Alex, in his misery, behind his closed bedroom door.

She could no more stop herself from going to him than she could stop the sun from rising that next day. Jill slipped from her bedroom, clad in heavy socks, a T-shirt, and sweats, tapping lightly on his door as she pushed it open.

One bedside light was on. He was awake, sitting up in bed, the covers pulled up to his waist, which was bare except for the bandages, his face still shockingly pale. He was staring at the fireplace on the facing wall. No fire burned there.

"Can I come in?" Jill asked softly, her heart twisting at the sight of him. In that moment she realized how deeply she cared for him. In that moment, she wondered if she could bear the burden of a life without Alex in it. She felt shaken and stunned and elated and afraid all at once.

He turned his head and almost smiled at her. "Sure."

Jill faltered, because it was obvious that he'd been crying. His eyes and nose were brightly red. He couldn't quite look at her.

Jill melted. She hurried to him, sat down beside him, and without even thinking about it, she took him into her arms, holding his head to her breasts as if he were a small child. "I'm so sorry," she whispered, gently rocking him.

"Yeah," he said roughly, a sob in his voice. "Me, too."

Jill continued to hold him. He did not move. She bent and kissed the crown of his head. His hair was thick and wavy and it teased her nose, and he smelled so good, a blend of talcum powder and musk, and for one moment, a jolt of need that was physical took her by surprise. She ignored it. He was so still that she wondered if he'd suddenly fallen asleep, right there in her arms.

But after another moment, he raised his head, trying to smile and failing, tears shining in his eyes. "Oh, Alex," Jill whispered, aching anew for him.

His left hand cupped her nape and he pulled her head down. Their lips met in a gently, barely-there brushing.

Jill felt tears form in her own eyes as she somehow slid down the bed so they were on a level, their lips touching tenderly again and again, a bubble of sadness and joy mingling and ballooning in her heart. Alex rolled fully onto his back and Jill didn't hesitate, moving so that she lay partially on top of him. In spite of the sheets between them, there was no mistaking that he was fully erect. Their eyes met and locked.

"Spend the night with me," he said roughly. "Please." Using his left hand to trace the line of her jaw, the tip of her nose, the shape of her lips.

"I want to," Jill said as roughly. "I need you, too."

She bent over him again, toward his mouth. This time they kissed with deep need and a deeper hunger. Hard. Alex's hand slid under her sweats and over her bare buttocks, then lower, down and behind them.

Jill tore the sheets and blanket out from between them; he pushed at her sweats with one hand. Jill shimmied out of the sweats as their lips locked again, with urgency and determination.

She tore his briefs off and slid on top of him. She gripped his full length and he pushed up, inside of her. And they moved as one, with desperation, with tears . . . until she was crying out, crying his name, spinning out of control, so wildly in love, into the far-flung universe, and he was coming too, hot and wet, deep inside of her, her name a sob torn from deep inside his being.

Afterward, he slept.

And Jill crept back to her own room.

The morning was cool and damp, the sky overhead partially overcast, with no real hope that the sun would shine that day. Jill stood staring at the manor and the tower behind it, braced against the chill of the breeze, glimpses of the steel gray sea flashing among the trees along the cliff's edge. Her hands were buried deeply in the fleece pockets of her red anorak.

Kate was in the tower. Jill felt certain of it. She had been imprisoned there and now she was buried there. But it didn't matter. Not anymore.

Because Jill was quitting and she was going home.

She had done enough.

She started past the manor, head down, tears in her eyes, trying not to think about Alex and failing miserably. She finally brushed her arm over her eyes. It was a bit late to have realized that she had somehow fallen in love with him. It was

too late to change the past. She couldn't undo any of the
harm she'd inflicted on his family. And nothing would ever
bring Lucinda back to life—and there would never be justice
for Kate.

Jill still had trouble grasping the fact that Lucinda would
have killed her last night without any remorse at all.

She paused before the tower, chills sweeping over her, hating the very sight of it. She wasn't sure she had the courage to
go inside. It was a place of death. First Kate, and now
Lucinda, and dear God, if Alex hadn't been there last night,
she might be the one who was in the Scarborough morgue.

"Hey."

Jill froze at the sound of Alex's voice, just behind her. She
hadn't been aware of his approach. She slowly turned and
met his brilliant blue regard. It was probing. And he still
looked like hell.

He did not smile. "You ran out on me last night."

She swallowed. "I was afraid I'd hurt you in the middle of
the night. Your shoulder." It was a lie. And she knew he
knew it. She'd been afraid to wake up beside him, afraid of
what would—or wouldn't—happen next.

He didn't reply.

"Shouldn't you be resting?" she asked nervously. He was
still pale. He'd forgone shaving, and he almost looked menacing. But his eyes, which were soft, negated that possibility.

"I feel fine," he said. "Well—" his smile was brief—"considering."

"I am sorry," Jill cried passionately, thinking about
William, sobbing over the death of his mistress, and Margaret, who must know and must hurt. "I never meant to hurt
you or your family. I never meant to do any of this."

"I know. I never meant to hurt you either, Jill. Please try to
understand, please try to believe that," he said as vehemently.

She stared, hands deep in her pockets, her heart thudding
with fear. They were at the point of no return. Finally, after
all the twists and turns that the search for Kate Gallagher had
entailed, it had brought them to this singular point and place
in time. The road forked here. Their paths would diverge—or
not. "You lied to me, Alex. You stole those letters."

"I know." His jaw flexed. "And I'm not happy about it."
She wanted to believe him.

"I was stuck. Between a rock and a hard place. Trying to head you off at the pass and protect my family while falling head over heels at the very same goddamn time." He made a sound, not quite a laugh. "Life sure has its surprises, doesn't it?"

Jill nodded, afraid now of the future—of a future spent alone, back in her dreary life in New York City. A future without Alex. "Did Kate ever write about being afraid for her life? Does she ever point her finger at anyone?"

"No. I'll give you the letters. Oh, I forgot, you have them." He sighed, the sound heavy and resigned.

Jill didn't like that sound. "Were you ever going to tell me about the DNA tests?"

"Yeah." He wet his lips. "Honey, I had to know conclusively that you were Kate and Edward's great-granddaughter. Things were getting out of hand. After Lady E., I got scared." He met her gaze. "I got scared as all hell for you—and I was scared about who was behind her death."

"So you hoped to pay me off so I'd go home."

"Peter's trust belongs to you."

"I didn't start this to find and claim Kate's fortune." Jill took a deep breath. "William's my half-uncle. Thomas and Lauren are my cousins." It had hardly sunk in.

"I know." His gaze veered to the tower. "I appreciate what you did last night."

Jill nodded, following his gaze and shivering. She could see Lucinda flat on her back, eyes wide, unseeing. "I don't think William really wanted to hurt me or anyone. I think Lucinda led him astray."

"I hope you're right." His expression changed, becoming fierce. "I know you're right! He told me she killed Lady E. He told me he hadn't any idea she would do such a thing. He was weeping, Jill. I think she flipped out and he feels as betrayed as we do."

"Will he be okay?"

"I don't know. He's aged, he's aged so much even since yesterday, not to mention since Hal died."

Jill closed her eyes, shivering, but not because of the cold bite of the wind. "Everyone knew, didn't they, about Hal's obsession with Kate? Everyone recognized me, didn't they, the minute I walked in the door?"

"Yes. We did. I did. I'm sorry. Everyone was scared, Jill. Scared of you and what you stood for and what you might do."

"Well, I'm not doing anything. Anne murdered Kate, she told William herself. But we'll never know where Kate is, or how she died. But maybe that's for the best."

"You don't mean that," Alex said.

"I don't know what I mean," she said, head down.

"Do you know how you feel about us?"

Her head popped up, her heart slammed to a halt before starting again. "What?"

He just smiled. It was sort of sad.

She stepped closer to him, gripping the left sleeve of his jacket. "You saved my life last night."

"I'd do it again," he said flatly. "I'd do it over a thousand times. That's how much you've come to mean to me."

Jill was overwhelmed. She couldn't speak. And his question echoed in her mind. But could he really forgive her for destroying his family? And even if he thought he could, would he, with his heart? Could two people start over when a past filled with lies and deceptions lurked just behind them— between them?

"Jill?" Alex finally said. "Thank you for last night. And I'm not talking about stopping me from calling the police."

Jill bit her lower lip so she wouldn't cry and she nodded.

"Hey." He put his good arm around her shoulder, hugging her to his body. "Everything's going to work out."

His tone was so firm that she started and looked into his eyes and saw a promise there. "I hope you're right."

He cocked his head behind them. "Shall we take one last look around before we go back to the house?"

Jill jerked. "What do you mean?"

"She's got her hooks in me, too. I want to know what happened. Even if I dared ask, which I won't, I don't think William will tell me what really happened."

"She's in the tower," Jill said, her hands deep in the pockets of her anorak. Her voice sounded odd, even to her own ears. "I'm certain."

Alex nodded.

Alex stood beside her as two gardeners continued to dig up the earthen floor of the ruined tower. Clods of dirt and stones flew off of their shovels. "I wonder if you're right," he said. "Maybe that's why, when I was a kid, the locals always said this place was haunted."

Jill felt her eyes widen. "Is that the village gossip?"

He met her gaze. "Yeah."

Jill leaned against the stone wall, continuing to shiver, watching as the two men who worked at Stainesmore steadily dug up the ground inside of the tower. They had gone several feet already, but had come up with nothing. Jill was beginning to feel dismay.

Maybe Kate was supposed to remain lost forever.

Maybe Jill had opened up a can of worms that fate had never intended to be opened in the first place.

"Me lord," one of the gardeners said. "Ain't nothing here but dirt an' rock."

Alex stepped forward, regarding the area. "It looks like you're right. Jill, they've gone a good eight feet. She can't possibly be buried in here."

Jill stepped into the tower, beside the two sweating gardeners, an odd desperation washing over her. "She has to be here, Alex. Where else would she be?" But she could see that he was right. Kate wasn't here. By now they'd have found something, anything.

"Maybe she was tossed over the cliffs."

Jill hated the thought. A moment later the two gardeners were being dismissed, Alex insisting they call him Mr. Preston, not "my lord," while pressing a few pounds into their palms. He came to stand beside her inside the four ruined stone walls.

"I guess this has been a wild-goose chase from the start," Jill said.

"Has it? She was an extraordinary woman, and she was your great-grandmother. Maybe that's all we were ever meant to learn," Alex said, his hand on her shoulder.

Jill smiled slightly. "You're becoming spiritual." In frustration, she kicked at the dirt at her feet and watched a rock roll away, hitting the bottom of the facing stone wall. Jill blinked.

And felt a pressure on her shoulder. For one moment, she thought Alex was pushing her, urging her forward. But then she realized she had walked away from him and the pressure was only her imagination.

Jill stared at the dull gray stone wall.

And suddenly, as she looked down, something caught her eye. Jill dropped to her knees, her pulse soaring, staring, wondering if there was a letter just barely visible on the stone wall, and thinking, No, it couldn't be.

"Jill?"

Jill didn't really hear Alex. She brushed the dust off of the rough stone, watching as the crude lines of the letter A emerged from the years' accumulation of dirt and grime. Stunned, Jill began brushing off the entire section of the wall with both hands, frantically, eyes wide, staring in disbelief as letter after letter was finally revealed.

"Oh, God!" she cried. "Alex, come here! It's a message— and it's from Kate!"

Twenty-Eight

THE EARLY AUTUMN DAY WAS BRILLIANT WITH SUNSHINE. IT should have been dismal and gray. For it was terribly painful being back at Coke's Way. Edward knew he shouldn't have come.

"Papa."

Edward realized that the sixteen-month-old bundle in his arms was squirming to be released. Gently, he set Peter down. The red-haired toddler swayed unsteadily, beaming at Edward, who could not smile back, before staggering off toward the boarded-up manor house. Abruptly tears filled Edward's eyes.

The grief would not go away. The grief, the anger, the confusion, and the self-pity.

There were times when he forgot, only to suddenly, violently, remember everything.

Like now.

He rubbed the sleeve of his hacking coat across his eyes, regained his composure, and started after his son. He had not been to Stainesmore in over a year, but affairs of the estate demanded his attention, and the earl had insisted he go. He had expected this, hadn't he? The sorrow, the angst, the memories of Kate. What he had not expected was for Anne to insist that she would accompany him to the north, or for the grief to be stronger than ever, the memories more insistent, more haunting, than in the past.

She was at the house right now, waiting for him to join her for tea, pretending not to be livid that he was with his son. His son—Kate's son.

Peter had wandered past the house and was ambling toward the tower. "Peter! No!" Edward called after him, lengthening his strides.

But Peter, who was a very happy boy, only laughed and ran faster, his arms flailing like windmills at his side. His cap fell off. Edward wished he could smile at his child's antics. He no longer knew how to do so. He had not smiled in what felt like an endless lifetime. He watched his son swaying precariously from side to side. It was only a matter of moments, really, before he fell. And just as Edward finished the thought, Peter went face down in the grass and dirt.

Edward reached him instantly, lifting him into his embrace. But Peter was grinning from ear to ear, in delight. "Run, run," he shouted, squirming enthusiastically. "Peter want run!"

He was exactly like Kate. Kate, whose will knew no force greater than her own, who had cherished and loved every moment life had offered her. Kate, who had disappeared without a trace, who had, perhaps, left him for another man.

Edward patted Peter's head awkwardly, hardly seeing him. *Damn it, but who could live this way, not knowing what had really happened?*

He had no choice but to release his overenergetic child, and he did so, dutifully watching him again as he staggered enthusiastically off. To this day his cloying, annoying wife, whom he had no interest in, insisted that Kate had run off with a lover. In the beginning, shocked, angry, betrayed, it had been easier to believe Anne than not. The anger had enabled him to go through with his wedding. And now, how he regretted that.

Had Kate run off with another man? His heart shrieked a No! at him. But he did not know what to think, dear God.

And he never would. Somehow, he must be resigned to that. For try as he might to will the truth to come to him in a flash of insight, he could not comprehend what had really happened to Kate, or why she had left him.

His mind had spun a thousand circles in the year since she had disappeared. Round and round and round, like a mouse on a treadmill, with no way to get off. Had Kate run away with a new lover? Or had some terrible tragedy befallen her? Or had she, being the Kate he had so thoroughly known and loved, run away in an ultimate act of self-sacrifice, refusing to stand in the way of the title and the fortune that he had been prepared to give up for her, for them?

He had finally ruled out the notion that Kate had been the victim of tragic circumstance. Because she had left Peter with his mother before disappearing, so that disappearance had to have been an act of her free will, a premeditated act of her free will.

"Oh, Kate," he whispered, a moan. How could she have done this to him? And the worst part of it was, he would never know if she had left him for someone else or if she had left him because she loved him so selflessly.

Edward suddenly realized that Peter was about to stumble into the tower. *The tower, which had always terrified and repelled Kate.* Seized with an unreasonable fear, almost a panic, Edward shot to his feet and ran after his son. "Peter! No! Do not go inside!" he shouted.

But Peter disappeared into the ruins.

His fear spiraled to terror. *He had lost Kate, he could not lose Peter, too.* Edward rushed inside the tower, only to find Peter sitting in the dirt, making mud pies. He relaxed, closed his eyes, and realized that he was shaking like a leaf.

His reaction had been absurd. He could not understand it.

Peter suddenly pushed up to his feet and toddled over to the wall, talking in gibberish, falling against it. For one more moment, Edward watched Peter, who was beaming, who looked just like Kate. He suddenly shivered and glanced warily around the tower, feeling as if he were not alone. As if he were being watched.

But no one was about.

Chilled and uneasy, finally understanding why Kate had always hated this place, Edward strode to Peter, lifted him up, and quickly left the tower. Outside, he began to breathe easier as he put Peter down. If anything had happened to his son, he knew he could not have borne it.

And suddenly a searing realization struck him. He had been so caught up in his grief and misery, in his confusion, that he had not only been neglecting the affairs of the estate, he had been failing his son.

Edward was stunned.

"Papa, down," Peter demanded. "Down!"

Edward slid him to the ground, staring at him as if seeing him for the first time. Peter toddled off to inspect a fallen tree branch. He quickly became interested in a nest of ants.

Edward stared, his life passing before his eyes, every wonderful, painful moment of it. He felt a hundred years old, but he wasn't even thirty—he was still a young man. A young man with a young son and a bride and a vast earldom to run. He had responsibilities, and this past year he had thoroughly shirked his duty to his family and the earldom.

"Papa, Papa, look, look," Peter chanted happily, pointing at the ants.

"Yes, I see," Edward said quietly. He might not be able to demonstrate his affection as he had once been able to, but there were other ways to care for one's family. "Peter, it's time to go home. I have much to do."

Duty. It was a terribly comforting thought, and Edward clung to it for the rest of his life.

*   *   *

ANNE KILLED ME
GOD SAVE HER SOUL

"Oh, my God," Jill whispered, her hand on the stone. Alex knelt beside her, shining his penlight on the coarse wall. "Anne killed me God save her soul." Goose bumps covered her entire body. Jill met Alex's gaze.

"Christ," he said quietly.

Jill's heart was pounding as she stood. "She was here. She died here. She wrote this message before she died. God." And Jill could see Kate, dirty and bloody, frightened and terrified, there in the tower, begging for her life. Tears filled her eyes.

Alex slipped his arm around her and Jill leaned into him without thinking. "I wonder if this would have held up in a court back then. I don't think so."

They stared at one another. "Anne was insane," Jill finally said.

"That's putting it kindly, don't you think?" Alex returned.

"And she's not buried here. And she wasn't buried in the grave. Anne must have erected that stone, don't you think?"

"Unless she had an accomplice."

Jill's eyes widened.

"You think she had an accomplice?" Jill cried.

"Honey, I don't want you to get started. But how did Anne get Kate up here? Maybe it was the hired coachman, but she had to have had help. Let's go."

Jill bit her lip. "She deserves a proper burial."

"We'll never find the body, Jill."

She hated accepting that. Jill walked past him, outside. The mist had evaporated. The sun was, miraculously, trying to shine through the overhead clouds. A gull wheeled above her head.

Alex was probably right, she thought grimly, staring blindly toward the house. Kate had been murdered by her best friend, she had died in the tower, but God only knew where she was right now. It was sad. Kate deserved a real burial, a real grave.

Jill paused, absorbed in her sorrow, her hands in the pockets of her anorak. A breeze was sweeping past her, causing tendrils of hair to tickle her nape. Suddenly Jill felt a tension settling over her. Suddenly she felt as if she were being watched.

Jill stiffened. The sensation of eyes trained upon her increased. She glanced first at the manor, then at the drive-way and road. Silver bark and pale leaves were shifting and shimmering in the glade ahead of her, by the cemetery. No one was present.

Her imagination was running wild again, Jill thought. But the hairs were now raised on her entire body, and she had forgotten to breathe. Abruptly she whirled, to see if someone was watching her from behind. It was only Alex, pausing beside her.

"You look like you just saw a ghost," he joked.

She faced him. "I just had the strongest feeling of being watched."

Their gazes held. "Kate?"

"Maybe." Jill realized how much she wished that she had seen her—and this time, clearly, so there would not be any doubt whether it was her imagination or not. "I think I saw her once, in town, at my flat."

Alex nodded. "I think it's time to let her go, Jill."

"Yeah," Jill said roughly.

"Are you about ready to go back to town?" he asked.

Jill looked around—at the tower, at the manor, and then at him. Alex was right. They weren't ever going to find Kate, but they had found the truth. And that was going to have to be enough—it was time to let go.

She met his gaze. "Should I take a train? So you can drive William back?"

"Would you mind?" he asked. "I really need to take care of him right now."

Suddenly Jill felt like an outsider all over again—even with Alex. But she was an outsider, wasn't she? She forced a smile. "No problem. I need to think, anyway, and the ride will give me a chance to do that." Abruptly she started toward the Land Rover, leaving him behind.

But she only took one step. Alex caught her by the arm, halting her in her tracks. "What do you need to think about, Jill?" he asked very quietly, his gaze boring into hers.

Jill stared. Did she dare be honest? How could she not? So much was at stake! She wet her lips, choosing her words with care—not being quite as brave and open as she could be. "I guess I need to think about going back home and getting back to work," she said slowly. When what she really needed to think about was her future, and him.

His face tightened. "What about us?"

Jill didn't breathe. "I didn't know there was an us," she finally said.

He rolled his eyes. But it wasn't comical. "If there isn't an 'us' then I don't know what the hell there is."

Her heart began to race. He had said "us." Which meant that a relationship was on his mind, too. But Jill was so afraid. "Maybe we both need to think, and carefully, Alex."

"Why are you being so cautious? Usually you don't mince words."

Jill hesitated. "All right. I care about you. I admit it. Maybe a lot. But God, look at what's happened—and it will always be between us."

"Why?" He stared.

Jill just stared back and then she had to smile briefly. "You can be succinct, Alex. Don't you think a foundation of lies just stacks the odds against us?"

"I think it can bring us closer together, if you want it to."

Jill froze. A long moment stretched between them. "I'm afraid," she finally said. "I don't want to be hurt again."

"Maybe I'm afraid, too. Maybe I've never felt this way before and I'm not sure of what to do or when to do it or even how."

She gazed into his soft blue eyes and realized he was as scared as she was. "There are no crystal balls," she whispered.

"Maybe we can find one."

Jill smiled.

He smiled, too. "You know, being as you are such a romantic, you can always look at this as Kate having brought us together."

Jill froze.

"In a way, it feels like she did bring us together," Alex said. And he flushed.

Jill couldn't needle him about his romanticism now. But her search for her great-grandmother had brought her to Alex. "Maybe we can finally end a terrible, destructive cycle of the Collinsworth men falling for women they can't have."

His gaze slammed to her. "I don't want you to go back to New York, Jill."

Jill inhaled. "I don't want to go back."

Their gazes remained locked.

He moved first, smiling a little, then a bit more, and then he touched her cheek briefly. "I believe you've got another two months at Barrows's flat before he comes back."

"I do." She knew where he was leading. In two months, she had plenty of time to find another apartment. "But I'm dead broke, remember?"

And Alex started to laugh.

"What's so funny?"

Tears of mirth slid from his eyes. "The trust," he said. "I hate to tell you, Jill, but you are now an heiress."

Jill stared. And slowly, she did smile. "My God, and to think I never thought I'd see the day where I could pay my rent in advance." It began to dawn on her what the financial freedom could mean. "Oh, God, I could even buy a flat."

He laughed again, the sound warm, sliding his arm around her. "Damn right you can. But I think you should wait." His eyes were intent. "To see what happens. With us."

Us. She was liking the way he said it, the sound of it on his lips. "Okay. I won't be rash."

He lifted both brows in skepticism, then said, "Why don't we start over with an old-fashioned dinner date? Say, tonight?"

She warmed, all over. "That sounds really good, Alex," she said, meaning it.

He smiled at her, and gestured toward the car.

Jill and Alex walked around the side of the house, arm in arm, not speaking, not needing to, and not noticing as they passed the barely visible door of the root cellar in the ground by their feet.

And behind them, maybe, just maybe, amid the scrubby trees, back-lit by the sun and the sea, Kate stood, watching, and as the cumulus clouds shifted, opening, the sun grew stronger, brighter, bathing the rough cliffs in its light. Kate turned, fading, becoming weaker and weaker still as she walked slowly away, past the cliffs, past the sea, until nothing was left but an old ruined tower that had once been haunted.

TURN THE PAGE FOR AN EXCERPT FROM

House of Dreams—

THE EXCITING NEW NOVEL FROM BRENDA JOYCE,
AVAILABLE IN HARDCOVER FROM ST. MARTIN'S
PRESS!

One

Just where the hell was her sister?

Cass had spent most of her life in her sister's shadow—Tracey was one of the most beautiful and glamorous women Cass knew, and unfortunately, she had a tendency to run late. Cass was a wreck. Surely today, of all days, Tracey could be on time. Just this once.

In another two hours the house would be filled with Tracey's guests. With Forbes 400 types, their fashion-plate wives, the odd Silicon Valley millionaire, celebrities, dignitaries, the press, two Japanese bankers, a couple of rock stars, an Israeli shipping tycoon, an ambassador, and a sprinkling of dukes, duchesses, and earls. The very thought caused Cass's heart to lurch unpleasantly.

But mostly, Tracey should be on time because she hadn't seen her own daughter in three months even if they did speak on the phone twice a week.

Cass stood nervously by the window, staring past the crisply white shell drive and across the green rolling hills of the East Sussex countryside. She was perspiring. Dairy cows dotted the fields spanning the distance between the house and the small village of Belford, which she could just make out as a jumble of pale stone rooftops. The day was gray, the threat of rain imminent, reducing visibility. Even so, she could see the nearest town—Romney, famous for its tourist attraction, an intact castle dating back five full centuries—as it sat on one of the surrounding hills. Cass could also see a thin strip of highway meandering through the countryside. No car was in sight.

"Where's Mother? Why isn't she here yet?" a small voice asked.

Cass's stomach was in knots as she turned to face her seven-year-old niece. "Your mom will be here at any moment, I'm sure of it," she lied. And she thought, *Please, Trace. For Alyssa, for me, just get here!*

Alyssa sat on her pristine pink-and-white bed, against numerous fluffy pillows, all beautifully embroidered and mostly pink, white, and red like the bedroom, wearing her newest clothes—a short, pale blue dress from Harrods, navy blue stockings, and chunky black suede shoes. Her raven black hair was pulled back with a tortoiseshell barrette, and her face was scrubbed and glowing. She was so pretty, but nothing like her mother—not in any way. "She was supposed to arrive an hour ago," Alyssa said glumly. "What if she doesn't come?"

Cass started and rushed to her niece, who had just verbalized Cass's own worst fears. "She is coming, sweetie. You can bet on that. This is Tracey's black-tie supper, even if Aunt Catherine is hosting the event. You know that. She *has* to show up."

Alyssa nodded, but did not seem convinced.

Cass knew that her younger sister was wild and irresponsible, but she wasn't that wild, or that irresponsible. The evening affair was on account of Tracey's new job with Sotheby's in London. The moment Tracey had asked Catherine if she could hold an event in order to display a very rare necklace to three dozen potential buyers—the crème de la crème of international society—Catherine had agreed. Their aunt rarely refused either one of the nieces. Cass's temples began to throb dully. Tracey would show up—wouldn't she?

Cass could not imagine helping Aunt Catherine to host this event. She was not a jet-setter like her sister. She did not frequent five-star hotels, fly first class, juggle playboys and polo players, or even own more than a single evening gown. She did not go to the weddings of supermodels. Cass's last boyfriend had been a journalist, not a rock star.

"Some people just can't help being late," Cass finally said, forcing a lightness into her tone that she did not feel. "It's a terrible habit," she added. And that much was true. Cass knew that Tracey did not mean to keep people waiting. It just happened. It was less about self-absorption than it was about disorganization and time management. No one lived life the way her sister did.

Still, Cass had been filled with a growing sense of dread all that day. The evening—or her sister's visit—was going to be a disaster. Cass had never felt more certain of anything, even if she could not pinpoint why.

Cass just hoped the premonition of disaster didn't have to do with her filling in for Tracey.

"She's so busy now with her new job," Alyssa said, her dark eyes lowered, her thick black lashes fanning out on her alabaster cheeks. She was the spitting image of her rock-star father, Rick Tennant, who was currently on a world tour and somewhere in the Far East.

Cass hoped that was so. Sotheby's seemed like the perfect job for her sister—she could mingle with the rich and famous, while her employers benefited from her celebrity status and her celebrity associations. Since her marriage, and even more so since her divorce, Tracey had been a fixture on the society pages of major magazines.

Tracey's marriage to Rick had been over in less than three years. Cass regretted, for Alyssa's sake, that it hadn't lasted. But Alyssa was the best thing that had ever happened to her, and she loved her as if she were her own daughter. In fact, sometimes she forgot that if Tracey wanted to, she could saunter into their lives and whisk Alyssa away without even an explanation. Which, of course, Cass prayed she would never do.

"I hear a car," Alyssa cried, leaping up, her entire face brightening.

Cass was flooded with relief. Alyssa ran to the window, her black hair swinging like a cape behind her, while Cass hugged herself, sighing, because she would not have to play hostess and Alyssa would see her mother after what had become an interminable separation—from a little girl's point of view.

"It's not her," Alyssa said, her tone flat.

Cass stood, her heart sinking, eyes wide. "What?" Where was Tracey?!

Alyssa seemed on the verge of tears. Cass took one look at her pinched white face and she reached for her hand. "She's running late. Should we take a walk? It might help pass the time," Cass said.

"I'd rather wait here. I don't want to miss her," Allysa said with a stubborn tilt to her chin.

Before Cass could suggest another diversion, there was a soft knock on the door and Aunt Catherine appeared, holding a silver tray in her hands. Her gaze instantly connected with Cass's, before she entered the room and smiled at Alyssa. "Scones and tea, my dear. You must be famished, Alyssa. You haven't had a bite to eat all day."

Alyssa folded her arms tightly across her chest. "Why does she have to be so late? Doesn't she miss me, too?"

Catherine slowly set the tray down on the Chippendale table in front of another set of windows, one graced by two pink velvet chairs. Although seventy, Cass's aunt was a tall, statuesque woman who looked no older than fifty. Her reddish hair was shoulder length and worn in a chignon, and she remained extremely handsome, a perpetual light in her blue eyes. Even clad simply in gray trousers, a white blouse, and a darker cardigan, she had the carriage of a very noble, self-assured, and self-sufficient woman. Cass admired her greatly, for her character, her generosity, and the many good deeds she had dedicated her life to. "Of course she does. Our guests will be arriving at seven, and knowing your mother, who needs a good hour or two to dress for this kind of event, she will have to arrive at any moment," Catherine said, smiling.

Alyssa wandered over to the table and stared at the scones. She had been so excited that morning she had gotten sick after breakfast, and Cass had let her stay home from the exclusive all-girls school she attended.

Cass went to her. "Of course she misses you, sweetie. She's your mother. No one is more special to her, believe me. But working for Sotheby's can't be easy; they send her all over the world. I think she was in Madrid just a few days ago. Your mom is probably very tired, sweetie—and really nervous about tonight."

Alyssa looked her right in the eye. "She was in *Vogue* again. With a new man. Does she have another boyfriend?"

Cass blinked. She'd obviously missed that last issue. Actually, she avoided the kinds of magazines and rags her sister usually appeared in. Cass wasn't jealous. It was just oddly hurtful to see her sister on those pages so often, surrounded by household names, looking so perfect. "I don't know," Cass said after a pause, truthfully. Tracey hadn't mentioned a new lover to Cass.

Catherine rubbed her thin back. "Do not fret, dear. Your mother will be here at any moment, and then you can ask her yourself about any new man that might be in her life."

Alyssa bit her lip, looking perilously close to tears.

Catherine said, brightly, "I think everyone in this room is exhausted. I do mean, we have had staff preparing for this evening for two days, not to mention the security from Sotheby's to make sure that ruby necklace is not stolen by some cat thief—those men swarming all over the grounds! Let's take some tea. We'll all feel better, and by the time we're done, I have not a doubt Tracey will be sailing through that doorway."

Alyssa nodded, lips pursed, sitting down in one of the pink velvet chairs, swinging her chunky platform shoes back and forth. As she reached for a scone, Catherine pouring the tea, Cass said, "I'm going to go downstairs and take a breath of air, if you two don't mind."

"I think you should take a long hot soak, Cassandra, and spend some time primping before the mirror for this evening's affair," Catherine said gently.

Cass caught the briefest glimpse of her own reflection in the mirror as she started and turned back to face her aunt. She was wearing not one stitch of makeup, and the Barnard sweatshirt she'd thrown on that morning was as old and faded as her jeans. Her honey blond hair was shoulder length and pulled into a ponytail. Like her aunt, she had strong, even features and good skin. Unlike her aunt, she did not turn heads.

And she knew exactly what her aunt meant—she should take extra care to dress up because one never knew whom one might meet.

"*Moi?* Primp? Would you care to define that for me?" Cass had to smile.

Alyssa even giggled. "I'll help Aunt Cass get dressed," she said. "She can use my lipstick. It would look great on you, Aunt Cass."

Before Cass could accept or decline, Catherine said, "You are far too young to own, much less wear, lipstick, Alyssa." Her tone was stern.

"Actually," Cass cut in, "I thought I'd go over the notes I made last night. I was so tired I feel asleep at my desk, and I want to make sure I can decipher my scrawl."

Catherine just looked at her, her expression a mixture of resignation, reproval, and respect.

Cass fled the room before they could get into an argument about Cass's single-minded focus on her career as the author of historical novels—she'd had four works published in the past six years—and her consequent, serious lack of a personal life—or even the mere pursuit of one.

Cass hurried downstairs in her rubber-soled loafers. They had been over the old tired argument a dozen times—she should get out more, date more, she should be married, she should have her own kids. Catherine just didn't understand. Taking care of Alyssa and her work was just about all she could handle. There was only so much time in every day.

A housemaid smiled at her as she hurried past, down a dim hall with stone floors, her mind torn between thoughts of Tracey's arrival and her departure, the desire to protect Alyssa from all of life's disappointments, both large and small, and her own inner voice, which agreed with her aunt entirely. Five years ago, when she had packed up her life and moved with Alyssa from her small apartment in New York City to Belford House, she'd given up her pursuit of a personal life and hadn't dwelled much on it since. There had been no choice to make. Alyssa had needed her from the day she was born, and the moment Tracey and Rick had decided to divorce, it had been clear to Cass that if she didn't raise the small child, no one else would. She hadn't had the means to be a single mother, and moving in with her aunt had been the perfect solution. There were no regrets.

Cass stepped through a pair of doors that opened on one side of her aunt's flower gardens, the driveway to her left and just within the range of her peripheral vision. She swung her head around and hesitated, noticing a black Citroen in the driveway. Her sister drove an Aston Martin. Or rather, her driver did. Tracey had made out very handsomely in her divorce settlement.

It was too early for any guests to have arrived, and just as Cass was pondering that notion, she realized that someone was standing in the gardens on her right, his back to her. For one moment she wondered if he was one of the security men from Sotheby's. He was tall, dark-haired, and well dressed in tan trousers and a black sport jacket. The tan trousers gave him away as something other than security, because the security men wore all black. Cass approached, clearing her throat, about to ask him if he needed help—or was even in the right place.

He turned.

Cass felt a flash of recognition even before his eyes met hers. She stumbled, for one instant lost in confusion.

Just what in God's name was Antonio de la Barca doing in her aunt's flower gardens? She did not know him personally, but he was the kind of man a woman would never forget, not having met him even once. Not that they had actually, really met. He was a professor of medieval studies, of international renown, tenured in Madrid, and Cass had attended a lecture series that he had given at the Metropolitan Museum in New York City seven years ago. She recalled the series so well: Medieval Myth, Fact or Fantasy, a Mirror to Our World. She had been researching her third novel at the time, and his course had been just after Alyssa's birth but before her sister's quickie divorce.

"Señora, I see I have startled you. Please, forgive me," he said, his smile slight. He had an intriguing Latin accent.

Cass tried to recover her composure. "I wasn't expecting anyone to be out here," she managed, her heart racing madly. This was absurd. Why was she so surprised to see him? Obviously he must be there to attend the dinner party. It was now clicking in her brain that the necklace that was the highlight of Sotheby's next auction was a period piece, dating back to the sixteenth century. Article after article had been written about the stunning find. Perhaps he had even appraised its historical value.

"A servant assured me that I could take a walk in the gardens without disturbing anyone, but I see I have disturbed you. Again, my sincerest apologies." He was wearing tortoiseshell eyeglasses, which hardly detracted from his strong, attractive Spanish features. His gaze was at once assured and questioning.

Cass knew she was blushing. He did not seem to remember her, but of course, he would not. Even if she had asked dozens of questions after each and every lecture. Her gaze slid to his hands, but they were tucked in the pockets of his trousers. He'd worn a wedding ring seven years ago, and the gossip among all of the women attending the lectures had run rampant, because supposedly his wife had simply disappeared without a trace the year before. Cass recalled the ceaseless speculation—was it even true? Had she run away? Or had some unspeakable horror befallen her? Of course, no one had had any answers. But it had certainly made him even more of a romantic figure in the eyes of the women attending the lecture series. Just about every woman there had been madly in love with him.

Cass included.

"I'm being a terrible hostess," Cass finally said, finding her tongue. "You must be here for the evening's dinner party. My aunt is Catherine Belford. I'm Cassandra de Warenne."

For one moment he studied her, not accepting her hand. Cass wondered if she had said something wrong, and then the moment passed—her hand was in his grip, which was firm and cool, and he bowed ever so slightly. "You're American?" he asked with some surprise.

Her accent was a giveaway. "My mother was American, and actually I was born in the States, but when she died, my aunt took us in. I was eleven at the time. I've spent so much time here, I consider myself at least half British." Cass knew she was speaking in a nervous rush.

He removed his eyeglasses, tucking them into the interior breast pocket of his impeccably tailored navy blue sport jacket. "You went to Barnard?"

Cass suddenly realized, with no small amount of horror, how she was dressed. Unfortunately, she could feel her color increase. "Yes. I graduated ten years ago," she said. "I took a year off, then went back for my master's."

"I've lectured several times at Columbia," he said with a smile. "I know both colleges well. They are fine schools."

Cass shoved her hands, which were damp, into the pockets of her jeans. Did she sound like an idiot? Or a blushing schoolgirl? "Actually, I attended your lecture series at the Met a few years ago."

He just looked at her, his expression difficult to read.

Cass felt like taking back her words. Should she have admitted that she remembered him? "You *are* Antonio de la Barca?"

"Forgive me again." He raked a hand through his jet black hair, hair that was even darker than Alyssa's. "I do not know what is wrong with me today." He shook his head, as if to clear it. Then he stared. "Yes, I did give that lecture, seven years ago." Something crossed his face, an expression Cass found difficult to read. "A great institution," he murmured, and he turned slightly, staring toward the rolling hills and Romney Castle. Cass realized it was drizzling.

She ignored it. She also ignored the slight twinge she felt because he didn't remember her at all. "It was a wonderful lecture, Señor de la Barca. I enjoyed it immensely."

He faced her, their eyes meeting. "Are you a historian?"

She hesitated, debating telling him the truth. "I majored in European history at college," she said. "My master's is in

British history. And now I write historical novels." She kept her hand in her pockets.

His eyes flickered. "How interesting," he said, and there was nothing patronizing in his tone. "I would love a list of the titles you have published."

"I'd be happy to give one to you before you leave," Cass said, wondering if he would really read one of her books, then worrying about any inaccuracies he might find. "Are you here to see the necklace?"

He nodded, eyes brightening. "A sixteenth-century piece? The way it has been described, it would be worth a king's ransom—and would have belonged to someone exemplary. If the piece is authentic, which clearly it must be, as Sotheby's does not make such grievous errors, then I am more interested in discovering who might have originally owned it than anything else." He smiled at her.

"It's stunning," Cass said eagerly. "Of course, I've only seen the photos. Those rubies are cut so slightly and so primitively that the average person would assume them to be glass. I can't wait to actually see the piece tonight."

He was nodding. "Rubies were very rare in the sixteenth century," he said, his gaze directly on her again. "Only the most wealthy and powerful possessed rubies. This necklace might have belonged to a queen or a princess. That the Hepplewhites discovered it in their possession is rather amazing."

"Can you imagine if Lady Hepplewhite had thrown it out as she first thought of doing, assuming it to be a costume piece?"

He was smiling, shaking his head. Cass was smiling, too.

"I'm writing a novel set during Bloody Mary's reign," she said impulsively. "It was a fascinating period in time, and Mary has been so stereotyped and so gravely misunderstood."

Both of his dark brows lifted. He stared. "Really."

Cass bit her lip. "I can't help it. My imagination runs away with me. That necklace could have been a careless gift handed down by Mary to one of her favorites. She was very loyal and generous to those in her household."

"Yes, it could have been." Their gazes locked. "Or it could have been a gift from her father to just about anyone—one of his wives, one of his daughters—or perhaps his son Edward passed it along in a similar manner."

"It would be very interesting to trace the lineage of the necklace," Cass mused.

"Very interesting," Antonio de la Barca agreed, his gaze still focused entirely on her.

There was something in his tone that made Cass tense. She could not look away, and now she remembered talking to him after a lecture and being as mesmerized by the brilliance in his hazel eyes. The brilliance and the intensity.

She had to take a step backward, away from him. Even if he was a widower, he was way out of her league. Besides, she had learned her lesson years ago. Eight years ago, to be exact—just before Alyssa was born. When you fell in love, all good judgment flew out the window, and the result was tragic. Having had her heart broken once and forever was enough. The man who broke it was a college love affair—but it had apparently been more important to her than it had to him. She knew she had moved past the heartbreak. She just never wanted to go there again. "It's raining," she said, to break the moment, which had somehow seemed far too intimate and even awkward.

He glanced up at the sky, smiled slightly, as the skies opened up and it began to pour. "Indeed it is," he said.

"C'mon," Cass said, turning to lead him inside.

But he was shrugging off his designer sport jacket and draping it over her sweatshirt-clad shoulders. Cass did not have time to gape. Taking her elbow very firmly, he hurried her back inside.

Once out of the rain, Cass handed him his nearly soaking jacket. "I hope you haven't ruined that."

"It hardly matters," he replied.

Cass hesitated, aware of the darkening shadows of the late afternoon, and as suddenly aware of the fact that this particular guest was several hours early. What was she to do with him?

Clearly her thoughts were written all over her face,

because he said, "I am meeting Señora Tennant here, but apparently she is somewhat late."

Cass stiffened. *He's meeting Tracey here?* "Tracey is my sister."

He started. "She never mentioned that she had a sister. I was assuming you to be her cousin."

How did de la Barca know her sister? "No, we're sisters, even if we look nothing alike," she said slowly. A new sense of dread, very different from the one that had been haunting her all day, was filling her.

In fact, her unease made it possible for her to not even notice a twinge of hurt at his surprised reaction to the fact that she and Tracey were sisters. No one ever guessed, because they were so unalike.

Why was he meeting Tracey? Before Cass could even begin to sort out what was happening, Alyssa came pounding down the stairs, crying out in excitement that her mother had finally arrived.

And the front door swung open behind them. Cass heard it just as she felt a gust of cold, wet air, but she was looking at his hands now, which were hanging by his sides. He was wearing a very bold ring with a blood-red stone on his right hand, but the slender wedding band she had seen seven years ago was gone. Well. He had not remarried. And that explained everything, she thought grimly. His involvement with Tracey had nothing to do with the sixteenth-century necklace. Cass knew it the way she knew she would have an awful time that evening.

"Hello, everyone!" Tracey cried from behind Cass.

A huge weight settled on Cass's shoulders, and she turned.

Tracey stood in the doorway in a pair of beautifully tailored white pants, an exquisitely cut short grayish white jacket with Chanel buttons, and a pair of high-heeled white boots. Her long, pale blond hair was loose, the dampness causing it to curl about her face and shoulders. She looked as if she had just stepped off a catwalk, or out of the pages of *Vogue*. Which, considering Alyssa's earlier comments, apparently she had.

Tracey was classically attractive. Her features were perfectly even, her eyes blue, her skin unblemished. She was one of those women who looked as good without makeup as they did with it. And while there might be more beautiful women in the same room with her, Tracey was always the most striking. She was the one who turned heads. Because she was model-thin and close to six feet tall. She also lived in drop-dead designer clothes. No one made an entrance like her sister did, Cass thought sourly. She realized she was hugging herself.

"Cass, how are you?" Tracey smiled, apparently not having noticed Alyssa, who stood on the lowest level of the stairs, clinging to the banister. She hugged Cass hard, but Cass hardly noticed. How the hell had her sister and de la Barca met? How?

Tracey's gaze became questioning. "Cass?"

"Hiya, sis." Cass managed a smile.

Tracey beamed at her, then turned to face Antonio de la Barca. The smile she sent him told Cass all she needed to know. They were lovers. This was nothing new—so why was she surprised? Dismayed?

"I see that the two of you have met," she said happily. "Don't tell me you're already dressed for supper?" she teased.

"Ha ha," Cass said, watching Tracey kiss Antonio on the cheek. At least she was spared the real thing. How *had* they met? *When* had they become lovers? And why, God damn it, did she care? Tracey changed men the way she changed her wardrobe—which was seasonally, at least. Cass was used to it—she expected no less.

Although if she were brutally honest with herself, she could admit how nice it would be to have an endless stream of boyfriends.

But she wasn't Tracey. She just couldn't settle for good looks and good times.

Tracey pulled on her ponytail. "Why are you so grumpy? I was only kidding, sis. In fact"—her smile widened—"I brought everyone presents!"

Cass stepped back a bit. "How have you been? You look great, Trace. I guess Sotheby's agrees with you."

Tracey beamed, which only made her lovelier. "A lot of things are agreeing with me lately," she said, her gaze locking on de la Barca. She stopped, spotting Alyssa with her nose between the bars of the iron banister. "Darling, come here!" Tracey cried.

Alyssa slowly stood, her face as red as a beet. "Hello, Mother," she said, her brown eyes wide and riveted upon Tracey's snow white figure.

Tracey pounced on her, embracing her once, hard. Cass watched. She watched Alyssa's body remain straight and hard and tight, and she watched Tracey's smile fade and finally vanish as she straightened, a look of hurt in her blue eyes. Alyssa climbed the stairs one step, a similar look of hurt in her near-black gaze. In the next instant Tracey recovered, the cover-girl smile firmly in place as she turned and rushed to Antonio, looping her arms in his. "I see you've met everyone," she said too brightly.

It was hardly noticeable, but he disengaged their arms. "I have met your sister, but I have not met your daughter," he said somewhat quietly. His smile was brief.

Cass's antenna went up. Trouble in paradise? Something was up, and she had to know what.

"Alyssa, come meet my boyfriend, Antonio de la Barca. Tonio, this is my beautiful daughter, who is seven, I might add."

Alyssa finally came down the stairs. "I saw your picture in *Vogue*. With my mother."

Antonio stooped so that he was not towering over her. And he smiled and it was wide and genuine, marking him as a man who liked children. "Your mother is the kind of woman that photographers wish to photograph. I have no doubt that one day you will be the very same kind of woman."

Cass fell in love with him in that moment. The sudden, shocking depth and intensity of feeling immobilized her. It was the kind of feeling she'd had once before—a sensation of absolute free-falling, a headlong plunge, into the abyss of emotional space.

Cass had gone there once before and barely survived. She

stared at her sister, her niece, and the stranger in their midst, paralyzed.

Antonio continued to smile at Alyssa. Very slowly, very slightly, Alyssa smiled back.

And Cass could not move. She could not even think, she could only feel. She was stunned. Terrified.

He was so gorgeous and so Old World, so masculine, so intelligent . . . Jesus.

And he was her sister's.

Which was just fine.

This could not be happening, she thought.

"I have a son," Antonio continued, "only three years older than you. Maybe one day you will meet him."

Alyssa's eyes brightened. And when she spoke, it was clear to Cass that she was doing all that she could to sound detached—but her tone was breathless. "What is his name?"

"His name is Eduardo, and he lives with me in Madrid, just a few blocks from the Plaza de la Lealtad. We live near a beautiful park, El Retiro, where many children play soccer and Rollerblade in the afternoons." Antonio straightened. Tracey was wearing four-inch heels. At that moment they were the exact same height.

"I would love to go to Madrid," Alyssa breathed.

It suddenly clicked in Cass's very befuddled and stunned mind why Tracey had sent Alyssa several postcards from Madrid. Now she knew why Tracey had been channel-hopping. And she had a very unladylike but very New York City thought. *Shit.*

Cass tried to get a grip. She tried to recover her composure. She did not know de la Barca, not at all, and it was insanity to think that she had just discovered some kind of profound feeling for him.

She was not falling in love.

No way. Not now, not ever, not today.

"Well, one day I am sure you will," Tracey said, moving into the center of the tableau. "Look at what I have brought you, darling," she said, digging four packages out of her Vuitton duffel bag and handing them all at once to Alyssa.

Alyssa clasped her hands in front of her, staring down at the gift-wrapped boxes. "Thank you, Mother."

"You have to open them!" Tracey cried. Then, "Aunt Catherine! There you are, and just in time. I have something for you, too!"

Catherine was coming down the stairs. She was smiling, and Tracey flew into her arms. They embraced warmly, and then Tracey handed her a small box that could only be from a jeweler.

Cass went to Alyssa, trying to avoid looking at de la Barca. "Do you want to take the gifts upstairs to your room and open them privately?" she asked softly, for Alyssa's ears only.

Alyssa nodded. Tears had formed on the tips of her lashes.

Cass wanted to hug her, hard. Suddenly she wanted to turn and shout at Tracey that all the gifts in the world could not make up for her absentee style of motherhood, that gifts could not buy love. She wanted to shout, *Wake up! I know you love her, but show it, Goddamn it! Spend some time here, with your family!* But she said none of those things. Alyssa's control was fragile, at best. And now, so was her own.

Wouldn't de la Barca want an intellectual woman?

"Oh, you have to open the pink package, you'll just love it!" Tracey cried, rushing forward and handing it to her daughter. It was one of the smallest packages present. In the same breath Tracey delved into her duffel and produced a long flat box for Cass. She smiled. "And don't you dare say no."

Cass knew it was clothing. Her sister had incredible taste in clothes, was the chicest person Cass knew, but Cass wasn't Tracey. She didn't wear miniskirts and she didn't wear stiletto heels. Of course, she was only five foot three. She wouldn't even be able to walk in the kind of shoes Tracey wore. "Thanks," she said.

"Are you all right?" Tracey asked with concern.

"Absolutely," Cass said, imagining that her smile was stretched wide and thin.

Catherine suddenly said, "Oh, Tracey, dear, how lovely." Her tone was odd. Cass looked up to find Catherine holding a stunning Elizabeth Locke pin, a large peridot stone engraved with the figure of a woman, set in a matte gold bar with a diamond chain. But she wasn't admiring the pin. Her brow was furrowed, and she was staring at their visitor. Cass realized she had forgotten to introduce him to her aunt.

But before she could do so, Tracey was speaking in a gay rush. "I was walking down the street when I saw it in the window and I just knew it was perfect for you," she said, smiling happily at her aunt.

"I wish you hadn't," Catherine said very softly, for the hundredth time, her gaze now on her niece. But then it veered back to de la Barca, and her aunt's expression made Cass concerned.

Alyssa had opened her pink parcel, and now she sat down on the second step of the stairs, clutching something to her chest.

Tracey turned eagerly. "It's a collector's item, darling. Her name is Sparkee. Isn't she just the cutest?"

Alyssa bit her lip, nodding. "Thank you, Mother."

Cass realized she was holding a Beanie Baby. Alyssa adored the small stuffed animals and had been brokenhearted when they had all been retired last year. Tracey had probably found the little toy in an auction, or even on the Net. She had gone to great lengths, clearly. But Cass could not focus on mother and daughter now. "Aunt Catherine? Are you all right?" Her aunt seemed oddly stiff with tension.

"We haven't met," Aunt Catherine said quietly.

"Forgive me, but I am intruding—and that is the last thing I wish to do," Antonio de la Barca said as quietly.

But Tracey was swooping down on her aunt, having looped her arm in Antonio's again. "How could you intrude, darling? Aunt Catherine, this is Antonio de la Barca, from Madrid. Tonio, my aunt, Lady Catherine Belford."

Cass started forward. Her aunt was immobile, as if afraid to move, the color having drained from her face. "Aunt Catherine? Are you ill?" she asked with alarm.

If Catherine heard her, she gave no sign. She stared at de la Barca, her expression strained. She could not seem to take her eyes off him. "You resemble your father," she said thickly.

He had been reaching for her hand, and now he froze. "You knew my father, Lady Belford?"

Slowly Catherine nodded, and something terribly sad flitted through her eyes.

"Many years ago," Catherine said. And suddenly her face crumpled with the onset of tears.

"Señora?" Antonio asked, alarmed.

"Oh! I just remembered—I need to ask the caterer something." Catherine turned, almost running, and quite shoving past Tracey.

"Aunt Catherine!" Cass had never seen her aunt act in such a manner before.

Tracey was also wide-eyed.

"Why don't you show our guest to his room?" Cass said. She didn't wait for a reply. She hurried down the hall after Catherine, pushing open the door to the kitchen.

Inside it was a flurry of activity, as the caterer and her staff were busy making the last-minute preparations for a cocktail hour and a supper that would serve forty. Catherine stood by the end of the center aisle, hunched over it, leaning upon it, her back to Cass. She was shaking.

Cass did not understand. She rushed to her aunt, slipping her arm around her. "What's wrong? What has happened?" Cass cried.

At first Catherine couldn't speak. She could only shake her head wordlessly, continuing to tremble.

"Aunt Catherine, talk to me, please," Cass begged. One of the staff handed her a tissue and her aunt accepted it, dabbing at her eyes.

"I never expected this," she whispered. "After all these years. Cassandra, we must get that man out of this house— and out of Tracey's life."

Cass was incredulous. "Why?"

"Why?" Catherine turned on her, and Cass was shocked to see both pain and fear in her aunt's wide eyes. Catherine was shaking. "I will tell you why, Cassandra. I killed his father."